E118/

THE LORDS OF AKCHASAZ
Murder in the Ironsmiths Market

by the same author

Memed, my Hawk
The Wind from the Plain
Anatolian Tales
They Burn the Thistles
Iron Earth, Copper Sky
The Legend of Ararat
The Legend of the Thousand Bulls
The Undying Grass

YASHAR KEMAL

THE LORDS OF AKCHASAZ

PART I
Murder in the Ironsmiths Market

*Translated from the Turkish by
Thilda Kemal*

COLLINS and HARVILL PRESS
London, 1979

This Book was first published under
the title of
DEMIRCILER CARSISI CINAYETI
by Cem Yayinevi, Istanbul

© 1979 in the English translation by
William Collins Sons & Co Ltd, London

ISBN 0 00 261518 5

Made and printed in Great Britain by
William Collins Sons & Co Ltd, Glasgow
for Collins, St James's Place
and Harvill Press, 30A Pavilion Road, London SW1

1

'They have mounted those beautiful horses, all the good people, and ridden away.'

The words were like a dirge on Dervish Bey's lips, a whispered lament for bygone days. Over and over again he repeated them, striving to recapture that enchanted dream of many years ago. 'Those good, good people . . .'

The rain was coming down in torrents, a stark yellow rain. There was no thunder, no flash of lightning. Just that monotonous, undeviating, steady downpour, never-ending, lurid, yellow. The night was like a wall and only the dull muted sound of rainfall filled the plain, dense as the earth, solid as the rocks.

Dervish Bey thought he heard a moan outside, a kind of strangled sound mingling with the noise of the rain. He ran to the window. There in the middle of the courtyard was the blurred silhouette of a man on a horse. His heart leapt and his hand flew to his revolver. He thrust the muzzle through a louver in the shutters and aimed. But just as he was about to press the trigger, he changed his mind. There was not the slightest movement from the shadow that stood there, hardly visible, like a darker spot on the night. Dervish Bey went from room to room and looked out of the windows, but he saw no other shadows, nothing, only the vast deep unmarred darkness and the yellow, murky rain that steamed from the earth as though it were falling over a red-hot sheet of iron. He went back to the window overlooking the wide front yard and peered out again. The shadow was still there. It had not even moved. Raising his revolver he turned the cylinder a few times and held it to the shutters. But again he hesitated. What was this man waiting for there in the yard? No enemy would expose himself in that way. But if he were a friend, a visitor, would he not call out instead of remaining like this under the rain? Could it be that he had met with some accident? Dervish Bey drew back and began to pace up and down the room, twirling the

5

cylinder of his revolver. A faint strangled whinny caught his ear. He rushed to the window. The shadow was even dimmer, hardly visible, stuck to the dark and the rain. Dervish Bey began to feel more and more curious.

Everyone was asleep in the mansion, perhaps even the sentinels posted inside and outside. Could it be that the horse was riderless? Once again, a chilled muted whinny trembled in the air, but the shadow remained quite still.

Strange blurred forms of birds began to fall, fluttering specks like balls in the darkness and the rain. Masses of them dropped from the sky, spilling in yellow spangles across the night and to the earth. Fascinated, Dervish Bey forgot the shadow in the yard. The very air was strange tonight, stagnant, steamy, wet, suffocating . . . Then the night paled and over the mountains the dawn sky, frosted and yellow, pulsed and steamed. The rain, the light that hit the fulvous earth, the streams and the trees, the hillocks, the marshes were all swathed in a yellow vapour. With daybreak the rain gathered strength and poured down, a shimmering golden smoking cloud, bright and sharp as the blade of a knife.

In the yard, motionless under the yellow rain, stood a long slim bay horse with a Turcoman saddle and seated on it a man wrapped in a black felt cloak. The horse's rump and the man's cloak were steaming and water streamed down them. The horse's head was stretched forward, nostrils wide open, as though sniffing the rain. Hunched over its neck the rider seemed asleep. His eyes were closed. The tinsel-tasselled cords of his cloak hung down, dripping. His shadow struck the earth, very black. Blood frothed out of his boots and a fusty odour filled the whole yard. Green flies in hundreds flashed about him, steel-green in the yellow brightness, quick as lightning. From the stirrups the blood fell to the ground, drip, drip, drip, denting deep into the dust of the yard. Slowly he raised his head, a hawk-nosed man with a curly green-tinged ebony beard and black mournful suffering eyes that stared at the mansion house, hesitant, disbelieving, as though in a dream. His limp arms moved, pulling the reins. The horse's head jerked up and a glob or two of almost solid froth spilled from its mouth.

On the boots the blood was clotting now, in streaks, and the froth drying, the drip-drip of blood over the dust lessening. The man's arms twitched several times, then his head fell to his breast as though it had snapped. In the shimmer of yellow rain the green flies flared and went out and flared again, a cataract of steel-green that died out in the blood-stained dust. Dervish Bey gave a sign to his men who were standing by. They rushed down the stairs and lowered the motionless rider from the saddle. His hands were clamped tight to the reins and it was with difficulty that they prised them open.

'Sultan Agha, Sultan Agha!'

They carried him inside, frozen, unconscious, and took off his dripping cloak. Under it was a German carbine and several cartridge-belts were strapped to his body.

Dervish Bey hurried down. 'Upstairs, quick,' he ordered. 'Undress him and get old Niné to see what she can do about his wound.'

They made him drink some tea, while the old woman found the wound, cleaned and poulticed it. He opened his eyes. They were black, coal-black and very large, with long curly lashes. Both eyes and lashes gleamed brightly. His black hair fell in wet curls down his forehead. His narrow face, the cleft in his chin, his long tapering fingers aroused Dervish Bey's respect and also his curiosity. Who could he be, this man who had alighted at his door in the middle of the night like a wounded bird?

'Sultan Agha! Those good people . . . Those good good people . . . Sultan Agha!'

The man muttered a few words. His teeth were snow-white and perfect as a child's, his lips full and shapely and stood out pink and fresh in his pallid face. His speech was foreign, with intonations of the far south or south-east. He smelled of sun and rain, of sun-scorched grain stalks in the rain . . .

'Sultan Agha, Sultan Agha! How can it be . . .'

As the warmth spread through his body the man relaxed and he slept. They made up a bed for him, clean and white and soap-scented, and laid him in it. Even in his sleep his hands were tightly clenched, the nails sinking into the palms.

Down Ayash and Zeytinbeli way, from the edge of the far Mediterranean a dust-devil appeared. Above, in the bright pure

7

blue of the sky white clouds were piling up, the puffed light-soaked cumulus clouds of the afternoon. The dust-devil, spinning on its axis, grew larger. For a while it tossed here and there on the shore of the Mediterranean, sweeping up straw and chaff that made it gleam and glitter in the sun with hundreds of thousands of tiny sparks. The dust-devil was as white as snow, like the bright clouds above, and as the south wind gathered force it swelled and lengthened and began to speed away from the sea, north towards the Binboga Mountains. That is how it is always in the Chukurova. Soon more dust-devils sprung up and one after the other, in a row, they surged on towards Kozan town. The mountain shadows lengthened towards the east and dark patches from the clouds above raced through the plain. The cloud-white dust-devils grew taller, twice, three times the height of a poplar tree. Spewing out dust, glittering with tiny sparks, following the dusty roads and tracks, they spread all over the plain, dispersing, uniting, dissolving and forming again. A few red-tinted dust-devils broke away from the foot of the red crags above Dumlu and came to a stop in front of the steep mauve cliffs of Anavarza. Up and down they wandered along the edge of Akchasaz swamp and the banks of Savrun River. Then leaping over Jeyhan River they reached the mulberry groves of Sakarjali that loomed like a dark hill in the distance. There they met with a group of green-glinting dust-devils and forged on together towards the Gavur Mountains. At Toprakkalé, at Telkubbé more dust-devils erupted, ten, fifteen of them, in a file along the railway.

The rain started again in a thin drizzle, amber-yellow, sheeny, not falling in drops but uncoiling in threads of light . . . Then it came down harder and puddles formed on the ground. The yellow mud leavened. The night turned yellow and out of the darkness a horseman skimmed into view. Three times he circled Anavarza hill. Nine men were riding after him in hot pursuit. They wore long silver-embroidered Arab headdresses and their Arab horses were lathered with sweat. Now drawing nearer, now dropping far behind they kept firing at the fleeing rider whose horse stumbled and rallied and streaked on, its belly razing the ground. They entered the dark curtain of rain and emerged steeped in yellow. Yellow their saddlebags and

8

horses, their headdresses, their cloaks . . . They rode through the dust-devils, in and out of the smoky whirling clusters, firing their guns all the time, the shining barrels catching the sun and flashing briefly. Out of the dust and into the rain again, vanishing into the woods, reappearing in great confusion, for their quarry has given them the slip, fanning out through the plain, then taking up the scent once more.

Blood gushed from the horseman's right shoulder, ruby-red, burning, and filled his boot. He dismounted and leaned against a tall mulberry tree, and the tree sweated. It sweated all over its dusty leaves, its gnarled hollow trunk, its branches and its deep-reaching jagged roots.

'Sultan Agha, Sultan Agha! My heart, my soul, they're coming, they're closing in on you. Quick, get on to your horse and fly. Draw your gun at least. Don't let them catch you like this. They're coming, they're here! Draw your gun!'

He pulled out his revolver and threw himself behind the tree, and the tree broke into a sweat again. Dust filled the air and a dust-devil rushed by. Sixteen bullets hit the tree-trunk and from the sixteen holes a yellow liquid spirted out. Swiftly the horsemen swerved towards the back of the tree. The man flung himself to the opposite side just as sixteen yellow bullets pierced the trunk again. He lifted his revolver and all at once three of the men were on the ground at their horses' feet. The horses reared and bolted eastwards, dragging the wounded men after them, their feet tangled in the stirrups, their heads raking the dust of the road.

Crouched against the tree the man's large coal-black eyes widened. Dazedly he stared as the horsemen fled all in a heap into the gully and out of sight. His wounded back hurt unbearably. His horse was munching among the fresh green grass a little distance away. Now and then it lifted its head with a snort to sniff at the air. Nostrils wide open, ears pricked, it tossed its long tail high up, then lowered it again over its rump, delicately down its hocks to the fetlocks. The man forced himself up on to the saddle and rode on. At the gully the horse narrowed its eyes, folded back its ears and took a flying leap. As they came to the woods thousands of orioles with long gracile beaks, blue, yellow, reddish, took flight and the limpid air was filled with

9

blue specks that flashed and died out and flashed again. Tiny thumb-sized yellow birds, thick as flies, covered the sky, flaring up, plunging, darting into the trees and zooming upwards almost in the same instant. A rabbit perked its ears. A fox waved its long bushy tail like a flame. A snake hissed and all the secret places of the forest rustled. Suddenly a hail of bullets tore at the leaves. The wounded man bolted.

The day was drawing to a close and the yellow rain fell faster now. The rocks and trees, the bursting rice, the sky, the loudly-flowing stream, the swamp with its reeds, the brake, the briars, all was dyed yellow.

A whinnying sound rose from the yard. Dervish Bey ran to the window, his hand on his revolver. Outside the wind was blowing strong enough to uproot the trees, a stark yellow wind. The horse's mane and its long tail were flying, and the yellow night fluttered, driven in the fore of the wind.

'Quick,' Dervish Bey shouted. 'Be quick . . .' And the men rushed here and there, but never got anywhere near the cloaked rider who sat crouched over his horse, motionless in the middle of the yard . . .

Day dawned and the east brightened. Long straight cords of yellow rain were falling, hurled on by sudden squalls to plump in cataracts way off. The wet blood-stained cloak, the bay horse, its ears pricked, alert . . . At last the men could draw near. And still the horse never stirred, but as soon as they touched it, the rider slipped to the ground into the yellow mud. He opened his eyes. They were large, oval-shaped and very black. His beard too was black, long and wavy. In his pale face the lips stood out red and full. They picked him up and carried him inside. He was tall and handsome with his silver-embroidered cloak and looked to be about thirty years old. They laid him down by the hearth. He opened his eyes again questioningly, but could not speak. They stirred up the fire and threw in heaps of wood. He slept, heaving deep deep sighs all the time. A bullet had pierced the shoulder-blade, shattering his shoulder.

The south wind began to blow and from Saricham and Misis giant dust-devils reared up, each one reaching to the peak of Mount Nurhak, multiplying as the wind quickened and spreading over the plain, a forest of many hues, red, mauve, yellow, blue, white, very pale, yet glinting with thousands of tiny sparks, a-quiver with light. Helter-skelter, at a dizzying speed, the whirling forest of dust-devils streamed through the flat polished plain, part of it swarming around Misis, another part making for the Anavarza crags that stood out like a dark island. As they passed Hajilar and Dumlu the dust-devils turned into a glittering spangled orange mass. The south wind blustered ever more forcefully over land and sky and herded the dust-devils north towards the Taurus Mountains that lay recumbent, an almost invisible girdle about the plain swathing it in a pale mauve veil.

'They have mounted those beautiful horses and ridden away . . .'

On they speeded, dense as a great forest, to gather at the foot of the Taurus, and it was as though the whole plain with its towns and villages, its trees and telegraph poles, its screeching birds, with all its things living and inanimate, was marching upon the mountain.

'Those good people, riding those beautiful horses . . .'

The mountains vanished behind the dust-devils and everything went dark but only for a moment, and then all was bright again as though the sun had only just dawned. The plain stretched out flat, scrubbed clean, calm and morning-fresh, faintly steaming and smelling of burnt grass, speckled here and there with shadows from the flowing clouds above. And far away in the distance a black dot crept along the plain towards Mount Hemité, the weary flagging rider and his horse, its head drooping, almost touching the ground . . .

They have all gone all the good people, mounted those beautiful horses and ridden away . . . Gone all those noble men, gone and taken their gazelle-like horses with them . . . Gone never to return. Never, never, never! What once was steel has turned to bronze and men are bastards now. A difficult world indeed that's left for us to live in, where one evil man can hold in thrall a thousand good ones . . . All alone, friendless, impotent . . . It hurts like the poisoned tip of a dagger plunging into your heart. And the emptiness . . . My heart burns, but not as of old with that glowing fiery flame, ardent and strong. If only it could be the same again, if only I could feel fear, like the fear of death, harrowing, making my heart burst at its very core . . . Every creature in this world has a bough to cling to. Only man is alone, abandoned, helpless, only man . . . Everyone, everything will live on, the trees and grasses, birds and insects, even serpents and creeping creatures, but not man. Only man is annihilated, because every man is his own beginning and his own end. Such solitude, such isolation is the attribute of God alone . . .

Ah, if a man starts to pity himself . . . Self-pity carries an undercurrent of cowardice, a cringing weakness. It is debasing . . .

Under his black bushy eyebrows Dervish Bey's eyes shone like flames. He had salient cheekbones, slanting eyes and a strong deeply cleft chin. The large forehead, the face, deeply lined, dark-complexioned and tanned even darker by the sun, revealed in all its fullness the self-confident nature of the man. When he spoke or laughed his white teeth would gleam and flash. His thin sparse mustache drooped slightly. It jarred with the thick black brows, the strong chin and lent a strange discordance to the face.

With his whip in his left hand and his right hand on the butt of the revolver over his hip, he paced up and down the large hall of the mansion in his dust-filmed shiny boots. His face was dark, sweating, the skin drawn taut in anger.

He always wore shalvar-trousers of blue broadcloth, with silver-fringed pockets. The large folds of the shalvar-trousers fell over the boots wiping the dust off the top and polishing them bright. No tailor was left in this part of the country who could make and embroider such shalvar-trousers any more, but by hook or by crook Dervish Bey would manage to obtain a couple of them each year, sometimes sending as far as Aleppo and Damascus and even Egypt for them. Over these shalvar-trousers he would wear a collarless striped shirt with a silk-embroidered front. But his jackets were made to the latest dictates of fashion, of the most expensive cloths by the most renowned tailor in Istanbul. And this heterogeneous costume suited him to perfection.

Though nearing fifty and his hair quite white now, he was

still straight and wiry and would mount his Arab horse with the nimbleness of a youth, splendidly upright, eyes fixed into the distance, chest thrown out and the left hand that held the whip resting on his thigh. His revolver with its finely chased ivory handle was always over his right hip, thrust bare into the sash of multi-coloured Indian silk that an old friend had sent him from Baghdad. And wherever he went, to the town, to Adana, to Ankara or Istanbul, in audiences with the Vali or with ministers, the revolver was always at his side. Once he had entered into the presence of the prime minister in this state. The revolver never left him, not even at night. It had been like this with him ever since he was a boy. His tall body was slim, even thin, matching the sharp, stern lines of his countenance which radiated a noble masculine spell. And yet the full fleshy mouth stood out pink and fresh as a child's in the dark face, and his teeth too were like a child's. It was a strange mixture, juvenile yet harsh, unfamiliar, enchanting, daredevil, free, un-confined, that riveted the attention of man or woman anywhere, haunting them long afterwards with an irresistible urge to look on it again and again. Dervish Bey was in love with his own face. He never had enough of gazing at the looking-glass, of watching himself change from laughter to sorrow and grief, and to joy again. But all at once he would stiffen and blench. 'Death,' he would cry and hurl the mirror away.

The spacious hall of the mansion was spread with *kilims*, leaving not an inch of floorboard uncovered. It was like a well-tended garden this hall, a marvellous exotic garden transported there from some other world, unknown, bountiful, unattain-able, like some strange thing, not real, nor a dream either, half way between day and night, green like no other green, studded with hundreds of embroidered flowers, the brightest of colours shining with the hardness of red copper on a vaporous spring morning, copper that has been polished new, smelted to a perfect fineness over the embers of a thousand years. In this vast hall of lights and designs a spring world was blooming, a world of long ago, like the beginnings of creation. There before your eyes was the wide world in all its mightiness, its green meadows, its springs and summers, autumns and winters, the snow, the cold, the storms, flowers, trees and woods, rocks,

13

mountains and seas, the rains, the clouds, the rivers, pomegranate flowers, water flowers, the trout in the mountain pools, the scents, the wonderfully bright days, the dark star-spangled nights, the deep impenetrable darkness . . . The slim-waisted, goggle-eyed bees with red-striped whirring wings, iridescent, the ants and birds and fishes, wolves and eagles, amorous tortoises and black-eyed gazelles, horses straight and graceful, poised on taut-stretched legs, and people, ebullient, overflowing with joy and happiness, hearty, lovable . . . Such was the great hall of Dervish Bey's mansion, in all its beauty, freshness and old-world charm, born anew every morning at the first gleam of day in a far-off play of lights, green and blue, orange and black, with its glowing copper and pomegranate flowers, a garden of *kilims*, alive, fluttering, seething, changing every moment into a thousand and one shapes, sparkling with a thousand and one lights, a place far away where the dawn is, a world created anew every day with each dawn, a hundred thousand years old, maybe older still, immemorial, the sweat of man's brow, the light of his eyes, the craft of his hands.

But Dervish Bey saw nothing of it all. Nor did he feel the warmth and softness of the fine wool under his feet. The mauve crags of Anavarza crackling in the heat, the faint outline of the Taurus leaning against the sky to east and north, the gently rolling plain that spread like the sea, he was blind to everything, and though it was long past noon, the thought of food never crossed his mind. Since daybreak he had been pacing up and down, up and down, and it had been like this with him for days now.

It was raining, a yellow viscid stream. Yellow sashes of rain swept wide bows from Anavarza to the Gavur Mountains, spanning the plain from one end to the other, orange-tinged, now faint and fading, now sun-bright over the blue of the plain . . . First it was the solitary horseman who came riding down the smoking mauve-cragged slope. Slowly, with hanging head he descended into the plain and at the same death-like pace crept on to the shelter of a plane tree. Then the horsemen appeared. They cataracted down the slope and galloped towards the plane tree, leaving long white walls of dust in their wake. There was not a breath of wind. The hot sun beat down, corroding the grass, blackening the leaves, dulling the glitter of the stubble and straw. As the horsemen pulled up in a bunch under the tree, the solitary rider materialized further off, springing out of the very ground it seemed, and galloped towards Jiyjik, disappearing into the gully of Yalnizdut. At once the horsemen scattered flat out over the plain, the silver harnesses of their horses glinting under the sun. The solitary rider emerged from the gully way off, near Jeyhan River. Like a shot the horsemen spurred on after him and coming within a range of five hundred feet fired their guns, eight shots all at once. Their quarry's horse stumbled three times, but rallied again and reached the steep yawning bank of the river. The rider turned and looked back, but only for an instant, at the swarming knot of his pursuers. The hoofbeats thudded, dull and muffled under the sun. His horse tensed, unfurled and leapt into the water. One by one the pursuing horsemen hurled themselves after him into the hot burning river that glowed as though on fire. The solitary rider surfaced first, then the others, and on they flowed in the direction of Anavarza, firing intermittently. The first rider's horse was swimming well and leaving the others behind. At the point of Anavarza it clambered up to the bank, shook itself, spattering water to right and left, reared and set off again at a gallop. The sky darkened. Black clouds rolled in from the north and overcast the plain. Lightning flashed, yellow, lacklustre, dyeing the clouds a dull orange. All the dogs of the plain fell to barking with one voice. Then the cocks began to crow. A blustery wind sprang up, fast whipping itself to a storm, blowing with equal force in all directions, tossing up grass and straw and dust. Big warm raindrops pattered down, bursting over the dust. The rain gained force and turned yellow.

The chase started again, more doggedly than ever. Shots rang out, javelins and even lassoes were thrown, but the first rider avoided them all and plunged into the dark green of the swamp, followed at once by the others. When he emerged he was caked with mud, green, mossy, musty-smelling, and so was his horse. After a while the horsemen reappeared, equally muddy, only their teeth gleamed.

The rain stopped and the sun came out. Steam rose from the

horses' backs. The mud dried stiff and flaked off and still the first horse streamed on, its belly razing the ground. Beyond Akchasaz swamp the grass was on fire, flames were rising high in the sky. As the first rider circled the ever-widening blaze, his pursuers began to catch up, shooting at him all the while. The horse stumbled, picked itself up quickly and dashed on, in and out of the flames. And so, on and on they went and in the afternoon the first horse began to falter. There was a burst of gunfire and the rider disappeared in a swirl of flames. Then the flames enveloped the other horsemen too.

It started raining again and the burning fields were smothered in dense yellow smoke. Out of this smoke they all erupted and galloped across the rice-paddies, one after the other. They were very close to the fleeing rider now, but for some reason they had stopped firing. Towards evening, under the driving rain they came to the mansion house and began galloping around it. The pitch-black night, tinted orange by the rain, was full of the sound of muffled muddy hoofbeats. All night through the mansion rang with their monotonous thudding. Then the hoofbeats stopped. There was a deep silence and morning dawned. A yellow curtain of rain, shimmering, iridescent, hung in the east and the top of the Gavur Mountains misted over and crystallized in a thousand and one colours.

In the yard was a man mounted on a slim elongated Turcoman-saddled bay horse. With his long sallow face, his upcurling lashes and his ebony beard he looked like a holy man, some kind of dervish perhaps. The collar and fastening braids of his felt cloak were embroidered in silver. The servants tried to help him down, but he slipped from their hands and crumpled limp and lifeless at the foot of the horse. His cloak, his beard were soaked with blood. Blood filled his boots. He was breathing yet. They carried him in and at that moment a piercing scream rent the air and the horsemen began to circle the house, howling like a pack of wolves. Round and round they galloped and in the end they drew up in the yard, quite still, a frozen row of black-cloaked men on snorting fuming Turcoman-saddled bay horses.

On the point of noon the first one, a white-bearded man, dismounted, laid his cloak on his saddle and walked to the door of the mansion. He knocked three times. The door opened and

Dervish Bey stood before him. He put his right hand to his heart and bowed his head. He had long horsy lashes, coarse and sparse.

'From Urfa we have come, from the plain of Haran, riding our mettlesome horses, bearing our deadly rifles and our swords, through thick and through thin, each one of us exhausting three horses on the way. Scaling the seven mountains, we passed over Amik plain, its lake and the Syrian desert and reached Hama city . . . Seven times we skirted lofty Musa Dagh and it is here our quest has brought us. Give him to us. If you don't, your hearth will be extinguished, the males of your race will be nipped in the bud. Blood will take them. Noble horses shall breed no more in your house. Give him to us!'

The door slammed shut, black, heavy as lead.

Then the second man dismounted. He came to the door and knocked four times. It was opened to him and he spoke the same words. Black, like the blade of a sword the door shut on him too. The third horseman came and knocked five times. One after the other they all got off their horses and knocked on the door. The last one knocked eleven times. The door opened and closed in the same instant. He did not have the chance to say a word. The nine riderless bay horses approached and rubbed their heads on the door. Tears of blood flowed from their large eyes and they wept until darkness fell. Then all at once they started to neigh and the Anavarza crags rang with their cries all through the night.

Day dawned. The noble horses fell back and the men began to beat on the door again. At mid-morning it was opened at last and three black-eyed, ebony-bearded, curly-lashed, long-faced men appeared. With slow, dignified, confident steps they walked up to the cloaked men.

'From the desert of Urfa we come, from Haran, from the mountains of Abdülaziz . . .'

The men jumped on to their horses. Round and round the mansion they went till it was night again and the horses neighed, the cocks crowed and the earth trembled and every living creature on the plain, bird and beast, serpent and insect, raised its voice in a cry.

The next morning, with the rain screening the eastern sky,

the men hurled themselves once more at the door. Their black, gleaming, flaming eyes were misty.

A huge dust-devil came storming along. It uprooted the cotton plants, sucked in tall heaps of hay, tore the roofs off the houses and snatched up chickens, ducks and birds. The roof-tiles of the mansion were tossed in the air and hurled to the ground. Everything went dark and Dervish Bey held fast to the door to avoid being carried away too. His mouth and nose filled with dust and chaff and for a moment he could not breathe. When he opened his eyes the dust-devil was speeding on towards the Taurus, swollen to giant size now. He felt a sudden emptiness and longed for the vortex to return in all its force, again and again. Desperately he fought against the yawning nothingness into which his body was dissolving. He gripped the butt of his revolver and squeezed it till his bones cracked.

The horse's head drooped to the ground. It was moving almost imperceptibly under the crackling heat. The rider had let go of the reins, inert, grieving perhaps, and the horse crept on steadily eastwards along the edge of the vast swamp. A long dust-devil, tenuous as spring smoke, enveloped them for a while and swirled away, but the rider's death-like stance never changed. Odours of scorched wheat stalks, of swamp, of pungent burdock filled the air. The rider paused under a clump of squat mulberry trees, and before him stretched the swamp, dark, murky, all the way from the foot of Anavarza crags right up to Jeyhan River that shone under the sun like a metalled road.

It was as though he had lost something, something very important that he could not remember. He began to search. He rummaged through his pockets, then drew out his revolver. It glistened, iridescent under the sun. He emptied the chamber and held the bullets in his hand. They were oily, lustreless. Loading the revolver again, he began to spin the cylinder round and round until, sick of it, he thrust the weapon into his sash again and wandered out of the room, through the house and into the garden. He stopped by the well and leaned over. Mirrored deep down he saw his face more clearly than in any mirror. He scrutinized it for a long time, but did not find what he wanted. He cast a pebble into the well. The smooth surface crinkled and rippled gently. He walked away to the road, then

18

to the house again, on to the fields and back to the vegetable garden. He could not keep still. Mounting his horse he spurred it to a gallop, then leaped off and swung up on the saddle at a run, riding on madly over the flat boundless plain, not knowing where he was going, what he was doing, plunging into thorny scrub that tore at his clothes and body till the blood flowed, clambering up the saw-like crags of Anavarza and jumping from rock to rock in the dark of the night. That is how Dervish Bey was these days, rampant, frantic.

He sat down on the divan, took off his boots and examined the inside of each one in turn very carefully. Then he went to his room where the thick rug-curtains were drawn shut. Only through a narrow slit did the light of day penetrate, casting a long track through the gloom. He liked to watch the strange particles that floated in this path of light. Here was this huge bee with red, green and blue rings that seemed caught in the bright path, sliding along it, up to the ceiling and down again in a flurry of whirring wings, its angry buzzing filling the whole room, struggling and straining as though trapped in a long closed tube, unable to break through the wall of darkness and slamming itself against ceiling and floor in turn.

'Stupid witless creature,' Dervish Bey muttered. 'Takes the dark for an insurmountable steel wall . . . Just like human beings . . .'

His palms were filling with blood. He could smell it, fresh, frothy, weird. He looked at his hands. There was nothing, no wound, not a scratch, yet they were bleeding, a viscid bloodless exudation. He let them fall slowly to his side. From his right palm blood trickled along the cold iron of the revolver, down his groin and his legs; it was warm, sticky. His whole body was wet with blood.

Then he forgot about the blood. That lost something he was unable to remember was plaguing his mind again and once more he felt himself draining empty. His eyes went black. He staggered, pulled himself together and began to walk as fast as he could. Suddenly the ancient dirge rose to his lips and it was as though he had found what he had lost. It filled him with the warmth and staunchness of an old friendship.

'They have mounted those beautiful horses, all the good

people, and ridden away.'

The sadness, the longing to weep . . . Like the aftermath of towering anger, of uninhibited tears, leaving you weak and soft and hurt . . . Over and over again he murmured the words of the dirge, fearful that this blissful emotion would leave him, that he would never be able to recapture it.

And then it was over. He was weary, empty, drained. 'God damn it all!' he shouted at the top of his voice. 'God damn everything . . .' His voice echoed way over from the other end of the dust-smothered village and he was shaken to the marrow of his bones by a burst of anger. He let himself go, trembling in all his limbs, anger and exultation clashing within him one moment and all over the next. Every day, over and over again the seething storm in him would dissolve into annihilating sadness and he would be left floating in the void, alone in the immensity of the world, sinking into emptiness, into nothingness, forever yearning after something that was gone, striving to recapture some forgotten joy. No, anger was the best, the only way, enduring, lasting anger, foaming at the mouth, quivering, wild, glaring, agonizing . . . Better, much better than this hollow, meaningless, loveless, friendless existence. Not even to be able to feel jealous of something or somebody . . . Without pity or anger, or sleep or dreams . . . Like a vegetable, a tree, an insect . . . Much worse . . . Oh to feel that racking fear of death, to be terror-crazed, desperate, to suffer grimly, bitterly that silent gnawing prescience of annihilation . . . Anything but this horrible numbness, blunting all fear, even of death. For him who had lived a life of high tension, wild, sanguinary, in hiding, on the run, with death ever present at his side and fear never leaving him . . . To lose it all, to be like this . . .

A dust-devil started up from Hürüushagi and swept on towards Jeyhan River. Another burst out below the Dry Jeyhan, another above Endel. In the twinkling of an eye they had speeded across the plain and reached Kesikkeli, whisking up stalks and hay and dried grass, spinning invisibly with their light load along the river, gliding on top of the water with the current and vanishing suddenly in the dark mulberry wood near Jeyhan town.

On the north side of the yard at the bottom of the wall were four deep well-like Kurdish-style *tandirs** set in a row from which rose flames taller than a man. All around women were busy kneading dough and slapping little round cakes on to the white-hot walls of the *tandirs*. They fell away as Dervish Bey approached, covering their faces and crouching side by side at the foot of the wall. He took the dough from the basins and the freshly baked bread from the homespun cloths and threw them all into the *tandirs*. Then he stood there, legs planted wide apart, breathing deeply. His face was slowly clearing up. 'Let them burn, women!' he cried.

A dense smoke spread through the yard. The bread, the dough were burning with thick tar-like fumes that swirled all about Dervish Bey almost choking him, making him sweat until his hair and clothes were as wet as though he had stood a long while in the rain.

The smell of burnt bread had carried him way back to his childhood days. Dragging his feet in the dust he walked out of the yard. He stopped before an ant-hole, scanning the long narrow white path that extended far out in the direction of the swamp and the string of ants, each one with a seed in its mouth. It was growing dark now. From the Anavarza crags a single bird's call rang out at intervals, unfamiliar. With the tip of his boot Dervish Bey raked the earth around the ant-nest and closed up the hole. The ants clustered about the heap, letting go of their seeds and probing anxiously at the earth with their delicate antennae.

What Dervish Bey liked most was to think back on the old days, to call to mind the Chukurova of the noble Turcoman Beys with hawks on their wrists, riding their Arab steeds and stalking the deer. The Chukurova as it was then, clean, wild, untouched, a vast garden of the gods . . . He would visualize it in times of stress, immortal in his mind's eye, and a sad bitter-sweet Turcoman lament would sound in his ears.

Covering his face with his hands he ran back to the farm. The place still reeked of burnt bread and the women were sweating over the *tandirs*, scraping out the carbonized smoking remains.

I am the most wretched of all creatures in this whole wide

**Tandir:* a kind of oven dug into the earth.

21

world. All men suffer, and the anguish of death is the worst for them. But what I suffer is far beyond all this. It is the agony of non-suffering, of not feeling anything any more . . . They stick out their long red tongues and laugh. They understand everything. They know. They have to know, and as they learn they shed their fears a little, but only a very little . . . Captives, toad-eaters, goggle-eyed. The most cowardly creature on earth, that is man, and pluck this fear out of him, then what is there left to show? Hardly anything.

'Get some axes and come with me,' Dervish Bey thundered. At once five men materialized in front of him. He grabbed an axe from the hand of the foremost. A huge plane tree grew on the edge of the stream that flowed dark and sluggish below the garden. Soon the night was ringing with the blows of the axe as a tough battle began between Dervish Bey and the mighty tree. The rapidly swinging axe traced glittering arcs of light through the air and in the dimness of the close silent night the thudding sound travelled far out to the Anavarza crags and echoed back. Overhead the spreading branches of the plane tree loomed dark and massive, like a stormy sky. As the axe sank into its broad trunk confused feelings, painful, nostalgic, gripped Dervish Bey, something stirred within him like the morning brightness, a light cleaving the darkness, a clear fluid breeze rocking the night, fish skimming in the water, blackberry bushes, plane trees with beds of pebbles spread under them, a fresh moist odour of swamp, pennyroyal and burdock, watermelons with wasps swarming all over them . . . At every stroke of the axe a sharp acrid smell gushed out of the tree. Like sounds, scents too can spread more easily, more distinctly in the night.

The village had woken up at the noise . . . All the dogs had started to bark, and an answering chorus of barks broke out in the village at the foot of Anavarza. As the night progressed the blows slackened and grew fainter. Dervish Bey could hardly lift his axe up any more. He swayed as though he would fall and at every hit he slumped over the axe with all his weight to wrench it out of the trunk. He was drenched in sweat and the odour of his own sweat mingled with that of the tree and the scents of the night, cool, chilling. In the end the axe remained stuck in the trunk.

'Leave it there,' he gasped out to the men. 'Go ahead now, starting on the other side.'

His chest heaving like that of a panting horse, he sat down against a tree. The earth was warm. He felt pleasantly drowsy, at peace with himself and he relaxed there, listening to his men pounding at the tree. There were no dust-devils to be seen now. How they would have gleamed, swelling to twice their size in the dusky light . . . Now they had subsided one by one, retreating into their lairs. The wind had dropped, not a leaf stirred. The air on this August night was soft, silken, cool, the sky laden with bright whirling sparkling stars.

He was rested now. Spitting into his palms he wrenched the axe from the tree and began again. The shining blade flashed blue in the starlight and died out. 'We've got to fell it tonight even if it takes us all night. Come on now!'

As the edges of the clouds above the mountains lit up and silvered, the huge plane tree toppled over. Its wide branches crackled as it crashed down into the dawn sky . . . Evenings as the sun was going down, mornings just at the peep of day, the lofty plane tree would fill up with birds, clustering, swarming over each other. Chattering starlings, spangled, green, with pointed beautiful bills and bright black eyes, would descend upon it like a black cloud, a deafening din, rousing earth and sky. All over its branches hundreds of nests . . . The nestlings, necks outstretched, yellow mouths opened wide, wriggling, frantic, all a-twitter . . . With a great crash, like a mighty world collapsing, the huge tree plunged into the darkness. Behind it, a light flickered like the first blush of day and masses of nestlings, their yellow mouths wide open, tumbled out, screeching, necks outstretched . . .

The sun rose and from the wide boundless steppe thousands of horsemen appeared and scattered over the open country. All of them wore long white robes. The rain was coming down, luminous, yellow . . . Behind the curtain of rain the Anavarza crags trembled, mauve and misty. On the ground thousands of nestlings, featherless, yellow mouths open, threshed about on the bare muddy earth, at their last gasp.

Round and round the mansion they circled the riders, their horses' legs caked to the knees with red mud, cantering, pacing, galloping, foaming at the bit, with eyes of glowing red.

The rider of the black horse entered the yard. He was wrapped in a grey mantle and wore an Arab headdress trimmed with silver and gold. His eyes were black, his beard crescent-shaped and his mustache drooping.

'He burnt down my house,' he said. 'Four brothers I had, he killed them all. Give him to me, Bey. If you don't, this mansion of yours will crumble down over your head.' He turned and with a flying leap scaled the high wall of the yard to join the galloping horsemen.

Another rider broke from the circle and came to a stop in the yard. He never spoke, only stood there, immobile, staring fixedly at the mansion. His was a bay horse, slender, long-bodied. Its eyes were coral-red. The rider was soaked to the bone and water like molten gold trickled down his horse's back. How long did he remain there? It was impossible to say. Suddenly, effortlessly he was over the wall and circling round and round the mansion together with the others.

The rider of the white horse sat very straight. Sparks shot out of his greyish-blue eyes. His fingers were long and slim, reed-like. The horse's mane flowed in the air and its tail reached down to its fetlocks, yellowing under the rain. 'Don't do this to us,' he said. 'How can we face our people back home if we return without him? The very dogs will spurn us. It's a matter of honour, Bey. You should know . . . Hand him over or kill us all, every one of us. All the way from Haran we have come and trailed him to your door . . .' He fell silent and waited, his glinting steely gaze on the window, then turned away, a blurred streak in the rain. And in the distance, the mauve crags of Anavarza undulated gently with the wind.

As night was falling they all trooped into the yard and stood in a row, their eyes on the mansion, never speaking, never moving, and the yellow glistening rain rattled down steadily, filling up the ditches and gullies and river-beds and cataracting down the Anavarza crags. All night through they remained there, swaying shadows in the dark. At the first ray of light they cleared the wall, one after the other, as though linked by a chain and began racing round the mansion, their horses sinking knee-deep into the mud.

Inside, wood was heaped over the fire. Sultan Agha shivered. He was burning with fever. His wound had swollen. It was still swelling and Abdo, the *hakim*, had been called in to tend it. And in the great hall Dervish Bey, in an angry mood, was pacing up and down, and the ancient floorboards creaked under the stamp of his boots.

And beyond, on the plain below Anavarza he saw again the Turcoman Beys of old, hundreds of them, all with hawks on their fists, flying their hawks, hundreds of hawks that whistled like bullets through the air, rising high in the sky, almost invisible, swooping down at the same furious speed to disappear on the ground. And the great hunts on the Chukurova plain ... Thousands of flitting, leaping, flying deer, and in hot pursuit, sprung from the past, the Turcoman Beys riding their sun-drenched horses, white, black, chestnut, stirrups of unalloyed silver, niello-mounted saddles and curb-bits, saddle blankets threaded with gold and silver ... Herds of deer licking the plain like lambent flames, wave after wave, and after them, streaming like the wind, the streaking horses of the old Turcoman stock, brought all the way from Khorassan to the Chukurova ...

And scattered over the plain, galloping, flying, thousands and thousands of saddleless horses ridden bareback by white-robed men with moss-green eyes ... The foremost horse stumbles. It falls. The one behind bumps into it and falls too. And the next ... On and on they rush like a white cloud over the plain, white robes, white manes, white tails flying, in hundreds and thousands, stumbling, falling, tossing their riders headlong to the ground, white robes whirling in the dust, a mighty torrent irrupting from the mountainside, inexhaustible, rocking the earth, hooves flashing, leaving snow-white tracks in their wake and turning the plain into a white-capped sea, into a dazzling expanse of sparkling hooves. A confusion of sprawling frantic horses overflows the plain in a tangle of manes and tails, heads and legs, bodies, hooves and coral-red eyes, as though an invisible dragon from Anavarza were pursuing them, as though they had come swarming from the four corners of the world into the Chukurova, as though this plain were their last refuge on earth. Ear-rending whinnies fill the air and all the birds burst out of their nests and boughs screeching, the sky is so black

25

with birds that the sun is hidden. And from the hills deer and mountain-goats, hawks and eagles, jackals and foxes, bears and wolves, insects and worms pour down into the plain, panting, their clamour adding to the outcry of the birds and horses . . . They are whinnying, but not like horses, not spiritedly nor mournfully, but more in the low tones of a broken lament . . . The vast Chukurova teeming with people roused from their sleep, with neighing horses, bellowing oxen, snarling leopards, with butterflies and insects, with deer and gazelles and polecats, the sky thronged with birds, wings touching, rustling . . . The Chukurova filled to the brim, rattling and shaking as though in the throes of an earthquake . . .

Suddenly all was quiet. The white cloud melted away and only one single horseman was left. His horse's head hung low. On he crept, listless, all by himself on the great wide plain . . .

'They have mounted those beautiful horses, all the good people, and ridden away.'

A young man was journeying through the world and he came to a beautiful city. His eyes were like the eyes of Emir Sultan, his eyebrows joined, his complexion was a burnt yellow, his full lips were pale. He was slim and tall. A handsome youth is the most beautiful of creatures in this world, like the foal of an Arab steed. The young man got off his horse and as he looked around he saw that this city was different from all the other cities he knew . . .

The horsemen came again and lined up in a row, silent under the pelting yellow rain. Every one of them to a man fixed his eyes on the big window of the mansion and there they remained till darkness fell. Rumblings rose from deep down in the earth and resounded all over the Anavarza crags.

Under the blazing heat, his horse's head hanging to the ground, he moved dully, torpidly. Perhaps he never stirred at all. His shadow fell very black at the horse's feet. Shielding his eyes with his hand he looked towards Dumlukalé fort that floated far out in the distance like a red ship anchored in the middle of the Chukurova plain, ready to hoist her sails and surge on southwards. Before him Jeyhan River, its banks overgrown with tamarisks, forest-like, tracing a long dark line over the water. From way off a dust-devil was approaching, whirling ever faster and larger. It swept past the rider, widening like melting blue glass, like water evaporating, and faded into the sky over the hills. The rider's hand fell. All about him, the whole world, the flowing water even, smelled of bitter burdock, dust, wheat stalks, mullein and swamp, the smell that pervades the whole Chukurova plain on days of intense heat.

In the yard the horsemen suddenly broke into a shout. 'Emir Sultan, Emir Sultan!' Then swiftly they cleared the wall and spurred on towards the Anavarza crags. The yellow rain kept falling thinly, imperceptibly.

... For in this city dwelt the friendliest, the most lovable people in the world. And the most hospitable too. Hardly anyone was poor and the rich were always generous. The very stones of the city spelt plenty and prosperity, and it was obvious that its inhabitants had lived happily like this for centuries. If they had anything to complain of, it was death. And even death must be something beautiful in this city. So thought the traveller ...

A herd of gazelles appeared in front of Hemité Mountain, making for Anavarza.

'Emir Sultan! Emir Sultan!' The horsemen in the yard were shouting. 'Is it worth suffering all these indignities just to save your miserable life?'

The rain had slackened. Glittering yellow layers of dust flitted thinly through the air.

'Emir Sultan, Emir Sultan, what have you done?' They repeated it again in Arabic and in Circassian, in Kurdish and Syriac, and for a long time their voices echoed and boomed over the Anavarza crags.

Crouched over his *saz** a very old minstrel is playing, and from way over Akyol a large Turcoman caravan is travelling, making for the high pastures, with its camels and noble horses and gaily dressed girls, a riot of colour. A new herd of gazelles follows the first, then a third ... Now they are five, all springing

Saz: a stringed instrument used in Anatolia.

27

out of the red and mauve valley of hawthorns on Mount Hemité and plunging down the slope like a long exuberant torrent of flames, bounding on towards Jeyhan River and Anavarza, Hajilar and Dumlukalé, fanning out over the plain, now gliding round the foot of Toprakkalé, towards Jeyhan-bekirli, now flowing below Kozan towards Merjimek farm.

It was at the close of February that they would arrive, the gazelles, migrating from the desert, and the whole of the Chukurova would be full of them. They would stray into the villages and join the flocks of sheep. And afterward they would slowly draw back again to their homeland in the Arabian desert. Once upon a time, a long long while ago, it was considered a sin to kill these gazelles. Nobody would ever dream of touching a hair of their heads. The first to hunt them was an officer of the Ottoman army. The upstart Beys followed suit, then their hangers-on, their retainers. Then the villagers, everyone . . . And so the whole race of gazelles was wiped out of the Chukurova, hunted, killed or forced to retreat into the desert. Last year, he had glimpsed five lone gazelles on the Anavarza crags, strayed from who knows what herd, long departed . . . Well, they too would soon be hunted . . .

The rider slowed to a stop at the foot of Mount Hemité. His shadow was a dark round blot stuck to the horse's hoof. His hand was on his temple. He was still as a stone and the horse under him was just as still, not even its tail moved. Nothing but the rider and his shadow in the solitary drowsy flatness of the plain. Not a breath of wind. Over the Anavarza crags was a sequined, glittering blue haze . . . Out of the emptiness there materialized the horsemen, slowly, one by one. They rode across the plain to the mansion and formed a circle. Very black they were, their horses, themselves, their shadows beneath the horses' hooves . . .

'Dervish Bey, Dervish Bey, you'll never get away with this. Give us Emir Sultan! A whole year we have trailed him, all the way from the Arabian desert. Dervish Bey, Dervish Bey! If you don't give us his life, then take ours . . .'

An orange dust-devil sprang up from Toprakkalé Castle. It whirled and grew and blazed. In a twinkling it had reached the foot of Mount Hemité. There it stopped, spinning, swelling, gathering within itself the thousands of gazelles, lifting them up high and sweeping them off into the faint blue gauze of the Taurus Mountains.

... And in this city were the most handsome horses he had ever seen. Purebred Arabs of every colour, the most resplendent chestnuts, bays, whites, duns, palaminos, roans, blacks, with coats glistening like no other, with eyes as soft as a gazelle's ...

'Dervish Bey, Dervish Bey, don't do this to us. Give us the Emir. Rather than go without him, we shall die here on the threshold of your door, we shall let our bones rot on this Chukurova soil.'

Tall and handsome the Emir was, like a slender-hocked Arab steed. His long slim hand would grip yours so warmly . . . 'Brother,' he would say and the word seemed to hold all the love in the world. Sometimes, leaning against the plane tree, never letting go of his mother-of-pearl inlaid gun, he would murmur a sad foreign lament, very low, and then he would weep . . .

'Dervish Bey, Dervish Bey, have you no pity? . . . Dervish Bey, Dervish Bey . . .'

Flurries of yellow rain swept obliquely through the air.

... The traveller was enchanted with the city, its good people, its noble horses, and so he dwelt there for as long as he could. Then he had to leave, but wherever he went, his whole life long, he told of this beautiful city, kindling admiration in the hearts of all his listeners . . .

The aged man with the curly beard got off his horse and shuffled up to the mansion on his knees. The door opened before him immediately. Still on his knees he mounted the stairs. Once in the big hall he leapt to his feet and drew out his sword. Shrinking into a corner, his eyes widening, Dervish Bey lifted his revolver and fired just as the man was hurling himself at him. The man doubled up over the *kilim* and his sword fell to his side. Blood flowed out of him, warm, foaming, yellowish, its odour spreading through the whole mansion. He opened his mouth wide again and again to speak. 'Give him to us, Dervish Bey,' he gasped at last. 'If you don't you will have to kill us all, like this. And in the end you will be killed too. And your wife and your daughter and son, and all those close to you. And this mansion will be destroyed. The wild fig tree will grow in its place . . . Give him to us . . .'

The blood gushed from the wound. He made a go for the sword.

'Throw him out,' Dervish Bey said.

They carried him down and set him on his horse.

'Dervish Bey, Dervish Bey . . .' The white horse was dyed red in an instant.

A deafening roar and thousands of starlings, iridescent, white-specked, scattered through the sky. The thud of many axes felling trees and myriads of chicks, yellow beaks open wide, necks outstretched, raising hell in their nests . . . The horsemen retreated into the woods, vanishing in the night, and from the heart of the forest a fire blazed out, the flames topping the crests of the trees. The forest was smothered in smoke.

. . . Many years passed. He was very old now. One day he said to himself: Before I die, before I leave this world and all its pleasures, let me have one last joy, the greatest of all. Let me see that beautiful city once more with its good people and noble horses. So he travelled up hill and down vale for days and days and one morning he came to the city of his dreams . . .

The men, the horses were steeped in mud. The scorching sun beat down upon them and dried the mud stiff. The horses' coats, the men's clothes, their swords, guns, silver-nielloed harnesses, gold chains all cracked under the sun. With drawn swords they rushed at the mansion. They poured in through the doors and windows, ransacking the whole place, but they could not find him.

'Dervish Bey, Dervish Bey you shall answer for this . . .' And jumping on to their horses they galloped off towards Jeyhan

River, while the yellow rain fell softly, imperceptibly, fine as the dust on a butterfly's wings. The horses' eyes glowed like flames, coral-red, as they plunged into the river and floated down to the point of Anavarza. From the crags eagles started up and whirled in the sun, broad black wings outstretched. Their shadows floated, very large, over the water.

Emir Sultan opened his eyes. The sun fell over him and the teardrop on his beard widened, his curly hair gleamed greenly . . .

. . . But when he looked about him, what should he see! Could this be the same city? The people were so different, and where were the horses? Everything had changed . . .

Again they came, at a gallop, and charged at the mansion, their bare swords flashing in the sun, uttering wild cries that beat against the Anavarza crags and died out over the plain. What were they saying, in what strange tongue? Round and round the mansion they careened, shrieking, brandishing their swords, firing their guns. Suddenly they leaped over the wall and stormed the house, opening doors and windows and carrying everything they could lay their hands on out into the yard. 'Emir Sultan, Emir Sultan!' An endless ululation all day long. And as the sun was setting, the broad-faced long-bearded man was the first to raise his sword and thrust it into his horse. Blood gushed out as from a tap and the animal toppled to the ground. Then one by one the others also ran their swords through their horses. Fitful agonized whinnies arose to mingle with the terrible screaming of the men. The yard was streaming with blood. They turned away and, still holding their bloodied swords, walked through the blackthorn thicket, barefoot, towards Jeyhan River, which flowed like pure light, shedding its glare far over its banks. Their voices rose in a deep-toned grieving dirge, immemorial, mellowed on the lips of millions of mourners.

Emir Sultan awoke. A fire of glowing embers was burning in the fireplace beside him. He thrust his hand into the embers, a smile flitting on his lips. His eyes, very black in his pallid face, darkened and gleamed greenly. 'Aah,' he moaned. 'Ah aaah . . .'

His head fell back over the pillow and he closed his eyes. Far and muted came the voices of the lamenting men and the faint spasmodic whinnies of the dying horses. 'Aaah, aah, ah . . .'

. . . The people, so friendly, so gentle-spoken of old, had no greeting for the traveller now, not so much as a glance. Their faces were sullen, bitter. The meadows and fields about the city were empty, and so were the vast stables. There was not a trace of those gazelle-like horses. Stunned, bewildered, the traveller was wandering aimlessly about the lonely dilapidated city when he saw an old man sunning himself against the wall of a tumble-down inn. His white beard was soiled and flies swarmed over his red-rimmed fevered eyes. Could this be all that remained of those happy days of long ago? . . .

It was raining. Naked to the waist, with brawny arms, thick necks, huge strong hands, their long swords flashing brightly, numberless, they rode in, from where the sun was rising, on horses that had neither saddle nor bit.

'Emir Sultan, Emir Sultan, you have laid ashes over our hearths, destroyed our homes . . . Do not think you can hide forever in the house of that Turcoman. No! We will smoke you out even though you sneak into the serpent's hole, the bird's nest, the wolf's lair, even though you flee to China and beyond, to the ancient isle of Serendip, to the land of the Franks, the steppes of Russia or the home of the slant-eyed Mongols. We have vowed to have you . . .'

The last faint whinnies of the horses were dying away as the men dragged their carcasses out of the yard and on to the Anavarza crags. There, they took off the saddles and harnessed them on to the barebacked horses. Then they returned and started riding round and round the mansion again at full gallop.

. . . The old man's white beard was dirty, but his wide-browed face was warm and open. So the traveller spoke to him. 'Once there were good, hospitable, friendly people who dwelt in this city. I saw then the noblest of horses, long-necked, slim-eared, coral-eyed, graceful as gazelles. What has happened to them?'

At that the old man stirred and sat up a little. His dirty white beard trembled, his face lit up with a ray of light coming from long ago. Then he sighed as though his lungs would burst and sank back against the wall.

'Aah, ah,' he moaned. 'They have mounted those beautiful horses, all those good people, and ridden away . . .'

From the sandy shores of the Mediterranean, from below Payas fortress they sprang up in hundreds, tall dust-devils, tapering into the sky, scintillating whirls of every hue and colour. And high above, white puffed cumulus clouds piled up, water-soaked, and loomed over the land. With frightening speed the dust-devils rushed on through the plain, spinning, flashing, sparkling, playing havoc along their path. They turned deep red, then bright green, and suddenly very black, and all the northern expanse of the plain beneath the Taurus range was covered by a tall black forest of dust-devils. Earth and sky were plunged in a dense, breathless, impenetrable darkness. From north and south, east and west, black churning clouds converged over the plain. A cold blast of wind was followed by a hot one, and then large raindrops began to fall, desultory at first, then gathering strength. Finally came a heavy yellow downpour. The horsemen in a long row, their horses' heads hanging to the ground, were heading south towards the red crags of Dumlukalé. Far and faint came the sound of their lament. Lightning flashed and a thunderbolt hit the crags of Anavarza, bathing the whole fortress in light. Thunder rolled through the skies. And Dervish Bey covered his face with his hands.

'Bring out my horse!' he called.

The black horse was out of the yard in an instant, carrying its rider far out on the Chukurova plain, a swift-moving black dot that left a cloud of dust in its wake. The ground unfurled under the horse's feet and Dervish Bey flew with the wind, a black dot flowing further and further out over the flatness of the plain, into its blue depths where a single tenuous dust-devil trembled . . . flowing, whirling, in a constant turmoil . . .

2

His heart bursting with impatience he watched the road that threaded across the plain like a thin white rope and disappeared among the crags of Kizilgedik Pass. His eyes were the eyes of a starving wolf, glowering, sullen.

Kizilgedik is a lonely unfrequented gorge, full of lizards. They crawled all around him, huge, scaly, their red tongues licking at his hands and feet. In the evening dusk, bats flitted by, so close it seemed they would hit him. Only a very few people were passing along the road, some on foot, a few riding donkeys.

It is not yet summer. The dust on the road does not reach to the ankles, does not hang for hours in the air like a cloud. The grass, the reeds, the bushes are all a delicate green. Tiny midges are swarming all over his face and large green mountain flies sting him, drawing out blood and forming boil-like growths. Horned snails with pin-point eyes, white, yellow, green, blue, creep over the mauve, white-speckled crags. When darkness falls all sounds merge, the susurration of the night, the call of the birds, the drone of tractors fallowing the land, dotting the plain, star-like . . . The smell of fuel-oil drifts in from very far and mingles with odours of swamp, dry crops, dust and burdock. All through the night this silent earth is astir, all its creatures abroad, swarming. At sunrise they will regain their nests and holes. And all the while strange sounds come from the distant swamp, as from a huge cauldron forgotten over a fire, boiling and bubbling.

In between the rocks grow the thorny blue cardoons of the Chukurova, moist and vaporous in the morning breeze. A hard thin thorn is sticking into his chest. He does not feel it. And the sunlight slits through the blue of the cardoon, its thorns gleam like glass. He plucks them off the bulbous fruit and munches it. It has a slightly acrid taste.

He could see the road very clearly as it stretched across the plain to the very foot of the Taurus, a narrow line, perfectly white, not like a road at all. It was as though a school-child had taken a pail of lime and traced this road over the flat plain just so that it should not remain empty, just to adorn it.

Towards evening a filmy veil of smoke sank over the plain and the white line grew faint and blurred. Then the moon rose and it was clear again, but strangely magic now, and the fear grew in him that it might soon be snatched away by some unseen hands. And what if he did not come by then? What if he took another road? What if his men had lied to him? . . . No! He had to come this time, he had to! This business must be settled once and for all.

Sparrows alighted on the road and a large eagle-like bird stood there swaying in the face of the wind, wings spread taut, intent, head tilted to one side as though it were watching the road too—waiting for something. Shreds of dry grass stuck to his clothes. His knees ached. His feet, his right hand were numb and his back felt like wool. He had large hands with long yellow fingers. They lay side by side, very still, like the hands of a corpse, mournful, dreary . . . Suddenly the right hand came to life, spectre-like, and seized the revolver. It was new and shining bright. The left hand went to the cylinder. It whirled swiftly and bullets gushed out like water. In an instant those deft hands had loaded them again. And so it went on, the bullets passing at lightning speed from hands to revolver, coming and going so fast that fingers and bullets seemed tangled into each other. Surely there was no other in all this wide orb who could beat the mastery of these hands . . . A monotonous noise came from the revolver as from the steady shuttling of a loom. Suddenly it slipped to the ground, neglected, and the two hands lay inert again. When he lifted his head Kizilgedik was in full sunlight and the veins of the mauve rocks flashed with dazzling brightness. A thick haze had sunk over the plain, hiding the white road. The shrill chorus of cicadas grew louder as the sun blazed over the earth, turning the rocks to red-hot iron. It was impossible to so much as lay a finger on them.

There was another road to his left that ran from Dumlukalé to Saricham. And another still, leading down to Chukurköprü, and dozens, hundreds of paths, as though a spider's web had been taken from a branch and spread over the plain.

The pummel of his Turcoman saddle would be of pure silver, and so would the stirrups and the reins. They would flash and sparkle from afar as the rider came.

A cloud of dust rose from the road below Kozan. Something flashed inside it. He sprang up, his eyes fixed expectantly on the dust. It subsided and there was nothing there. In a fit of anger he threw himself on to the rocks, cutting his knees until the bones showed, knocking his head until his hair was wet with blood. Then the lifeless hand moved swiftly to the revolver, and the monotonous rattling began again, unremitting, maddening . . .

The sun was noon-high, striking up blinding sparks from some split straw on the road. A man came into view, but this could not be him, not this drooping dirty dusty creature. He would never go walking like this, his tongue hanging out in the heat. He watched as the man reached the stream and jumped in with a great splash, clothes and all. The revolver hurtled through the air and fell far away.

His skin was burnt red by the sun, as though marked by a fiery brand, the flesh almost flaking off. The sweat ran all over his body. Stifling, panting for breath he leapt to his feet and bared his breast to the breeze. Then he saw the rider, proud and erect on a handsome steed. Trembling with excitement, he scrambled down the crags to the road, just as the rider was drawing near. The revolver exploded and the rider slumped off the horse to the ground. He ran up, grasped his shoulders and looked into his eyes. They were large with fear.

'Do you remember me, Fiend?' he cried. There was no answer. 'What, have we hurt you a little?' The rider was still as a stone. Angrily, with the accumulated spite of many years, he hauled him to his feet. The man toppled over at once like a rotten tree. 'Get up, Fiend, up, up! Ten years I've waited for this day, fifteen, twenty years, a hundred years . . .' He dealt him a piercing kick in the ribs. 'A century . . . For this day . . .'

Suddenly a drowning rain poured down, green as poison, and the day turned greenish black. Smoke spurted from the crags and swirled with the green rain in furious squalls towards the swamp. With all his strength he grabbed the man again, but he slipped from his hands and rolled away down the road at a dizzying speed. He threw himself after him, but lost his hold again. On and on the man rolled, eluding his grasp, until the rain let up and the crags were smoking no longer. A scorching sun came out, drying everything in an instant.

The man was now quite dry. He held him by the neck and propped him up against a rock. His eyes were closed, but he was breathing. His horse was there, still as a statue. He stripped it of its saddle and harness and gave it a kick to make it go. The horse reared a couple of times and galloped off, tail erect, towards the Chukurova plain. Then seizing the man by the ear he thrust the bit into his mouth. Next he tied the saddle over his back and mounted him, driving him on towards the stream that sparkled far in the distance like pure molten silver. As he was in a hurry and the stream was a long way off, he led him through a field of thistles. At first the Fiend balked, but calmly, without a word, he drew his dagger from his belt and pricked him in the hip. The Fiend gave a bound and spurted forward. He was streaming with blood when they came out of the thistles. Next he forced him into a clump of burdock, and soon he was a mass of burrs from the waist down. He felt him tremble beneath him and spurred him on towards a stretch of blackthorn. There the Fiend stopped short and threw himself down.

'No, nooo! None of that! Up you get, my stout fellow! Don't push me too far or I'll strip you naked to drag you through that blackthorn. How shall I kill you, how, how? By what means? I'm at a loss. For twenty years, day and night, I've thought about this, but I've still not found a fit death for you.'

The bullets were in his hands again. They came and went, came and went from one hand to the other, wet with his sweat. He picked up the revolver. In a trice he had loaded it and just as quickly he emptied it again.

So the Fiend would not get up, eh? He went up to him and pulled off his shoes and socks. Then with his dagger he pierced his ear. Oh, only a little bit, and just look at him, up and away, running for his life right into the blackthorn scrub! He caught up with him and mounted on his back again. How he was trotting, the Fiend! He always called him the Fiend now. He did not want to remember his name. The very sound of it made him retch. With a desperate effort the Fiend hurled himself into a blackthorn bush, striving to creep down to its deepest roots. He dragged him out by one leg. The blood was flowing from his body now like water from a thousand springs. He rubbed the wounds with earth which turned to blood-soaked mud and dried stiff in the sun. Again the Fiend made a run for it, but barefoot, how far could he go! His silver-embroidered shalvar-trousers were hanging in tatters now and his legs running with blood again. With a leap he was on his back once more, lashing at him with his powerful whip made of a bull's organ.

And now it was night. The Fiend's cheeks and mouth were torn to shreds by the bit. If he let him slip through his fingers now, in the darkness of the night, he might never get hold of him again. He tied the strap of the reins to his wrist. And so, the Fiend moaning louder and louder, they went round and round in the blackthorn scrub until day dawned. And then what should he see! The Fiend, quite naked now, his skin torn and gory, had no nose at all . . . It had fallen off somewhere. As for his ears they hung like a cord and wound round his neck. They came to the road and there the Fiend threw himself down, senseless into the dust. Dead? What if he were dead? He was struck with dismay. The Fiend should never be allowed to die so quickly . . .

His grip on the revolver tightened. He shook out the bullets, filled the cylinder again, but with trembling hands now, unsteady, clumsy . . .

He bent over, put his ear to the Fiend's heart, then gave a cry of joy. 'Ah, you don't die so easily, Fiend!' He trussed him up securely with a coil of rope, got on to the horse and strapped the other end of the rope round the horse's neck. Then he rode on very slowly, dragging the Fiend through the dust of the road.

Yes, he was strong, the Fiend, not one to die readily . . . And so they came to the stream and stopped in a wooded place. He filled a large can with salt, poured water into it and stirred the mixture thoroughly. When the salt had melted he emptied it all over the Fiend, who gave a spring and plumped sprawling to the ground, jumped up again, rubbed his eyes as though roused from a deep sleep and took to his heels. He followed him on the horse, but the Fiend hurled himself into the stream and sank like a plummet. With a thousand difficulties he fished him out, half-drowned and for a long while contented himself with watching him as he lay there in a faint, on the bank, his blood dripping steadily to the ground, draining out of his veins.

All at once the Fiend came to and bolted once more. It would have been easy to catch him, but he just went after him, pretending to fall behind whenever the Fiend looked back, letting him hope, even rejoice. On and on he kept up the chase, until the Fiend stopped dead in his tracks. 'Here I am,' he panted. 'Do what you like to me. I can bear everything, but not this death by slow degrees.'

'Is that so? Oh, is that so?' How he laughed . . .

This time he tied the rope round his arms and again about the knees and lugged him to the water side. And now the Fiend was begging. How he begged! Like no one ever begged since the beginning of the world. This was the best of all, to have him there grovelling like a dog. He decided not to do anything to him so long as he begged. The Fiend soon caught on to this. He was still begging as the sun went down, his voice hoarse now, unintelligible.

All through the night he let him whine like a cur. Then, as day was dawning he seized his little finger, twisted it back and broke it. The ring finger, the middle finger, the index, the thumb, one after the other he broke them all to pulp and went on with the other hand. Then he forced the forearm back from the elbow until it broke too. The Fiend was silent now, his face racked with pain. He took the razor from the saddlebag on the horse, honed it well and, slowly, carefully, carved the ear into a long thin strip that he twined round his neck. After doing the same with the other ear, he set to stripping the skin off his chest and back. He worked quickly now and when he had done, he sowed the raw flesh with salt and nitric acid. The Fiend's body tautened and stretched rigid on the ground, without a sound.

Swiftly the bullets poured out of the revolver into the palm of his hand. Then back into the cylinder and out again, blithely. He tossed them high in the air, catching them as they fell, expertly. They were shining brightly from so much handling. At last he let go of the revolver. It dropped at his feet. He was tired.

The sun was growing hot. The earth cracked open and the

39

stream evaporated in swirls of smoke vanishing into the sky. 'Ah,' he sighed deeply. 'Aaah . . .' his cry resounded in the distance. What if someone had heard him? . . .

He threw himself upon the Fiend and snatched at a tuft of his hair. It came off, scalp and all, and he flung it into the dry bed of the stream. Then he saw the hanging tongue and, grasping it with his two hands, he pulled. He pulled and pulled. It was midday and still he could not tear it off. It only stretched longer and longer in his hands. In the end he cut it off with the razor. Then he broke the toes one by one, then the legs. All the bones in his body he ground to powder, but the heart was beating still, very fast. Slowly he began to gouge the right eye out with a twig. At every poke the Fiend tensed as though he would sit up. As he was starting on the left eye the Fiend was seized with a fit of trembling. Terrible spasms shook his whole body. Just then the yellow ants appeared. They poured in from the dry river-bed, from the grass and trees until the ground was all yellow with them, and made for the gouged eyes, the torn lips, the flayed broken body that was soon nothing but a seething quivering yellow mass. He sat down on a stone and watched. This was the crowning victory. He closed his eyes. But he was not one to die easily, oh no! The ants would devour only a half of him, still alive . . .

There was a loud noise. He opened his eyes and saw the Fiend on his feet before him. It startled him out of his wits. Was this man the devil himself? How many lives did he have? Only a couple of seconds and he had crashed lifeless to the ground. Yet his heart was beating, quickly, quickly . . .

The Fiend's black horse was running wild. That horse would never let itself be caught by any stranger. It would run wild for months, for years and only fall into somebody's hands if shot at. He lifted up the Fiend and threw him on to the horse. His head dangled to one side, his mangled limbs to the other. With a long long rope, maybe a hundred yards long, he strapped him to the horse's back. His heart was beating still . . . And now for days he would be carried on the back of this untouchable horse to be devoured piecemeal by vultures and eagles and other birds of prey. With all his strength he brought the whip down on the horse, who bolted in full career. 'I know how you love horses, my stout fellow. Well, let it be a horse carries you to the last . . .' He would have no grave either, every piece of him would be ground in a bird's gizzard . . .

He was tired out now, exhausted, with hardly strength enough to lift his hand. Slowly he took a few sips of fresh water. He longed for a good meal.

The black horse was kicking and rearing, bounding backward and forward, neighing wildly in a frenzied attempt to throw off the thing on its back. All of a sudden the sky was overcast with angry screeching eagles. Then from way over Anavarza came the vultures. A slow-moving eagle gathered itself up in a ball, swished down like lightning over the horse, tore off a piece of flesh and rose up again just as swiftly. At once the horse disappeared under an agitated mass of wings. It tried to make a dash for it, but the eagles and vultures swooped down in throngs, tearing at the Fiend's flesh, never letting go. On and on the horse galloped, like the wind, and in the Chukurova sky crowds of eagles, vultures, kites, hawks, buzzards swarmed above it wherever it went. Steadily, like rain, the blood dripped from their beaks on to the earth and the dust of the plain. Drip drip, drip . . . Endlessly . . .

3

It was raining, a thin steady drizzle, and the rotting leaves, the summer-long dried grass, all smelled of rain. The night was utterly black, not a tiny light, not a single star to be seen.

Apprehensive, ashamed, yet vaguely exultant Mahmut went up the stairs of the mansion into the presence of Dervish Bey who had been expecting him for the last two days.

'What news? Good, let's hope, at last.'

Mahmut was silent.

'So you let him get away again?'

'He escaped. He's the very devil, that man. It would take forty devils to catch and kill him. No man could. I waylaid him just where they told me, in the gully of Yalnizdut. I fired twice and he fell, but just as I was going up to him, he leapt on to his horse and galloped away. Five shots I fired after him and all five hit him, but still he got away. Bullets don't work with this man . . .'

Dervish Bey snorted. 'What d'you mean, bullets don't work? You can't hit him, that's all.'

'Bey, don't you know me?' Mahmut said. 'Do I ever miss? No, forgive me, Bey, but there's something about this man, some magic . . .'

Dervish Bey was incensed. 'If bullets don't work with him, why don't you catch him, why don't you tear him to pieces with your bare hands? Does it have to be with bullets? Five years we've been after him. Not to be able to kill a man in all this time! What kind of people are you anyway? A man who murdered my brother, and with the greatest of ease! Ah, my house is dishonoured. Everyone's turned coward on me.'

'Don't say that, Bey,' Mahmut said. 'Not to me. My life is yours. I would die for you.'

Dervish Bey fell silent. Nothing could make him open his mouth now. He would remain there stiff as a ramrod, not even dismissing Mahmut, who would have to stand before him and wait.

Mahmut blamed himself. In all these five years he had not been able to kill Murtaza Bey, though he could have done so a dozen times. Always something had paralysed his hand and stopped him from pulling the trigger. I'll do it next time I catch him, he would resolve, without fail . . . Slowly he lifted his head. Dervish Bey's face was twisted in a frozen mask of grief and rancour, a pitiful sight. 'But why doesn't he kill him himself?' Mahmut wondered. 'Back east where the Fourth Army is stationed a man kills his enemy with his own hands. Here, people use others to avenge their blood. They train them from childhood just to kill.' His thoughts dwelt on his own predicament, on his father and mother, how they had come to settle in this Chukurova plain. A strange languor overcame him, but he chased away these memories. 'What kind of men are these Chukurova people? What kind of Beys? I'd wish them on my worst enemy . . . Come, Bey, kill Murtaza Bey yourself if you've got the guts.' But he knew there was no choice for him. Sooner or later he would have to do it, and either get away to spend the rest of his life a fugitive at Dervish Bey's beck and call, or be thrown into prison, there to be killed in his turn by the Akyollu family's men. There was no third way.

Day was dawning when Dervish Bey's lips moved at last. 'Go,' was all he said, but the word pierced Mahmut to the heart. He dragged himself back home. Meyro was waiting for him, anxious, dishevelled, as she always did when he went out after Murtaza Bey. She would neither sleep nor eat until he returned. The children were asleep. Mahmut drew back the coverlet and, bending his huge head, kissed and fondled them, without caring whether he woke them up or not.

'Good news?' Meyro asked.

Mahmut shook his head.

'You'll never kill that man,' she cried, 'because you don't believe you can do it. Let me go to the Bey and tell him to find someone else. Let me, please, Mahmut. You know as well as I do that you don't intend to kill Murtaza Bey.'

Mahmut leaned closer to the children. 'My little ones, my babies,' he murmured. The children's arms lay over the cover-

43

let, locked into each other. 'My dear little ones, my babies . . .'
Mahmut had a beautiful voice. Meyro was as much in love with
his voice as she was with him. Over and over again he repeated
'my little ones, my babies' in a sing-song lullaby, then drifted
into a long plaintive nostalgic Kurdish song, and Meyro began
to weep. It made him weep too.

It was nothing to him to kill a man. After all, this was what
the Bey had been keeping him for all these years, him and
others too. But why had he been chosen to kill Murtaza Bey
and not one of the others? 'It's because I'm the one he trusts
most,' he thought with pride. 'And yet for five years I've done
nothing. I'm not worthy of his trust. Meyro's right. I never
really believed I would kill Murtaza and that's why each time
I had the chance I failed, but I will now, I will! I can't bite the
hand that feeds me. I can't go on deceiving my benefactor.'

'Whoever kills Murtaza Bey will be killed in his turn. The
house of Akyollu is the most powerful in all the Chukurova.'

'I will kill him!'

'Murtaza Bey never did anyone any harm. He's a kind gentle
person, a friend to the poor and the destitute. And though he
has such a blood enemy as Dervish Bey he never even carries a
gun. How can you raise your hand against such a man?'

'That's a lie. He does have a gun. And it's a lie too that he's
a friend of the poor. No Bey ever can be. No Bey has ever even
considered the poor as human beings. I'll kill this Murtaza Bey.
Didn't the Akyollus kill Dervish Bey's big brother?'

'Well, Dervish Bey hasn't been gathering pears either!'

'What about Dervish Bey's family? Didn't the Akyollus kill
all of them?'

'They gave as good as they got . . .'

If Murtaza Bey was killed wouldn't his older brother Mustafa
Bey kill Dervish Bey in his turn? Wouldn't it be a pity for the
Bey? On the other hand, if no one killed Murtaza Bey then the
Akyollus would make no move to further the feud. Because it
was Dervish Bey's turn to kill now. Because one summer night
Mustafa Akyollu's man, Bald Muharrem, had shot Dervish
Bey's brother, Jevdet Bey, from under the trellis on which he
was sleeping. Jevdet Bey had sprung more than two yards in the
air and with a terrible cry had crashed dead to the ground, his

44

thorax shattered by three dumdum bullets. Not two months afterwards Dervish Bey had Bald Muharrem killed in the prison. But Murtaza Bey must be killed too, because it was he who had ordered his brother's murder. Brother for brother, and according to tradition he could not do it himself. It must be done in the same way . . . What tradition? Hadn't Dervish Bey made up this tradition himself? Murtaza Bey, who knew how it would be, had vanished without a trace on the day after Jevdet Bey's murder. But no place would be safe for him henceforth. He was inexorably doomed. For just three years he managed to avoid detection, but in the fourth year Dervish Bey's men ferreted him out. 'Don't on any account kill him,' was Dervish Bey's message to them. 'Now he's discovered, he'll come back home. He must be killed here. But keep a close watch on him.' And indeed, terrified at finding himself exposed and defenceless in a foreign place, Murtaza soon returned to the Akyollu mansion where he could guard himself better.

'I will kill him.'

'You have to. Killing's your job in life and Murtaza Bey has fallen to you. You must kill him and try not to be caught. And if you are, I'll maintain you in prison like a king. I'll bring up your son like the son of a Vizir. Remember? Who arranged your marriage? Who protected you all your life?'

For a whole month Dervish Bey took no notice of him at all. He never stirred from the mansion either, nor spoke to anyone. He ate his meals alone. It was as though he was in mourning. Mahmut was ashamed. He tried hard to whip himself into a state of anger, to make himself believe he would kill Murtaza Bey, but it all seemed unreal to him.

In the end he plucked up his courage and went to Dervish Bey. 'I give you my word, Bey,' he said. 'I won't let this gun out of my hand before I've settled his account. I won't set foot on this farm. I won't lie with my wife. I won't rock my children's cradle. I swear it.'

Dervish Bey's face assumed a look of contemptuous disbelief. 'No, my poor Mahmut, I don't think you've got it in you to cope with that devil. I must find another man for the job. It's not your fault. There are some things some men just can't do. Anyway, take this. Since you say you won't be coming to the farm for some time, you may need it . . .' And he held out a handful of money.

'Thank you, Bey, but I don't want it,' Mahmut said.

Dervish Bey frowned. 'Take it!' he ordered sharply.

Mahmut's young face flushed scarlet. 'Don't, Bey,' he said. 'I'd die rather than take this money. I won't touch any money before I've cleaned up this business.' He stepped up to the Koran that hung on the wall in a silver-embroidered velvet case and laid his hand on it. 'By this holy book I swear I'll kill him. I swear it on the heads of my wife and children, on your dear head, Bey . . .'

And still it all seemed a game to him . . . But he had sworn on the Koran . . . He rode home and repeated his solemn pledge before his wife, beside his children's cradle. Now he was saved. He could not go back. Even if he doubted, he would have to kill Murtaza Bey. He had always wondered what kind of man he really was, this Murtaza Bey. He looked so young with his pale smooth hairless face. Sad too . . . He never laughed. Why hadn't he been able to kill him all these years? Who knows? Anyway he was going to do it now. For three years he had trailed him like a shadow. He knew what he did, where he went every hour of the day. He could find him this very minute as though he had placed him there with his own hand . . .

A slow steady drizzle fell over the night and a dizzying odour rose from the earth. He spurred his horse towards the Akyollu farm. He felt no fear, no faintness, no emotion. Too many times, for too many years he had lived through all this. He tied his horse to a tree in the reed-bed below the farm. It was the same tree he had tied his horse to, maybe a hundred times. There was no danger. Even the savage hounds of the Akyollu farm had grown accustomed to him over these many years and never barked at him. The farmhands too were familiar with him and had even forgotten that Mahmut might kill, that it was for this he had been trailing Murtaza Bey all this time. People who looked on Mahmut's child-like, innocent face could never believe he could kill anyone. No one paid much attention to this timid shrinking man who blushed crimson when addressed and never knew where to put his hands. And it was the same at Dervish Bey's farm. No one in the world thought Mahmut of

46

any importance and this hurt him to the core.

Unhurriedly he made his way into the farm. The dogs, recognizing him, came up and rubbed themselves against his legs. By their presence he knew he was near the mansion now. He found the wall and groped his way along it. The sentinels were always posted beside the door. They must be there now, though he could hear nothing but the drizzling rain and saw no cigarettes burning. Not even the men's silhouettes could be discerned in the darkness.

In the end he found the window and with the nimbleness of a cat hoisted himself up along its grille to the balcony. Murtaza Bey slept on the upper floor of the house, in a room like a garret. He slipped in. It was very dark. His heart began to beat faster. He picked out two figures in the bed and knew the man by his breathing. Murtaza Bey lay only a couple of feet away from him. He drew out his gun, but his hand trembled. What would happen when they heard the sound of shots? Wouldn't they come rushing up from everywhere, blocking the stairs, surrounding the whole house that very instant? He replaced the gun. Suddenly there was a flash of lightning. It illuminated the whole room, and he saw Murtaza Bey's pale narrow face, sad, pearly with sweat, and his wife beside him, one large breast sticking out, bare. A sudden frenzy of lust swept over him and in an instant he had drawn the gun and fired again and again. With a terrible scream Murtaza Bey vaulted high in the air. Coolly Mahmut thrust the gun into its holster and walked down the stairs without hurrying. The mansion was in a turmoil. People were rushing all over the place, but nobody had the presence of mind to light a lamp. He heard Mustafa Akyollu scream three times: 'My house is ruined. Ruined, ruined!' Mahmut walked out of the front door through the frenzied rushing to and fro of shouting people and barking dogs, and at the same unhurried pace came to the reed-bed. He untied his horse, leaped on to the saddle and rode away. After a while, as the pandemonium at the farm died down behind him, he lit a cigarette and began humming a mournful tune. Far in the distance Mount Hemité was lit up by flash after flash of lightning and the thunder rolled through the sky.

Meyro was waiting at the door. She took the horse to the

47

stable and Mahmut was asleep the minute he lay down on his bed.

The next morning, very early, he went to the Bey. He was tired out, as though a load of a thousand years had only just dropped from his shoulders. 'May all your enemies live just so long,' he said, and he laid his gun down before Dervish Bey.

Dervish Bey embraced him and kissed him on the forehead, three times. 'Bless you,' he said. 'Bless you. You have accomplished a sacred task. You have more than repaid me for all I've done for you.'

It was raining, a thin clammy slow drizzle, as though it was not raining at all, as though the rain had frozen in the air, as though this rain had been falling for a thousand years and would go on for ever, murky, muddy, glaucous, ash-like . . .

4

From far and wide, from the remote mountain hamlets of the Taurus, the most renowned keening women had come to hold the wake. Their heads swathed in white shawls, they swayed and beat their breasts and wailed, and the mansion rang with doleful voices, shrill or low, spirited, timid, fiery, monotonous.

The yard in front of the mansion had turned to viscous mud. And still the rain came down, slow, clammy, a dirty yellow rain. The windows and doors, the stairs, the trees were steeped with mud and so were the people who came and went, not knowing what to do, their faces long, yellow and grieving. Now and then one of the keening women would utter a piercing shriek that could be heard far out on the plain, and the people in the yard would start up with dread.

The wailing and lamenting of the women never stopped for even one moment. They huddled around the dead man, who lay stretched out under a sheet, and extolled his life and deeds, his ancestry, his goodness, every single thing about him. And the rain kept falling, miry, viscid.

Mustafa Akyollu had shut himself up in his room, deaf to the keening, blind to the rain. He was thinking, planning. His nerves, his veins were strained to snapping point. An ominous blackness filled his heart. He must set to work now, tonight. Dervish Bey must be killed before the week was out, before Murtaza's body was cold in its grave . . .

In the yard a cart had been prepared, laden with myrtle branches, the leaves crushed, dark green under the rain. Mustafa Akyollu caught their bitter scent and he thought how all the deaths ever since his childhood had carried this same odour of myrtle and blood. And always the endless screaming of women . . . The huddled mourners . . . The incredible hatred, the lips pinched with outrage. And the clammy endless rain, dirty, yellow. And the white headcloths, swaying like a field of grain in the north wind.

All at once the keening stopped. The yard was suddenly very quiet and even the rain let up. The funeral procession set out. The graveyard lay on the slope of an old Hittite tell. A single aged mulberry tree stood there, half its bark rotting away, the other half decked with leaves as green as fresh young shoots. The ground was clayey, sticky as glue. They began to dig. Steam rose from the clayey earth, the gravestones, the rotting mulberry tree, the Hittite tell, the reed-bed and the men's backs, a bluish vapour, blinding, like a cloud. They laid the corpse into the gluey grave and fitted in shafts of resinous pinewood over it. Then they heaped myrtle branches on to the shafts and shovelled back the earth, while the *hodja* recited verses from the Koran and the mourners listened with folded hands. The bitter smell of myrtle was everywhere. The rain began to fall again. From the wounds of the dead man a yellow serous fluid would be oozing, warm as blood, and soon it would fill up the whole grave . . .

Mustafa Bey turned and dragged himself away, weighed down by a single thought, not the dead man, not death, just one overriding thought: Dervish Bey must be killed at all costs, and before the week was out. For years now Mustafa Akyollu had been preparing for this. He knew by rote what Dervish Bey did, where he went, every minute detail of his life. The enemy never forgives and he knows his foe better than any other. For the Akyollus, the mansion up on the hill west of the Savrun River was a dark fearsome mountain of death which they had to look upon the minute they opened their eyes. And for the Sarioglu household too, the Akyollu mansion, also built on an elevated mound, held the same gloomy foreboding of death. None of the Akyollus had ever seen the inside of the Sarioglu mansion, but they knew every corner of it as if they had lived there all their lives. And it was the same with the Sarioglus.

The rain fell with slow persistence. It had a dirty oily consistency. Now and then the sun would appear and a slimy sticky vapour would rise from the ground. Then again that hot, thick, dirty rain would begin. A bald-headed bird was perched on the old leafless fig tree in the yard, its neck drawn in under the rain, wet through, its feathers matted and stiff.

Mustafa Bey called to one of his men. 'Big Hassan,' he said, 'get hold of that bird and dry its wings so it can fly again. It looks like a young bird.'

'It's only an old vulture,' Big Hassan said disdainfully, but he ran up to the tree and caught the bird. 'It's been shot in the wing, Bey.'

'Well, make a salve and see if you can heal it.'

A flight of bedraggled sparrows swept down over the mulberry tree by the window and flew off again, twittering noisily.

His eyes were dry, his face as stern and rigid, as stony as it had ever been. It was as though the death of this brother, who had been so dear to him, had left him quite indifferent. He sat in the room, his head in his large hands, and stared at the gleaming new revolver that lay on the table beside a big heap of bullets.

'Big Hassan!' Hassan was waiting at the door. He came in at once.

'Yes, Bey?' he said.

'What's Dervish doing?'

'Doing? That you know better than I do, Bey! He won't stir a step out of his house now, that one!'

'Then how are we to kill him? We have to, in not more than four or five days.'

'Yes, Bey. Black Hüseyin . . .'

'How long has he been gone?'

'Three days. I've sent word to Saribag village. He'll be here any time now.'

Rain was seeping into the room from under the window. In the flickering light of the oil-lamp his face was longer, yellower, the lines of his brow deeper. His one-day growth of beard seemed to be a month old. But only his trembling hands revealed the turmoil of his mind.

How to catch him, that was the problem. To kill him was easy, but to get hold of him alive . . . To take him to Murtaza's grave, Murtaza who was so young, so handsome, so sad, to kill him there, a long slow death . . .

Though he had never spoken to him and only seen him once, he knew Dervish down to every quirk of his character. He was proud to have such an enemy: generous, brave, an upholder of the old traditions, an island of righteousness in the mire of wickedness, depravity and dishonesty of present-day Chuku-rova. An island, yes, and only two such remained, where probity, honour, human values were still valid, the two houses of Sarioglu and Akyollu, and both were doomed to extinction, living out their last days. Within a week Dervish would be gone, and then it would be his own turn. Their children? Of what good were they, each one emulating those upstart Aghas . . .

He opened the window and leaned out. A few cool drops of rain touched his face.

What was Dervish thinking now, what was he doing, knowing that his death warrant was signed, that if not this night, then the next, the sentence would be executed? Ah, but what had Murtaza done, who had lived so long with the same knowledge, what but bow his head like a sacrificial sheep? Why had he not locked his door? Why had he not changed his room every night? He had been weary, his own dear brother, weary of dying every day a little bit. He could not stand it any more. One could read it in his eyes. He had been almost ready to rush over to the Sarioglu mansion and beg Dervish to finish him off quickly. Yet how afraid he had been at first, how he had fled to Istanbul and kept moving to a new house every week. To what avail . . . The enemy had tracked him down in the end, and he had come back to his homeland, resigned to his fate.

The rain was gathering strength and beating down ever more loudly on the roof tiles. The door opened and Black Hüseyin appeared, wet to the skin, the water streaming down his body.

'Well?' Mustafa Bey said.

'It's Mahmut who killed him, as you must have heard, Bey. I kept a good watch on him and I can tell you he's half dead already that one, weeping, his face yellow. How could I have killed him, so brave, so handsome, he was saying. Let me go and kiss the threshold of the Akyollu mansion. Since they're going to kill me anyway, let them kill me there and lay me in a grave beside Murtaza Bey, paradise and hell side by side. He cast his gun to the ground and began to trample on it like a madman until the gun had sunk deep into the mud, out of sight. I don't want to see it ever, he shouted, the gun that killed Murtaza Bey. Then he set out. He was coming here. Dervish Bey's men were trying to stop him, but he would let no one come near. He was so strange, singing a Kurdish lament, and the Chiyanli Kurds there told me it was all about Murtaza Bey. May they turn blind the eyes that look on you, may they rot away the hands that are raised against you, may his house be ruined who has caused your death . . . And his voice rang out all night all through the Anavarza plain . . .'

At first Mustafa Bey had been listening to him impassively. Then his face began to pale until it was white as parchment. 'Stop,' he cried sharply. 'That's enough, Hüseyin.' There was a long death-like silence. When he spoke again his voice was calm, as though nothing had passed. 'What shall we do about that Fiend?'

'He hasn't stirred from his house, and won't for a long time,' Hüseyin said.

'Can't we lure him out, somehow?'

'Not for the moment.'

'Then how are we to kill him? We must do it quickly, before the week is out.'

'They know me too well,' Hüseyin said. 'I couldn't take a step into the Sarioglu estate again.'

'How to smoke the wolf out of his lair? How to kill Dervish quickly? Think, say something!'

Hamdi was sucking fiercely at his thumb as always when perplexed. 'We've got to kill him, yes, we've got to.' He was trembling all over. 'You know best, Bey. Just tell us what to do.'

'Who's ever heard of a man remaining shut up all his life?' Big Hassan said. 'He's bound to go out some time. Then we'll lay a trap and kill him.'

'I can't wait,' Mustafa Bey said.

'Then,' Hüseyin said, 'there's nothing for it but to set fire to his house . . .'

'We can't do that,' Mustafa Bey said. 'Go now, all of you, and think of some other way. He must be killed this week.'

'Bey,' Big Hassan said, 'it's not easy to kill an old wolf like Dervish in just a couple of days. Let's see if your life will be long enough for that!'

'It has to be this week, d'you understand me, Big Hassan?'

Hassan left the room without replying. Mustafa Bey picked up his revolver, loaded it and fastened it to his belt. The rest of

53

the bullets he fitted into his cartridge-belt which he strapped to his waist. Then he went down the stairs. 'Bring my horse,' he called.

The rain fell on, unabating, monotonous, neither increasing nor decreasing. Slowly he rode down the slope to the plain. Then, spurring his horse, he crossed the Savrun River and galloped on through the darkness. The ground was muddy and the horse sometimes tripped and sank knee-deep. After an hour of this it stopped altogether and would not take another step forward. But Mustafa Bey did not turn back. There in the distance, towering over the plain shone the light he knew so well, watched through the years, recurring in his dreams. As the day began to break he drew nearer. The light went out and out of the greying dawn Dervish Bey's large house emerged amid the plane trees on the hill. His throat tightened and his eyes began to ache. How many, oh how many brave men of the Akyollu family had been swallowed up by that house . . . Two warm tears rolled down his face. And now Murtaza, his dear brother, was lying in the cold slimy ground, while his enemy lived on in that huge mansion.

'No, no, I'll kill you, whatever it costs me, before the week is out, before the rain stops. Yes, before this deadly rain lets up you too will be laid into this black earth.'

Slowly the walls of the mansion whitened and sounds rose from the surrounding farm. Then a deep voice boomed out above all the other sounds . . .

And still the rain fell on, as though it would never stop, dense, foggy, slippery, cord-like.

5

A phalanx of cranes was flying in from the Gavur Mountains, gliding over Anavarza, westward in the direction of the Gülek Pass.

It is not every day that you can spot cranes in formation. Maybe it is a good omen. How marvellous they look, all in a group like an embroidery over the sky. Like a nostalgic promise of reunion, of long life . . . Their haunts are wild and lonely, near lakes and marshes, and when they fly they rise high, very high in the sky, tiny black spots stringed out over the blue.

There was a cool gust of wind and clouds came moving in, very black, from over the Mediterranean, north towards the mountains. The day grew darker. Violent blasts whipped up from east and west. The phalanx of cranes was broken up, thrown into confusion, reduced to a single ball tossed right and left, helpless, defeated. Then the wind dropped and the phalanx formed again. A furious rain began to fall, but the cranes flew on and vanished into the clouds.

The crane is a greenish colour. Its voice is harsh and sad . . .

Dervish Bey saw it with his own eyes, how it fell into the yard, the wounded crane, with a dull noise like a stone. They brought it to him, its feathers matted, wet to the bone, smelling dank and sour like human sweat, still warm . . . Its mouth opened and shut several times, and then it died. Dervish Bey examined it carefully, but found no trace of a wound. He put it down gently, and they took it away.

They are looking at me as if I were already dead. With pity, with awe as before the sacred mystery of death . . .

The rain was coming down in torrents. And under the rain a group of bare-bellied children were playing with the dead crane. Two little boys had grabbed it by the wings which were stretched wide open, two more by its long legs and they waded through the mud, dragging the limp bird along, followed by a howling mob of children each holding one of the crane's

55

coloured feathers and prancing about in a weird wild dance. On they went, the rainwater streaming down their bodies, until they came to the stream. There they washed the mud-caked crane clean. It was nothing but a skeleton now, with a few matted feathers stuck to its body.

Why do they keep looking at me, with huge eyes, wide with grief and pity? How difficult to bear the weight of those eyes, staring in superstitious fear as at a consecrated beast! They all know I shall be killed, if not today then tomorrow. But I'm alive, alive now, even though I may be dead tomorrow. They'll all die too sooner or later, but I don't look at them in that way. They don't look at each other like that. The crane falling to its death never knew it was going to die. And if you don't know you will die, you know nothing. You're not even alive. Think, what if death did not exist and the fear of death . . . How tedious life would be! It's the inevitability of death that makes us want so much to live a little longer. Cranes never feel that passionate longing, so utterly human. No one can avoid death. Mine will come earlier, that's all. All I can do is try and gain a little time. A few days, a few moments . . . A year at the most, and then inexorable death . . .

He shivered and a trembling that was warm and bitter and voluptuous spread through his body. 'I shall become extinct, perish from the earth, be no more. Years and years will pass over me, hundreds and hundreds, millions and millions, and I shall feel nothing, a blank, a vacuum. Never, never shall I exist again. This falling rain, this blowing wind, the rising sun . . . The rebirth of spring, the warm handshake of a friend . . . But why, why did I have Murtaza killed, inviting death, why, for what reason? If he were living now this business would have been done with once and for all. Mahmut didn't want to kill him. I forced him to. He knew it would be the end for him too. So why did he do it?'

The stark awareness of death, of annihilation struck him to the depths of his being. He began to shout out loud. 'No one, no single creature on earth has ever suffered what I'm suffering. And they say that what makes men bear it all is that no one believes in his own death. What a lie! Even the most witless of

56

human beings know they will die one day. They would never be so attached to this world if they didn't. I, Dervish Sarioglu, know that I shall die, that I shall be killed, that I am doomed, irrevocably. But I can do nothing about it. And because I know, I die and die anew every minute of my life. No one on earth has ever suffered such torment.'

How horrible these death-games that mankind have invented! And the worst is this blood-for-blood game, elevated to the rank of a tradition too! How disgusting . . . And it was in my power to have ended it all. So why then did I hound Murtaza to death, like the hand of fate? Why didn't I allow him the slightest chance to save himself? Is there no alternative in this terrible game of death? They killed my brother Jevdet and I killed their brother Murtaza. Here it should all end . . . But it won't. Though Mustafa Akyollu is a clever man, he will never have the strength to desist. Just as I did not have the strength . . .

'But I won't let myself be killed!' he shouted suddenly. 'I will defeat fate. I'll do what no one for centuries has been able to do.'

But how? That he didn't know. Only a voice inside him kept repeating, you'll escape, Dervish, you'll escape . . .

'Hatun, Hatun!' he called to his wife. 'I'll not let myself be killed, d'you hear me? He won't be able to kill me. Never! I shall live out my full life, till I'm seventy, a hundred years old, like my grandfather. They couldn't kill him and they won't kill me either. What are you looking at me like that for? As though I were dead already . . . What's the matter with you all? I'm not dead and I'm not going to die. D'you understand that, Hatun?'

'Aaah, if only . . . If only . . .' The words came out like a moan. 'If only it could be like that . . . I'd give an arm, a leg, my two eyes . . . If only we two could go away hand in hand and beg our way through the world . . . Ah, if only . . .'

'Don't worry, Hatun. Come, cheer up now, no one can ever kill me.' But even as he spoke these words, he thought how a bullet shot through the window might hit him this very minute.

What if he killed him first? Why not? Why not kill them all, children and old, men and women, wipe out the Akyollu race once and for all, and then take to the mountain? The idea fired

57

his imagination for a while. One night . . . Towards dawn . . . Everybody would be asleep. A few sticks of dynamite . . . That would be the end of the Akyollu mansion . . . Of Mustafa Akyollu, of all of them . . . And afterwards? Every day of that fugitive life would be a new reprieve for him.

'Hidayet!' he called.

Hidayet responded at once from the garden. 'Here I am, Bey.' In a moment he was in the room, standing at attention, a shining German carbine in his hand. He was a diminutive man with a smooth hairless face like a girl's, marred only by a few wrinkles that spoke of bitter experience, a face that was a mixture of cunning and innocence, of ferocity and childishness. Three cartridge-belts were strapped one over the other round his waist and two more crosswise over his breast. They were of silver and ornamented with niello, surely very old and valuable, so utterly at variance with Hidayet's casual aspect that they lent him the air of something out of a fairytale.

'Everything all right, Hidayet?'

'Yes . . . Only last night, just before dawn he came and stood there under the rain, his eyes fixed on the house, without moving.'

'Was it Akyollu himself?'

'None other. I went right up to the horse, but he was like a frozen man, deaf, blind . . . I saw his eyes as day dawned. They were like glass. Suddenly he gave a shout because he had seen me at last and he rode away like a madman.'

'Was it eight years you worked for him, Hidayet?'

'Eight years, my Bey, and I know him through and through. When he's like that, he'll do anything. If only I'd killed him there and then.'

'Perhaps it would have been a good thing, Hidayet.'

'But I couldn't do it without your permission, could I, Bey?'

'Well, if you have the chance to again, then kill him.'

'Ah, but when will we ever get that chance again? . . .'

'What news of Mahmut?'

'He's taken to the mountains with his gun and some ammunition he got from our villages and he won't give himself up. I've got children, he said. I don't want to die so young. If the

58

Bey's going to help me, let it be here in these mountains. And come summer, I'll take my wife and children and go to my own country, east, to Van . . .'

'Send word to the villages then, that he's to be helped in every way. And now tell Muharrem to take your place at the watch and come with me. We're riding into town.'

It was raining very hard, so they kept their guns hanging mouth down. The horses' hooves squelched through the mud.

'Bey,' Hidayet said as they were crossing the stream, 'we must be careful. Akyollu could catch us here.'

'Nonsense, Hidayet.'

'But, Bey, I know him well. From now on he'll follow you like your shadow. We were wrong to go out today.'

Yet, though he did not show it, Dervish Bey was on the alert. There were fresh hoofprints on the road beyond the stream, and floating on the water, tangled in a mass of branches and pine-cones, was the body of a dead eagle.

Dervish Bey reined in on the brink of the turbid reddish stream and stared at the bird. 'Odd,' he said. 'Very odd. First the crane that fell into the yard this morning and now this . . . Who could have killed this eagle?'

'Eagles aren't easily killed, Bey. They die of themselves.'

'No, no, Hidayet. Eagles too can be killed. Even eagles . . .'

The current bore the dead bird to the shore where it was stopped by overhanging tamarisk branches. Another current snatched it away and carried it to the opposite bank. On and on it went from bank to bank until it was caught in a bubbling eddy in the middle of the stream and washed away in an instant. 'Strange,' Dervish Bey said in a sigh. 'Very strange.' He spurred his horse, feeling suddenly very cold inside.

They left the stream behind and rode on, the horses' hooves sinking deep into the gluey mud. It was as though they were not advancing at all. Night was falling when a bird flushed up in front of them and almost at once a gun exploded. Hidayet threw himself down, but Dervish remained on his horse, as though nothing had happened. 'What's that, Hidayet?' he said. 'Are you afraid?' Bullets were whizzing about him. One bullet grazed his right ear. He felt nothing.

'Bey, get off the horse. It's the Akyollus . . .' Hidayet had taken shelter behind a blackthorn bush and was firing away furiously at their attackers, giving them no time to breathe.

The skirmish lasted till it was too dark to see.

'Come, Hidayet,' Dervish Bey said at last. 'Let's go back. He's raving mad, that Mustafa Akyollu.'

6

He could not sleep. His uncle kept rising before his eyes, a man like an Arab steed, so tall, so reckless, so daring . . . He saw him coming down the hill that day, blue thistles stuck all over his woollen stockings, walking with that springy gait of his, and the goats and the mist descending from the mauve crags into the gloaming with him. Then the sudden flash among the scrub oaks and the white shirts vanishing behind them. He fell, his hand pressed to his neck, and rolled down a rock. After a while he lifted his hand and the blood jetted out forming a pool on the dark earth. He rose, he fell, but he reached the village and dragged himself up the slope to the mansion through the masses of prickly pears in bloom, yellow, blue, pink, the spines piercing his body. And then he sank there in the dung and dust of the yard among the cattle.

'Water,' he said, and everybody rushed about in a panic. He leaned against a tree. It was a pear tree. And still the blood gushed from the wound, spreading through the dust. 'You know,' he said, 'who did it.'

Shots rang out in the night, endlessly. The yard, the village, the prickly pears, the rocks, the stream, even the moon above, were smothered in dust and smoke. And that moist scent of sweet basil . . . Suddenly, the shooting stopped and from the village came the thundering beat of hooves, shouts and screams. A group of sleeping eagles started up from the crags into the black sky. On and on the horses galloped through the village, vanishing into the darkness beyond the great river. And then that terrible silence. No sound but the swish of the eagles' wings.

The sun when it rose was blood-red, like a heap of glowing embers, and the mauve crags began to sweat. They sweated so, it was as though it had rained. Soon they were quite dry, glinting and sparkling with tiny pinpoints of light. And he lay there before the door of the mansion, in the dust, in his own blood that frothed and steamed under the sun, his legs drawn up to his belly, and fluttering about him a brood-hen with her newly-hatched chicks, yellow, fluffy. A huge fly, gleaming greenly, entered his nose and flew out again. Then there were three, persistent, untiring, buzzing round and round his head.

Mustafa Akyollu saw it all as though it were happening now, his father standing there motionless, his eyes glassy, staring from their sockets, fixed unblinkingly on the corpse, his face rigid, his lips blue. All under a searing sun, and not a breath of wind . . . And no one dared take the corpse away, nor touch this man of stone beside it. Towards noon a black cat approached, sniffed at the pool of blood, then settled down at his father's feet in the shelter of his dark, dwindling shadow. It had eyes like green glass.

The dust storm had broken out very suddenly. The black cat made a dash for the roof of the mansion and perched there, nervously flicking its long tail, like a green-tinted black serpent. The sun was blotted out and everything turned a murky pink. Dust filled people's mouths and eyes and noses, almost stifling them. It penetrated into the houses, into closed coffers and chests, insinuated itself under the tree-barks and people's skins and when the storm subsided everything was smothered in layers of greyish-pink dust, the trees, the grass, the mansion, people's faces and clothes, the cattle, the chickens and the dead man where he lay on the ground. And yet his father never moved, a statue of dust, his eyes always on his dead brother.

Many long years had gone by, but still he stood there, his father, in the yard before the mansion, his eyes wide open, staring . . . And the dust sweeps over him, cloud after cloud.

Mustafa Bey jumped on to his horse and galloped across the plain, followed by his men. It was raining, a slow thin dusty drizzle like the fall of dew. They dismounted on the edge of the blackthorn scrub, near the mill. Further away stretched the swamp of Sekizgözü, and the road passed between this swamp and the mill, and on towards Savrun River. The swamp merged into the river. It was a wild place which man and beast could hardly penetrate and where the narcissus bloomed in abundance. Here the road was very narrow and ran uphill. They drew the horses out of sight into the blackthorn thickets. Black Hüseyin was carrying a machine-gun. Mustafa Bey was armed with a German carbine and Big Hassan with a huge Russian-model rifle.

The sun began to shine through the dusty drizzle. The slow, imperceptible drops turned to vapour as soon as they hit the ground.

'Big Hassan, you're not to fire at Dervish, only at whoever's with him . . . Black Hüseyin, if he comes in his car, you'll aim at the tyres. Be sure you take a good aim. As soon as we've got hold of Dervish, you'll take the others away and lock them into our cellar. But truss them up well first . . .'

They had taken up positions behind a clump of reeds, their rifles at the ready, their eyes on the road. Mustafa Bey lay down behind another clump.

Once he had seen Dervish face to face. His hair was very black and his cheekbones jutted out. A dark-complexioned man, with large slanting black eyes, always uneasy, always on his guard. It was in Istanbul, under the great plane tree in Beyazit Square. How elegant he had been that day, in that dark blue suit, cut to the latest fashion and the well-starched, impeccably white shirt . . . It was before the First World War when Dervish was studying law at the University of Istanbul. Everybody had thought then that he would never come back, that he would forget the family estate, the blood feud, everything, and become a judge.

Mustafa Bey smiled. A column of ants had traced a path for themselves and were hurriedly carrying wheat-seeds to their hole.

'I'll kill him with this hand, as sure as fate . . .' He himself had only finished high school, while the other was a university graduate . . . 'Well, it won't save him. All his learning will be buried in the black earth.'

Was it jealousy? Could he be jealous of Dervish? He ground his teeth and grasped his gun more tightly. His hands trembled. 'I will be the one to kill him!'

It filled him with pride, a kind of bitter joy. This feeling had been with him ever since his brother's death. He was ashamed, he hated himself for it, but he could not chase it away. He had loved Murtaza more than anyone in the world, more than his wife, his children, more than his own soul. Was it because he had always seen him under the shadow of death? And now, this insidious, unavowed feeling of joy, more terrible even than the death of his brother . . . It made him want to weep. He saw again the dead body steeped in blood, the wife and children clinging to it desperately . . . And yet he could not help it, that strange exultancy persisted. It was madness.

'I shall be the one to kill him!'

The best horseman in the land, it was said of him . . . A lie! Such a marksman, he could shoot out his own name in the most ornate Arabic script from a distance of forty yards . . . Another lie! All the women would spring to their windows when he passed through the streets of the town . . . It wasn't true! The most handsome of men . . . Dervish . . . Lies, lies, lies! I'll show him!

'Listen, I want to catch him alive. And then . . .'

'That's what a Bey should do,' Big Hassan said. 'A noble Bey like you. And then wipe off old scores face to face . . .'

'It's not easy to catch a man that way,' Black Hüseyin objected, 'as you would any old jackal. And a man like Dervish Bey too . . . He'll be passing by like the wind in his car. Say we hit the wheels . . . He'll soon have taken cover in the reed-bed. And then it'll be just another skirmish, till night falls and he gets away. If we're three, they're three too. An ambush should be to kill at once. Or the bird will fly from the cage.'

'He must die . . . All right, Black Hüseyin, let it be as you say. Fire away as much as you like. But the first shot's mine, don't forget. We'll make a sieve of that car of his. Aaah, if only I could catch him and make him beg for his life . . .'

'Dervish Bey would never beg,' Black Hüseyin said. 'He wouldn't be worth having as an enemy if he did.'

A light flared up over the swamp in the direction of Jeyhan River and burst into a thousand shivers over the green water-gorged reeds. Far and faint came the rumble of a motor.

'I'll kill him . . . I'll tear his tongue out . . .' How he would pull and pull and pull, and the blood would drip on to the dust of the road, drip drip drip . . .

His heart bursting, his hand ready on the gun, he waited for the car that would be passing like the wind. He would never miss, not even the driver, not anyone . . . 'If only we could get hold of him . . . Wounded . . .'

The day was drawing to a close. Mustafa Bey watched the road, trembling with a strange unaccustomed fever, a keen, terrible, intoxicating sensation that shook his body in a paroxysm of voluptuous joy, never to be attained again in a whole lifetime. The sinking sun glowed red over Anavarza. He shivered and burned all over, and the lights and colours began to dance before his eyes.

And the car came to a dead stop right in front of him . . . Out of it stepped Dervish, his bare revolver in his hand, his eyes blinking rapidly to right and left. His face was white as parchment, drained of all blood, pitiable, the right side twitching uncontrollably. Slowly he began to walk along the road, trying to hold his head high, yet reeling like a dying man. His eyes bulged out, as lifeless as those of a three-day corpse. His left hand hung down, yellow and trembling, his legs quivered, as though every step was bringing him nearer to death.

Suddenly there was a peal of thunder and everything grew dark. Slow and warm, large drops of rain began to fall with loud plops. Straining his eyes, Mustafa Bey could barely make out the figure that moved along the road like a condemned man to the gallows, with the car creeping behind him.

'Say the word, Bey, please . . . I'll riddle him with bullets. Please, Bey . . .'

Mustafa Bey was in a transport of joy. He wanted to throw himself at the neck of that living corpse. His hand went out, restraining his men. Just then Dervish stumbled and fell. Two men rushed up and lifted him to his feet. His legs were weaving into each other. They had to support him back to the car almost in a faint.

Night fell. At last Big Hassan spoke: 'But why, Bey, why?'

'I don't know . . .' Mustafa Bey's voice was buoyant, triumphant.

Without another word, they mounted their horses and rode into town.

The Public Prosecutor put him the question: 'We have received a denunciation to the effect that your brother, Murtaza Bey, was killed at the instigation of Dervish Sarioglu, because

65

of an old feud between your two families. What have you to say to this? It is said that Mahmut the Kurd, your brother's murderer, is one of Dervish Bey's henchmen, that he grew up on his farm. Is all this true?'

Mustafa Bey's eyes shone with satisfaction. 'It's true,' he said, 'that there has been since quite some time a small difference between our two families. But why should Dervish Bey have my brother killed because of that? I wouldn't give credence to such a rumour. As for Mahmut he grew up not in Dervish Bey's house, but in mine. It must have been some private quarrel between him and my brother. In all conscience I think we must absolve Dervish Bey from any participation in such a base ignoble act.' When he walked out, he was very straight, his gait as springy as though he were dancing.

One hour later Dervish Bey arrived at the Public Prosecutor's office. His face still held an earthen hue, his eyes were dull, like a dead sheep's.

'Who said that?' he cried, his voice trembling with vexation. 'Such a thing's quite impossible. I know Mahmut the Kurd of course, but there are two hundred peasants like this Mahmut working on my farm. Is it for this that you summoned me to town, Prosecutor? Or has Mustafa Akyollu lodged a complaint against me?'

'No, he hasn't . . .'

Dervish Bey left the Public Prosecutor's office even more haggard then before. He covered his face with his hands in shame. This 'no' had dealt him the finishing blow.

7

A feverish activity reigned all over Dervish Bey's house. In the big hall a group of farm women were busily cutting out endless bolts of cloth and sewing them into large and small bags on the sewing-machines before them. Outside, farmhands were bringing in cartloads of sand and emptying them into the yard, while a group of boys and girls filled the sand into the bags and more farmhands loaded the bags on to their backs and carried them inside to Dervish Bey who had them placed in the door-ways and window embrasures.

This went on for three days. In the end the mansion was as strongly barricaded as any fortress. Let Mustafa Akyollu do his worst, he could not even approach it now. Night and day watchmen were posted everywhere under the supervision of Dervish's most trusted men, Muharrem and Hidayet. As evening fell Dervish Bey would lock himself up in his room, turning the key three times, and pile up the sandbags against the door. The windows were kept closed with a rampart of sandbags. At first he could hardly sleep, but after a week he grew accustomed to his new surroundings. He did not take a step out of the house, neither by night nor by day, and whiled away the time talking with his sharecroppers and farmhands and listening to their news and tales.

Two months passed by without a sign from Mustafa Akyollu. It seemed as though he had vanished from the face of the earth. He was not at the farm, Dervish Bey had soon found out, nor was he in his town house. He had not gone to Adana, nor to Ankara or Istanbul. What could have become of him? This unaccountable absence disturbed Dervish more than anything else. Obviously Akyollu was preparing to strike, and such a blow that no one would know whence it came.

Summer came, and the terrible yellow heat set in, turning the house into a real inferno. Dervish Bey would retreat into the coolest corner of the big hall and play games with those of the farm children who had not gone to work, for in the summer everyone else was in the fields and it was only in the evenings that the labourers came in to see him. All the farm people, even the children, were angry with the Akyollus for having brought their Bey to this. It hurt their pride, it stung them to the core that he should not be able to stir from his house, nor even see the light of day. They had begun to be afraid too, like him, of going abroad at night, and even in the fields the slightest noise, the sudden flight of a bird flashing by them, would make them start nervously. They were confused, on tenterhooks, living in the same dread of death, the same state of tension as their Bey, without knowing the reason why, without wanting to know.

The summer nights were hell. He would eat his dinner in company and chat with his sharecroppers. Towards midnight, after everyone had left, he would go to his wife's room and kiss her goodnight, then lock himself up in his own room, with the sandbags all around and not the slightest aperture to let some air in. Sleep evaded him. He would throw off his clothes and pace about the room like a drunken man, and when morning came he would rush out to the big hall and, throwing himself on one of the divans there, would fall fast asleep. And he never stopped sweating. It was as if his whole body were dissolving into sweat. Sometimes he would ask himself if death would not be a good thing rather than go on living like this.

'It would be better, yes, but I have to live, to stick it out. I can't resign myself to an inglorious death . . .'

And so life for him was reduced to a single sweating stand. Everything about him smelled of sweat, the rugs, the walls, the people, his own wife, all his clothes were impregnated with a strong sour odour. Everything, the whole world, whatever he touched was streaming with sweat.

One night he could stand it no longer. He threw himself out of the room shouting: 'I'm burning, stifling! Burning . . .'

They poured pails of water over him. He came to and went back, locking the door behind him again.

In spite of all these precautions he lived in constant fear, and when he laid his head on the pillow it was with the thought that he might never wake up again, annihilated, a thing that had never been. Only a few people would remember him, his wife, his children, his people, some friends . . . And then they too would die . . . But there was one person who would never forget, who would carry his memory in the very core of his heart right into the grave, and that was Mustafa Akyollu . . . But he himself would be dead . . . The world would cease to exist, the whole boundless universe would die with him. Everything would die in the end, so why this will to live a little longer? What magic did life hold, what potent, inexhaustible, elusive enchantment? The strange thought came to him that it was with Akyollu he could best talk of such things, of life and death, and several times he was on the point of riding over to him, then changed his mind. What madness this, obstinately, perseveringly killing each other through the years! To kill and be killed in turn, whether you were brave or a coward, and nobody daring to be the one to end it . . .

One morning they had to break open the door of his room. They found him lying in a faint, quite naked, the sweat pouring from his body like a fountain. The whole floor was wet with it. They bathed him in cold water, pail after pail drawn from the well. He regained consciousness at last, but this was too much for his wife.

'It's not a bullet that's going to kill you, but your own stubbornness, Bey,' she exploded. 'Why don't you leave a little opening to get some air? Why don't you sleep in a different room each night?'

Dervish Bey flared up. 'Be quiet, Hatun,' he cried. 'I know what I'm doing. D'you think I want to die?'

'Well, you'll die asphyxiated at this rate.'

'So long as I don't die of a bullet, I don't care.'

'But, Bey, what harm would there be in making at least a small hole in the window? How would your enemy find that hole and shoot at you?'

'He'd find it, never fear. Besides, I've got used to sweating. It does me a world of good. And with the windows shut I'm not plagued by mosquitoes.'

And so it went on. Night after night Dervish Bey remained shut up in his room, panting for breath, sweating like an earthen

69

jug full of water, pressing his flaming body from wall to wall to imbibe some short-lived coolness from them.

And all the time he heard those galloping hoofbeats in the night, that never stopped until dawn.

The mansion was built on an elevated mound, fifteen to twenty metres high, and the whole mound was surrounded by a two-metre stone wall. All along the top, the wall was stuck with broken pieces of coloured glass. It was an old wall, mossgrown in patches, its original white weathered by rain and dust and heat, as were the walls of the house. A gravelled path overhung with vines led to the mansion. Large trees grew in the courtyard, fig trees tangled with vines, some of them so old that their trunks were hollow, and huge plane trees where countless storks had their nests. A large part of the garden, to the east, was planted with pomegranate trees. And all along the wall were tall poplars and masses of large bright-flowering prickly pears.

The Bey's farmland lay south to the right of the big gate. And on the left were the houses of the sharecroppers and farmhands, a whole village. There too lived Dervish Bey's men and also a few families not attached to the farm but owning small plots of land thereabouts. There was not a single tree to be seen in the whole farm.

The horses would approach each night along the cotton fields, east of the mansion, always passing the big white solid block of stone on the way. It was such a huge block that nothing had ever been able to move it. How, why had it come to rest on this black loamy soil where hardly a single small stone was to be found? The white slabstone was famous in all the countryside and many were the legends and songs that had been woven around it.

'Muharrem,' Dervish Bey said, 'haven't you found out about those horsemen yet? It's a whole fortnight now they've been riding like this. One can't sleep all night for the noise of their hoofbeats.'

'The nights are too dark, Bey. We have to wait for the moon to find out. It's always at the same time they come, towards midnight, riding towards the mountains, then back south towards the river. And just before dawn they ride off into the

70

mountains again. If you like I can follow them . . .'

'No, let's wait for the moon.'

The people on the farm would wake up every night, just as the horsemen were approaching the white stone, and would listen anxiously to the beat of their hooves, but no one dared voice a suspicion as to who they might be.

8

It had not taken long for Mustafa Akyollu to pull himself together and restrain the blustering rage that was ravaging him like a prickly blackthorn. He began to think things over more coolly. Dervish Bey had turned his house into a fortress and would not take a step out of it at any price. How unexpected had been the fear, the palpable terror in his face, in his whole body as he had stepped out of the car . . . How wonderful, oh how gratifying! So much for his vaunted bravery! He could be as cowardly as any other man, but with him courage and cowardice were both tinged with a mad inconsequence. It was this trait of his character that must be exploited.

Whirlwind Veli was a long thin man. He could scour the breadth of the huge Chukurova plain and back again in only a couple of days. Once he had raced with a man on a horse, and the horse, a real Arab steed, had collapsed of exhaustion. He was a legend on the tongues of men and it was said that even bullets could not catch up with him. He was also the best tracker in the land and could pick out the trace of a bird's wing wherever it had grazed the ground. He had never married and his large hazel eyes were always sad.

'Muharrem is on guard till midnight at the big entrance gate. Then he turns the watch over to someone else and goes straight to his *chardak** where he falls asleep at once, between his wife and his youngest child. He never lets go of his gun. The boards of the *chardak* are of stout thick wood, but the mattress he sleeps on is thin. Even a pistol bullet would be enough.'

'If Muharrem goes, then they'll kill you too, Veli. What d'you say to that?'

'I'll say it's fate. But I'll also say this, Whirlwind Veli's not one to give up the ghost so easily!'

Chardak: a summer sleeping shelter, built on stilts away from the ground.

'Black Hüseyin, you'll take a horse . . .'

'I don't need a horse, Bey. It's better not for this business.'

'But you'll never keep up with Veli.'

'Let him keep up with me.'

'Why you black dog, how can I ever keep up with you!'

They both knew this Muharrem very well. He was a thin short man, but quick and wiry, always on the go, always smiling, one of the best marksmen in the countryside. Nobody knew when he had joined Dervish Bey's household, nor from where he had come. Perhaps he didn't know it himself. He had been Dervish Bey's crack shot ever since anyone could remember. The most beautiful horses at the farm were his to command, and when he went into town he never left the saddle, buying and selling, even eating on horseback. He had six sons, the eldest twenty years old and studying in Istanbul.

Black Hüseyin felt a twinge in his heart.

It was a dark night. Black clouds were rushing across the sky from the Mediterranean to the Taurus Mountains. Black Hüseyin and Whirlwind Veli were making their way along a gully to Dervish Bey's farm. They were both sweating. A fresh rain-heralding gust blew in and Black Hüseyin shivered. Yet it was stiflingly hot. Even the earth had not yet cooled off. It was like red-hot iron. They had been on the road for two days now, hiding during the hours of daylight and only stopping in secluded places to eat from the food bundles tied to their waists; neither the one nor the other uttered a single word.

They entered the village. The dogs never barked at Whirlwind Veli and Black Hüseyin had brought some meat to throw at them. A couple of cows were chewing the cud beneath Muharrem's *chardak*.

'This is it, Hüseyin. Muharrem will be coming any minute now. He'll climb up that ladder there. You'll aim straight up, at the fourth board of the *chardak*. He always sleeps there. Don't hit the wife or the child. If you aim well, right at the centre of the fourth board, you'll nail him through the heart. Good luck. I'll be waiting for you on the edge of Akchasaz swamp, under the single mulberry tree.'

And suddenly he was not there, already gliding out of the farm and away. Black Hüseyin knew that Whirlwind Veli could

73

move faster than anyone, but not as fast as this.

He inspected the *chardak* cautiously and located the fourth board. Then he went to the hedge that surrounded the house and hid behind a pile of sesame. And now, for the first time in two days, he began to think about this man he was going to kill. So in a little while Muharrem would be dead. His children would be orphaned . . . But supposing it was the other way round? What if Muharrem killed him instead? Would he give a thought to his orphaned children? Tomorrow this place would be astir with people, women and children, weeping, cursing, and with gendarmes from the town, doctors, government officials . . . Blood would be dripping from the *chardak* over those ruminating cows, over the crowd, hard as rain . . . Only the swamp could save him. Otherwise Dervish Bey's men would hunt him down like a partridge on this flat plain . . . Thank God for the swamp . . . A vast boundless expanse, where only Whirlwind Veli knew his way about. Without him . . . Not even the creeping snake, the flying bird could penetrate this swamp, and it was there, at a short run's distance, and Whirlwind Veli was waiting for him under the mulberry tree . . . What could be easier?

It was past midnight and still no sign of Muharrem. What if he didn't come at all? That would mean another night of waiting here like this . . . He put out his hand and picked at a plant. It was a nettle and he smarted at the sharp sting along his hand and arm. What if Muharrem spotted him when he came? There was no trifling with Muharrem. He'd shoot at once, and shoot again, every single bullet in his gun, and not one would go astray . . .

The black clouds parted and a small bright patch appeared for a moment, then vanished. The odour of fresh cow dung was everywhere and from the swamp came whiffs of rotting vegetation, dank and clammy.

He rose, then sat down again. Muharrem was wiped from his mind now. Bey, he was saying, after this business, won't you give me some land, just fifty *dönüms** off the side of the swamp . . . I'd plough and sow it. I could grow cotton, as tall as myself,

---

*Dönüm: about a quarter of an acre.

74

each boll would be as large as my fist. I'd sell it and make a heap of money. Damn this Chukurova . . . A thousand curses upon it! A furnace, that's what it is, not a place to live in . . . I would take my wife and children and move up to the highlands. What's this life worth anyway if you can't live it the way you want? There among the junipers . . . The thyme on the mountains . . . The marjoram-scented springs . . . That's what I call life! Even if only for a single year, for one short summer . . . A man's life is tied to a gossamer thread, here today and gone tomorrow . . . If only the Bey would give me that fifty *dönüms* of land and set me free at last . . . I'm growing old . . .

Someone was drawing near, a short man, the stature of a young boy. It was Muharrem and no other. With weary floundering steps he reached the *chardak* and stopped at the foot of the ladder, his head sagging sleepily. Why not now, Hüseyin thought. Must it be when he's in bed? But he's got that deadly Mauser in his hand. There's no evading Muharrem's aim . . . He was climbing up the ladder now, very slowly. He did not even undress, but pitched on to the bed just as he was. Black Hüseyin noted which side his head lay. He waited a little longer. With growing excitement he recalled the Muharrem of many years ago, riding a chestnut horse at full gallop along an orchard into the mountains and firing madly at the empty road before him. Very young he had been then, Muharrem, not the balding ageing man he was now. What on earth had he been firing for into that empty road? It was only now, so many years later, that Hüseyin asked himself this. It was crazy . . .

A few cocks crowed and a foal whinnied. From Akchasaz came the harsh shrill cries of swamp birds. He rose and walked to the *chardak*. Raising his rifle he held it straight up and pressed the trigger. The German carbine was like a machine-gun. It spewed out five shots all in an instant. Muharrem uttered a strident scream and was hurled three yards into the air. When he fell back he was dead. The *chardak* groaned and rocked like a cradle. His wife sat up, dazed, unable to move. By the time she had lit the lamp, the whole farm was roused. People were rushing up and a loud wail rose from the women and children.

'God, Muharrem's done for,' Dervish Bey groaned. 'I never

thought Akyollu would stoop so low . . . Lashing out at an underling when he can't get the Bey!' He was about to go out, but checked himself. What if this was a trap to lure him out? Grabbing his revolver, he began to pace up and down the room. 'Get a doctor, quick,' he called out.

There was a pause. Then the answer came: 'Muharrem's dead.'

Poor poor Muharrem . . . Like the others the innocent victim of jousting lords. How unjust . . . And now it would be Whirl-wind Veli's turn. He was the only one of Akyollu's men who could compensate for Muharrem. Whirlwind Veli would die, killed by someone as good as him, just because the great Beys willed it. So it was with all the wars of mankind too, millions killed each other because great Beys wanted it so . . . 'Because we wish it . . .' That was the fixed order of things. What an abject world . . . 'It's our social order. But what about those new upstart Aghas? Their social order is bloodier, more odious by far, the order of unscrupulous greedy new merchants . . .'

He went to the door. 'Who did it?' he called.

It was Hidayet who answered him from outside. His voice sounded subdued, frightened. 'Nobody saw him. It was too dark.'

'Have you sent men after him?'

'Yes, but he'll be sure to hide in the swamp and escape.'

He was dying to go out, but he had sworn to himself not to take a step out of this room at night, not even if the world came to an end. The heat was stifling, more than he could bear. He cast off his underclothes. They were wringing wet.

'Hidayet . . .'

'Yes, Bey?'

'Have you got your gun? Is it loaded?'

'Of course, Bey.'

'Look, I'm opening this door or I'll die asphyxiated this minute.' Quickly, he knocked down the sandbags, drew open the door and stood on the threshold, his mouth open, gasping like a fish out of water. 'I'm going to faint. Quick, get a pail of water, Hidayet.'

After Hidayet had emptied a large pail of cold water over him, Dervish Bey felt better. He went back to his room, locked

76

the door and piled up the sandbags again.

It won't be so bad when winter comes, he thought. We won't let anyone into the house, that's all. And I'll have everyone searched who wants to come near me. That man will stop at nothing. He could very well suborn one of my men even. Hidayet? No, never!

'Hidayet,' he called out, 'Whirlwind Veli has to be killed. Who'll do it?'

'I will, Bey, if you please. My heart burns so for Muharrem . . . I can't let his death go unavenged.'

'All right then. Set out first thing in the morning. Ah, Muharrem was worth a hundred Whirlwind Velis, but what's the use . . .'

Black Hüseyin arrived panting at the appointed place. Veli was waiting for him under the mulberry tree. 'I heard the shots,' he said. 'And the shouting from the farm. Is anyone following you?'

'There are five of them after me.'

'To the swamp then, quick . . . A whole army wouldn't find us there among the brakes and briars.' He seized Hüseyin's hand and drew him into the swamp. The mire was knee-deep, but firm underneath. They did not sink, and with sure feet Whirlwind Veli led the way into the thick of the vast gloomy brakes of Akchasaz.

And from afar they heard the voices of Dervish Bey's men who had traced Black Hüseyin to the lone mulberry tree.

9

Dervish Sarioglu was the Bey of the Sarilar tribe. Until the settlement ninety years ago, this tribe had led the life of the nomad tent-dweller. They would winter on the land between the rivers Savrun and Sumbas, and the Bey's tent would always be erected on the flat-topped mound where the mansion now stood. Their summer pasture was the Binboga Mountains. Though not large, the tribe was rich and powerful, reputed for its honour and fidelity to the old traditions. After the settlement, when the world about them was changed beyond recognition, the Sarilar tribe remained the same. But the suffering was not forgotten. Forever in their hearts, from the Bey to the humblest shepherd, they carried the memory, bitter as poison, of their subjugation to the Ottomans. Dervish Bey's grandfather had taken part in the revolt of the nomads against the Ottoman state. Like the other Beys, he had been defeated and this defeat had rankled to his dying day. Yet he bore a grudging admiration for the commander of the conquering army, Dervish Pasha, and because of that he had named his grandson after him.

After the Kozanoglu revolt had been crushed. the tribes were scattered far and wide, and those who had not fled were resigned to a ruthless domination. But what came to them was worse than they had expected. Some were exiled to alien lands, to Bozok, Diyarbekir, Kayseri, Sivas. Others, and the Sarilar tribe was one of these, were forcibly settled in the Chukurova plain, never again allowed to migrate to the highlands at the first blush of spring, prisoners all summer long in the burning hell of the Chukurova. All the roads and passes that led into the mountains were guarded by Ottoman soldiers and not even the flying bird could get past them. And so they died by the hundreds, unable to withstand the heat and fever of the plain, and many were the corpses that were left to stink in the open for lack of someone to bury them.

The Ottomans had assigned fields to them on the fertile

Chukurova soil, but who cared for sowing and reaping! They hated the plain. Every tree, every bird, every blade of grass was an enemy to them. They knew nothing of tilling and crop-raising. They were breeders, and they saw their livestock being even more decimated than their people in the cruel, fever-infested Chukurova. And death and pestilences were also taking their toll of the age-old traditions and customs of the tribes, playing havoc with the relations of father to son, wife to husband, tribesman to Bey.

In all this upheaval Süleyman Sarioglu found a way of saving himself and his tribe. He went straight up into the mountains to the commander of the Ottoman force, an open-minded, kind-hearted major, and told him of their plight. 'Ask what you want of me, major,' he said, 'livestock, gold, women, and I will give it to you.' And the major accepted. It was already July and the Sarioglu tribe lost no time in taking themselves up to the Binboga highlands.

In the years that followed the settled tribes began to learn how to sow the land. They made houses out of reeds and rushes and brushwood, and grew to love the soil. Although the patrols in the mountain passes were relaxed and finally lifted, many were the men who chose to stay the summer in the villages to guard the corn, sending their wives and children up into the highlands alone. It was only after the First World War that people gave up their semi-nomadic ways and stayed all the year long in the Chukurova.

The Sarilar tribe, because they did not spend those first summers down in the hot plain, were not decimated like the others and their old customs and traditions too were less impaired.

The present imposing mansion had been built by this same Süleyman, Dervish Bey's grandfather, long after the settlement, when the tribe was growing used to ploughing the land and growing crops. He had gone to Marash on business, and there he had talked with the Bey of the Beyazitoglus. 'Süleyman Bey,' Beyazitoglu had said, 'it's no use nursing a grievance against the Ottomans. Nomadism is over and done with. It's not civilized. Look about you. Are there any nomads in the land of the Franks? We have to settle for good, Süleyman. I've done so, and what harm has it done me? On the contrary, from being the Bey of a trifling little tribe I am now Bey of this huge Marash. And you too can become the Bey of the whole Chukurova, Adana, Tarsus and even Sis if you want to. Stop being obstinate. Get out of that tent and build yourself a house, a large mansion where the Ottoman officials and the great people of this world can come and visit you. Things will be easier after that . . .'

Süleyman Bey had long been aware of this. There and then he engaged a master-mason and a carpenter from among the Armenian artisans of Zeytin, and brought them back with him, together with as many apprentices and builders as were necessary. That very winter the foundations of the big mansion were laid. As the workers dug into the mound a profusion of marble stones and statues were brought to light. The stones were carved in relief with human and animal likenesses and inscribed in a strange alphabet. They uncovered ruins too and substructures of ancient dwellings. Süleyman Bey ordered all these marble stones to be sent to the limekiln. Graven images and human likenesses were a sin before Allah and could not be used in the groundwork or the walls of a Moslem house . . . So this place had once been inhabited, Süleyman Bey marvelled. People had lived here in this infernal heat, they had built houses, inscribed stones, sculpted their idols of stone . . . What madmen there were in this world, what erratic creatures . . . But what had Beyazitoglu said? 'You just build that house of yours,' he had told him, 'and don't live in it if you don't want to. It's the house that makes a Bey nowadays. It'll serve to enhance your consequence in the eyes of the Ottoman rulers. The bigger it is, the richer, the more they'll respect you. Your tent may be all of pure satin, and supported by posts of solid gold, with hangings of coral and pearl, it's still only a tent, and though the Bey's tent, of no more value than that of a gypsy. Ah, Süleyman Bey, they are gone those days, the glorious days of the tent, have vanished in a puff of smoke. We can beat our breasts in grief, but they will never come back.'

The Armenian master-builder from Zeytin had worked in Sivas in his youth, as an apprentice in the building of the Bey of Sivas's mansion, and had been filled with wonder at the work of his master. Ever since then he had been obsessed with one idea, to be able to build such a house himself before he died, if possible one still larger, more imposing, with an even finer finish to it than that of his master. And now here was his chance, the chance of a lifetime. Prove yourself, Master Omnik, he gloated, show what you can do and your name will live on till kingdom come. And what a splendid location for a building, on that tell in the middle of the plain . . . It would dazzle all eyes for miles around . . . But where was he to find the stone for the mansion? The Chukurova is all rich loamy soil with not a stone bigger than a fist. The marble and stone that lay buried in the tell could not be used, so what was Master Omnik to do? He needed stone and lots of it. Then his eyes fell on Anavarza Castle. For days he inspected its walls and ruins and aqueducts. Here were stones galore, but how to bring them down these steep crags into the plain? It seemed an impossible task.

'Is that all you want, Master Omnik?' Süleyman Bey said. 'The stones of Anavarza Castle? Leave that to me.'

And he proceeded to line up the whole tribe, men and women, young and old, all the way from the tell to Anavarza. But still the line fell short, so he got more people from the Sumbasli tribe, the Jeritlis, the Lek Kurds and the Tatarlis. And so the stones of Anavarza ruins were passed from hand to hand and heaped at the foot of the tell, stones of every kind, square, round, shale, granite, marble, some heavy, some light, hewn, unhewn, yellow, dark blue, white, greenish, crystal-veined. The long file stretched for miles, very black, almost like a wall, but swaying slightly, bending, straightening. For months on end the stones flowed like a river from Anavarza down into the Chukurova plain and people's hands began to peel. The stones gnawed into palms and fingers and nails leaving them raw and sore. People were dropping out of line. Some died, others ran away, never to be seen again.

The master-builder was struck with awe at this proof of the Turcoman Bey's practical mind. Who would ever have thought of such a thing, to line up people for miles on end and bring the stones of Anavarza Castle down into the Chukurova! He was fired with fresh ardour and burning to start. Legends were springing up about the projected mansion, and many were the minstrels who came to the Bey's tent to celebrate his enterprise in verse and song and to extol his lineage. He welcomed them all and showered them with gifts. These stones, hewn in days gone by, carried from hand to hand the distance of a three days' journey, at the cost of so much blood and of so many lives . . . The patience, the toil, the sweat . . . For these Turcoman nomads, uprooted from their native Khorassan, swept about from land to land, cast up on this Chukurova plain, oppressed, humiliated, dispersed, defeated, the mansion was a thing of pride, a victory, a final revolt, a vengeance, a resurrection. The very last . . . Their backs were sore and calloused from carrying loads of stone, sand, lime and timber, but they did not complain, they asked for nothing in return, they put themselves heart and soul at the Bey's service and waited with growing excitement for the mansion to be finished. Even if the Bey had for some reason or other changed his mind or said he could not afford to go on, they would have sold their souls and found a way to complete it. Who knows, they might even have killed the Bey in an agony of frustration. Their fever and enthusiasm spread to the other Turcoman tribes. They too brought in stones from the ruins of Sis, from the Castles of Bodrum and Hemité, from Yilankalé and Misis, so many that two mansions could have been built with them. These stones can still be seen lying in a heap at the foot of the tell.

Süleyman Bey had a master-craftsman fetched all the way from Sivas to paint the mansion. The stones chiselled by the mason, the doors, windows and eaves were things of beauty. All the skill of the most famous craftsmen in Anatolia, all the efforts and zeal of a whole countryside had gone into this mansion, and when it was finished a bounteous feast was laid out and the festivities lasted for a week. Invitations were sent out to the Beys of all the tribes in exile and in the Chukurova, to the Beys of Marash and Antep, to the Ottoman Pashas in Adana and Aleppo. This unparalleled event is still remembered in the Chukurova as the 'Festival of the Mansion'. The Sarilar tribe, the other tribes who had helped to build it were bursting with pride. How it glowed in the middle of the wide Chukurova, like a pearl! How brightly its windowpanes shone at sunrise and sunset, illuminating the whole plain!

Although the mansion was ready at last, Süleyman Bey had

never meant it for a dwelling. It was furnished and fitted out to perfection, but not once did he sleep in it, nor spend a day there. Only when high-ranking officials came to visit him were its doors thrown open, and after their deparature they were locked up again. For his part, he had the ancient Bey's tent set up in the mansion's vast yard and continued to live in it. He simply could not warm to his new house. He loved it and was proud of it, but for him it was just a place for important guests. The Bey's spacious tent was as renowned as the mansion, if not more so. It was supported by seven poles, each a marvel of woodwork and encrusted with a profusion of precious stones. The inside of the tent was spread with tiger-skins and adorned with beautiful old rugs that were said to have come with the tribe all the way from Khorassan. Such were the colours and designs that had been woven into them by the Khorassan masters of old that they seemed to contain all the colours, flowers and smells of their ancient land. Süleyman Bey would gaze at them again and again, and marvel, 'All the colours, all the light of this world have been captured here. Look at these rugs and know what a great land Khorassan was, a land of saints and brightness, a holy land. Look at them and know . . .'

And so, until his death no one lived in the mansion. It remained closed and untouched as a young virgin, and as long as no one lived there, the people of Anavarza plain looked upon it as their very own, and it would shine upon them from its heights, morning and evening, like the enchanted palace of a fairy king.

The Akyollus, too, built themselves a house on Küp hill on the other side of Savrun River where the tribe had settled, but it had not the grace and beauty and splendour of the Sarioglu mansion. It was certainly large, perhaps even larger, but something was lacking. It did not impress minds and dazzle the beholder like the other one. And then the Bey of Akyollu had moved into his house as soon as it was finished, and this the tribes could not swallow. 'Like the simpleton who had a son and tore him apart by the legs to make two!' they sniffed.

The Beys of Sarioglu and Akyollu were sworn enemies, ready to kill each other on sight without any more ado. Nobody knew when, where or why this feud had started. The cause might have been some raid or other, or a quarrel over a woman. Maybe the feud had started way back in distant Khorassan. Maybe it had flared up somewhere over grazing ground and winter quarters. Even after the Kozanoglu revolt, which had reconciled many a foe and put an end to age-old feuds, the Beys of Sarioglu and Akyollu refused to bury the hatchet. People said that not even on Doomsday would they make the peace and that the feud would last until both families were exhausted, stock and stem. The Savrun River was like a state boundary between them. Neither would venture on the wrong side of it. During the First World War when refugees were pouring in from the Balkans, a great number of them had been assigned to the Anavarza district, and a commission was appointed to settle them. The head of this commission was Dervish Bey's brother, Jevdet, and he manoeuvred to ensure that all the refugees, enough to form ten villages, were located east of the Savrun on the Akyollu side, although there was just as much empty land on the west bank of the river as on the east. This infuriated the Akyollus.

When the Sarioglu mansion was built and finished Süleyman Bey had three members of the Akyollu family killed, as offerings, so to speak, for his glorious enterprise. The Akyollus were powerless to retaliate. For years and years they stalked him without success. 'There's some magic about him,' they said. 'It's so strong that you cannot even draw out your pistol, let alone fire at him. It's those strange eyes of his that paralyse you.' To cover up their mortification they spread legends about him that travelled all through the Chukurova and ended by inspiring the minstrels in the land. In one of these tales five members of the Akyollu family were travelling along a rugged mountain pass when they came face to face with Süleyman Bey. Swiftly the five of them whipped out their pistols and fired. And what should they see! There was Süleyman Bey standing laughing before them and holding out the five bullets in his open palm . . . Still another tale had it that, having caught him at last, they strapped him to a log and lighting a huge fire, cast him into it, then went away. A few days later, walking along the same mountain pass, he suddenly appeared before them, large as life, and they turned and fled.

84

Süleyman Bey lived to the ripe age of ninety. His back was stooped, his eyes dim, yet he still kept a firm seat on the saddle. One day he fell sick, but refused to be laid up. 'Bed is for women to die a-farting in,' he said. 'No man worthy of the name would let himself die in a bed.' They wanted to bring a doctor, but he would have none of it. 'My doctor is Allah,' he said. A few days later his legs failed him. He sat propped against the wall. Then his head drooped and he was too weak to lift a spoon and had to be fed. When he could no longer open his mouth, he called his sons. 'Dress me in my best clothes,' he said. 'And saddle my bay horse with the silver and gold harness.' They dared not disobey him. Even dead, Süleyman Bey could make the world too hot for a man. He tried to rise, but failed. 'What are you standing there gaping at me for?' he said sharply. 'Help me get up and take me to my horse.' They supported him out of the house. 'To the mounting-block,' he ordered. And without assistance he climbed up the block and on to the saddle. He sat there for a while gazing around. His last look before he spurred the horse was for his sons. Like a black cloud the horse glided out of the yard and across the plain towards the blue shining hills. For days, for months, his sons together with hundreds of men searched for him in the mountains. They never found him, neither alive, nor dead. The horse too had disappeared without leaving a trace.

Süleyman Bey's sons remained faithful to their father's traditions, although the first thing they did was to strike down the big tent and move into the mansion. 'Be always careful to keep up our good relations with the Ottomans,' had been his frequent enjoinment. 'And never ill-treat the tribe. The tribe is our earth, the Ottoman our arm.'

Until the First World War the land hereabouts was not worth much. Sowing and reaping being almost unknown, its value was just that of grazing ground. But things were beginning to change just a little before the war. Cultivation made its appearance in the region of Anavarza. Dervish Bey's father took good stock of this wide plain, then spoke to his sons. 'You will put a stake right there, under that single mulberry tree,' he said, pointing in the direction of Jeyhan River. Then he turned north. 'And on this side we can have the whole land beyond the house. Go and have all those fields registered in our name. It looks as though we shall be needing them in the future. D'you think that's enough?'

'More than enough,' his sons said.

The Beys of Akyollu at once followed suit and staked their claim on their former wintering lands, and also on their pastures in the highlands.

Dervish Bey was only eight years old when his father gave him his ivory-handled pistol, and before he was ten he could shoot a sparrow on a bough. His instructors were the most renowned outlaws of the Taurus and handle-bar mustached Kurdish sharpshooters from Dersim. By the time he was fifteen his fame as a marksman had spread all over the Chukurova.

And so, raised in the midst of shots and gunpowder, with black-mustached, bloodshot-eyed, rocky-faced rough outlaws as teachers, he lived not the life of a child, but one of constant fear that seeped into his veins drop by drop like poison, penetrating to the very marrow of his bones. They were training him not to be afraid of death, to face it with courage, but the fear was stronger than all, and as the days and years went by, the dark wall before him soared higher and thicker. Every minute, every second, tense, quivering as a drawn steel bow, he waited for the shot that would kill him. Death was stalking in every nook and corner, on every path, under every bush, behind every door and wall and shadow. He must be ready to draw his pistol before death struck. Quick as thought he must shoot at those shadows, living or inanimate, before they had time to kill him.

He was growing up. How old was he, he could not recollect, fifteen perhaps, when the Akyollus killed his father? All he remembered was the red gleam of marble under the dust, only the wall and the flickering flames. His father on a horse that galloped like the wind, out hunting the deer, and himself riding a hundred paces behind him, and suddenly the crackle of shots and his father's long rending scream, the horse rearing again and again, its forelegs stretching up to the sky, and the thud of his father's body hitting the ground. And behind a thicket, lying in a ditch, the ambush, the large eyes, the long black drooping mustaches. He sat frozen to the saddle, unable to move. His hand did not go to his gun. He did not flee or speak or scream. He only stared at the men, at their trembling hands, their rigid faces, their ears, their black eyes boring into his. On the ground his father was writhing, his hands clawing the grass, his teeth clinched to a bush, jerking it this way and that, raucous sounds issuing from his throat. Then the men's eyes widened. His father made a sudden spring at them. Three shots from the three guns and his father dropped again and lay there in all his length, lifeless. The three men clambered out of the ditch and ran through the cotton fields towards Jeyhan River.

How long he stayed there frozen to his horse, he did not know. The blood gathered in a pool, frothed and was sucked into the soft earth. Then he was whirling desperately about his father's body. He remembered following the men down towards the river. He could even hear them talking, loud, insistent. But he stopped and turned back, running for all he was worth, shouting at the top of his voice. When he came home his tongue was tied. For a long time, perhaps a whole year he could not utter a word. Even now, closing his eyes, or awake in the dark of the night, he saw as clear as day his father's threshing body at the foot of the red-veined rocks, the blood-stained cotton bolls, the engraved white stone spattered with blood, his father clinging to it, gnawing at the stone, pathetically small now under the tall wild mass of flinty red crags. Blood everywhere, and a mighty swirl of dust, blood-red . . .

After his father's death it was his older brother, Jevdet Bey, who became the head of the house. On him too fell the task of carrying on the feud. Dervish shared the cold horror, the incredible mixture of resolution and vacillation, afraid to kill, afraid to be killed in turn, he lived through it all intensely with his brother, as did the whole tribe with them. And in the end Jevdet Bey had the eldest of the Akyollu brothers killed. They tied the body with a long rope to his horse's neck and let it go, and the horse, maddened by its burden, dragged the mangled mass back through fields and marsh and thickets to the Akyollu mansion.

After finishing elementary school in the town Dervish Bey had attended the high school in Adana, and in all these years the pistol never left his side. His teachers and the other pupils knew this, but no one ever mentioned it, nor did anyone ever dare make the smallest joke about Dervish. There was something in his bearing, proud, confident, rock-hard, that kept people at arm's length. And when they heard about the circumstances of his life, they looked upon him with a different eye altogether, as if he were dead already, pity was in their gaze and fear too, a feeling of awe as if in the presence of a holy man, of some magic, or a taboo. All through his schooldays he bore the weight of anguished eyes forever expressing the same horrible emotion. And now even the people in his own house were looking at him like that . . . It was only during the first two years of his law studies at Istanbul University that no one knew about his pistol or his family feud. He was careful not to betray himself. But his luck did not hold. One day he was sitting in the café under the big plane trees of Beyazit Square with some friends, and at the next table were two other acquaintances and a stranger, a young man with a thin pale face and large coal-black eyes. The two tables soon joined up.

'Don't you know each other?' one of Dervish Bey's friends said, indicating the stranger. 'How extraordinary! You're both from the same town.' And Dervish Bey was just holding out his hand when he added: 'This is Mustafa Bey of the Akyollu family.'

Dervish Bey's extended hand snapped back as though it had touched a live ember. Without a word, he left the table and walked away, and Mustafa Bey with an identical gesture did the same. Their friends were astounded, but soon ferreted out the reason for this strange behaviour, and so, from the paradise it had been, Istanbul turned into a hell for Dervish. Everywhere he met with the same looks, even from the girls he made love to, awed, frightened, recalcitrant. Again he was a dead thing, a strange marked creature . . .

Dervish Bey never had much inclination for studying and only just managed to get by. His two passions were women and foreign languages. At least once a month he would fall madly in love with some girl, Turkish, Greek, Jewish or Levantine, but would just as quickly tire of her. He would spend huge amounts of money at such an incredible rate that he often found himself with empty pockets. Yet inexhaustible funds poured in to him from the Chukurova and his lavish extravagances were the talk of both Istanbul and his home town. He had a generous nature. His money, his life, his affections, whatever he possessed, he would give with both hands. Handsome, large-hearted, passionate he was always giving and never taking, and for this reason women doted on him.

Languages came easily to him. French he learnt in six months and at the same time took lessons in English, Greek and Arabic. He frequented fashionable circles in Istanbul and was much admired. Few people could speak French as perfectly as he did and his good looks and dramatic background added to the aura about him. He took it all as his natural due. He came from a race of men used to dominating and being looked up to.

He never finished his studies. He did not want to. In his last year he left to fight in the Chanakkalé war where he was wounded. Later, during the War of Independence, he formed a band of guerillas and fought against the French in the Taurus Mountains. When he came back to settle on the farm, it was with the rank of major and with an Independence medal shining on his chest. His mother and grandmother had chosen a bride for him. She was the daughter of an important Turcoman Bey from Amik plain, in the south. Dervish never even had a glimpse of her until the wedding-day. The wedding was held on the Sarioglu estate. The festivities lasted for a fortnight and there was not a Bey or Agha or important government official for miles around who did not attend.

Dervish never looked back again on his life in Istanbul. Only two habits remained with him from that time, reading and the study of languages. His predilection was for philosophy. He read and meditated on life and death, the human being, the world, the universe. A full five years, the question, where do we come from, where are we going, troubled him and after long tergiversation he reached the conclusion that God did not exist. There was no God, only the human being counted. Nothing existed in the whole universe, only death, and for a long time he moved in a world of death. People, animals, insects, the trees, the grass, everything he looked upon was dead. He pitied every living thing, beautiful or ugly. Alone, lost in a vast endless graveyard, he felt nothing, neither pleasure nor anger, not even envy.

Many years passed before he met the venerable Alevi Sheikh, with the long white beard and whiskers, and the beautiful eyes, who reproved and shamed him. 'It is evil the way you consider the world,' the Sheikh told him. 'No, let me not say evil, that's wrong. Only one-sided . . . Don't you see there's one thing stronger than death, and that is life? If there were no life, then there would be nothing. Death exists because there is life. Life is the source of everything, of the whole universe. It is not death but life that endures. Your outlook is all wrong, Bey, upside-down. And if I am wrong, still my error is better than yours, for it's life creates death . . .'

In all his life this was to be the only man whom Dervish would value, in whom he would have faith. He held the vital spark, this Sheikh, a light shining above death. Dervish, a sceptic for whom nothing but death had ever existed, henceforth accepted the Alevi Sheikh's conception as a glimmer of hope in life.

10

Day was glimmering when they came to a shadowy brake. Both were ready to drop after having run all night through the viscid mud of the swamp. The noise from the Sarioglu farm, instead of diminishing, was growing louder and nearer as they fled, the sounds booming off the Anavarza crags and echoing back many times amplified.

'I'm sinking, Veli! Help!'

Whirlwind Veli turned and saw Black Hüseyin floundering waist-high in the water-logged brake, sinking deeper and deeper the more he struggled. He hopped on to a bush and clinging to a stout branch with one hand he held the other out. 'Grip this, you damned fool,' he said. 'Hold tight . . .'

Black Hüseyin seized his hand. 'Something's pulling me down, Veli, tugging at my legs . . .'

'Hold fast! Don't let go, you miserable wretch!' And he wrenched him out.

Black Hüseyin was steeped to the waist in clinging mud. 'If it wasn't for you, Veli, I'd have been stiff dead and buried in that slime. It would've been all over with Black Hüseyin! Look, if the swamp is everywhere like this, we'll never get out, not even dead. Let's go another way.'

'Man alive! Have you lost your wits? It's this swamp that'll save us, if anything. Any other way means death for us. Why, the whole plain and surrounding hills are full of people searching in every nook and cranny. Every one of the Sarilar tribe, from seven to seventy, must be out now, and you can be sure they're looking for me too. It's my turn . . .'

'Then let's hide in this brake here.'

'Idiot, what's the matter with you? Is it the blood that's gone to your head? Is it blood-guilt you've got?'

'Shut up, Veli,' Hüseyin shouted in a terrible voice.

Startled at this outburst, Whirlwind Veli held his peace for a while. Then, very softly, he spoke again: 'Think, you blockhead, don't they know we're here? Won't they search the swamp? Why, Dervish must have sent out a hundred of his brutes after us already? We have to reach the farm today, this evening. It's our only hope.'

But Black Hüseyin did not move. He stood there blinking dazedly in the face of the rising sun. 'I can't see a thing, Veli. It's the light that's dazzled me. Let me get used to it.'

Whirlwind Veli took Black Hüseyin's rifle from him, grabbed his hand and drew him along. His eyes, sharp as a wolf's, were not likely to be dazzled by anything. The rays of the sun were heavy, razor-sharp. The mud reached up to their knees, but where Veli stepped the ground was firm underneath.

'D'you hear those voices, Veli? They're drawing nearer.'

'Yes . . . They know this swamp like the inside of their houses, how many reed-beds and brakes there are, how many bees . . .'

'Go on, Whirlwind Veli, you're just spinning tales! How can they be counting bees and flies?'

'I'll swear to it!'

'Look, give me that rifle and stop your chatter. What if they do know? That doesn't mean they'll catch us, not while I have this gun in my hand.' And he snatched the rifle away from Veli.

'Well, if we don't step on it we'll be needing that rifle of yours soon,' Veli said. 'They're in the swamp already and on our track. Come on.' He spurted forward, making for the centre of the swamp. Black Hüseyin followed some hundred paces behind. The sun was growing hotter and the briars and brambles tore at their legs, but they kept on until they came to a brake so dense it seemed quite impenetrable. Yet to circle it would take them at least one day. Suddenly they stumbled upon a clearing in the brake where the ground was not at all swampy, but dry and cracked. Even the grass had withered here. At once they were assailed by tiny midge-flies that stuck to their eyes and faces and would not be driven away. With his huge hands Veli swept them off every minute or so, but they swarmed back ever thicker and faster. Soon their hands and hair and backs were black with them. Seen from afar they looked just like two Negroes. A hot clammy haze was forming and the all-pervading odour of the swamp pierced their lungs. The sun was dim, like an ash-skimmed heap of embers. Black Hüseyin turned his head and saw the wasps, the hundreds of combs massed in a clump of reeds and the thousands of yellow wasps seething all over them. In such stifling clammy weather wasps can be particularly dangerous, even deadly, should they spot a man and attack him.

'Hisht Veli, look at that! If we can slip by without rousing them it's a day of grace for us.'

'Devil take it! A real death-trap! Quick, Black Hüseyin, quick . . .'

Carefully they tiptoed away. Stuck to the reeds and the combs, the wasps stirred sluggishly under the sun, their trembling, whirring wings glistening with thousands of hues and tints.

As soon as they were at a safe distance they broke into a run. On and on they ran until their breath failed them and they stopped, panting, their chests heaving and making a rasping noise.

'Which way now?'

'East. We'll never get through this brake. We must skirt it and still be out of the swamp by tonight. Quick!' But at the first step Veli took he had plunged deep into a quagmire. Hüseyin just stood there dumbfounded, until after a while Veli re-surfaced and, catching hold of a branch, drew himself out.

'I'm sorry, brother,' Hüseyin said. 'I was so rattled I couldn't move an arm.'

From somewhere on the brink of the swamp shots rang out. Hüseyin clung to Veli's arm and they pressed on. The heat grew stronger, more clammy as they advanced. It was almost impossible to breathe. The dense humid air would not pass through their noses. They had to open their mouths wide to gasp it in.

'I'm suffocating, Veli. What is it? There's something . . . and you?'

'Me too, me too . . . Stifling . . . Heavy . . .'

Not a single living creature was abroad, save an occasional turtle that slid out of the reeds into the water at their approach. But there were flies in plenty, of all kinds, some as large as bees, some noisy, some soundless. The sedge, the rushes, the squat thick-leaved trees, all the vegetation of the swamp had a saturated, bloated look, as though if a leaf, a branch, a stalk or a flower were plucked, green water would gush out of it for days on end.

Now it was high noon. They were bathed in sweat and the midges and flies gave them no rest.

'They're devouring me, Veli, tearing me to pieces.'

Their hands came and went like machines, chasing off the flies. The swamp had begun to boil and bubble making rumbling sounds that seemed to come from the far depths of the earth.

It was a good thing they both had stout *chariks* on their feet. Whirlwind Veli never set a foot out of the village without those thick rawhide sandals and made everyone else do so too. It would have been impossible to walk through this swamp in anything else. The *chariks* protected them from the leeches too that would otherwise have sucked their veins dry in a morning.

The whole swamp was crackling in the noonday heat. Sweat was gushing out from their shoulders, and their eyes were burning with running sweat.

'I'm feeling faint, Veli. Let's find some dry shady spot or tree to climb into and rest . . .' He pointed to a group of trees that loomed tall and black in the distance, south of the swamp. 'There, have you seen that?'

'I've seen it.'

'Couldn't we go there?'

'We could, but . . . There's a spring there too, so cold it can freeze a man's teeth, but . . . It's not safe. That place always tempts fugitives, then it turns out to be a death-trap. What if we're encircled? Have you got enough ammunition to hold on till nightfall?'

'Plenty,' Hüseyin said. 'Can't you see?'

Whirlwind Veli hesitated. 'Let's not be tempted by the devil. A cool drink, a good sleep up in the branches of those trees, it'll put fresh life into us, but . . . Give it up, friend. Better by-pass the bush than be bitten by the cur . . .'

'But I simply can't go on. And I'm dying of thirst, my lips are all dry and cracked.' He bent down and drank a little from the muddy swamp water. It was like hot blood. 'God, it stinks! I feel sick. It's not water this, just poison.'

The distant trees were growing ever brighter, shining like an

94

oasis in the eyes of the weary flagging men.

'What if they're lying in wait for us there? . . . That's what I'd do.'

'All right then, let's rest a little at least in the shelter of those brambles.'

They crawled into the bushes. The ground was muddy. They spread some branches and sat down careless of the prickly thorns. At first the shade of the wet bushes felt cool as a mountain wold. But gradually the heat closed in again, oppressive, stifling.

'Once safe out of this, I'll go to Mustafa Bey and say, pension me off now, Bey. I've served you faithfully, killed for you, sweated for you . . . He should give me land, a hundred and fifty *dönüms*, Veli, shouldn't he? I'd till and sow it . . . And in the summer I'd go up into the cool mountains . . . I'd be able to buy things I want, to send my children to school so they can be somebody and not remain asses all their lives . . . The land should yield thirty or forty to one . . . And there I'd be, rich in a single year. I'd build a house then . . . Isn't that so, Veli? The Bey should help me retire at last. I've earned it.'

'Indeed! He should grant you a pension like the Government does . . . Just as any high-placed Kaymakam* . . .'

'Don't make fun of me, Veli! It's bad enough as it is. And I'm hungry too . . . I'm sure there are watermelons growing beneath those trees.'

'Are you off your head? Who'd go planting watermelons there?'

'Well, I thought perhaps they might, near that cold spring . . .'

'Nobody ever sets foot there except runaways . . .'

'Then nobody would think of it . . . Besides, we're strangers in these parts. What would we know of any tree-grove in the middle of Akchasaz swamp?' And like a smoked-out fox Black Hüseyin darted from the bushes. Veli followed him.

It was only as the day drew to a close that they reached the grove, utterly spent. The trees grew on a slight elevation. The ground was quite dry there with fresh green grass everywhere.

*Kaymakam: a district governor, coming after the Vali who is the governor of a province.

Joyfully they stepped over the soft turf, feeling cooled already in spite of their burning thirst.

'The cold water's over there, at the foot of that big willow tree.'

Hüseyin summoned his last remaining strength and spurted forward. He stopped before the spring. It flowed clear and crisp, ice-cold, from the roots of the tree, shedding a dancing play of lights on to its massive trunk. Just as he was bending down two rifles burst out and bullets began to rain about him. He dropped to his knees on the very edge of the spring and stretched over. First his hand touched the ice-cold water. Then his lips. Feverishly he drank, and as he drank the fire in him increased. Two more bullets hit him. His blood spouted into the water and the little spring soon turned bright red. Black Hüseyin's body shook once or twice and quivered. Then his head drooped and sank, immersed in the blood-stained water.

At the first intimation of a shot Whirlwind Veli had flung himself behind a tree, and almost in the same instant had waded into the swamp and speeded away, gliding serpent-like through the reeds and rushes, the brambles, briars and wild vine of the brake.

Hidayet and his companion pulled the dead man out of the spring, tied a long rope about his shoulders and dragged him off to where the swamp ended, not very far from the clump of trees. Then they tied the corpse to a horse and rode off towards the Akyollu farm. It was nearly day when they reached the stream below the farm. On its banks were tall, very large plane trees. They hung Hüseyin's corpse on to the highest branch of the tallest tree, and mounting their horses again galloped madly away.

In the first light of day, in the soft breeze of dawn the corpse swayed to and fro, naked, with yellowing feet.

11

The story goes like this:

Many years after the settlement there lived among the Afshar nomads a Bey called Amber Agha who would winter with his tribe in the Chukurova plain, erecting his tent near Vayvayli, and in the summer would repair back into the Binboga Mountains. The Bey's tribe was not very large, but he himself was shrewd and quick-witted, always full of new ideas.

And one day he had a brainwave. 'Look at this Chukurova plain!' he said. 'Think what a paddy it would make! I'm going to sow rice here.'

Straightaway he sent men to Aleppo to bring back rice-experts and seeds. The experts were open-mouthed at what they saw. Here was an untapped vein such as they had never seen before. They struck a bargain with Amber Agha. Instead of money they would take a portion of the crop. Amber Agha had a long canal built, starting about a mile south of Sülemish. All the men of his tribe worked on it for nothing, and to the men of other tribes he paid the equivalent of a packet of cigarettes daily. The canal extended from Sülemish way down to Vayvayli, so that the Aleppo experts had a huge plain as far as the eye could see to sow their rice. That year when Amber Agha returned from the Binboga Mountains he found such a crop that his storehouses were not enough to hold it. He had it all transported to Aleppo on camels, and in return got bags and bags of gold coins.

A few years later he died, and after him rice and rice cultivation fell into oblivion. But the canal was left intact, and also the dam he had built over Savrun River. Every winter the river used to overflow its banks, but now most of the water poured into the canal and filled up not only the disused paddies, but the whole Anavarza plain as well. The flood that winter had been such that the soil remained wet even through the summer.

97

The Amber Agha canal continued to feed the flood over the years, and the next winter three villages were completely submerged. The villagers had to abandon their homes and move elsewhere. The winter after that more villages were forced to evacuate. Another winter, and the whole plain was inundated. In a few years a large swamp came into being. They called it the Akchasaz swamp. It grew and grew until it reached the place that now bears the name of Amber's Ark. South-east it stretched to below Jiyjik, and south to Kesikkeli, Endel and Jeyhan River. Mosquitoes made their appearance, and with them malaria. People began to die of the fever and those who survived fled into the mountains. The already heavy climate of the Chukurova became even heavier because of the swamp, making it a veritable hell to live in. It was impossible even to approach Akchasaz in the summer.

In the course of years rice began to be cultivated again, this time by the Kadirli Aghas. They opened up innumerable canals from the Savrun River, and the result was that new marshes were formed, even larger than Akchasaz, marshes good for rice-sowing . . . And indeed so much rice came to be grown that Savrun River was no longer enough for all and big quarrels broke out among the rice planters. Even blood was shed over water. The river itself began to dry during the summer months. And so from June to October Akchasaz swamp was deprived of its mother source, the waters of the Savrun. Slowly, year by year, its vegetation withered. Land appeared again and was immediately snapped up by villagers and Aghas alike. The villagers were soon ejected from their new-found land by the Aghas and the rice planters who became rich, even millionaires thanks to Akchasaz swamp. Later they built factories, they took up politics and for a while these Akchasaz Aghas, joining the group of men who directed the fate of the country, played out their most negative and disastrous role.

And all the time this was taking place, while the land of Akchasaz was being avidly appropriated, fortunes being made, new Aghas and rich planters springing up, Dervish Bey and Mustafa Akyollu were thoroughly engrossed in their own private feud, blind to the world, locked in a struggle for life or death. Akchasaz was at their door, its stranglehold tightening, but they saw nothing, heard nothing, knew nothing. And even if they had been aware of what was happening, it would have made no difference. Nothing was of any interest to them but each other.

12

'He was running so fast, Bey,' Hidayet said, 'a bullet wouldn't have caught up with him. I saw him. I was just pressing the trigger, but he had vanished. There never was such a man, the devil's own brother he is! I'd heard tell about this Whirlwind Veli, but I didn't believe it till now. Don't worry, Bey, I'll catch him sooner or later and send his soul to hell, I will. I won't let Muharrem's murder go unavenged.'

It was hot. The mansion, the trees in the garden, the grass, the cotton plants, even the earth, everything was in a sweat. Dervish Bey too was sweating profusely. His clothes were wringing wet.

Suddenly, a shot rang out and a bullet came and planted itself right beneath Dervish Bey's window. This had been happening for some days now. The first shot was fired at eventide, the second just as the midnight cocks were crowing and the third at the peep of dawn, and all the bullets lodged in the same place, below Dervish's window.

Dervish Bey was furious. His first impulse was to rush out and catch the sniper, but he could not take a step out of his self-imposed cage. He stayed where he was, in that stifling, steaming room, boiling with rage. Neither Hidayet, nor any other of his men succeeded in even getting a glimpse of the sniper, or at least that is what they told Dervish Bey. He did not believe them. At last he nerved himself to make a little opening among the sandbags, only the size of a hand, and set to watch. As darkness was falling he saw a horse emerge at full gallop from Akchasaz. The rider reined in on the far bank of the stream near a casuarina tree. Quickly as he dismounted, he fired a shot, then jumped back and rode away like the wind. But why had he got off the horse in the first place? Couldn't he have aimed just as well from the saddle? Or was it that he had never dismounted at all? Was it an illusion? He had only caught a blurred glimpse of the rider. Perhaps he was imagining it all . . .

That night the rider came again with the crowing of the cocks at midnight, and once more at break of dawn. Only a vague silhouette, that is how Dervish Bey saw him. He said nothing to his men, not even to reproach them for having lied to him. Now, every night, he would watch impatiently for the rider and, at the slightest delay, a strange feeling of emptiness would take hold of him. Even deep in sleep he would wake up on the stroke of midnight and again just before dawn, and running to his peephole would wait with thumping heart for the rider to come and shoot at the mansion.

And then one day instead of the single rider there were three, then four, then five. They came the same way, at a gallop in the night, stopping only an instant beside the casuarina tree, discharging their rifles and dashing off again. And still the number of riders increased. The sound of hoofbeats haunted his sleeping and waking hours. Sometimes he could hear them from very far off, clattering over the Anavarza crags. There was nothing for it but to wait for the full moon. Perhaps then it would be possible to identify them.

'Do you see those riders now, Hidayet?' he asked.

'I see them, Bey.'

'Who can they be?'

'I don't know.'

'Couldn't we ambush them?'

'They never come the same way twice . . .'

'But they stop under the casuarina tree . . .'

'It seems to at this distance, Bey, but it's another place every night. Maybe they want us to go after them. Maybe it's a bait . . .'

'That's it! He wants to provoke me, that Mustafa, to draw me out. But I won't be drawn. I won't! Let him come here if he's got the nerve. It's driving him mad not to be able to come to grips with me. He has had one of my men killed. Well then, I'll have two of his. If only you'd got Whirlwind Veli, Hidayet, that would have done the trick!'

'I caught sight of him, lifted my rifle and he wasn't there any more, all in the same instant! It's uncanny.'

The moon rose and the Anavarza crags, the trees cast their shadows westwards. The night became bright as day, and every detail of the plain stood out, perfectly clear. And from far in the distance a group of horses sprang into view, galloping towards the mansion. They came right up to the wall of the yard, dismounted, fired several times, jumped back and rode away, full tilt, towards the Taurus Mountains. Though they had come so near, he had not been able to see their faces, but he had noticed that the horses were thoroughbreds. All through the night the beat of hooves rang in his ears, mingling with a far-off baying of dogs. But over and above all was the croaking of the frogs from Akchasaz swamp; so loud was it, that it seemed that earth and sky must be crawling with them.

Then one day, he waited and waited and the horsemen did not come. The dogs too were silent and even the frogs had stopped croaking. A vague apprehension filled him, deepening into fear. If the riders did not come, if they did not appear this instant a great catastrophe was imminent. He was sure of it, ready for it.

And just as he had expected a roaring sheet of flame burst up into the sky from below Anavarza hill, and, fanned by the madly blowing south wind, began to spread over the plain. The harvest was on fire.

'They've set fire to our crops,' Hidayet groaned. 'Bey, we'll all go hungry. How can we put the fire out in this wind? . . .'

'So you've stooped to this, Mustafa! Burning the bread and portion of the poor, of the little children . . . And here I am, taking you for a man, acknowledging you as an enemy!' Nothing could have wounded Dervish Bey more. That an enemy of his should lower himself in this way! Round and round the room he went, bathed in sweat, strangling. 'It can't be, it can't! My personal enemy over so many years, a man of honour, he wouldn't do this . . . No enemy of mine could degrade himself so. Impossible, impossible . . ' He simply could not believe it. 'If this really is your doing, Mustafa, then I'll come out and give myself up to you. Do what you like to me then . . . Have me shot even. I shan't turn a hair. I'll cast all my weapons at your face. There, you wretch, I'll say, after what you've done you're not my enemy any more, you're just a despicable executioner, and an odious one at that. What can life hold for you or for me now? A man loses all self-respect when he has such an enemy. I don't care what happens to me after this. Take my life if you wish.' Beside himself with rage, he beat his fists on the wall

'Traitor, traitor! Traitor to the blood our fathers shed, to everything that's good and honourable in our traditions. No, I have no enemy any longer. There's only a petty low-down murderer who wants to kill me.'

The sharecroppers, the farmhands had crowded into the yard, silent, still as statues in the moonlight. Dervish Bey went out on the balcony, gripped the balustrade and waited a while. Then he spoke. 'It's not often that a human being can sink so low. You are being made to suffer because of me. But I won't let you go hungry. I shall have your losses evaluated and everyone will receive his due. The blow is against me. Never before this mad dog has any one of the Akyollu family stooped to such an ignominy. We have always been proud to have them as enemies . . .'

As he spoke there was an ear-splitting explosion at the back of the mansion and a long flame lapped up the wall. The men in the yard rushed over to try to put the fire out, but Dervish Bey did not stir from the balcony. His wife grabbed his arm. She was trembling. 'Come, Bey, let's go in. They'll see you here and fire at you. They're doing this on purpose to smoke you out. Let's slip away, Bey, and hide in some house in the village.'

He waved her away as he would a fly. 'I don't care, Hatun,' he said. 'It makes no difference to me now whether I live or die. Not after this . . . Not after my enemy's degraded himself so shamefully. It's a terrible blow, Hatun, it's agony. I never expected this of an Akyollu . . .'

He fell silent and would not say another word. He just stood there, his long tapering fingers clutching at the railing so tightly that the blood flowed from under his nails.

The flames swirled over the roof now, almost reaching him and the huge mansion crackled ominously. The labourers were all over the place, fighting the fire with water, earth, wet cloths and rugs.

'Bey, you'll burn! You'll burn to death! Let's get out of here.' His wife was shaking him, shouting into his ear. But he heard nothing, saw nothing.

13

They had taken up positions in the reed-bed at Akyar. Not the slightest breeze stirred the tall tufted reeds, so thickset that they hid the water in places. The heat weighed down, sultry, steaming, sweltering.

Mustafa Bey rose and went to the water's edge. He bent down and clearing away the chaff from the dust-skimmed surface, splashed his face and neck. The water was as warm as blood. Then he went back and sat down again, leaning against a clump of reeds, his rifle on his lap. Big Hassan was dozing, the nostrils of his sharp eagle-beaked nose flaring wide. His large dark face with the jutting cheekbones had a yellowish tinge. Blinding flashes shot out from the straw that floated on the water. An enormous bird of prey was flying above the reed-bed, its wide wings outstretched, not really flying, but seemingly nailed to the blue of the sky, immobile. Another bird came to spread itself out beside the first one. The heat frazzled away and crackling sounds came from the baked, cracked earth, the sun-scorched grass, the trees and the reeds. Not a soul passed along the dusty wheel-marked road that ran along the reed-bed.

Then they heard the car, and Uncle Hamza's Ford came into view, squirting dust to right and left like water. It passed in front of them and they saw that there was no one but Uncle Hamza in it.

'What's happened?' Mustafa Bey said to Big Hassan. 'The car's empty.'

'Dervish was going into town today. I'm sure of it,' Hassan said. 'He had to, there's no mistake about it, to draw money from the bank. He needs it badly. He was going to sell his farmland at Kurtkulak too, to Adil Agha, the Circassian. They're expecting him in town. Let's wait a little more.'

'All right, let's wait.'

A bright scintillating cloud rose above Dumlu Castle and moved in their direction, just a single cloud in the spotless blue, but gathering speed like a great bird and floating ever higher into the sky. Hard upon it, the wind blew, churning up the dust of the roads, gaining strength until the plain was smothered in dust. Then it dropped. Slowly the dust settled back and it began to rain, a dusty clammy drizzle, yellow, dirty as water draining off a heap of straw, smoky as steam gushing out of a boiler. The heat was even more oppressive now, the sun a vague drift of embers behind a veil of vapour . . . Water poured down the reeds and Mustafa Bey and Big Hassan were drenched to the skin.

'If only I could get hold of him . . . If only . . . I wouldn't kill him. Oh no, I wouldn't! Would you, if you caught him, Big Hassan?'

Big Hassan roused himself with a start. 'Never,' he shouted. 'What I'd do is make him beg.'

'Dervish is not a man to beg for his life.'

'But I'd know how to make him beg. Ah, just let me get hold of him . . .'

'He'd never beg, I tell you.'

'No? Not if I took him up into the Anavarza crags and stripped him naked? Slashed a knife down his back and sprinkled salt deep under the skin . . . Strapped him tightly to a tree and poured sweetened water over him . . . Think of the bluebottle flies of Anavarza, of the wild bees, how they'd infest the wound, devour it. Wouldn't he beg then, d'you say?'

'Not for anything, he wouldn't!'

'I could also drive in thin strips of reed under each of his nails. That would do the trick.'

'No, it wouldn't.'

'Well then . . . I'd loose him from the tree and ram a stake down his back, hammer it into the ground and leave him standing there in the sun, with no water to drink . . . Only a drop of very salty water I'd give him from time to time. And a little bread baked with a lot of salt. I'd sit before him all day drinking cold water . . . You know, Bey, how hot the Anavarza crags can get of a summer noon, like iron in a furnace . . . Won't he beg then for a drop of water? He will, Bey. A man can bear anything except thirst, especially when he's licked all that salt.'

'Dervish would never beg anyone for anything. Look, Hassan,

if he were to send me word now, if he said, not begged mind you, just said, I'm in your power, think of my family, my children, only that, I'd give up this feud, though he did kill my brother, though he were to kill my son even. Aaah, if I could only catch him and make him say, don't take my life, Mustafa!'

'I'll make him say it . . .'

'Oh be quiet, Hassan. Don't talk about things you'll never be able to do. Now, if I were to catch him, I wouldn't do anything at first. I'd take him by the hand and make him sit down and show him the utmost courtesy. Then, in the middle of the night I'd go to him and say, choose your own death, Dervish. Of course he'll say, shoot me. All right Dervish, I'll say, and I'd blindfold him and take him up to the top of Mount Teké. There I'd rope him to a tree and shoot at him the whole day. But I'd be careful not to hit him. Oh no! Maybe just graze his skin now and again, his hair, his ear . . . If he asked to drink I'd give him water, and food too if he was hungry, and if he cried out at last, enough, Mustafa, don't take my life, I'd set him free. But he'd never do that. So, the second day I'd start firing at him again, hundreds of bullets, between his legs, over his shoulder, on a level with his brow, his eyes. Ask me to stop, I'd say to him, and I'll stop this minute, just ask me . . . I'd go on the third day, and the fourth, the fifth, the tenth, for a hundred days, until I made him say it. And all the while he must never know when I'm going to kill him.'

'That he'd never bear!' Big Hassan said. 'No human being could.'

'But he would. He's not a human being, he's Dervish . . . Ah, if only he'd say, enough, Mustafa, kill me . . . Yes, I'll tell him that too. Say it, I'll say, and I'm going to let you go. I don't care if he kills me afterwards, once he's begged.'

The yellow rain fell on, a steady drizzle, pus-like, evaporating in smoke the moment it touched the ground as though it had hit a red-hot metal sheet. The dust turned to yellow viscous mud and even the clouds were a clayish yellow.

In the afternoon they left their hiding-place in the reeds and, climbing on to a monticule, began to scan the plain in the direction of the Sarioglu farm and of the town. But a heavy almost man-high haze hid everything. Then, from where the plane trees floated above the haze, they saw the horseman emerge at a gallop. He was coming from the town, along the river, huddled flat over the horse, cleaving sword-like through the mist-swathed plain, growing smaller and smaller until he was only a tiny dot in the distance.

'Look, Big Hassan! See that? He's already been to town and he's going back. We've missed him again, the heathen. We set an ambush here and he takes another way. Aah, I'll never be able to catch him, never! Aah, Big Hassan . . .'

'Bey, it mayn't be him at all. Just some man on a horse. Maybe he's sick and couldn't go out.'

Mustafa Bey's face turned yellow and he glared at Hassan with hostility. 'Shut up,' he growled. 'Don't you dare say such a thing. He couldn't be sick. God, let him not fall sick . . .'

Realizing he had dropped a brick, Big Hassan hastened to make amends. 'What I meant was that he may have a cold, or be a bit tired . . . Just one of those little things . . . What else could be the matter with him? He's still young . . .'

'It's him all right . . . What if I had a shot at him?' He put his right knee to the ground, aimed and missed.

'It's much too far, Bey,' Big Hassan said. 'Shall I try?'

'No.' He fired again and again, trying to aim at the speeding horse's belly, but the horse went on galloping at the same breathtaking pace. 'It's Dervish, it's him all right! But he's out of our range.' He rose.

Overhead three eagles with widespread wings floated darkly immobile in the sky, wet under the yellow steamy drizzle. Mustafa Bey lifted his rifle and aimed at the long-pinioned eagle in the middle. He stood there for a while, his finger on the trigger, staring at the eagle, then he lowered the rifle very slowly, a mocking smile flitting on his drooping black mustache.

The hovering eagles never changed their stance and the yellow rain fell on relentlessly.

14

The refugees assigned for settlement on the east bank of the Savrun had begun to establish villages. One of these villages was situated below Bozkuyu on the site of five former Armenian villages.

It was early spring when the refugees first arrived in the Chukurova and they were overjoyed at the prospect of living on such a land. Their joy lasted only until summer came, when the fiery yellow heat of the Chukurova hit them and mosquitoes infested the sultry nights. These refugees had come from the Balkan highlands. They had never known such heat and mosquitoes and very soon they were falling prey to malarial fever. At first three children died and the refugee graveyard was inaugurated. There were no doctors, there was no quinine. The refugees appealed to the authorities in the town, to anyone they could find, but they always received the same answer: 'You must be resigned, there's no doctor or medicine that can cure malaria.' Then it was the turn of the old people. The number of dead increased day by day until the refugees could barely find time to bury them. In the end, not one person was spared. From morning to night, they lay there in the heat of the sun, on the black burning earth, old and young, trembling in all their limbs, racked by violent spasms, with no one strong enough to take away the corpses that were left to stink wherever they dropped, huddled up by their hearths, on their thresholds or in some ditch or other.

Then the rains began, and once the summer rains start in the Chukurova they do not let up easily. On and on it rained, a yellowish, dirty, murky, clammy, dusty rain, steady, persistent.

Mustafa Akyollu was on his horse riding around the village under the rain, inspecting the houses, looking at the shivering, moaning refugees, at the unburied dead. He was silent, with not even a word of sympathy for their affliction. Accompanying him were Big Hassan and a few other men. Once in a while he would turn to spit on the ground. He was wet through by the time he spurred his horse and rode away.

That night the village was attacked by bandits, who abducted five girls and took them into the mountains. Some days later the head of the village, young Idris Effendi, was shot dead on his threshold. The refugees were stunned. They had managed to obtain a few cows, horses and donkeys. These too were lifted one night. Weak with fever as they were, they decided to apply to the authorities. For days on end they waited at the gates of the town hall, a palsied ragged huddle. Three of their group had already died, when some honest citizen took pity on them.

'You'll get no help from the government or anyone else here,' he told them. 'All this is Mustafa Akyollu's doing. You'd better appeal to him, throw yourselves at his feet.'

So this time they collected at the gate of the Akyollu farm, but Mustafa Bey refused to see them and ordered his men to drive them away. After this they could only curse their fate.

At last the rains let up and the sun shone again . . . The refugees had built their houses out of reeds and rushes and two days later a fire broke out, turning the village into a heap of blackened ashes in a single night. When day dawned they discovered that five bed-ridden villagers had perished in the fire. They gathered together in the middle of their ruined village and wept.

'We came here to be in the fatherland,' they kept on saying, 'to live with our brothers . . .'

That night they spent in the open, shivering with fever, and towards morning they heard a mysterious voice ringing through the darkness. 'Refugees, you are occupying the land of Mustafa Akyollu. Get out of here. You have two days to leave. If not, worse things are in store for you. This is just a warning.'

The voice boomed on till daylight and the shuddering refugees huddled closer and closer to each other like a flock of sheep. All day long they did not speak or move, not even to eat or drink. No one was hungry and, anyway, where were they to find food in the burnt-down village? So they just remained there in the heat of the sun, and when evening came they took to the road, not knowing where they were going, but running for all they were worth, still keeping together in a close cluster.

Nothing was left of the village but a large fig tree leaning against a crumbling wall, nothing to show that there had been houses there once, no trace of human habitation. Nobody knew where the refugees had gone, what had happened to them, whether they died or survived. No one asked, no one ever heard of them. In the space of two or three months the inhabitants of this large village had melted into thin air.

For some time after this, Mustafa Akyollu was nicknamed 'Village Shifting Mustafa' and this fame of his spread through the Chukurova. Young and old, rich and poor, reasonable or not, they were all of one mind.

'Good for Mustafa Bey,' they said. 'That's how a man should act. He did well not to allow foreign heathens to settle on his land.'

And Mustafa Bey was proud of what he had done.

15

In those times the great blackthorn scrub stretched from the farm's sheepfolds far out to the edge of Akchasaz swamp, a wide dense expanse that a tiger could not have penetrated. Every spring, like a well-tended garden, the blackthorn would come into bloom with yellow flowers, bright as the sun, and all summer long the air would be fragrant with their strong heady scent. It was only in the autumn when the shrubs shed their leaves that the blackthorn showed its true face. Then the flowering fragrant garden would vanish, as though it had never existed. The tallest blackthorn bush does not exceed the height of a man, but it has hundreds of offshoots, bristling with spines, needle-sharp and hard as an eagle's talons. Their points shine like steel, and in the noonday heat the whole blackthorn scrub glitters with millions of tiny sparks of light. No bird can alight on this thorny mass, but when the blackthorn is in flower all the bees of the Chukurova seem to gather there, filling the air with a deafening drone.

Dervish Bey was black with rage. He sat his bay horse, holding a long whip made of a bull's member. Kamil was brought out of the stables, dishevelled, shreds of clothing hanging about his naked body, a bundle of rags. Blood was trickling down his right temple. He was a fine handsome man, Kamil, blond, green-eyed, open-browed . . . They led him to the edge of the blackthorn scrub, then coming from a distance Dervish Bey spurred his horse and galloped straight at him. The horse just grazed Kamil who fell to the ground, then stood up again, very straight. Dervish Bey reined in and rode hard back. As he passed Kamil he lashed at his back. The crack of the whip resounded from the Anavarza crags.

The force of Dervish's anger, the speed of the horse rendered the impact of the whip as sharp as a sword's, slashing a deep welt into the flesh. Again and again, furiously, he lunged at

Kamil, driving him into the fierce blackthorn scrub. Kamil was bleeding. His face, his head, his arms, legs, back, chest, all his body was streaming with blood. He made a spurt for the inner reaches of the scrub, running for his life. But Dervish Bey rode after him, swinging his whip mercilessly, on and on, deeper into the dense scrub, right up to the foot of Anavarza. The blackthorns had plucked the last strip of clothing from Kamil's body and the blood poured out of him as from a fountain.

The people from the farm, others from neighbouring villages, who had got wind of what was happening, women, men, children, all crowded on the edge of the blackthorn scrub to watch. Some even penetrated into the scrub, following Dervish Bey and Kamil wherever they went.

It was well into the afternoon when Dervish Bey, too exhausted to lift an arm, called out to Hidayet. 'Go and get a horse and come here,' he ordered. 'Find yourself a stout whip, and let two other men come with you, also with horses.'

Hidayet was quickly back with the two men.

'You're to whip him to the very end,' Dervish Bey said, and he turned Kamil over to them.

All through that night the Anavarza crags rang with the crack of whips and with deep-sounding moans. As day dawned they brought Kamil's body, a lacerated mangled mass of flesh that had nothing human left about it, and cast it down at the gates of the sheepfold. Dervish Bey emerged from the mansion.

'Is this Kamil?' he asked.

'May all your enemies live just so long, Bey,' Hidayet said. 'Every bit of his flesh is hanging on some bush. We could only bring in this much of him.'

Dervish Bey smiled. 'Take it away,' he said, touching the mass of flesh with the tip of his boot, 'and throw it to the dogs outside the farm.'

Kamil was the husband of Dervish Bey's sister, whom he loved more than anyone else, and she had sat all through this scene watching from the window of the mansion.

The news of Kamil's death in the blackthorn scrub travelled all over the Chukurova. Everyone heard of it, from the Vali to the deputies, from the commandant of the gendarmes to the chief of police.

'Good for Dervish Bey,' they said. 'There's a real man for you. He took the matter into his own hands and did what was necessary. Only he was a tiny bit too hard.'

And Dervish Bey was proud of what he had done.

16

Hidayet was standing at attention before the Bey. 'How could he do this?' he kept repeating. 'How? The man must be really mad.'

Dervish Bey did not lift his head. He preserved a gloomy silence.

'No one would do what he's done. No one but those new-rich Aghas . . .'

At last Dervish Bey looked up. He fixed a piercing gaze on Hidayet. 'I still can't believe it,' he said. 'The great Mustafa Akyollu of such noble ancestry, my personal enemy . . . Would he fall so low as to burn the crops of the poor and needy? What difference is there between this and butchering a man in his sleep? Mustafa Akyollu, my enemy . . .' He stressed the words again: 'Yes, my enemy, Hidayet, could he turn out to be such an abject person? Couldn't it be someone else who set fire to the mansion and the crops?'

But Hidayet was positive. 'Who else in the whole Chukurova plain would dare do this to us, Bey?' he said. 'Is it possible? Can you think of anyone but him?'

Dervish slapped his hands to his knees and rose. He began to pace the half-burnt room from wall to wall. 'I can't believe it! I can't, I can't! It hurts me to see my enemy come to this. Hatun, what d'you think?'

She was standing by the fire-blackened stairs and came over to the door at his call. 'I keep on telling you, Bey,' she said, 'but you wouldn't listen. Times have changed. Men have degenerated. Akyollu has become like everyone else. If I were you I wouldn't call Akyollu my enemy any more, now that I cannot look on him as a man of honour. Whatever he did after this, I wouldn't answer back. It would be degrading myself to his level to do so. But you never listen to anyone. You'll never conquer your anger and you'll find yourself doing to him just what he's done to you. And after that, Dervish, don't look for a man of

honour in this Chukurova any more.' She turned away and
began to descend the stairs. The burnt timber flaked off under
her angry step. 'And don't you see,' she added as an after-
thought, 'that it's impossible to go on living in this house? We
have to move to town at once. I'm going, with the children.'

'She's right,' Dervish said. 'I'll never conquer my anger. I'll
fall into the same pit as Akyollu and be dishonoured for ever in
the eyes of all the world. Yes, I know. I've thought about it for
days, Hidayet. For days I've tried to curb myself, but it's no
use. If only I could find it in me not to retaliate, it would be the
death of him. He did just that when we fell into his ambush.
How he controlled himself, knowing exactly what a humiliation
it would be for me to be let off! I was a hundred percent certain
he'd shoot as I was walking in front of the car. I never imagined
he had it in him to resist. How can this same man, a man who
has the strength not to pull the trigger when his quarry is right
in front of him, how can he stoop to setting fire to poor people's
crops? Ah, if only I could simply ignore him! Ah, Hidayet, if
only . . .'

He fell silent and went on pacing through the burnt room.
The mansion's big hall, the bay window, the rooms, nothing had
escaped the flames. The whole place was now but the blackened
skeleton of what it had been. Only the furniture and other
movables had been carried out and saved from the fire.

Dervish looked about him and suddenly a smile lit up his
face. 'I'll show him,' he cried. 'He'll see!' There was not a trace
of anger or dejection in him now. 'Go and tell the Hatun,
Hidayet, that we're leaving tomorrow for the town house. And
send for Zülfikar. Let's see what news he has.'

Zülfikar was the farm overseer. No one knew when he had
arrived on the estate, nor when he had become the overseer. He
himself would have been puzzled if asked. He seemed to be
forty years old, but he had looked exactly the same ten years
ago, and would undoubtedly still look forty in ten years' time.
Everything about him was long, his size, his face, his arms, his
neck. A scar from some old burn shone down his right cheek to
his neck. His eyes were tiny narrow slits, almost invisible, his
lips a thin straight line. A few sparse strands of hair hung from
his chin. When he spoke or looked at something, he would

stretch his neck out as far as it would go and, his head tilted bird-like, would gaze out sideways with one eye. All the business of the farm passed through his hands, selling the crops, employing seasonal hands, supervising the work. Dervish would never be bothered about anything. Zülfikar was an expert on matters of land cultivation. If Dervish Bey had left him to himself, this Circassian from Uzunyayla, would the estate have come to this, short of funds and dwindling steadily in size year in year out? On the contrary, he would have managed to annex new land until it was five times, ten times its present size.

'Have you closed that deal with Rüstemoglu? When is he going to pay? I need the money at once, not later than tomorrow. Look, the mansion's burnt down and the villagers have lost their crops because of me. If he wants to buy the land, then he must pay cash tomorrow. Have you measured the Sakchagöz place? How much is it?'

'Seven hundred *dönüms*. It's a splendid piece of land, Bey. Sow a man on it and he'll take root . . . The soil is so fertile it'll yield a hundredfold for wheat. And for cotton four hundred kilos per *dönüm*. How can you do this, Bey? The bulkiest tree can only roar with its branches. A landless man is worse than a shepherd without a flock.'

'How much is he offering? You tell me that.'

Zülfikar clasped his hands and just stood there, his neck stretched out pleadingly towards Dervish Bey.

'Don't you hear me, Zülfikar? I'm asking you how much Rüstemoglu's offering for the Sakchagöz land?'

'Nothing, Bey. Nothing to speak of . . . He wants to get it for nothing . . .'

'How much?'

Zülfikar hummed and hawed. His long neck lengthened still further and flushed red. 'For that much land, Bey . . . Only twenty thousand liras. So I spat in his face and sent him packing.'

Dervish Bey burst out laughing. 'You did well to spit in his face. He's just the kind of rascal that should be spat at. But you shouldn't have turned him away, Zülfikar. Twenty thousand is good money. Who'd pay out like that on the dot nowadays? Did he bring the money with him?'

Zülfikar seemed to wilt. 'Yes, he had it all in a bundle . . .

But what is twenty thousand for a place like Sakchagöz? You don't realize this, Bey. Seven hundred *dönüms* of good land . . . A huge farm . . . And he can then reclaim land from Akchasaz swamp, two thousand *dönüms*, five thousand . . . Any amount, and there he'd be, a huge landowner right next to us. That upstart!' Zülfikar drew himself up in anger. His tiny eyes widened. 'That upstart!' he shouted. 'Who's he to buy land off the Sarioglu estate? Not a jot of land would I give him, not for a million liras! He's nothing but a wretched nobody. Only yesterday his mouth reeked of hunger as he drove that lame donkey before him from village to village, peddling ginger, cloves, henna, beads and glassware . . . Only yesterday! I can't let this man settle there as a neighbour to the Sarioglus, not if they cut my head off I can't. Don't insist, Bey, don't press me too far or I'll do something crazy. Don't let me soil my hands with the blood of that son-of-a-bitch!'

But Dervish Bey knew his man. 'You're right,' he said mournfully. 'What you say is only too true. But what can I do? Those cowards have burnt my house as you can see. Shall I leave the great Sarioglu mansion like this, just a shell of four walls? What will people say? And those poor peasants, their crops and fields destroyed because of me, their children hungry . . . People will say I'm no different from those new-rich Aghas . . . Will we find better than Rüstemoglu? They're all the same these Aghas, all cast in the same mould . . . We need that money badly, unfortunately. If not, do you think I'd give them an inch of my land? Or even let their filthy feet step on it? But we have no choice, have we, Zülfikar? So send somebody and have Rüstemoglu bring the money. We're going to the town and you'll see to it that the mansion's repaired and ready in a month. You know I can't stay long in town, Zülfikar, so for heaven's sake try to be quick about it . . .'

Zülfikar's eyes had been filling with tears, just as Dervish Bey had expected. He knew that only soft speech could draw anything out of the man. If contradicted he was apt to become more and more stubborn. Time and again Dervish Bey had made him weep by deploring his bad fortune. If there was one person who was sincerely attached to the family and the land, it was Zülfikar. He could not bear to see Dervish Bey weak. It would send him into paroxysms of grief and he was happy only when the Bey was happy.

'I'll kill him,' he mumbled angrily as he left the room. 'I'll kill that Rüstemoglu. I will, I will!'

After Zülfikar had gone, Dervish Bey called to Hidayet. 'Saddle my horse,' he ordered. 'The black one.' Then he turned to his wife. 'I'm going now,' he said. 'You can come afterwards. I'll send Uncle Hamza's car.'

The horse was brought to the door and Dervish Bey jumped on to the saddle. For one minute he hesitated there, in the middle of the yard. Should he ride by Sögütlü? They could easily ambush him there . . . Across Savrun River ford? The Aktash road? Along Yalnizdut or below Vayvayli? . . . No road, no place was safe.

Suddenly, closing his eyes, he spurred the horse and in no time he found himself riding on the road below Vayvayli. With the wind pelting at his feverish body, expecting a bullet shot from behind every bush, he whipped up the streaking black steed beneath him.

17

'Damn you, Rüstemoglu, you low-down son-of-a-bitch, wasn't it you, you filthy microbe, went tramping up and down the Chukurova roads from village to village at the heels of that lame donkey? Wasn't it you, you double-dealer, who would haggle for three days running over one single needle? Wasn't it you who practised every kind of skulduggery by what sleight of hand, God only knows?'

Thus grumbling on interminably, Zülfikar mounted his horse and rode over to Rüstemoglu's house.

Rüstemoglu had arrived in the Chukurova at the age of fifteen from Darendé. The inhabitants of this barren unproductive place had for years made it a custom to move to other parts of the country, where they would set up a small trade and soon make good. In all the important provinces of Anatolia some of the wealthiest citizens would be found to have originated from Darendé. His name then was simply Memet, but later he changed this to Memet Zeki Rüstemoglu, which was more suited to his new social status, and whenever he heard himself addressed as Rüstemoglu he felt a glow of confidence inside him.

At first he had engaged himself as farmhand to an Agha who had promised to give him twenty-three liras after one year. Memet knew very well he would never be paid, but for him one job was as good as another. What he needed was capital, and that he would never get by working just anywhere. As soon as he joined the farm he began to perform the *namaz* prayer five times a day, though he did not know a word of a single prayer, nor anything about the ritual of genuflections. For the rest of his life he could never memorize a prayer, nor did he want to, but at this time in a matter of a few weeks he did learn to make the semblance of the *namaz* so well you'd have thought he had been born to it. And sure enough, its effect soon made itself felt. Two months later the Agha entrusted him with the supervision of his cotton-pickers. This was the chance Memet had been waiting for. He succeeded in turning the head of one of the labourers, a sharp-witted youth, but this was not easy and he had to talk himself out of breath for three days before he could convince him that stealing cotton was not the same as stealing anything else and should not be rated a sin.

It was one of those black nights with a slight drizzle in the air when the darkness is like a wall and a man cannot see an inch before him. His hands and legs were shaking, his heart hammering. He felt so faint he could scarcely hold up the sack of cotton, let alone lift it on to his back. The labourers were asleep only a little way off. What if one of them should wake up and see him? He would be done for, his whole life ruined. The very thought made him sick. In the end, straining every nerve, he swung the sack up and ran after his companion. It was nearly day when they came to the stream outside the town.

'You wait here,' Memet said, 'and I'll go and find a buyer. We'll get nabbed if we go into town with these sacks on our backs.'

An hour later he was back with a man who agreed to take delivery of the cotton on the spot and told them to bring more every night. He would load it on to a cart and take it into town and no one would be the wiser. After this, each night the two youths filled up five to six sacks with pilfered cotton and hid them in a brake near the stream where the buyer would come to fetch them with his cart.

By the time the cotton-picking was over Memet had made quite a pile of money. So he went to his employer. 'Agha,' he said, 'I can't bear the heat and mosquitoes down here any longer. I'm very grateful to you, but I must go. It's five months I've been working for you and I have much to be thankful for. So you can pay me my wages or not, as you wish.'

The Agha was truly sorry. A man who had kept faithful watch over his cotton, a good Moslem, where would he find such a one again? He tried to dissuade him, but in vain. So he gave him a full fifteen liras for the five months and Memet kissed his hand and took his leave. He made straight for Adana and looked for a shopkeeper who might be from Darendé. They pointed out a place to him. The shopkeeper was a sallow man with huge mustaches that were quite white. Memet showed him his money and told him what he wanted.

'Nothing could be easier,' his compatriot assured him.

They bought a handsome sturdy three-year-old donkey and had two glass-panelled cases made which they proceeded to fill with every knick-knack imaginable. And even then Memet had enough money left to equip another such donkey if he wanted to. He then set off to hawk his wares in the villages, never forgetting whenever he saw a group of people to first make his *namaz* prayers whether it was the right time for them or not. Come rain come bad weather, untiringly he kept up a constant round through all the villages of the Chukurova. And when at last he had made enough to set up shop in the town, he paid a visit to his native Darendé and got married. A week later he left his wife there and went back. His shop was the best supplied one in the town and, as all the villagers around knew him well and trusted him, he had no difficulty at all in building up a roaring trade.

It was the days of the black market. 'Stock up, stock up as much as you can,' the Darendé merchants living in Adana town urged him. He followed their advice and in a few years his capital had increased tenfold, so that he was able to open a shop in Adana itself. By then his wife had borne him three girls, but he could now afford to marry again, and so he did, taking another wife from Darendé.

After this it was as if Allah had given Memet Zeki Rüstemoglu a blank cheque. The number of his wives increased to four and of his children to eleven. By a stroke of luck he was able to appropriate, title-deeds and all, a farm belonging to an Armenian on the Anavarza plain, near Hajilar. It was one thousand *dönüms* large and the whole transaction only cost him seven hundred and sixty liras. And now he was toying with the idea of building a factory. But first and foremost he must extend his land holdings and develop them. Anything could happen to factories and shops, but land was land and could expand infinitely and much more quickly than capital and factories. And what a sense of security it gave a man! Rüstemoglu had never felt so good in all his life. There is nothing like security to make a human being of a man. He was seized with a dizzying appetite for land, as though the more he had the better he would feel his own being, joy and hope, affection, beauty, things he had never known or long forgotten. In trade there was nothing to bind you but money. All the rest just came and went, a bad dirty business. But land was firm, wholesome, lasting.

And now he had set his mind on Dervish Bey's estate. 'The land's simply slipping under the feet of the brainless fellow. He's going to lose it all and soon, so why shouldn't it fall into the hands of someone like me, who knows its worth, who'd give his soul for just a span of land?' And there was Akchasaz too. Times were changing. Inevitably one day that swamp in the middle of the Chukurova would be drained and reclaimed into thousands of *dönüms* of fertile soil. It was imperative to stake a claim to some little bit of it now, at once. A clever man is one who looks ahead and Rüstemoglu could see the future of Akchasaz as plain as the palm of his hand. If he could have just five hundred *dönüms* off the border of the swamp, then he could turn it into five thousand, even ten thousand in just ten years, not more. And Dervish Bey's lands encompassed all the swamp, east and north . . .

Rüstemoglu's farmstead consisted of a windowless structure, one metre high and a hundred and fifty metres long, with a roof of rushes and walls of reeds. A small hut, also of reeds and rushes, was set some fifteen metres to the north, obviously new to judge from the freshness of the reeds. A long poplar swayed high above the hut.

'Rüstemoglu, Rüstemoglu!'

He rushed out at once, dressed in patched shalvar-trousers, bleached grey with wear and an equally frayed tattered dirty shirt. His feet were bare and on his head he wore a battered old hat with a hole in its crown. He had a huge head with a tiny face and black eyes that kept spinning restlessly in their sockets. A finger-thick grizzled growth of beard covered his chin. His brow, his neck, the corners of his eyes were a maze of wrinkles and his back was slightly hunched.

'Welcome, Zülfikar Bey! Welcome, brother. You were in my dreams all through last night.' With one hand he grasped the horse's head and with the other the stirrups. 'Come, my dear esteemed guest, get off and let your blessed feet step on my land and bring bounty to my crops.'

Zülfikar dismounted and Rüstemoglu drew the horse into the long building. Then he brought out a straw mat and laid it at the foot of a fence. 'Here, sit down, light of my eyes,' he said. 'Excuse the state of the farm. We haven't had time to put it into shape yet. The family don't want to live here, what with the fever and mosquitoes. We come from the highlands, you know. My people would die in this heat. One has to get used to it, dear Zülfikar Bey. I've heard that you too come from the far highlands, of a great family which has seen better days, that you're one of those noble eagle-like Beys . . . But fate . . .'

Zülfikar could not resist this. He sighed. 'My father, in his lifetime . . . When I think of the horses we had, not one herd, not two, thirty-five herds we possessed. All of the Caucasus was ours, at our beck and call . . . And now . . . Aaah ah . . .' His tiny button eyes filled with tears.

'But you must never say die, Zülfikar Bey,' Rüstemoglu said anxiously. 'The wolf-cub's always a wolf, as the saying goes. If it wasn't for you Dervish Bey would have been on the rocks long ago. All the Chukurova knows you for a loyal honest person, one of the best. What man can say as much? Last night in my dream a clear stream was flowing and, riding over its surface on a dazzling bay horse, was a tall man holding a hawk. He came floating with the water, nearer and nearer, and stopped at my door. There he dismounted and the stream, too, gathered at the door, foaming, rising like a mountain . . . Now what does that mean? It means a rich harvest. It means that a great noble person is showering abundance and plenty on this house. That's why I've been on the look-out ever since early morning, wondering who it was that was going to come. And here it's turned out to be you, dear brother! How happy I am! Light as a bird I feel now. What news? Good news, I'm sure. Would a good man ever bring bad news? The Bey's agreed, hasn't he? He couldn't find a better neighbour than me . . .'

He was very short, Rüstemoglu, and scraggy, with hollow cheeks and he looked at Zülfikar from below as at a high mountain-top.

'I don't know,' Zülfikar replied. 'They do say you're a good man . . . The Bey's going to sell, but I wouldn't buy any of his land if I were you. Remember what happened to Halil who'd bought two thousand *dönüms* from Dervish Bey? You've heard of Halil from Tarsus, haven't you?'

'Yes,' Rüstemoglu said faintly. 'Yes, but . . .'

'Well, if you've heard of him, then you know,' Zülfikar pressed on. 'Two thousand *dönüms*, and before he ever set foot on the land . . . He sent the money to the Bey that evening and the next morning he was found dead in his house, his head chopped off . . . No, no, God forbid! I'm not saying the Bey had him killed. What I'm trying to tell you is that these Beys' lands are unlucky. And then there are the ghosts that haunt our farm every night . . . It's different with us, we've got used to them . . . And then there's the dragon of Akchasaz that devours any stranger who dares set foot in the swamp . . .'

Rüstemoglu swallowed. 'Don't worry about me. The land will stop being unlucky as soon as I've stepped on it. The ghosts will go too. As for the dragon, that's an old tale, don't you believe it. And anyway, I've got a powerful charm for that. I'll bury it on the edge of Akchasaz and the dragon will find itself imprisoned in the swamp. It'll never come near the border again.'

'So you're set on it, eh? Aren't you a bit afraid?'

'No, I'm not. As for Dervish Bey, he's a noble man. He won't do anything to me, nor allow anyone else to do so.'

'So you're buying it, eh? Well, I'm sorry for you, Rüstemoglu. You're a good man, but what can we do, it's your look-out.' Zülfikar talked on and on until his mouth was dry, inventing the most terrible things to frighten Rüstemoglu. He even fell to pleading with him, but the other would not be swayed. In the end, he decided on another course. This accursed man must have some very special reason for wanting the land, so why not take advantage of that, at least? 'The Bey has changed his mind,' he said. 'He's selling only three hundred *dönüms* and wants eighteen thousand liras for it.'

The two men began to haggle. This went on all day and well into the night. They shouted at the top of their voices and hurled the most unholy oaths at each other. Zülfikar would not retrench by one kurush. In fact he was beginning to be sorry he had not asked for more. It was obvious that he could have got any amount of money from Rüstemoglu for this land.

At last Rüstemoglu held out his hand. 'It's a bargain then,' he said. 'But only out of consideration for you. We'll start the formalities for the title-deeds right away. Tomorrow I'll go to town and bring the money with me.'

Dawn was breaking when Zülfikar rode away tired to death, very small now, huddling on the back of his horse as though folded in two. There was a lump in his throat. Not since the death of his eldest son, shot at the age of eighteen, had he felt such a burning agony. Soon he was sobbing away like a little child.

It was the same every time land was sold off the Sarioglu estate.

'For sure, for sure the Bey will do something! He won't let that Rüstemoglu get away with it. He'll find a way to get his land back from him some day.'

Even this thought in which he believed implicitly, was not enough to comfort him and he wept uncontrollably all the way back to the farm.

18

Ibrahim Ibo arrived in a simmering temper. 'It's impossible, Bey, impossible,' he cried. 'He's shut himself up in the town house and doesn't even put his nose out. Three days I've been waiting there. He's posted four guards at the door and, except for the Circassian Yagmur Agha, no one's been allowed inside in all these three days. Now, what am I to do with such a man?'

Mustafa Akyollu blanched. He tugged at his mustache. 'If only we could abduct him from his town house . . . If only . . . It's so much better than if it were done from the farm. We have to find a way . . . Don't you see, it would be in all the newspapers. And afterwards, when we've carried him up into the mountain . . .' He closed his eyes for a moment and his nostrils quivered. Thousands of long needles stuck into Dervish's back, glinting under the sun . . . Round his neck a rope, tied to a horse . . . And Heko riding it, whipping it on . . . Dervish suffocating, his tongue hanging out . . . 'No, I don't want to just shoot him like that in an ambush. I want to catch him. And then for days . . . With my own hands . . . I'll make him die with tortures such as the world has never seen before. How long is he going to stay in town?'

'They've started repairing the mansion. It'll probably be ready in a month or so. Dervish Bey's been selling land again. To that Rüstemoglu. And he's given money to all those whose crops got burnt.'

'A pity,' Akyollu said in a moan. 'Ah what a pity that . . . But we can still get hold of him one night, can't we, Ibrahim Ibo?'

Ibrahim Ibo pulled himself together. 'Yes, Bey.'

'We'd be safe if we went up to Aladag. Nobody would suspect that we'd taken him there. And then . . .'

Hamdi leapt to his feet. He was a very small man, almost a dwarf, and had been a bandit in his time, notorious as the butcher of Kirkayak's gang. 'And then . . .' he said, licking his lips. 'Then . . . Come here, you, Dervish Effendi. Come come

come, don't be afraid, apple of my eye, don't be afraid, you cock of the gypsy village . . .'

They moved over into the shade of a clump of trees and sat down, leaning against the trunks.

'Come, brother, come, come here . . . What's that? You're all yellow! Now now, no pleading, no, no! I've got a soft heart, I couldn't bear it.' And as he spoke he mimicked Dervish crying, laughing, pleading, suffering . . . It was as if Dervish was there before them, he did it so well. 'So you've come, eh? Good, that's spared me some effort. Now, strip! Come on, man, strip! Bashful, eh? What next! Why, man, haven't you ever undressed since you were born? Quick now, strip, you son-of-a-bitch! None of your Bey-like airs here. So you won't, eh?'

'Here's something new!' Mestan laughed. 'Let's see what this wretched dwarf's going to do now. The fellow simply won't strip.'

'All the better,' Hamdi said defiantly. 'I'll get a can of treacle, very sticky, and pour it all over him. Then I'll open up as many hives as I can find. Of course, all the bees will head straight for Dervish, swarming all over him . . . He'll make a dash for it, the treacle dripping down his body, the bees sticking to him like hell . . .'

'That's not good enough, Hamdi,' Akyollu said. 'We might as well shoot him down right away.'

'Not good enough?' Hamdi said. 'Have you ever seen how bees can tear a man to pieces. And anyway, these will be special bees. Wasps . . .'

'No, no, it won't do at all,' Mestan seconded Akyollu. 'It's not worth taking him all the way up the mountains for that little bit of torture. Now, what I'd do is this . . . Strip him naked myself, then sit him down against a tree and tie him tight to the trunk. And then . . . With a knife . . . First I'd slit into the skin between the toes, then up his feet, the calves, very thin slices, right up to the waist. Here I'd sprinkle salt and there honey, so that we'd have yellow ants crawling over one part and flies over the other, the flies nibbling up the honeyed flesh and the ants the rest. You know how flies can make you itch, a man could never stand it. And the yellow ants would gnaw and gnaw away . . . Eh, what could be better? To be devoured before his own eyes until death comes!'

'That's good,' Akyollu said. 'Very good. The best so far!'

'I'm so full of revenge,' Mestan said, 'it keeps me awake at night, just imagining all the things we'll do to him when we catch him, that man who took our brave Murtaza Bey's life. Even this is too good for him.'

Hamdi was aggrieved. 'As if I get a wink of sleep,' he said, 'thinking what could be the best death for Murtaza Bey's murderer! I was only trying to decide what we'd do next if he didn't take his clothes off . . .'

'Don't worry, Hamdi,' Akyollu consoled him. 'Just let's catch him and the rest will be easy.'

'Just let's catch him,' Rejep said. 'I've got something in my head that's never been thought of before, not in all the world. Just let's . . .'

'Say it, do, Rejep,' Mestan pleaded. 'I'm burning to know.'

'I've got a little something in mind for him too,' Heko said.

'Rejep's never told us his idea,' Akyollu remarked. 'It must be something quite uncommon, a really good death.'

'You'll see, Bey,' Rejep said. 'Let's just get hold of him . . .'

'Ibo waited there three days, in vain,' Akyollu said. 'Supposing we tried breaking into the house one night, ten of us . . .'

'We can't do that,' Mestan objected. 'They've got just as many men and weapons as us. And anyway, the gendarmes would be there in no time. What I suggest is that three of us should disguise ourselves and . . .'

'Are you mad?' Hamdi broke in. 'Dervish won't even let the flying bird in, let alone strangers.'

'I have a plan,' Rejep said. 'Suppose we go to Dervish and say, Mustafa Akyollu wants to see you, to talk to you. We could bring him a letter and fix a place. And Mustafa Bey would write in the letter that he's coming alone, and Dervish should be unaccompanied too. Wouldn't he come?'

'He'd come,' Akyollu said. 'And then?'

'We'd hide in the bushes and as soon as he came we'd pounce on him.'

Akyollu took his head between his hands. 'It's a plan,' he conceded, 'and Dervish would never refuse to come, but . . .' He looked at Ibrahim Ibo. 'Does he think I had his house and fields set on fire?'

'What else can he think? He'd blame us even for a slight puff of wind blowing over his farm.'

'He could have retaliated by burning my house and fields too, but he didn't, just to humiliate me, the dog. Well, if that's what he thinks of me . . . He'll see what's coming to him!'

'I've got it!' Hamdi burst out excitedly. 'Something new. When we catch him . . .'

'Later, later,' they said. 'You'll tell us later.'

It was too hot to talk any more. They could hardly breathe. Then a yellow gluey rain began to fall, dark and slow, not like rain at all. A warm foggy wetness.

19

It did not prove difficult for Ibrahim Ibo to gain admittance to Dervish Bey's presence. First he was searched from top to toe at the door. His gun and dagger were taken away from him and he was led upstairs. He held the letter out to the Bey and stepped back, standing with folded hands in a bowed attitude near the door.

Dervish Bey's face changed as he read the letter. He flushed and turned pale in turn. Once or twice he looked up and scrutinized Ibrahim Ibo, then went on reading. When he had finished, he fixed his eyes on him, a killing gaze, and Ibrahim Ibo shivered.

'Speak out now. Wasn't it you who started the fire on my estate?'

Ibrahim Ibo thought for a moment. 'It was me,' he said at last. 'Mustafa Bey knows nothing about it.'

'Why didn't you tell him?'

'He wouldn't have let me . . .'

'All right. I'll meet him alone and wherever he wishes. Only you're to come back here after you've given him the message. You look like a ruffian, but a brave fellow too. Tell me, d'you love that Mustafa so much?'

'Yes, I'd give my life for him.'

'And would he do the same for you?'

'That I can't say. But why should I come back here? You can agree to the meeting or not, that's your concern, yours and Mustafa Bey's. I don't deny I set fire to your house. I have no scruples about such things, nor would I balk at shooting a man in the back or raiding or setting ambushes. I go straight for my goal without looking to right or left. If, to get you out of the house, I had to kill everyone in the Chukurova, children and all, I would do so.'

Dervish Bey was not surprised. 'I know you very well, Ibrahim Ibo,' he said. 'And how is Hamdi? Kirkayak's Hamdi?

Still as cruel and ruthless as ever?'

'A thousand times more. From morning to night he keeps thinking up ways of killing you.'

Dervish Bey laughed. 'So he hasn't found a way yet!'

'He's got a new one every day, but he doesn't find it good enough the next day.'

'But what has he got against me? You know how much I did for him. And three times at least I saved his life.'

'He's angry at the whole world. He hates the human kind and every living creature too. Just show him a man he can harm, you or anyone else, and that's enough for him. He can't live one day without killing something, a bird, a cat, a dog, or even an ant, a fly, a bee . . . Once I went to his house and what should I see! He'd strung up hundreds of bees on a long thread and left them to buzz away to death in the sun. They're still hanging there all dried up.'

'So that's the kind of men the noble Akyollu employs?'

'Anyone would want to have such a man.'

Dervish Bey walked up to Ibrahim Ibo and put his hand on his shoulder. His right hand was on the butt of his revolver, where he had kept it ever since Ibrahim Ibo had entered the room. 'Tell Mustafa that I shall meet him alone at Tilkitepé, though I hold him responsible for burning my mansion and the crops, even if it was you who did it, and this is just as bad as if he were one of those unscrupulous, upstart Aghas. Because of that I had every right to refuse his proposal. But I accept. Give him my compliments and tell him I want only one thing, that my enemy should not resemble those new despicable Aghas.'

'All right, Bey, I'll take him the message.' And Ibrahim Ibo rushed down the stairs, retrieved his gun and dagger, jumped on to his horse and was off at a gallop.

After he had gone, Dervish Bey began to have second thoughts. He went to his wife's room and told her about the whole business. She read the letter and uttered a cry. 'But you mustn't!' she exclaimed. 'You can't do this! How can you trust a man who set fire to your house and crops? If he wants to talk to you why doesn't he come here? Why does he insist on seeing you alone on top of that hill? This is just a ruse to capture you.'

'You're right, Hatun,' he said despondently. 'But how can I

draw back now?'

'Put it off to a later date . . .'

'That's exactly what I'll do, Hatun. How are the children?'

'Muzaffer's gone to the town square. Jeyhun's down in the garden.'

Dervish Bey's town house was a present from an Armenian friend. Long before the days of flight and exile the Armenian had come to him one evening with the title-deeds of the house. 'There's no future for us here,' he'd said. 'The end is death or exile . . .' They would tell everybody that the transaction had cost Dervish three thousand gold coins. The Bey had been astounded. 'But, my friend, what are you saying? Who's going to kill you or drive you out?' He had tried to dissuade him, but the Armenian would not listen. 'I put such love and labour into building this house,' he had said, 'but I've been able to live in it only two years . . . And since I must leave, I don't want any vulgar worthless person to take possession of it. So I thought, now who deserves to live here? Only the Bey of Sarioglu . . . Take it, Dervish, enjoy it and may you be happy in it.'

The garden was planted entirely with pomegranates, a pink variety not to be found anywhere else. They were in flower now, a vast rippling redness . . .

'Would he try kidnapping the children?'

'Not even those upstart Aghas would stoop to that . . .'

'I expect anything from him after he had the crops of all those poor people burnt,' Dervish Bey said and left the room.

Dervish Bey not only admired his wife, but was also still madly in love with her, although the marriage had been arranged for him without his even having had a glimpse of her. This daughter of a noble Turcoman Bey was true to the traditions of honour and valour of her fathers. She was tall and willowy, dark, with huge coal-black eyes and a pointed chin. Her dimpled cheeks would easily assume a rosy flush. Her thick lips were red and sensual. When she laughed she would relax a little, then quickly regain her usual reserved composure. Her every motion radiated grace and gentleness. She spoke very little, and did not need to. Her eyes, face, hands, gestures spoke for her. She still wore the traditional costume of the Turcoman women, a silver-embroidered fez on her head decorated with rows of gold coins, a necklace of gold coins, a wide shirt, shiny slippers and coiled bangles on her wrists. Though her nose had been pierced she did not attach her golden nose-ring any more, nor did she wear anklets in spite of Dervish Bey's insistence.

The menace of death that hung over her husband had never daunted her. Blood feuds were an old accursed tradition in her father's house too. Even before the marriage she had known that her husband was marked for death and her chief concern had always been the upbringing of her children.

She followed her husband out of the room.

'Don't send me to him, Bey,' Hidayet was begging. 'Please don't. He'll kill me. There's no trusting the man.'

'Good God!' Dervish exclaimed. 'I can't believe it. How can my enemy have fallen so low as to be spoken of like that?'

'That I don't know, but I can't put my life into his hands, a Bey who burns his enemy's house, sets ambushes, destroys people's crops. If you trust him, Bey, that's your business. But I can't. Forgive me, I know it's not right to speak like this of an enemy of yours, but I can't help it. When it comes to one's life . . .'

Dervish Bey was angry, but he did not show it. Every disparaging word against Mustafa Akyollu pierced him to the core. 'Well, let Alijik go then,' he sighed. 'I can't blame you, Hidayet, but what can I do?'

'Good,' Hidayet said jubilantly. 'Alijik's just the man for this job. Mustafa Bey will go raving mad when he learns who Alijik is.' He began counting up something on his fingers, stopping now and then with his eyes fixed reflectively on the ceiling.

'When shall it be, Hidayet?'

'Not next year, but the next, in September . . .'

'Are you mad? He asked for a meeting at once. What are you saying?'

'I know, Bey. But what else can you do with a man who burns houses and crops and sets ambushes all the time? You can't refuse to see him, for that would mean you'd make a mistake in taking him for a worthy foe. You can't meet him tomorrow either. To get even with him you must fix the meeting for the twentieth of the month of September, two years from now. You'll write a very polite letter, very condescending, saying it's quite impossible to meet him now, but, not next year, but the year after, on a sunny September day . . . He'll go raving mad if you write like this, he will. After all if it wasn't he who set fire to the mansion and crops, it's his job to prove it. If it was *his* mansion that had got burnt, wouldn't we have been obliged to find the culprit to clear ourselves?'

'That's true enough,' Dervish Bey laughed.

'Well then, let him clear his own name.'

'Hidayet's right,' the Hatun said.

'In September of the year 19 . . , on a bright balmy morning at break of day, say the twentieth, not at Tilkitepé, but on another hill, at Kushtepé, just the two of us, alone, each carrying the Holy Koran with the stamp of our family on it, red, so it can be seen at a distance . . . And a banner, no, that's forbidden . . . A flag won't do either. The flag is Ismet Pasha's . . . I know, a kerchief, but a very large white one that'll flap like a flag in the wind . . . That's how we shall meet . . . Write just that, Bey.'

'You've got it all confused, but I see what you mean.'

'We're not educated folk, Bey, not book-learned like you. But that's what you have to write. You can throw it in his face too that it's not worthy of a Bey to spend his time setting ambushes and the like, or is it that the noble order of Beys is dead? If so, then let's put an end to this whole business and call ourselves plain murderers and act like them too. Why should we stain our hands with blood if it isn't for the glory of manhood? You could write that beautifully, Bey.'

'If I write him such a letter I can't consider him as my enemy any longer. I wouldn't even write to such a man, Hidayet.'

'Well, leave that out, but fix the meeting like I said, for two years later. I'm really furious with that man. The way he had our Muharrem killed . . . He's just a low-down coward . . .'

'Be quiet, Hidayet,' Dervish Bey shouted angrily. 'If you speak once more like that of Mustafa Bey, I'll tear your tongue out.'

Hatun intervened at once. 'He *is* a coward,' she said in a calm firm voice. 'A low-down coward, and a crafty scoundrel too, evil, wretched . . .'

Dervish Bey blanched. His hands trembled. 'Don't, Hatun!' he said. 'You're killing me. God damn such a friend or foe.

Don't say any more. It's too shameful for me.'

Hatun put her hands on her hips and faced him coolly. 'Then write that letter, Dervish,' she said. 'Write it so it should pierce his soul and teach him how one should behave with the Sarioglus. If he's not up to it, then let him renounce the feud. It can't go on like this.'

'No, it can't,' Dervish Bey agreed.

'If a man wants to come face to face with a Sarioglu, he should do it in all honour or not at all . . . Is it easy to call a Sarioglu your enemy? If he can't, then let him give up.'

'Yes, let him give up,' Dervish said.

'Let him give up,' Hidayet echoed.

20

The rain started again, a warm, yellow drizzle . . .

Süleyman Sami was on the warpath. For days now he had been scouring the town, buttonholing whoever he came across. 'It's impossible, impossible!' he kept saying. 'Quite impossible, gentlemen. They'll exterminate their families stock and stem, killing each other like that. And all of them men in their prime. It's a whole army that's been wiped out already! What's an army, what's a human being? An army's an army and a human being's a human being! Why should he be killed? Isn't that so? Yes, gentlemen, the time has come to put a stop to this savagery, this ferocity, this treason to the fatherland. What's treason to the fatherland? It's treason! We've got to get them reconciled and put an end to all this killing.'

It was the third time that he had tackled Mahir Kabakchioglu in his home. 'You're right, Süleyman Sami,' the other said as he accompanied him to the door. 'This business is unworthy of our time. If a European were to hear of it, he wouldn't understand at all.'

Süleyman Sami took the words from his mouth. 'He wouldn't!' he cried excitedly. 'And since he doesn't understand, it means he simply doesn't! Because it's not easy to understand savagery in our epoch. And when we're all spending every effort to lift our country to the level of Europe, putting our heart and soul into the task of development, on the march towards a bright horizon . . .'

'Yes, Süleyman Sami, yes my friend, I sympathize with these humane sentiments of yours and will do everything I can to second you in your enterprise.' Mahir Kabakchioglu spoke without emotion, composedly, stressing each word deliberately. 'But I don't believe these monsters will ever stop killing each other. It's been tried before. Why, the whole of the Chukurova has been on its feet at one time or another to patch up the quarrel. Even the Minister of the Interior came here once, all the way from Ankara, for this business, but they would not listen. And I? Five times I've been to both their houses with delegations of notables from the town and the rest of the Chukurova, but in vain. It's a hopeless business. Still . . . One must trust in God. It's worth trying again, a hundred times, in order to wipe out this stigma of backwardness on our country's name. I'm ready, my friend, if you can persuade the others. I'm ready to tackle the two of them. After all, they're both educated men who've seen the world. They should be made to understand that such behaviour in our epoch is uncivilized, backward, inhuman, that the whole affair is a mockery, a hollow pretence, a disgrace, a black stain on the brow of our fatherland. I'll do my best to convince them. Tell me, what happened after Murtaza Bey's death?'

'Akyollu had one of Dervish Bey's men killed, Muharrem. He was a great horse-trainer, the best in all the Chukurova. And hard upon this, Dervish Bey had Black Hüseyin murdered, the one who killed Muharrem . . . Isn't it a pity, tell me, for this country's army? An army's an army, our country's our country. No one should be killed. Muharrem and Black Hüseyin were still young. So was Mahmut. And Murtaza . . . Count their sons, and there you have a whole squad, haven't you? One can't decimate a nation's posterity like that! No, Mahir Bey, let's go and deliver an ultimatum to them in the name of this nation, let's put some sense into the heads of these lunatics. What's sense? It's something that has to be put into a man's head.'

'I've not much hope, but I'll come all the same.'

They shook hands. 'Thank you, thank you,' Süleyman Sami exclaimed. 'I knew you wouldn't refuse me, Mahir Bey. A man who's been educated in Europe can't allow an open wound like this in the heart of his fatherland to go on bleeding for ever.'

'That's true,' Mahir Kabakchioglu said, hiding a smile.

The whole town was talking of nothing else but this reconciliation. It must be done. This couldn't go on, this killing of each other day and night. It was barbarous, not worthy of human beings. And so on and so forth, tongues wagged, but deep inside no one wanted a reconciliation. They had got used to discussing year in year out the feud between the Akyollu and Sarioglu families, to this exciting, extravagant, crazy saga of courage and cowardice. Damn Süleyman Sami! What had got into him? People killed each other everywhere. And this was an age-old tradition that had gone down from father to son. How could one cut it short just like that? And there were all these men who were employed by both families for this kind of job only. What would happen to them? How would they earn a living? They would die of hunger, for what else had they been taught to do but wield a gun? Yes, one had to consider that side of the matter too . . . And what would Dervish Bey and Mustafa Bey do with their empty time? Spend their nights gambling at the town club? And the townspeople, left with nothing to talk about? Why, they'd start tearing each other to shreds, that's what!

'I won't do it,' Veli Hassan Agha shouted at Süleyman Sami. 'They're used to it. They'll go on killing each other to the bitter end. It's their life. And a good thing too that Beys should kill each other so poor folk like us could take a breather, or they'd soon be killing us! And anyway, what business is it of yours, Süleyman? You're just a down-and-out pauper without a penny to your name. How d'you live, eh, tell me that! Just by being the fly in the horse's ass, that's how! And who told you to act the peace-maker, tell me that . . .'

What a battle it had been, many years ago, in the time of the tribes! For a full ten days they had fought, the Akyollus and the Sarioglus in a bloody encounter on the Anavarza plain. The waters of Sumbas Stream had flowed red with blood and the eagles had gorged on human flesh. All the Chukurova had crowded in to watch the fray. Such a turmoil, with the tents on fire and the whole plain too, forest and all, and the sheep and horses and camels plundered . . . Nobody had attempted to separate them. The battle had just petered out of itself, the warriors too exhausted to go on, dropping to the ground, their weapons still in their hands. For three days and three nights they had slept there in the middle of the plain . . .

'Let them fight! I wouldn't interfere, never! They're mad. They've been mad for a thousand years. Yes, my lad, I know them through and through. There's not a particle of good sense in any one of them. Just pure showing-off. Killing each other to show off, that's what. Well, let them. They'll either get sick of it or finish each other off. I won't go to those stupid fools, damn

138

them.' He wrinkled up his face in disgust. 'And as for you,' he added, waving his hand as if to chase away a fly, 'get the hell out of here. Go, go, don't bother me any more.'

Süleyman Sami was breathing hard. His long neck stretched still longer, the veins swelling out. He glared down sideways, bird-like with one eye, at the frail doddering figure of the old man, then he tossed his head. 'Just thank your great years,' he said. 'To think I expected . . .'

'Wretch!' Veli Hassan shrieked. 'You're just a good-for-nothing, low-down worm, only doing this to show off, so that people should pay attention to you and take you for a man . . . But that you'll never be. A horsefly, that's what you are. A horsefly's always a horsefly whatever it does, and everyone knows where it lodges too . . . Now get out of my sight. I don't want to soil my hands, even if it's only with the blood of a horsefly . . .'

Süleyman Sami flounced away with long angry strides, twisting his long neck this way and that, his large ox-like eyes bulging with shock. 'You old dotard,' he muttered. 'Damn you and your wife and family too . . .'

Peace-making had always been Süleyman Sami's speciality. Everyone has a job to do on this earth and Süleyman Sami's was to redress the wrongs and dissensions of the human kind. There are so many things in life unworthy of the dignity of man. Shouldn't someone take it upon himself to do something about it? But in all the years that he had managed such affairs no one had insulted him like this doting old fossil.

'I'll give up, that's all. Let them go on killing one another. What do I care? As if I'm obliged to go like this from door to door, begging people . . . There, I give up, you old dotard, I give up!' He stood there, under the huge plane tree in the market square, ruminating bitterly. He was very tall, and his long shadow reached right up to the lower branches of the tree. With his stooped back he was like a bow, a thin curved line. 'So I'm doing this just to show off! Because I've nothing else to do! Well then, I give up . . .'

What about Abdülhalik Effendi, the registrar, that canny man? All his family are statesmen. A tall distinguished man, carrying a silver-topped cane . . . So eloquent you can hardly follow what he says . . . Eh, Veli Hassan Agha! Remember how you used to carry wood to his house before you became an Agha? And how you would bring Rose Fatma to him? With her cheeks the colour of a rose, her green eyes, her strong body? How much did he pay you for this? Wasn't it Abdülhalik Effendi who gave you the title-deeds to the land of the Sazanli farm? You'll realize the value of this land later, he'd said. Your children and grandchildren will bless me for it till kingdom come. Go now and build yourself a hut on the Sazanli marshes and take Rose Fatma with you. She's a real stallion of a woman. Have as many children as you can. To me she's given a lot of joy, God bless her . . . She's added years to my life. But mind you marry her so she shouldn't be made miserable by wicked tongues. She's a real elixir, that woman . . . So you married Rose Fatma and had many children, seven boys and seven girls. And they all grew up on Sazanli farm. The swamp was drained, but your sons were no good, dissipating all your money in the Adana bars, and the eldest was shot dead over a whore in one of the brothels of Tashchikan. As for Rose Fatma she still visits Abdülhalik Effendi in his house. They're old now, both of them, but the whole world knows that their love is stronger than even that of Kerem and Asli*. They've been on fire with passion these forty years, and Rose Fatma says, it's him and him only, even if I live to be a hundred, and when I die the grass that grows out of my grave will cry out his name. And you, what are you, Veli Hassan? What's your business in that house? D'you even know which of the children are yours and which are Abdülhalik's? Well, if you don't, everyone else can tell the short dark skinny ones from the tall fair hazel-eyed slim-fingered ones! How can you even sleep, you worm?

'I'll get even with you!' Süleyman Sami shouted out loud. 'Who are you to live on the Sazanli land? If those Armenians hadn't fled, you'd have been licking your empty palms, you and that Abdülhalik too. Just a plain woodcutter you'd still be and Rose Fatma the most notorious whore of the Chukurova. Thank your lucky stars for that Armenian, Serkis Haznejiyan . . . If it weren't for him . . . What a man he was, Serkis, with his bushy

*Kerem and Asli: lovers in a popular Turkish folktale.

140

mustache and gold teeth, and that large ring he wore, engraved with the figures of a man and a lion. My father still keeps it. No, my father didn't kill Serkis Effendi. He just took his ring and gold teeth, and fine Bulgarian revolver. They say he took his gold too, bags of it, but that's a lie. Would we have been like this if we'd had all that gold? Aah, Serkis, ah!'

But Veli Hassan was still Veli Hassan Agha, insult him as he might, a man who had been able to send his sons to study in Istanbul . . . And soon Süleyman Sami was standing again at the gate of his house. There were large mulberry trees in the yard, dating back to the Armenians. The house, too, had been built by Serkis Effendi. How long is it, Süleyman Sami mused, that they went away, these Armenians? It can't be very long. Look how the whitewash is still fresh . . . He pushed the gate open angrily and found himself face to face with Veli Hassan who started hurling abuse at him on the spot. Süleyman Sami listened in silence, his neck stretching out longer and longer as the other cursed and swore. 'All right, Agha,' he blurted out at last. 'Since you take it so much to heart, I give it up. Let them go on killing each other.' And he turned and walked away, his back more bowed than ever, tripping against the large white cobblestones in the market square. What about tackling Haji Osman Agha? Another of those old Aghas who had got hold of his lands by God knows what intrigues . . . But at least he was good-natured.

For a long time he hung around Haji Osman Agha's house, blowing hot and cold. Then suddenly he found himself inside, already on the first floor, and before him was a beardless old man with a myriad-wrinkled neck and one eye set high above the other.

Soon Haji Osman Agha was laughing away. 'Certainly, certainly, Süleyman, my son,' he was saying. 'You're a charity-loving person. This whole business is a great shame. Murder is the worst of sins and whoever prevents it will earn himself countless merits in the eyes of Allah. Of course you mustn't give up. Never mind what Veli Hassan says. He's always been a contrary-minded fellow. As for his relations with Abdülhalik, is there a soul left who doesn't know? And about the children too? But what's it to us? You just do what you have to. Charity is charity and if no one else goes with you, I will. I'll get Rasim

Bey to come too. We have to stop this. It's a bad example for the whole town. Murder is contagious and if it once begins to spread, then people will soon be killing each other all over the place. Nobody will be safe . . . Only don't go repeating those things about Veli Hassan anywhere else, Süleyman, my son. He's quite capable of having you bumped off by some mountain Kurd. That kind of thing doesn't cost much you know, between five hundred and two thousand five hundred, according to your man. Ah, if Kurdish Temir had been alive would I have let that Veli Hassan sit on forever on the Sazanli land! Aaah . . . When shall we go?'

'Tomorrow, Agha. The sooner the better . . .'

'Yes, but our delegation should include people from Adana and Kozan. Those Beys are sticklers for high birth and pedigree. Kurdish Ali Agha, for instance, he must come. And try and get Hurshit Kurdoglu too . . .'

'We've had enough of people shedding each other's blood for nothing,' Süleyman Sami cried. 'Enough, enough!' he repeated several times at the top of his voice. 'I'm going to end this tyranny. You've given me confidence, uncle. With great men like you supporting me, I know I can pull it off.'

'People of rank you must find, people of old families . . . And members of parliament. Don't forget Mad Halit. And if you can get the Vali to come . . .'

'I'll tackle him too. Either I finish this job or I die. Death or . . . Or an end to this killing.'

He was in an exultant mood. Haji Osman Agha had offered him a good meal with a cup of coffee to crown it, and he had also slipped a fifty-lira note into his pocket. If only everyone could be like him! True, he had the murder of four persons at his door, but he'd long given up that sort of thing . . . His two sons were lawyers and members of the Democrat Party. Soon they would be elected to parliament, both of them. Why didn't Dervish Bey enter politics too and be useful to his nation instead of wasting his time on feuds? But then one never knew with these feudal lords. He might support Ismet Pasha instead. These old families were all for him. Fools! What good had Ismet Pasha ever done them? . . .

'Rasim Bey, Rasim Bey . . .'

142

'Certainly, my friend, willingly . . . And Dervish Bey and Akyollu will both kill a calf in our honour. And I expect there'll be *raki* too. We're going to be quite an important group of guests. They're not boors . . .'

'Quite, quite . . .' Süleyman Sami stammered, affronted. What babblers there were in this town! No one took anything with proper gravity. That night he did not sleep a wink. Here were human beings killing each other, and the townspeople were concerned only with their own well-being!

The next day he went to Haji Osman Agha. 'Uncle,' he said, 'I need a horse.'

'Certainly, certainly, my son.' And Haji Osman Agha saw him off. 'May your holy venture prosper,' he encouraged him. 'Once you've brought this business to a finish, I'll have something to say to you.'

'Many thanks, Osman Agha . . . I understand. You'll see.'

It was nearing sunset when he rode up to Kurdish Ali Agha's house. The Agha met him at the door with a smiling welcome. 'So you're still at it, Süleyman Sami Bey?' he said.

'Aaah,' the other sighed, 'ah, Ali Agha, is there ever an end? You finish one problem and five more spring up before you. There are bloodthirsty monsters inside every man and if one's asleep a thousand are awake. Ah, how can we cope with them all?'

He spent two days in Ali Agha's house, sleeping on a feather bed in a room hung with Turcoman rugs, eating and drinking his fill, but unable to obtain what he had come for. 'Aah, Agha, if only you could come,' he repeated for perhaps the hundredth time as he was making ready to leave. 'Then we'd have got the better of them.'

'I'm much too old, son,' Kurdish Ali Agha said. 'Much too old. Or I'd never have declined such a noble proposal. Why, I can hardly stand upright. But you go on and make the peace between them. The time is past when noble families carried on feuds with each other. Tell them there are no noble families any more. What's left of the Turcomans? All degenerated now. So tell them to stop killing each other. We've had as much of that as we can bear.'

'I'll tell them,' Süleyman Sami said as he rode off. He was

143

grinding his teeth. 'Miserable wretch,' he muttered. He rummaged through his pockets. They were empty. 'Miserable wretch, sending a man away with empty pockets, a man who's come to him on such a mission!'

Three days later he arrived in Adana. Leaving his horse at an inn, he made straight for a tailor shop, and taking his navy blue suit from his bag he had it pressed. Then he changed quickly, on the spot, behind the tailor's workbench, stuffed his old clothes into the bag and went to have a shave and his shoes shined. After having combed his hair with great care, he hurried to Government House and asked to see the Vali, but the interview was postponed till after noon. So he decided to have lunch at a nearby *kebap* restaurant. Adana *kebap* was served without onions, but still it was Adana *kebap* and quite delicious. At three o'clock he was summoned at last. With his long figure he prostrated himself almost flat before the Vali as many times as he could. This pleased the Vali and he showed him a seat.

'I know,' the Vali said, when Süleyman Sami had stated his business. 'This is a cancer that's gnawing at our country. The best solution would have been to exile the two families, Dervish Bey to Van, Mustafa Bey to Aydin or Edirne . . . The pity is that we don't have enough proof to apply the law.'

'No,' Süleyman Sami said, trembling with excitement. 'And even then they'd find each other wherever they were and start killing again. Once, long ago, Mustafa Bey's great-grandfather, sick of all this killing, fled to Salonica. As you know, honourable Vali Pasha, Salonica was ours at that time and Mustafa Bey's great-grandfather settled there with all his family. The Sultan gave him a huge estate as large as this Chukurova, and a palace in the town. Not a year had passed when what should they see! Mustafa Bey's great-grandfather's brother lying dead in a pool of blood in the big square of Salonica, and over the body, a letter. Death will track you down even if you hide in an iron chest, even if you flee to the other end of the earth. You are every one of you marked for death. The best thing for you is to go back to the Chukurova, to your home, so as not to be branded as cowards who run away, so that your bodies should not lie in alien soil . . . No, we have no other choice but to reconcile them.

It's such a pity, Vali Pasha, for this country's fine young men
... If at least they had fallen on the battlefield ... In my family
all the men lost their lives at the wars. Who knows, maybe I
shall be the first to break the noble tradition of my race, to die
in my bed without ever seeing a war, a blot on the family
escutcheon. Ah, Vali Pasha, aaah!'

Much affected, the Vali tried to comfort him. 'Don't worry
so much, my dear sir, please don't,' he said. 'You too are a man
of honour. Look what a good cause you've embraced.'

'Aaah,' Süleyman Sami sighed, his neck thinning out, his
veins swelling, his pointed nose turning crimson, 'aaah, how I
wish I could die on a battlefield. This is a battle too, yes, but
isn't it humiliating for the last offspring of a race not used to
dying in a bed? It seems so to me ... Yes, Vali Pasha, when
will you do us the honour of coming to our town? If we put it
off too long, a few more men will be lost. When they see you,
they'll desist, I'm sure ...'

'Do you think so?'

'At once!' Süleyman Sami cried.

'Then I'll come soon,' the Vali promised. 'Convey my
greetings to the Kaymakam.'

'At your service,' Süleyman Sami said.

It was soon all over the town that the Vali was coming with
other notables of the Chukurova to intercede between Dervish
Bey and Akyollu, and that this was the work of Süleyman Sami.

'That Vali will do the trick,' some opined. But others thought
different. 'Not the Vali, but even Ismet Pasha, or the Padishah
himself wouldn't stop those two. What Beys and Valis and
Pashas haven't we seen that tried, and what happened? They
pretend to make peace for a couple of days and then they're at
it again, worse than before.'

'This is like a law. Would the big fish give up eating the
small? Or the falcon his prey, the wolf the lamb?'

Yet there were some who said: 'Who knows, who knows ...
Perhaps ... A new day, a new harvest ... One should never
lose hope.'

And everyone waited impatiently for the day of the Vali's
coming.

Just at that time two bodies were discovered on the road that passed by Anavarza, each with a dagger planted deep into the heart. The daggers were exactly the same size with the same inscriptions, and the dead men too were alike as two peas.

'Thank goodness!' Süleyman Sami rejoiced as he scoured the town again, buttonholing people in coffee-shops and stores. 'Thank goodness we're putting an end to all this. Our noble countrymen will stop killing each other. They'll be good citizens from now on. There are so few nobles left anyway. What would we do if they perished all like this? Tell me, friends, can a nation exist, can it survive if it's composed only of common people, like a flock of sheep? Noblemen are a nation's blood, its pride. We can't allow them to destroy each other, even if it is one of their traditions. No, we must put a stop to this noble behaviour. Our Vali, too, is of noble stock. He's had to become a Vali because times have changed, poor man, and we're a republic now.'

Slowly, Aghas and notables from Adana, Kozan and some other places began to converge on the town. Süleyman Sami took it upon himself to welcome each newcomer whether he knew him or not, and to find lodgings for him according to his rank. To Veli Hassan Agha he assigned the care of no less than six guests. Veli Hassan had never reckoned on the Vali's really coming, but it seemed now that this was a certainty, and he was doing his best to ingratiate himself with Süleyman Sami. Moreover it was essential that he should not be left out of the peace commission which was to accompany the Vali. That dog, Süleyman Sami, was quite capable of doing him just such a dirty trick.

And then at last, early one morning, the Vali's automobile drew up in the municipal square, and the Kaymakam, the Captain of the Gendarmes and the Mayor rushed out to welcome him.

'We're going straight to Akyollu's place,' the Vali said. 'It's shameful, disgraceful, shocking . . . Such uncivilized ways! In our epoch! We can't allow this, gentlemen.'

'We can't, sir,' the Captain of the Gendarmes said, standing at attention.

'No, we can't,' the Kaymakam said.

'Indeed, indeed we can't, sir,' the Mayor said.

The Vali stepped out of the car. 'I'll just stop for long enough to drink a coffee,' he declared. 'Let those who are coming with me get ready at once. Shameful! Impossible! Thank goodness the Europeans don't know of this or what would they think of us? Shameful! Impossible!'

'Shameful! Impossible!' they all echoed in one voice.

As the Vali was drinking his coffee in the Mayor's office, Süleyman Sami made his appearance. The Vali rose and greeted him with great cordiality.

'I've something to beg of you, sir,' Süleyman Sami said.

'But certainly, please, Süleyman Bey . . .'

'Will you allow us just a short half-hour, sir? There's quite a crowd coming with you. Beys and notables from Adana and Kozan. They'll follow in a bus. Everyone's interested in wiping off this stain, so that we too can attain civilization in this civilized world. Some high-ranking personalities have come to our town just for this . . .'

'We'll wait,' the Vali said, sipping his coffee.

Mustafa Akyollu had long been informed of the Vali's projected visit and he had made preparations accordingly. The mansion had been cleaned from top to bottom, the floorboards scrubbed, the big hall repainted and old Turcoman *kilims* spread out in all the rooms and hung on the walls. Old Turcoman *kilims* seemed to have gone up in value these last years, especially among the educated classes, who would fall into raptures when they saw one, expatiating learnedly on our traditions and virtues. There was a newfound predilection for folk-minstrels too among these people, so Mustafa Bey invited the Bald Minstrel from way off in the Taurus Mountains, who prided himself on having played for Mustafa Kemal Pasha* in Tripoli, when he was not yet a Pasha and was having trouble with the Arabs. He would summon the minstrel to his tent on those desolate desert nights. 'Play minstrel, play,' he would say, and there would be sadness in his blue eyes, 'we're lost, finished.'

But what could Mustafa Akyollu say to the Vali? How could

*Mustafa Kemal Pasha: Atatürk.

147

he explain to this prestigious official of the Republic, who was taking the trouble to come to his feet, that he would not accept a reconciliation? Ah, if only it were all over and done with . . . Anyway this was the end. They were the last, he and Dervish. One of them had to die, or both together. Nobody would be left after them to carry on the old tradition of life or death. The Ottoman had crashed to its downfall, and the proud Turcoman was now agonizing with its ancient customs and people and way of life . . . This was the end . . . Why didn't they leave them alone, him and Dervish, to finish off their lives as they wished?

There's no one in my family to carry on the feud, nor in Dervish's. Our roots have decayed. Not our roots, no, it's a slow rot setting in at the branches, creeping down the tree to its roots . . . If Dervish were to come to me, with a smile, a little sad, not looking at me, his head bent . . . If he were to extend a hand, tremblingly, expectantly . . . And if I were to take it, without a word, without even looking each other in the face . . . If we were to stay like that, hand in hand, for a long long time . . . Till the hate of a hundred years, of centuries, should melt in that grip and turn to a warm firm friendship such as the world has never seen . . . If we could be friends with Dervish . . . Who knows what kind of man this Vali is? Can he touch a magic wand to the earth and air, to our hearts, our hostile hands? Yes, Vali Bey, only two people can be friends in all sincerity, with all their soul, Dervish Bey and I. That race of men is no more that could be friend or enemy without reservations, to the bitter end. Men live like weeds now. All they can think of is to buy at five and sell at ten. They can never know friendship, staunch to the marrow, intoxicating, nor enmity unto death . . . Neither love nor valour . . . Only fear do they know . . . Fear is all over them, in their hands and feet and nails, in their hair and teeth and eyes . . . Fear is their food and drink and the air they breathe. They sleep and dream in fear. The sky over them spells fear and they trust not even the earth they step on. They are sick, no longer human, a tribe severed from humanity, the buy-at-five-sell-at-ten tribe. So, let us be, Vali Bey . . . Leave us alone with our folly, to live it through like men. Death? Death will always exist, Vali Bey. And fear too. But not as now, not like with these men who know only fear . . .

In a strange euphoria this peace-making scene and the image of Dervish, his head bent, holding out his hand to him, kept rising before his eyes.

'It's impossible, Vali Bey,' Mustafa Akyollu said. 'You are most welcome here, indeed you have honoured us by coming, but it's quite impossible. We cannot be reconciled with Dervish Sarioglu, not at any price. This quarrel is not of my making that I should put an end to it. It goes right back to the days when we lived in Khorassan. Nobody has been able to settle it since then, so how can we? It's part of our existence like our hands, feet, eyes, head, and even worse, for you can live without a hand or an eye, but this is our lifeblood.'

'So you think that under our modern republican regime you can go on killing each other endlessly and, what's more, force your farmhands to do the same, and that we shall turn a blind eye to it, is that so?'

Mustafa Bey blanched and was silent. He could have answered back just as sharply, he could have made him sorry he had ever been born, but the Vali was a guest in his house. 'The finger sundered by the law does not hurt,' he murmured at last very quietly.

'Perhaps not, but the head sundered by the law will hurt,' the Vali retorted angrily.

Mustafa Bey's head whirled and his eyes went black. He sank on to the sofa. 'Vali Bey,' he said forcing a smile, 'the head wouldn't hurt either, if a head can be found . . .'

The Vali embarked on a long tirade. He expatiated on modern civilization, Europe, the world, the under-developed state of the country, and on murders in general. 'I will not take a step out of this house,' he concluded, 'without ensuring this reconciliation.'

Mustafa Bey sat on, crouched on the sofa, his face yellow, staring unseeingly before him.

After the Vali, Kurdish Ali Agha began to speak. He was old and gaunt, a relict of the old Turcomans, but when he had heard that the Vali was leading the peace delegation, he had changed his mind and come too. 'Don't, Mustafa,' he pleaded, his voice hoarse with emotion and tears in his eyes. 'Look at me, look, look! Am I in a condition to travel here? But still I've come, come to save you, and Dervish too. There's no sense in going on with this business . . . Make the peace, son, you've got to. The world's just swamped with pimps and perverts now, and if you two kill each other, it's to them that the world will be left and all human dignity will be wiped out. Look, just look about you . . .' With a sweeping gesture he indicated the guests sitting about the room. 'This scum, these burrs . . . Look, look at them well. Are these people men, Mustafa, my son? Isn't it a pity that men like you should disappear and the world be left to the likes of these? Look, look at these womanish creatures . . . Hah hah hah hah! Bless you, Mustafa!' Wrapping his old thick capote tightly about his body, he rose and surveyed the company sternly, his eyes bulging out of a skeletal face. Then he looked at Mustafa Bey again and his voice rang out, harsh, authoritative. 'Don't abandon this world to these people, devil's spawn, jinn in human shape. D'you hear me?'

Mustafa had slowly revived with Ali Agha's blasting attack on the buy-at-five-sell-at-ten. 'Thank you, Ali Agha,' he said softly, his colour returning to normal. 'I'm very grateful to you.'

Then the Lady of Gözükara spoke in her strong calm masculine voice. 'Here we are, so many of us, come to make a request of you, Mustafa. A great Chukurova Vali in person . . . Kurdish Ali Agha, despite his hundred years of age, one of the last great Turcomans . . . Death is hard. Enough! What right has a man to take a life that God has given? Even God should not have that right. Death is a great injustice. D'you understand that, Mustafa? Life is precious, only a mother knows how precious, Mustafa. Even God ought not to take it away, to annihilate the most beautiful, the most splendid, the most noble thing he has created. Strange indeed are the ways of God . . . And, you, Mustafa, you are destroying God's beautiful work even before its time! How can you have the heart to do this? Look how Murtaza was killed . . . Stop it, Mustafa. Death is an accursed thing.'

The Lady of Gözükara was the daughter of an eminent

Turcoman Bey and the wife of another Bey. After eleven years
of marriage her husband was found murdered on the crags of
Anavarza, his body half devoured by birds of prey. As her sons
grew up they too were killed one after the other on the same
spot as their father. When the Lady went up the crags to take
away the body of her last son, she did not weep or keen. She
drew the mangled body on to her lap and began to rock it,
singing a lullaby. For three days and three nights she remained
there, and from all the surrounding villages people gathered
about her. When at last she rose she was perfectly composed.
She walked down the crags to her horse, upright, proud, aloof,
alone in the world now, still beautiful, still desirable, with
bright black eyes and the gait of a gazelle. A year or two after
her last son had been carried down from the crags and buried
in a grave covered with myrtle branches, all the inhabitants of
a neighbouring village were found dead one morning, together
with their livestock. How this came about no one was ever able
to fathom, though the investigation lasted for months, with
doctors and gendarmes and police searching every inch of the
village for a clue . . . The Lady of Gözükara had a beautiful
voice, but now she sang only about death, sad haunting dirges
and epics. 'Curse death,' she said. 'Curse death to the bottom
of the earth. When my son breathed his last, the flowers burst
open and wept.'

After the Lady everyone in the room appealed to Mustafa
Akyollu in turn. The last to speak was Mahir Kabakchioglu,
and as he spoke he worked himself into a state of anger, waving
his hands, shaking his head, shouting, his neck swelling, his
ears getting redder and redder. 'That executioner,' he cried,
'that mad executioner Dervish! What right have we to ask this
of Mustafa Bey? Only yesterday that executioner had Mustafa
Bey's brother murdered, and only yesterday too, poor Black
Hüseyin, Mustafa Bey's best man, the father of fourteen
children . . . But Mustafa Bey is a magnanimous noble Bey, of
high and rare extraction, the last of his kind, so what else can
we expect of his generous soul but forgiveness? Yet what can
he do when confronted with that savage, ferocious, bloodthirsty
monster who is sparing no effort to root up his family? I know
one thing, so long as that monster is not thrown out of the

Chukurova nothing can be put right here.'

Ümmet Agha suddenly turned on Mahir Kabakchioglu. 'You shouldn't speak like that of Dervish Bey,' he said. 'It's an insult to Mustafa Bey.'

'Not at all, not at all,' Mahir Bey cried, startled. 'God forbid. It's only that I resent all this killing by Dervish Bey . . .'

Mustafa Bey got up, pale with rage, his hands trembling. 'Dervish Bey is not a bloodthirsty monster,' he said. 'Nor is he a savage. He was not responsible for my brother's death, nor Black Hüseyin's. Dervish Bey is a nobleman and a man of honour.' And he sat down without another word.

'But . . . But . . .' Mahir Bey stammered looking dazedly about him. 'But what have we said against Dervish Bey? God forbid, God . . .' He was shaken. How could he put this right? What if it went to Dervish Bey's ears? 'Yes, yes of course Dervish is a man of honour. It's all this excitement, the emotion, the longing for peace . . . It's just a slip of the tongue . . . For the sake of peace . . . Peace . . . What I meant to say is that killing is a savage thing. I didn't mean that for Dervish Bey. He's a noble Bey.'

The Vali rose to his feet impatiently, a cigarette trembling on the edge of his tobacco-stained lips. He stood very straight, hands in pockets, with a disdainful expression as if to say, now what am I doing here? The others rose too. 'Don't distress yourself, Mahir Bey,' he said. 'You were quite right. These people, these people here . . .' And he flung his hand out resentfully towards Mustafa Bey. 'They're savages. And mad too. Only let them be warned. Our Government is strong and will descend on barbarous feudal lords like a sledge-hammer. I'll show them. If they won't be reconciled, I'll have a word or two to say to these ravening hyenas.'

He crossed over to Mahir Bey, took his arm and murmured something in his ear, laughing. Mahir Bey laughed too and they both looked contemptuously at the *kilims* on the floor and walls, smiling broadly at the sight of the Bald Minstrel crouching in a corner. The minstrel, seeing that they were looking at him, smiled too and went after the Vali who was now making his way to the staircase.

'I am Mustafa Kemal's minstrel, Vali Pasha. Are you going

without listening to me?' he said humbly, expectantly. 'A whole year I played for Mustafa Kemal Pasha . . .'

The Vali stared him up and down. The minstrel had a huge jutting nose, even larger than his face, with a knobby tip. His clothes were old and ragged and his feet bare. The shalvar-trousers under the dirty shirt hung in tatters from the knees down. His hands were abnormally large. But his eyes were beautiful, and so were the mother of pearl-inlaid body and neck of his instrument and the delicate pegs.

'Weeelll!' the Vali said. 'Is that so?'

'That is so!' the Bald Minstrel said defiantly, the humbleness, the smile all gone, a different man altogether. 'Yes, son, who did you take me for?' His voice rose. It rang out, clamant, thunderous, crashing against the Vali's face. 'I am Mustafa Kemal's minstrel. Go your way in peace, Vali!'

At once Mahir Bey disengaged himself from the Vali's arm. 'Come here, minstrel,' he said, and drawing him into a corner he slipped a folded note into his pocket. Then he turned back and held out his arm to the Vali again. 'It's the custom,' he said as they descended the stairs. 'It doesn't do not to treat minstrels well.'

The Vali only smiled contemptuously.

They got into the car and drove away.

21

Alijik stood before Mustafa Bey. 'Not this year,' he was saying, 'but the next, in September . . .' His eyes were spinning like tops in their sockets, uneasy, wary, sharp. His hands were very small. Men with such hands are generally clever, Mustafa Bey thought as Alijik went on talking, and also treacherous, two-faced, dissimulating. Were his eyes green or blue or black? It was impossible to tell. Even his mother would not have known. They were the colour of a traitor's eyes, impenetrable, shifty. Mustafa Bey was an excellent judge of people. He would take stock of this man and weigh him up on the spot. Alijik's possibilities struck him at once.

'How many children have you got, Alijik Agha?'

'Seven, Bey, may they be your slaves.'

'And how many wives?'

'Two.'

'Where are you from, Alijik?'

'From Kutuderé, beyond the mountains.'

'And how do you earn your bread?'

'Dervish Bey keeps me . . .'

'Are you a good shot?'

'Not bad . . .'

'Do you love your Bey very much? Does he trust you.'

'I'm devoted to him. And he trusts me.'

Mustafa Bey fell to thinking, his eyes fixed on Alijik who stood stiff as a statue before him. 'Sit down,' he said at last. 'Why has Dervish Bey sent you and not someone else?'

'It's because I speak well, Bey. And I can also lie like a trooper. Besides, it seems I've bad blood in my veins. The Bey sets no store by me. Even the dogs of the farm have more value in his eyes.'

'And what have you to say to this?'

'I'll show him. He'll see who's a man in this Chukurova . . . I heard it with my own ears.'

'What did you hear?'

'Dervish Bey saying to Hidayet that he would send me to you. Alijik's just right for him, he said, a man who burns crops and houses and kills farmhands . . . We couldn't have found a fitter person than Alijik if we searched the whole world over.'

'Is that true?'

'It's true, Bey. It seems there's not a more utterly shameless wretch than me anywhere on earth.'

'And what exploits have you to show for it?'

'I can steal a man's lashes from his eyes and he be none the wiser. For seven years I led Yagmur Agha's band of reivers. I abducted women and committed countless murders. Nobody can imagine with what coolness I'm able to butcher a man. Anyone else couldn't even kill a sparrow so easily.'

'What else, what else?'

'I've raped young girls, children really, and was in prison for six years.'

'What else?'

'I'm the one who killed Turgut Bey, and very slowly, making him beg for three days . . .'

'What do you want?' Mustafa Bey said impassively.

'Why, only your health,' Alijik laughed. From the waist down his body was strong and shapely with long sturdy legs. But the head, shoulders, trunk, arms and hands were those of a child of ten and his tiny face was covered to the eyes with a furry fuzz. Just now he was bursting with joy and pride. Here at last was his chance to show his Bey of what stuff he was made.

'Well then, Alijik, you prince of liars, say it. What do you want?'

'Just your health . . .'

'Alijik, if ever you lie to me or play any of your tricks I'll have you killed instantly.'

'I know, Bey. You wouldn't give it a second thought. I know you very well. But that won't prevent me from lying or cheating, nor from killing you like Turgut Bey if I get the chance.'

'Very well then, what do you want, Alijik?'

'What do *you* want, Bey?'

'To get hold of Dervish.'

'I knew it. Dervish Bey knows it too. I'll help you.'

'There's five hundred *dönüms* of land for you . . .'

'Yes . . .'

'A tractor.'

'Yes . . .'

'Ten thousand liras.'

'Yes . . .'

'Anything else?'

'I want an Arab horse. And a German carbine. And also a real good suit. Made to measure, in Adana.'

'It's a deal.'

'Yes, but how am I going to get all this? Once Dervish is in your hands you could very well send me packing . . .'

'I wouldn't.'

'But your heirs might . . . And anyway, excuse me for seeming to want to meddle in your affairs, but why don't we kill him right away instead of kidnapping him? It would be the easiest thing in the world for me. I'd do it before the week is out. Eh, Bey? What d'you say?'

'I must get hold of him, Alijik.'

'All right then, Bey. Now, who d'you trust most in the world, Bey?'

Mustafa Bey looked at him thoughtfully. 'I see what you mean,' he said after a while. 'You know Kurdish Ali Agha? I'll hand over the money and title-deeds and everything else to him. As soon as you've delivered Dervish to me, you can go and get your due from him.'

'That's good!' Alijik said joyfully. 'And we can be quite sure with Ali Agha. He's close as wax that one, and wouldn't breathe a word to anyone. But what if he dies suddenly?'

'We'll think of something then,' Mustafa Bey said. 'I'm going to town right away to draw up the transfer documents and get the money. What's your family name?'

'Write Ali Daglarashan, son of Durmush and Elifché.'

'Good.'

'I can only come here in the night,' Alijik said. 'Once a week, just before dawn.'

'Contact Ibrahim Ibo,' Akyollu said.

'Ibrahim Ibo is Dervish Bey's man, though the Bey himself doesn't know it. I know it and so does Dervish Bey's sister,

Jeren Hatun, who owns the Yalija farm.'

'Are you sure?'

'We grew up together on that farm. Like brothers we were, both of us orphans. It's Jeren Hatun who placed him here with you without telling Dervish Bey. He wouldn't have allowed it. He'd never put spies in the house of his enemy.'

'Really?'

'Never,' Alijik said.

'You don't say!'

'Bey, this Ibrahim Ibo's very smart, but if you have him watched closely you'll find that he visits the Yalija farm once or twice a year.'

'Indeed?'

'And then it seems to me that . . . But my conscience . . .'

'Speak! Go on . . .'

'My conscience . . .'

'Don't beat about the bush. You don't even know the meaning of the word!'

'That's true, but . . .'

'You've no respect even for Allah's holy book.'

'That's going too far, Bey . . .'

'Well, speak!'

'It's Ibrahim Ibo who killed Murtaza Bey. Haven't you ever thought, Bey? Those dogs, each one as big as a horse, the guards . . . And Murtaza Bey on the very top floor of the house . . . How could a man break in and kill him? I should know, for I was after him too. Oh how I tried to kill him . . . What favour I'd have won in the Bey's eyes! He'd never have refused me anything after that. But it was impossible. One night I managed to slip into the mansion and up the stairs to his room. I pulled and pulled at the door, but it was locked. People were roused and I would have been caught if I hadn't hid in the attic. Three days I stayed there, hungry and thirsty until I got a chance to get away in the night.'

'You're making all this up, Alijik.'

'If you like to think so, Bey.'

'You want me to kill Ibrahim Ibo, who's my most faithful man.'

'You'll kill him one day, whether you like it or not. Anyway, don't speak of me to him, or that'll be the end of me. That hell-hag of a woman will get wind of it and have me killed without even telling Dervish Bey.'

'You're lying, Alijik!'

'All right, Bey, I'm lying . . . Good-bye now. Meet me on Sunday morning, under that plane tree.'

'You're going to kidnap me, Alijik.'

'I could always do so, Bey.'

'All right then, under the plane tree.'

'What shall I say to Dervish Bey?'

'Tell him I'll be waiting to meet him in September of the year after next . . . Is the house nearly finished?'

'Yes. Anyway it was only the stairs and doors that got burnt. The mansion wasn't really damaged. We'll be back there by September.'

The truth was that Alijik had never known when or where he was born nor who his father and mother were. His earliest memory was of himself lying under a plane tree, his face and head a festering wound, crawling with black flies and midges, the soles of his feet so flayed he could not step on them, his body full of sores, his eyes scabby, suppurating . . . And then a woman with a white headscarf was leaning tenderly over him, her long slim hands warm and white, relieving his pain at a touch . . . And soap, lots and lots of soap, a mountain of lather . . . The rustling of branches, the strong scent of honeysuckle . . . A garden, a large pink rose in full bloom. The soapsuds getting into his eyes, stinging. Alijik jumping up and down, screaming. The white headscarf, the lovely fingers also screaming. And the tree, the water, everything crying out. 'I'm hungry, Mother Selvi. I'm starving.'

'Here, child.'

The butter melting in the piping hot *tandir*-baked bread, dripping . . . Alijik's mouth opening wide. A huge morsel . . . And another, and another . . .

'Mother, I'm dying of hunger. Mother Selvi, darling mother . . .'

And sister Kudret would sing her beautiful lullabies, and the crying child would be soothed, the wounded man would hold

158

his moaning, and the sick forget their pain and suffering.

'Sister Kudret, sing another lullaby, please, sister!'

'Get away, you hairless monkey!'

'Please, sister, oh please . . .' And the flowing water stops its flow, the blowing wind is lulled and even the fast-galloping steed is frozen in mid-air.

Alijik is good at reaping. He can plough too, and pick cotton. There is no harder worker in all the Chukurova. Alijik is Mother Selvi's very own. He's the son of the house. He works till his bones creak, in that land of huge stars, of dust, of long winding roads. And the hair begins to grow on his bald head. He gains flesh. His wounds are healed.

'Alijik! Where's Alijik? Alijik's gone . . .'

Mother Selvi is in a taking, scolding the whole household. 'A tiny chit of a child! Making him work like that! Of course he'll run away . . .'

'Don't worry, Mother, he'll come back. Where will he find a better place than this, a kinder person than you?'

'Poor, poor little Alijik . . . Poor little orphan . . .' Mother Selvi has nine children of her own, all tall and strong and lusty. 'He's so small, so tiny, not like you all. He's frail as a bird. Of course he couldn't stand it, the way you worked him to death. Ah, poor mite, what if he's dead? Ah, what sinful creatures we are . . .' And Mother Selvi wept for Alijik and mourned for him for months on end. Long afterwards Alijik was told of this.

And then one morning, as Mother Selvi was putting the bread to bake in the *tandir*, the girl Telli rushed up: 'Mother, Mother! Alijik's back!' And Mother Selvi took him in her arms. 'Alijik, my child!' she exclaimed. His eyes were red, sealed with scabs, his clothes in tatters and stiff with dirt, his feet torn, crawling with worms, nothing but skin and bone, scarcely a breath of life in him. 'Don't run away again.' Her voice was warm and soft. Alijik would have wept at this welcome if he had had the strength. He had not slept for days. At Mother Selvi's touch he relaxed and dropped down asleep right where he was.

'He's dead,' Mother Selvi screamed.

'No, no, he's breathing. He's fainted, or just asleep . . .'

How old was he? Seven? Ten? Seventeen? He looked a hundred. His skin was black and shrivelled, as though it would fall away from the bone any minute. Mother Selvi boiled a huge cauldron of water and laid him down on the marble stone under the aged pomegranate tree, thick with flowers, humming with bees. The marble stone, Alijik, the roots of the tree were drowned in soapsuds. She applied her own homemade salves to his head and body. His wounds were deeper this time, festering. They would not heal easily. But she spared no effort and in a month's time he was restored, eating ravenously, putting on weight, full of life again.

Then he began to work. He had to in order to pay for his food. He rose in the grey dawn and fed the horses, watered them with the water he drew at the pump till his arms snapped, and harnessed them to the carts. Ant-like, he hoed the cotton field, reaped the corn, and threshed and winnowed. He could do all this perfectly. The girl, Telli, was thin like Alijik and not yet sixteen. She worked just as hard, rising in the grey dawn too, washing the dishes, cooking, mending and toiling in the fields. 'Alijik, you'll die if you go on this way,' she would keep saying to him.

'I know, sister Telli,' he would answer, bowing his head helplessly.

Autumn came, and the work in the fields was over. Now, Alijik had only the horses to tend to. All day long he would roam about the ruined Armenian estates in the town, eating figs off the trees. He had grown now, and Mother Selvi had sewn for him a new pair of shalvar-trousers and a shirt. She had also bought him red leather boots, but Alijik could not bring himself to wear them and went about barefoot.

And then one day he vanished again. Mother Selvi could not believe it. 'You must have done something to that child,' she said. 'Or why should he run away?' Her husband, the second wife, her children, everyone assured her that not a hair of his head had been touched, but she would not believe them.

A few months later he turned up, once again covered with sores from head to foot, worse than ever before . . . And so it went on until he was twenty. He ran away countless times. Mother Selvi never scolded him, nor was she cross or angry. He must have some secret trouble, this child. Perhaps he was searching for something. Perhaps he himself did not know what. She never asked him. And when he was twenty he disappeared for good and never returned.

Years later Alijik came back, spick and span, his pockets full of money, and at his side a ravishing blue-eyed fair-haired girl. He sat down under the same tree and leaned against the huge trunk, so wide that three men could not have joined hands around it. His wife sat down beside him in her bright brand-new dress. That is how Alijik had dreamed it should be. They would see him there and take the news to Mother Selvi. She would come running, grumbling: 'What's this I have to put up with year in year out!' And then: 'Now who are you! Where's Alijik?'

'I'm Alijik, Mother!'

She would stop there quite dazed, tears of joy springing to her eyes. 'Thank God, thank God,' she would **cry** and throw her arms around him. 'Thank God for letting me see this day!'

'And this is my wife, Mother.' She would kiss her too. 'There, wife, this is my good brave Mother. We haven't sprung out of just any old hole!'

She would take them into the house, glancing out of the corner of her kind laughing eyes, as if to say, I like your wife, yes, yes indeed! And she would hold a feast for them, killing a sheep and blessing them by marking their foreheads with its blood . . . 'Here, this watch is for you, silver, with a chain. It belonged to my father . . . And for you, this gold bracelet and these coins . . .'

'Hah, who says I'm a nobody!'

They waited there under the plane tree and noon came and still no one appeared. Where were they all? It was very hot now. He rose. 'Come, wife,' he said in a dead voice that seemed to sink like dregs into the earth. Slowly he went to the gate and opened it. The marble stone was there under the pomegranate tree, glinting palely, and the flowers were alive with buzzing quivering-winged bees. And bending over the *tandir* was a woman baking bread. Alijik felt the stab of its odour deep in his lungs. His voice came out as a shout, sounding dully in the noonday heat. 'Mother Selvi? Where is she?' The unknown woman looked up at him. No one but Mother Selvi should ever be baking bread at this oven, no one . . . Her lovely face shining

161

with sweat . . . 'Where is she? Mother Selvi?'

'Mother Selvi's dead.'

The south wind is whipping up the dust of the road. And mangy Alijik all primped up, as though no one else but him had ever got married before! And does a man shoot his gun at the house that fed him? Emptying all the cartridges at one go? Ungrateful wretch! Does a man rush to the graveyard like a racehorse with his wife panting at his heels? Does he cast himself on to the ground there rolling and rolling all over the place?

The leaves of the plane tree are motionless, stagnant in the dark night.

'Mother Selvi's dead.'

'What can we do . . . Let's go, wife.'

'What did Mustafa Bey say?'

'He laughed.'

'Didn't he say anything?'

'He laughed a lot. He held his sides. Then he said, I'll wait. I'll wait till next autumn, if he's still alive then, and the next and the next too. He roared with laughter. Tell Dervish, he said, not to be so frightened.'

'And what else?'

'A body torn by fear is worse than a rotten tree-trunk, though it be the trunk of a plane tree . . .'

'And what did you say?'

'I said, you know only too well, Mustafa Bey, who's afraid of whom and how much.'

'So he's going to wait?'

'I'd wait a thousand years if I could live that long, he said. I wouldn't leave this world without even once seeing my only enemy.'

'Well, he *will* leave this world,' Dervish Bey said. 'And before autumn comes. I'm sick and tired of this business. It's enough.'

'It's enough,' Alijik said triumphantly.

22

That dull yellow rain had started again. On and on it fell, brightening suddenly southward in an orange glow that faded and lighted up anew, sheet after shimmering sheet. And the Lady Karakiz gazed out at the Anavarza crags, immobile on her sofa, old, wizened, thin, her fingers crossed over her lap, her large hazel eyes widening under the masculine brows, her mouth a puckered thin line. A white headscarf was tied under the small pointed chin. Hers was a face that was all eyes, only eyes, wide-open, haggard, bitter, gleaming moistly, mirror-like, staring straight ahead in an agony of yearning.

And the yellow clay, porous, viscid, stuck to the green myrtle leaves and branches, like molten gold. And always that odour of myrtles everywhere, emanating from the anger and keening, the screaming in the night and the grey dawn, from the blood-stained yellow clay, the withered plants, the dead . . . Damp, like frothing blood . . . Bitter, acrid, a virulent green.

And Murtaza Bey's still unburied corpse, yellowing, the long narrow feet livid, oozy, the green-tinged black hair springing from the pallid brow, trailing out of the white shroud . . . And the keening, wafting from one swaying woman to another, without a pause, peal after peal, soaring, bursting to shivers, spilling down, and picking up again, unremitting, mature, knowing exactly where to begin, when to stop, monotone, modified only by the colour of each individual voice. And over long distant roads, in deserts and mountains, in innumerable forays, all through that centuries-long, never-ending journey, under white shrouds, red *kilims*, embroidered rugs, in majestic pavilion tents, yellowing feet always, emaciated, and black locks over pallid brows, all slain, and always the frothing blood, the frothing horse-flanks, the long wailing, the long long laments, all alike, varied only by the quality of the voice, deep or shrill . . . In the old country of Khorassan, in the Arabian desert, always fighting, always moving, subject to nature's will, from one place to another . . . The land you step on today is your homeland, yours today, but not tomorrow, this land for which you shed your blood, over which you chant your age-old immutable laments, persistent, clamant, this land whose very name you will never know, as you rush past, not even stopping as long as this flowing river, only gleaning a few legends and songs, this land you will forget tomorrow, or if the grazing was good, the plunder rich, the black-eared wheat abundant, forever treasure in your memory, retelling from generation to generation over the years the plenteousness that you left behind, the tart pears, the fragrant wild apples, and forever afterwards, opening your miniature chiselled chests, your saddlebags with their little bells, your embroidered sacks, you will breathe in the warm accumulated scent of wild apple, of wild roses, of salep orchis, strong, musky . . . And always death and bloodshed, and swollen sinews straining at the strings of crossbows, quivers and arrows, the smell of black powder, of blood . . . And the sea of white headcloths, the long long keening . . .

The Lady Karakiz did not weep over Murtaza Bey's corpse. She did not cast herself upon her son, kiss him, cling to him. She did not claw her cheeks, tear her hair, rend her clothes, nor did she clutch his bloody shirt to her breast and intone a lament, swaying wraith-like to the age-old rhythm of grief. Deaf to the keening, blind to the livid feet and the black locks under the white shroud, the frothing blood, the steel-green flashing flies, the relentless yellow rain, she crouched in a corner, legs crossed under her, narrow shoulders hunched, immobile, silent, drained of all blood, her hazel eyes frozen wide, her lips pinched in a thin hardly perceptible line, unseeing, unhearing. She did not eat or drink or pray. She did not complain, or curse or say it cannot be. She did not think. She did not even see out of those ever-widening eyes, riveted in a glassy darkening stare.

Mustafa Akyollu could not look his mother in the face after his brother's death. He never even once went to her, nor did he ask anyone after her. He knew. It had been the same ever since his childhood. He knew that she would come to life in the end, and rise and roam aimlessly from room to room, rigid, unseeing, and then after a few days, one morning at break of day she would walk out alone to the Anavarza crags, to the spot

164

where that ancient engraved, mauve-flowered white stone lay, and sit there and brood. She would accept food then, and drink. Tears would flow down her face and her sealed lips would break into a lament. She would be thinking then, and dreaming . . .

Of the untamed horses, roaming free on the plain . . . The Anavarza plain, that age-old wintering ground of the ancient Turcomans . . . And the high pastures up on Binboga Mountain with fragrant bluebells growing around the fresh springs. 'Ah, they have stained his shirt with blood, oh do not hurt him, tribes, oh cruel tribes, do not touch the blind old woman's staff, her one and only . . .' And defeat, again defeat, always defeat for the Turcoman . . . Plucked up, eradicated, sapped to the core a thousand, two thousand years ago, powerless to take root anywhere . . . Wanderers about the world with their long-drawn-out laments, their noble horses, their herds of sheep and goats, their flutes and crossbows and arrows, and their banners, tall and white, always present in peace and war, in wake and wassail, in triumph and defeat. And the horsetail crests, simple, unpretentious . . . Dashed to the ground . . . And always the laments . . . Striving to retrieve what is gone forever, to bring back the dead, to last on even in death, not to be extinguished, death and killing the only testimonials to this will to exist, blood and revenge . . . 'Ah, they have smeared him all over with blood, my dear one I hardly dared to kiss . . .' To keep alive even in death those who are no more . . . The tall young men with raven locks and crystal-clear moss-green eyes, mounted on sunny-flanked horses, galloping day after day, night after night, starting where the sun rises, stopping only where it sets, tempered to a serene acceptance of death, confident in their affirmation of life, proud in the certainty of life immortal.

And her breasts would ache and throb, her aged, cold, extinct breasts. Her eyes would kindle, as she sat there among the mauve-dappled crags of Anavarza, redolent of sun-dried wild thyme. And her lament would drift out over Anavarza plain, flowing down the rocks, sinking into the earth, faint and muffled, as though coming from a thousand years ago, exhausted, forever lost, never to be recovered, never till the end of time. She would mourn for all her race, the Lady Karakiz, sitting as on the very brim of the world, for the hundreds of thousands slain, for all the bloodshed, for the exodus from Khorassan, for those cast into the desert, up the high Caucasus, over mighty seas, dying like flies, their graves unknown. And she would sing of the revolt and subjugation to the Ottoman, of treason and defeat, of the great tribes of old, Kozanoglu, Sarioglu, Payaslioglu, Jadioglu, of the seventy-two branches of the Turcomans, the trials, the exile, the slow extinction. And lastly she would kneel down on the timeless earth of Anavarza and keen for her own, her slain husband, her grandfather killed in a raid, his body never recovered, for her brothers, for all her loved ones, for their violent untimely deaths. How she clung to her dirges, the Lady Karakiz, as to a life-giving elixir, in a desperate attempt to preserve something of the long-lost, forgotten Turcoman traditions, as though she could thus resuscitate what was gone for ever, as though survival depended on Dervish Bey's killing Murtaza Bey and Mustafa Bey killing Dervish Bey! How she held out, doggedly striving to implant her resistance into some settled patch of land, an old lament, a flagging blood feud!

Mustafa Bey avoided his mother. He could not face her these days. He would leave the house very early and return only late at night. But one morning as he was groping his way through the house before daybreak, a long thin shadow trembled in front of him and a white headscarf gleamed out of the gloom. Off his guard, trapped, unable to think how to escape, his mouth going dry, mesmerized by the swaying shadow that barred his way, knowing full well what she would say, yet powerless to move, he heard her voice, soft, muted, gentle, yet cutting knife-like through the dead silence in which a bud could have been heard bursting open.

'So, my son? Haven't you been able to kill him yet? Ah, but you can't . . . Would he ever let himself be caught? It's we who get caught, we who get killed. Yes, Mustafa, any stranger can enter this noble mansion and kill anyone he chooses, and get away with it.' She paused. Mustafa Bey faced her, not daring to move. Suddenly the voice lashed out again: 'Kill him! Kill him! What are you waiting for? My time is drawing near. Kill him, so that I should not pass away, my eyes open, into the other world, open and mourning for ever for my poor brave handsome Murtaza. Kill him quickly, or I will soon be keening over you too and wild dogs will be tearing at my corpse on the crags of Anavarza. Kill him! Kill him!'

The shadow swelled and lengthened, then subsided and faded into the darkness. The voice was silent. Mustafa Bey never realized when and how she had left him.

23

What d'you say to Ibrahim Ibo, Hamdi? He's an impostor, brought up by Dervish Bey's own sister! What's to be done then, Hamdi? We could have killed Dervish long ago if it hadn't been for him. D'you think he can do us any harm? Harm? That's putting it mildly! Who set fire to Dervish's house? Who? And to his harvest? The very thing to disgrace your name . . . Wasn't it Ibrahim Ibo? Your best man, egged on by Dervish . . . Now, hold on, hold on, that's going too far! Didn't I myself encourage him to do it? Burn his house to smoke him out . . . Burn his fields to make him go mad with rage . . . And didn't you help him do it too, Hamdi? I ordered it, I! All of you . . . Ah, Mestan, ah, you alone were against it. You alone said, it's beneath you to set fire to your enemy's house, to burn the crops of the poor. But I was lost to shame. I'll catch him, I thought, or shoot him as he tries to escape from the flames . . . The glaring brightness, the smoke . . . The whole plain, the Anavarza crags, all bathed in the glow. That huge mansion ablaze, crackling, and all about it the crops, the harvest up in flames . . . Dervish Bey will be burnt, burnt to ashes! Oh dear, why did I do it? Hamdi, it's a mistake! Heko, he's burning! My mother! She must never know I did such a shameful thing! Never! And then he comes, from out of the fire, perfectly calm, indifferent. So tall . . . Very slowly he steps down the stairs, stands there, scornful, etched out in the night, red flames roaring up behind him. He grows taller and taller, swaying like a crimson flame himself, soaring to the sky . . . They tell me he sweats a lot in that closed room of his, Hamdi? Sweats? He sits there stifling all through the night, crazed with fear. It's much better than killing him outright . . . The flames are all about him, he's sweating. His eyes gleam . . . Wait, Hamdi, don't shoot! Let him go down the stairs. Ibrahim Ibo, set fire to the huts, burn the whole village! The stairs are collapsing, the stairs! Heko, what are you waiting for? Shoot! Fire away at those stairs. It's too dark . . . The day is dawning. Smoke rises gently from the purple crags. The blackened ash-covered plain, the huge charred carcass of the mansion, everything reeks with wet wispy smoke. There he is now, crouched low on that bay horse, streaking like the wind! Quick, on your horses, he's riding Sögütlü way . . . And that Mahir Kabakchioglu, what a low-down wretch. He's the one who ought to be killed. All that land he's buying up! Where does he find so much money? Turn back, Mestan, it's no use . . . Turn back, Hamdi, don't you see the horse he's riding? It came to him as a present from his friend, that Arab Sheikh in Urfa. A real thoroughbred . . . Here, Hamdi, here, this is where we'll lie in wait for him. He'll take this way back from Sögütlü. Get off your horses all of you. We must catch him this time.

Another rider springs out of the charred smoking ruin and flares down the plain. Then another, and another. Where can they be going, Hamdi? You tell me, Ibrahim Ibo. They're going after Dervish Bey . . . Why didn't you let me shoot, why, Bey? It's all been for nothing, burning the house, all for nothing . . . He rose from the flames, from the smoke. And now the smoke is lifting, the sun is silvering the plain, sucking up the smoke. The riders are gone from sight. Whose idea was it, this burning of house and fields? Whose, Ibrahim Ibo? Whose, you traitor? Won't he burn my house in turn? Never, Bey, you can burn his town house too, his summer place, all his villages, but he'll never set fire to a single stick of yours. It'll rankle with him that an enemy of his should stoop so low. He'll sit there ruminating in that room of his, barricaded with sandbags and not a ray of light filtering through, sweating in mortal fear. A pity, he'll say, it's a great pity for Mustafa. And then perhaps one day he'll suddenly turn up before us, here I am, he'll say. There's no need to resort to such base tricks, here shoot me, shoot me, he'll cry at the top of his voice . . . Ibrahim Ibo, Ibrahim Ibo, who made me do this crazy thing? What made me consent? When will the mansion be ready, Hamdi? It's finished, Bey. Only the carpenters are still there. Yesterday they were repairing the carvings of an old oak chest that Ahmet Kozanoglu Pasha had given the family before he went into exile. A chiming chest that would smell tartly of wild apples . . . No, it's not good

169

what we've done, Hamdi. Not good at all. Ibrahim Ibo, you wretch, just you wait, I'll have something to say to you . . . What's happened to those riders? How hot the sun is. It's making the wasps mad. How heavy the air in this reed-bed, sticky, stifling! It's fire that's pouring in from the swamp, ravaging the plain, fed on by the parched grass, the bushes, the blackthorns, the reeds and rushes . . .

'I know it for sure, Bey,' Hamdi was saying. 'He'll come this way today. He dashed off early last night, riding so hard that his men couldn't keep up with him. His horse's legs simply streaked along the ground. I've been checking on this for days and I'm sure he'll come under our guns today. The rest is in Allah's hands. He's got two men with him. We are four, they are three. We're in ambush, they're in the open.'

Bubbling sounds rose from Akchasaz swamp, with its slim long-necked, long-legged blue birds, their brilliant plumage assuming a hundred different hues of blue in the sun, in the shade, in the starlight, in the dark of night, its flittering, droning thousands of huge bumble-bees, iridiscent-winged, waggle-tailed, red, yellow, blue, its panached migrant-birds, its pink herons, its large pulsing-eyed butterflies, broad wings outspread under the sun in a welter of colour and design, its jackals, frogs, wild boars, arrow-snakes, tortoises . . . And as the day waxed hotter, the bubbling grew louder. Mustafa Bey knew this swamp like the palm of his hand. So did Dervish Bey. Just before daybreak the swamp is silent, but for a moaning undercurrent and, now and then, a plopping, bursting sound. Then, as the sun rises, all hell breaks loose. The swamp is in a whirl, seething, throbbing, its every reed and rush, flower and tree, bird and insect swelling the noise with a separate sound. Even the sunlight can be heard. And as the day grows hotter and the swamp dissolves into a thick haze, as all things, live and in-animate, droop and languish, as the Anavarza crags fade away, lost behind the haze, the swamp begins to boil and bubble and pant as if shaken from the depths of its being.

Mustafa Bey and his men had taken up positions behind a clump of bushes. They lay in wait, their guns resting on a tussock.

She's never been like this, never, my mother, Mustafa Bey was thinking. She's dying. But she won't die, she won't before seeing a Sarioglu dead in revenge for Murtaza. The circles under her eyes are deepening every day. But that's nothing. With some people it's the eyes that survive to the end. Though they be sunk in wrinkles, though all the light be extinguished from the pupils, there is something left alive. Perhaps in the flutter of a lash, the lifting of an eyebrow . . . It's the hands that die first, and her hands are dead already, skeletal, jaundiced, shrivelled, inert . . . Yet she hangs on, dreading to die before seeing her son avenged. And she waits, her withered hands pressed to her flagging, fainting heart. Is there no way of putting an end to this? Couldn't I offer her the life of some other Sarioglu instead of Dervish? What if I killed his son? Wouldn't he kill my Memet Ali in his turn?

He smiled at the thought of Memet Ali, tractor-mad Memet Ali . . . Haunting the tractor agency day after day, caressing the tractors like a man in love, like a man would a girl. Then making his choice . . . My father's greetings and you're to give me this tractor . . . And here he comes, driving the tractor, a different coloured one this time. For a whole week he will drive it round the farm, up and down Anavarza plain, from village to village . . .

'What are you going to do with so many tractors, Memet Ali? Look, the yard's full of them . . .'

'I'm going to till the land, father. I'm going to plant cotton all over Anavarza plain. I'm going to drain that swamp and fill it up with orange groves.'

And will they kill my Memet Ali too? On a green tractor, on an orange tractor . . .

'Kill, my Mustafa, kill! Don't let my wrong go unavenged. Kill, kill, kill . . .'

Suddenly he heard the hoofbeats and turning saw the three horsemen almost upon them. 'Quick,' he shouted and the shots burst out, the four of them firing again and again. The smoke of gunpowder rose in the air.

It was almost evening and the shadows were stretching far out. The first horse toppled to the ground and a bellowing blare sounded and resounded from the crags. The second horse had bolted into the swamp, his rider's foot tangled in the stirrup, dragging him along. The third horseman just stood there, frozen on his horse.

'Mestan, Mestan, after that horse!'

Like a shot old Mestan was on the saddle and riding into the swamp.

'Hamdi, quick, catch the man in the ditch . . . Heko, you get that fellow on the horse.'

It was only then that the horseman moved, his arms outspread like an eagle's wings. 'Don't shoot,' he cried, flapping his arms desperately, 'don't shoot! I surrender.'

'Get off that horse,' Heko said, 'and throw down your gun.'

Mestan was soon back with the runaway horse. Its rider was dead. As for Hamdi's quarry he was firing away like mad from the ditch.

Mustafa Bey was exultant. 'Mestan, Heko, truss this man up and tie his horse to a tree. We mustn't let Dervish get away.' And swiftly he crawled over to Hamdi. 'Well?' he asked. 'Won't he surrender?'

'He won't,' Hamdi replied. 'He's a formidable shot, this Dervish Bey . . .'

'We'll shoot to kill only if he tries to get away. Heko, go and fire from the other side of the ditch. Mestan, come with me. And aim only at the legs.'

'He can't get away,' Hamdi said. 'I think he's wounded.'

'We'll wait until he's run out of ammunition.'

It was dark by now and the moon had not yet risen. Only the outline of the bushes and the crests of the trees and tall rushes swaying in the warm breeze could be distinguished. The four of them opened fire and blasted away. The man fired back. Mustafa Bey emptied two rounds of ammunition upon him. 'Surrender, Dervish!' he cried out in ringing tones. They waited, but there was no sound from the ditch. 'I hope to God he's not dead, Hamdi . . .'

'He can't be dead,' Hamdi said. 'We'll get hold of him alive. For sure.'

Mustafa Bey was exultant. Dervish could never escape now, even if he were not wounded. As soon as it was light he would slash off his head and take it to his mother. He would throw it

172

down before her and disdainfully prod the gory head with his foot.

The moon rose and at that moment the man in the ditch straightened up and springing over to his dead horse fired at Heko, who fell to the ground bellowing, but still firing back. The man slumped over the horse.

'Aah,' Mustafa Bey cried, 'aah, Heko, you've killed him!'

Heko was moaning. He was wounded, but only slightly. They put him on his horse and sent him back to the farm.

'Don't say anything to my mother,' Mustafa Bey told him. 'I'll bring his head to her in the morning.' He began to walk up and down on the edge of the swamp. 'Hamdi,' he said, 'is he really dead?'

'I think so,' Hamdi said. 'I went to within ten paces and he was lying quite still over the neck of the horse. But one never knows with Dervish. Let's wait till it's light.'

At last the east began to pale. Hamdi's eyes, keen as a wolf's, were fixed on the figure lying prone over the horse. 'He's dead, Bey!' he shouted suddenly, his voice ringing out in the stillness of dawn, and in an instant he was at the horse's side and had turned over the corpse. Then he recoiled. 'But this isn't Dervish Bey,' he cried and his arms fell to his sides.

'What!' Mustafa Bey exclaimed. He rushed up and stopped dead at the sight of the corpse. Then he sank to the ground. The dead man's eyes were open, black and glassy. He had a long pointed mustache, very black, and thick eyebrows that joined over the nose. Three small pockmarks, vestiges of the Aleppo boil, studded his left cheek. A handsome man, not more than twenty . . .

Hamdi slumped down beside Mustafa Bey.

The Bey looked up. His eyes were bloodshot. 'Who on earth are these people?' he said.

'Smugglers from Antep,' Hamdi replied. 'This one's name is Abbas. I knew him. A brave lad. He's got thirteen brothers, smugglers too, daredevils every one of them. This is a bad business . . .'

They rose and went to the trussed up man. He looked at them, his eyes starting from their sockets, his face yellow. 'Don't kill me, Mustafa Bey,' he moaned.

'Who are you?' Mustafa Bey asked, his mind already made up.

'Don't kill me, Mustafa Bey,' the man repeated, his voice only a whisper now. 'I won't speak of this to anyone.'

Mustafa Bey's eyes went dark. His head whirled. There was a rush in his ears as he turned and signed to Mestan. Mestan thrust his gun to the man's temple and fired.

Just at that moment Hamdi gave a shout: 'Look, Bey! Look, look!' He was pointing to a clump of trees in the distance. And Mustafa saw the rider galloping full tilt, followed by two other horsemen way behind him. 'It's him!' Hamdi said.

'Dig a pit here,' Mustafa said, 'on the edge of the swamp. Make it very deep. Mestan, throw them in, just as they are, clothes and all, and be back at the mansion by tonight.' He put his foot to the stirrup and heaved himself up with a great effort. Dully, his head hanging low, he spurred the horse on towards the farm.

The sun was blazing down now and Akchasaz was on the boil again, with deep rumblings that shook the earth. Seething masses of bees squirmed over their combs, their red-veined flashing wings taut and quivering. They swarmed before Mustafa Bey's eyes, buzzing angrily, long after he had passed them by.

24

'Have you buried him? Well and deep?' Mustafa Akyollu asked. 'What about the horses? And the smuggled goods?'

'We brought them along,' Mestan said.

'Take the horses to Jiyjik village, to Veli, and let him sell them. You can share out the goods among you. How's Heko?'

'His wound's not serious, just a scratch. He'll be all right in a couple of days.'

'Mind you don't forget his share. And tell him to keep his mouth shut. There's no proof, no witnesses, but we've got plenty of enemies . . . Now tell me, Ibrahim Ibo, what are we to do?'

'Dervish Bey goes out every day. He takes the Chinarli road.'

'Shall we ambush him?'

'Tonight?'

'Yes, tonight!' Mestan broke in.

'It's never at the same time,' Ibrahim Ibo said. 'Sometimes he gallops off in the middle of the night. But as far as I've found out he always goes to Anavarza and clambers up the rocks on his horse.'

'We'll lie in wait for him there, ride after him . . .'

'Yes,' Ibrahim Ibo said. 'If we can only get within firing range . . . A shot at the horse, and the rest is easy . . .'

'The rest is easy! . . .' a voice spoke up behind them. Mustafa Bey started to his feet. His mother was coming towards him, bent in two, tenuous, wizened, a figure of wrath. 'So, Mustafa, you've killed at last! So, instead of Dervish or his sons you've sacrificed three poor beggars! Everybody says you just don't dare kill him, that you couldn't raise an arm against a Sarioglu. It's the talk of the whole town, how your hand trembles and shakes until you drop your gun the minute you come face to face with Dervish.'

Mustafa Bey was silent. He could not lift his head. He could not look at her.

'Murtaza's body has mouldered away in its grave and still no Sarioglu has followed him! His bones are aching. crying for revenge, your brother's bones . . .' Her face was pitiless, withering. 'How many days, how many months since Murtaza was laid in the black earth? My time is drawing near, Mustafa. How can I go like this? What shall I tell my Murtaza? That he'll have to wait a long time yet there, under the black earth? Because it's as difficult to kill a Sarioglu as it's easy to kill one of us? What shall I say to him, what, Mustafa, when I'm laid beside him in the black earth?'

'Come with me, Ibrahim Ibo!' His face rigid, his lips purple, he rushed down the stairs and made for the stables. He was mounted and waiting outside the yard when Ibrahim Ibo joined him. 'Let's go,' he said, and spurred his horse.

They dismounted at the crags and settled down to wait. The moon rose, travelled across the sky and set, but still there was no sign of Dervish Bey. Then, just as day was about to dawn, they heard the galloping hoofbeats.

'Didn't I say so, Bey?' Ibrahim Ibo said. 'Here he comes. He'll take that path down there to get to the crags.'

Murtaza Bey began to tremble. 'Aim at the horse,' he quavered. 'We'll capture him as soon as it's light.'

The rider was drawing near. He was within shooting range now. Mustafa Bey took his aim with meticulous care and pressed the trigger. Ibrahim Ibo did the same. The horse toppled down, and almost in the same instant a volley of shots burst out in the direction of their two rifle flares, splintering the rocks about them.

The shooting went on until daylight.

'Mustafa Bey,' Dervish shouted, 'it went against the grain with me that you should stoop to burning poor people's crops. That's what I've come to tell you. Night after night I've waited here for you to come, but your information is so poor . . . You even slaughtered those poor innocent Antep smugglers, all in vain. And isn't it a pity for my horse? A purebred Arab! How can a man stoop to killing a poor mute creature? Is it worthy of your race? It's a curse on me to have such an enemy, who kills the horse instead of the rider . . .'

On and on he talked, and Mustafa waited, silent, stretched

full length behind a rock, his hand on the trigger, bitterly sorry now that he had not aimed at Dervish. You just wait, Dervish, only let me catch one glimpse of you and you'll soon join your horse . . . But it was he himself who must have moved a little for at that moment a bullet whizzed over him grazing his hat. He ducked just in time to prevent a second one from shattering his brain.

'Don't you worry,' came Dervish Bey's mocking voice. 'Your horse is untouched. You won't have to walk. I would never kill a horse.'

Goaded beyond endurance, Mustafa Bey let fly a volley of shots to right and left of Dervish's position.

The sun rose the height of a poplar and the rocks steamed. White clouds swirled over them, then cleared after a while. No one stirred from his place.

That yellow rain falling . . . And in Beyazit Square, under the huge plane tree a tall slim young Mustafa Akyollu . . . Thunderstruck . . . Leaping up from the table . . . And Dervish Sarioglu too . . . At the same instant the two identical reactions . . . And now what? Killing horses, burning crops and houses, murdering retainers . . . What a change the long intervening years had wrought! And now this game of death that had lasted a hundred years, maybe two hundred, was ending. Mustafa or Dervish, one of the two would be killed, and afterwards whoever was left would die a natural death. None of their children would ever carry on the feud. Their sons laughed up their sleeves, and even openly derided this game of death of their fathers . . .

He's sweating there, in the hollow of that rock beside his horse's carcass, Mustafa Bey was thinking. Crazed with fear. I've never seen a man so afraid of death. One shouldn't kill such a man. Better to let him live with his fear, better than killing him a thousand times that he should breathe fear, sleep in fear, lie with his wife in fear, his whole life nothing but one all-enveloping fear . . . I'll kill him in this way till nightfall. I'll kill him with fear at every blink of his eyes. He won't be able to stir, to move a limb, not even to smoke a cigarette. Sweating fear under the sun, utterly drained, unable to face death wherever it may come from . . .

'I'm going to kill you,' he shouted out loud.

177

At once Dervish Bey's laughing voice responded: 'What's that, Mustafa? I didn't quite hear you.' Coward, he was thinking. Low-down coward! Two against one . . . Surely Hidayet and the others would be looking for him by now . . . The Hatun would know something was wrong. But didn't the man want to kill him? Why had he shot the horse and not him? It was obvious that it was the horse he had aimed at. Suddenly a bullet pierced through his hat and lodged itself in the dead horse behind him. This time Mustafa must have aimed to kill. All at once he was weak with fear, stung to the heart by the imminence of total annihilation, the senselessness of being and not being. Then everything was wiped out, and he was rolling blindly as though in a dream towards a rock some way off, and a long-tailed lizard was gliding over his hand. He saw the lizard's bright beady red eyes and only then did he realize that bullets were raining all about him. But his position was more sheltered now. He looked at the lizard with affection. All in a flurry it was, under the hail of bullets, among the splintering rocks. It had sensed something. Some instinct was making it shelter here beside him. It knows, he thought. This lizard knows what death is. Any living thing who can feel fear knows death. Even insects and butterflies, trees, plants know death. But they cannot know of its emptiness, of the agony, the void beyond all suffering. So blissfully, happily unaware . . . Most men too have never realized this emptiness, the vanity of vanities . . . They, the happy ones, they, the living . . . The lizard, its red tongue sticking out, was racing round and round. It darted up Dervish Bey's back, streaked down again, ran over his hand and right up to the muzzle of the gun, then quickly shied away. Its back was slowly turning red. The devil if it isn't red with fright, Dervish Bey marvelled! Two more huge lizards fell into the hollow, running for their lives. Then, at a lull in the shooting, all three of them quickly scaled the rock and vanished. They're afraid of death, yes, he thought, but if they really knew what it meant, the emptiness, they'd never be able to move. They'd die of fright where they are. Like me, dead, dead, I feel dead. It's worse when the shooting stops . . .

He raised himself slightly and fired a volley at his assailants. Anything was better than this killing suspense. He reloaded the gun and fired again. Then again, madly. Round his waist were two cartridge-belts. His bag too was full, and there were more in the saddlebag. He could always slip over and get them.

There was a sound a little way above him, and he caught a glimpse of Ibrahim Ibo's head behind a rock. Swiftly he fired. 'Dog!' he shouted, gritting his teeth. He was stirred back to life now, all fear of death and emptiness wiped away. 'Out you come, you rat!'

Ibrahim Ibo threw himself into the open. 'Don't kill me, Bey!' he cried casting down his gun. 'You're a Bey and I'm only a servant . . .'

'Go! Go back to your Bey then. Run before I . . .'

Ibrahim Ibo dashed off to Mustafa Bey's side.

For the first time Akyollu spoke. 'Listen, Dervish,' he said. 'Let's come out of these holes, the two of us, and fire at each other the minute we're out.'

Dervish pretended not to hear. Suddenly Mustafa Bey let fly again. He's mad, Dervish thought, raving mad . . . He began to sweat again.

At last the sun set and the night crept slowly down the Anavarza crags. Soundlessly, slithering like a snake, Dervish slid away into the valley below.

25

Mustafa Akyollu's life was poison now. He could not keep still, his house, his fields were too small to hold him. His son had bought a new tractor. 'This one's different, father,' Memet Ali told him. 'It's got blades. Like a tank it is. These ploughshares at the back can reach down to the heart of the earth.' At any other time he would have run his hands over the new tractor and lingered on to watch Memet Ali driving it, pleased and thinking, this lad will be somebody.

But now, night and day, something, some invisible string, some chain dragged him to the Sarioglu mansion. At first he would stop under the plane tree, his eyes fixed on that faint glimmer of light, dreading to be discovered there as though gaping in admiration at his enemy's house. Later he drew nearer and sat his horse, dreaming, wondering about the sweating cloistered man behind the sandbags, appealing to him, pleading, laughing, scorning, humbling himself, shivering under the raining dew. Then he had found this ditch, with briars looming over him, wide, like a dark precipice. Wet, clutching the gun, his hands and arms numb, leaden, he would wait for the flickering light in the mansion to fade, and when it had gone would aim his gun at the window and fire a volley and the bullets would shatter on the sash and patter to the ground. The ditch must be about six hundred paces from the mansion . . . No, no, not so near . . . Impossible to judge distances in the dusk with the mansion melting into greyness . . . Just before sunset, and the evening star a shuddering vortex in the sky . . . A flight of birds burst from the ditch, scattering in separate dots through the clear air, clustering again and falling to the earth like a bolt from the sky. And then again the lonely plain dreaming on as though nothing had ever moved at all . . .

Every day, as dawn breaks Mustafa Bey fires at that window, then gallops off down the plain in the cool wet half-light, his horse's legs spanning wider and wider, its rump stiffening, the earth and horse shaking beneath him and the wild bitter-smelling flowers and branches trembling, and he trembling and shaking too, and looking back again and again at the mansion until it is lost to sight.

And every night too, he came to the ditch, drawn there inexorably, like a sleepwalker . . . And there stopped . . . And the mansion before him was swathed in fear, cowering, sweating, its tiny pale light shivering. And there drained of all thought, forgetting his revenge, his pain, his every desire, forgetting his dreams, he would sit on the horse as though he had nothing else to do in life any more. Then suddenly he would draw his gun and fire at the window. There . . .

He did not want to go. All day long he brooded and vowed to himself: never again! But in the evening he would find himself in the saddle. The horse would gallop straight on and when the flickering light of the mansion came into view, it would stop of itself at the accustomed spot.

First it was one horseman who joined him and, as the morning star whirled and blazed in the east, together they held up their guns, fired at the window and started galloping in circles about the mansion. The next night there were two horsemen, then three, four, five, their numbers growing night after night, careening round and round, firing incessantly, silent ghostly apparitions out of the darkness, the dusty earth, the foggy dew.

But when at daybreak he turned away he would be quite alone in the brake. And the heat would sweep down upon him like murky water. There . . . As the yellow-jacket bees clung to their combs, too weak to move, as the birds struggled upwards through the sheet of murky stifling heat, languid, hardly able to lift their wings that seemed to be embedded in the hot air . . . There . . .

The groaning of a wounded man . . . The warm blood unctuous, greasy, maddening . . . And the earth swallowing up everything, the blood and the moaning . . . Sweltering, sweating, wounded, the man in that mansion, his face running with blood, his eyes wide open, bereft of hope, wild . . . Wild, wild! Wild with the fear of death . . . Cowering in the dark, bathed in sweat . . . Huge open eyes, wild, lacerated, sinking slowly into the swamp. Lacerated bodies, infested with flies, acrid, sour, putrid . . . And a horse, its head drooping in the heat, its neck drawn out. And its rider, empty-eyed, exhausted, but still plodding on . . . And in the distance, dust-devils whipping up at the slightest breeze . . . There . . .

Suddenly, a loud report broke the stillness. The Anavarza crags cracked and resounded. The morning star whirled in the east and Mustafa Bey's horse stumbled. 'Wait! Wait, don't go!' The horse stumbled again as bullets whistled through the darkness. Then it fell and stretched itself out in all its length. The men's horses were floundering on the ground. Sheltering behind them they managed to reach the muddy bed of the stream. 'Wait, wait, don't go! Coward! Wretch! Don't run away . . .' He felt a burning pain in his left shoulder, as though something had bitten him. Long, shrill whinnies filled the night.

Mustafa Bey was wading down the stream, up to his waist in the water, bullets whizzing all around him and behind the hard persistent breathing of his pursuers. The very banks of the stream were breathing with a thousand pairs of lungs.

'He's here! He's in the stream!' The voice was jubilant. How dark the stream was . . . 'Shoot! So, you dog, you think you can fire at my house day and night and get away with it? Eh, you cowardly scoundrel?'

Mustafa Bey shivered. His heart began to beat faster. Quickly, more quickly . . . He lay back and abandoned himself to the swift current. And all about him the sound of thousands of feet, walking, crashing among the bushes, the reeds, wading through the water. And always that panting breathing, angry, furious . . .

'Wait, you dog, just wait! I'll catch you yet. It'll soon be day.' It was true. Behind his closed eyelids he felt a murky, timorous intimation of dawn. 'I'll catch you. I'll kill you just as you were dreaming to kill me, not in one day or two, not in five days or fifty . . . A hundred . . . I'll hack your ear off and make you swallow it, bit by bit . . . I'll make you eat your own body, piece by piece. Until there's nothing more left of you . . . Until you're finished.' The water was flowing more swiftly now, sounding loudly like a waterfall. A deadly pain stabbed through his shoulder, cutting his breath, and the stream bore him on, half in a faint, towards Akchasaz swamp. A willow branch caught him prisoner. The darkness on his eyelids was paling. It would be light soon. With a tremendous effort he shook himself free of the branch and floated on. The footsteps came louder and louder. Shots were fired. And the voice rumbled on. 'You've asked for it. All these months I've been holding myself in check. I've given you a chance to stop pestering me. But there's a limit to how patient a man can be. This time I'm going to kill you. No, no, not just kill you. I'm going to make you eat yourself piecemeal as you would have done to me.'

Suddenly it was light. His shoulder ached unbearably, but his head was clear now. He saw that he was knee-deep in the middle of a wide stretch of muddy water surrounded by tall reeds with long leaves that rustled and gleamed in the wind. From deep deep down the swamp soughed and boiled like a giant cauldron. And louder and louder came the footsteps, the hoofbeats. And the voices, clear now. He cast himself into the reeds. His wound was bleeding. How to bind it, how to staunch the blood? Then he heard a voice almost under his nose and his knees failed him. 'Bey,' it was saying. 'Bey, it's me. Me . . .' The voice was familiar. It held a promise of rescue. 'It's me, Mestan.' The pain stabbed into his back, harrowing. 'Mestan!' he moaned. 'Here, Mestan, I'm here.' Then he fainted. The noise of footsteps was very close now, feet splashing through mud and water, angry voices, panting horses . . . Mestan stopped short, then slipped back into the cover of the reeds. He was steeped in mud. An orange butterfly with wide bird-sized wings sparkling like gold was flitting from spike to spike, weaving orange patterns against the blueness of the sky. Then, slowly, the sky turned pink, and still Mestan could not drag his eyes from the butterfly. It came and settled on his head, but started off almost in the same instant.

26

Mustafa Bey's shoulder healed in a couple of weeks. There was nobody like the Kurdish Physician for curing such wounds and he had insisted on having him instead of a real doctor. The Kurdish Physician was a thin, puny, ancient—old as Methuselah—with a sparse white beard and a swarthy complexion. A taciturn man, he had kept to himself ever since settling in the Chukurova. He would spend his time gathering herbs, flowers and insects, that he set to brew in copper cauldrons under the large plane tree in front of his house.

He tended Mustafa Bey's wound with bitter- and sweet-smelling many-coloured salves. He spoke only once and said: 'You will be all right again in seven days, Bey. A wound always heals more quickly with persons of noble stock. You must be of older and nobler stock than I thought.'

Mustafa Bey was well aware of his noble descent and proud of it, but still it pleased him to hear this from the lips of such a venerable ancient.

The Kurdish Physician stayed ten days in the Akyollu mansion, and only when he left did he speak again. 'Bey,' he said, 'way back east where we come from, in our ancient tribal tradition a blood feud is no longer that when a man shoots you from behind. Dervish Bey has gone beyond the line. It's too shameful. So don't kill him. It's not worth it. He can't be called your enemy any more. That's all I have to say.'

Mustafa Bey rewarded the Kurdish Physician with a pile of money and also, in accordance with the old Turcoman tradition, bestowed on him a handsome steed.

And all the time he was laid up Mustafa Bey could think of nothing but how to catch and kill Dervish. In the night some voice would be whispering new methods of torture into his ear. In the day Ibrahim Ibo, Mestan, Hamdi, and the others would come to him with ideas. He would listen enthralled and in turn would tell them what he had thought up. But it was the Lady Karakiz who came up with the fiercest, the most ruthless ideas. She would sit at his bedside and live through the scene, shouting, weeping, storming, crying revenge. 'That's what you'll do to him,' she would say. 'They've killed so many of us, those heathen Sarioglus . . . You must kill Dervish like I tell you, so we can get even with them and I may die in peace.'

And Mustafa Bey would smile. 'Soon, mother,' he would say with conviction. 'We'll get even with them soon.'

Ibrahim Ibo burst into the room.

'He's there, Bey,' he cried. 'Galloping along the road. And he keeps looking this way. What shall we do, Bey?'

Mustafa Bey rushed to the balcony. In the distance a black spot was streaking towards Jeyhan River. 'It's him,' he said. 'Where can he be going?'

'Shall we stop him?'

'He never went that side of Anavarza before . . . What can he want there? Is he trying to draw us into a trap?'

'You can expect the dirtiest tricks from a man who shoots you in the back. What shall we do, Bey? The others are all waiting downstairs.'

'Let's wait and see,' Mustafa Bey said, his eyes on the galloping horse. 'You're right, he'll stop at nothing that man, after this.'

He spent a troubled night, not knowing whether he was asleep or awake. One moment he would be on a wide flatland, trapped in dazzling brightness, naked, all alone, and the next rolling down a pitch-black bottomless pit, unable to breathe, unable to stop. And suddenly Dervish would materialize before him, laughing, his white teeth flashing, light and springy in his high boots, his ivory-handled pistol gleaming, the stock of his German carbine inlaid with mother-of-pearl, his stiff mustachios . . . Now who had told him that? Did Dervish really wear mustachios? . . . Visions of the dead would arise before his eyes, of the smugglers he had buried in the swamp, the straining, thrashing, gory limbs, the twisting, squirming bodies on the blood-stained green of the grass, all blurred in the heat-haze, and the ear-splitting screams rending the heat like bullets.

There . . . Would Dervish betray him to the authorities? There
. . . That Dervish . . . That swarthy face with jutting cheekbones . . . Traitorous, bold, cowardly . . . The kindest of men
and the most cruel . . . A stickler for honour, yet capable of the
basest acts. Scorning death, yet cringing in a dark closed room,
sweating it out for days, for months on end in the fierce
Chukurova heat. His wife, following the old ways, never
showing her face in public, his sister, sleeping with every man
in the Chukurova, even casual labourers and shepherds, even
smugglers . . . And how he had killed her husband in front of
the whole Chukurova, the cruel, rabid madman, hounding him
through the blackthorns with a bull's member whip until every
bush held a piece of his flesh . . . And without reason seemingly.
But Whirlwind Veli knew. He made it his business to know
everything.

'I saw it with my own eyes, heard it all with these ears,'
Whirlwind Veli had sworn, and with his hand on the Koran too.

The Lady Sabahat—she had forbidden anyone to call her
Lady—had been educated at the Adana high school for girls,
but had been expelled for seducing all the young men of Adana.
As soon as she returned to the farm, they had married her off to
Kamil, a handsome strapping lad from Bitlis, and indeed,
during the first year of her marriage Sabahat had seemed a
reformed character. Dervish Bey, all the family had heaved
sighs of relief. But this was short-lived. Sabahat was soon abroad
again, sleeping with whoever took her fancy in the farm, in
the villages, all over the place. More often than not she would
go up into the Anavarza crags with five or ten men, strip naked
and dance, and remain there for days, sometimes weeks and
months. Then she would return to the Sarioglu farm, half-
naked, her body covered with bruises, her lips bleeding, her
hair in a tangle, her eyes circled with blue, not caring who saw
her in this state. She would eat and recover and be off again as
soon as it was warm. In the winter months she would repair to
haylofts and stables, anywhere . . .

'Kamil, Kamil, you must take that wife of yours in hand,
Kamil.'

'But she isn't doing anything, Bey. My wife's as pure as
snow . . .'

'Kamil, she's my sister, but only you, her husband, can do something. She's disgracing us all.'

'But, Bey, she's my wife, she wouldn't do anything dishonourable . . .'

'Get out of my sight, Kamil!'

Mustafa Bey sighed. The Lady Sabahat . . . Her full body, her long white neck . . . Those slanting moss-green eyes fringed with black lashes, her raven hair . . . If they could get hold of her it would be a thousand times better than killing Dervish. That his sister should be made to dance naked in the house of his enemy . . . Perhaps his daughter, his wife too . . . Suddenly he was ashamed of himself, but still he could not drive the thought of the Lady Sabahat from his mind.

The day was just dawning when he jumped from his bed and, dressing hurriedly, rushed down into the yard. Under a huge hangar-like awning a number of bright-coloured, brand-new tractors were lined up in a row and Memet Ali was there, inspecting his newest acquisition. He started when his father came up to him and laid a hand on his shoulder.

'Father!' he exclaimed, somewhat annoyed at being shaken out of his contemplation. 'Look at this one, Father. There isn't another like it in all Turkey, so solid, so beautiful . . .' He retreated and gazed entranced at the tractor. Then he began to explain to his father all its particulars with a profusion of technical terms and the only thing Mustafa Bey gathered from all this was that his son had spent the better part of the night gloating over his new tractor.

Someone had told him that Memet Ali was on friendly terms with Dervish Bey's sons. Could this be true? Or was it just slander spread by his enemies? Could the Akyollu family ever be reconciled with those accursed Sarioglus, forgetting all the past? Could they ever shake hands and sit at the same table?

He left his son to his tractors and walked on towards the darkly-looming swamp, hesitant, feeling his gun for assurance. That Memet Ali, his face and hands always soiled with machine grease, what kind of an Akyollu was he? He cared nothing for horses and traditions. His only concerns were tractors, harvesters and combines. And money. Day and night his head was busy calculating. If I buy at five will I be able to sell at ten?

How much will this tractor or that harvesting machine bring in before it must be scrapped? How can the farm be brought to twice its size? And the labourers, how to make them work for less? And when, when the factories in Adana? How many? And when the new house, modern, with a swimming pool, electricity, hot water, refrigerators? . . .

His other children were just the same, taking their cue from the new rich, the upstart Aghas. None of them had ever so much as mentioned the name of Sarioglu, not even on the day their uncle had been murdered. Their attitude was one of disparagement, of disdain for the whole business. Nothing stirred in their hearts any longer, not pity, not anger. They had lost some human faculty, something was lacking in them. 'They'll never carry on the fight,' he said and spat angrily on the ground. 'Blood does not speak in them. And they say it's the same with Dervish's children too. When Dervish dies, or either one of us, it will be all over. We are the last of a different age, another species . . .'

His mother rose before his eyes, the incarnation of revengeful wrath, her thoughts, feelings, her whole existence centered on the enemy, waiting, taut and vibrant as a drawn steel wire, waiting . . . If they told her now that all the Sarioglus had been wiped from the face of the earth she would die too, she wouldn't live another moment. And to think Memet Ali was her grandson! Only two generations! And they talked sometimes, they loved each other, but with condescension on Memet Ali's part. And it was the same with her.

Suddenly Mustafa Bey realized that he had been muttering aloud for some time and he smiled. I'm growing old, he thought bitterly. Old . . . He felt crushed, humiliated. Why, oh why had he failed? Why had he not been able to kill Dervish? Never before had he wanted anything so much and not been able to do it. What if his mother died without seeing vengeance? The very thought sent a searing pain through his body. He lifted his head and fixed his eyes straight at the rising sun. I'll kill him before she dies, he vowed. The light of the sun blinded him. He turned and walked rapidly back to the mansion. I'll kill him, he repeated. I'll kill him before she dies. There . . .

He found his breakfast laid for him on the low table, the

warm milk steaming, the butter, freshly churned, in a copper bowl. He sat down at once and made a large roll with the flat bread and butter. Mustafa Bey was in the habit of eating breakfast alone, unless of course there were guests in the house.

Just as he was about to retire to his room, Ibrahim Ibo burst in. 'Bey, Bey,' he said breathlessly. 'Look look, there he goes. Look! If we shoot at him from here we'll get him.'

Mustafa Bey went to the balcony. He was livid. 'The man's mad,' he muttered tonelessly. 'Raving mad.'

'Shall we go after him, Bey?'

Mustafa Bey was silent.

'Bey, what do you say?'

It was as if he did not hear him.

'Bey, say something. He's going. We won't be able to catch up with him . . .'

But Mustafa Bey still stood riveted, silent as a stone, his face drained of blood, his eyes on the swift-vanishing rider.

Ibrahim Ibo's arms fell to his sides. 'He's gone,' he sighed. 'Oh dear, to think we could have caught him this time, and alive too . . .' Suddenly he brightened. 'Tomorrow!' he exclaimed. 'He'll come this way again tomorrow. We can lay an ambush for him.'

'Would he ever go the same way twice, Ibrahim Ibo? Now, would he? It isn't as if we don't know the man . . .'

'He's gone mad, Bey, I swear it. See if he doesn't come this way again tomorrow . . .'

'He won't, Ibrahim Ibo, he won't.'

Mustafa Bey turned and saw his mother standing right behind him, her eyes starting from their sockets, trembling of all her limbs. 'So you won't kill him, Mustafa,' she said in a muffled hopeless voice. 'Not even when he comes to flout you on your own doorstep. I see now that you'll never kill him, my Mustafa. Well, I only want your good, my son. If it's for your good, so be it.'

She reached out and stroked his hand, then turned away, a tiny bent figure, and shuffled off like a grieving lament.

Mustafa Bey swayed and caught at the balustrade. His eyes met Ibrahim Ibo's. 'Go,' he said, fighting for breath.

Mestan and Hamdi were waiting downstairs. 'It's no use,'

Ibrahim Ibo told them with curling lip. 'He just hasn't got it in him to kill. He's only deceiving himself. And here we are knocking ourselves out, all for nothing. The man's been passing under our very noses these past three days and he doesn't even make a move. What should we care!'

'What indeed!' the others said.

That night too, Mustafa Bey was assailed by nightmares. Benumbed, dazed, in a state of half-sleep, he saw great lights blazing out on the Anavarza crags, illuminating the whole of the Chukurova plain. Then everything would be plunged into darkness, stone-like, impenetrable, clammy, but pierced by a dazzling beam of light through which Dervish Bey was galloping with whip and spur. And after him he saw the Yörüks, the people of the black tents, like so many black eagles alighting on the Chukurova plain with their camels and horses, their bright-coloured rugs, their red boat-shaped mocassins, their wide handwoven woollen shalvars, their long sorrowful songs, their deep-toned pipes. And the Yörüks were plundering his land and Dervish Bey's too, wild-eyed, desperate, ready to die for a scrap of land to call their own. Then the circle of light would tighten upon them and the new-rich Aghas and the merchants would be there, each grabbing a piece of the Chukurova plain, tearing the land apart, dividing it among themselves, this land that belonged to the Akyollus, the Sarioglus, the old old families.

'Aaah, Dervish!' Mustafa Bey moaned. 'It's your fault. You've ruined us all.'

Soon only the wind would blow where once the Sarioglu mansion had stood. He had no brother, and his sons were only spiritless good-for-nothings. 'With my own hand, Dervish, with this very hand I'll tear your heart out and throw it to the dogs, to the dogs!' He shouted this out loud and started up in his bed gazing wildly about the room, his face haggard, greenish, still seeing a confused rushing of shadows in the bright beam of light.

'Mustafa Bey, Mustafa Bey!' He sprang out of bed at Ibrahim Ibo's cry and went to the balcony. 'Look, Bey, look! There he is again!'

He was passing even closer to the house this time.

'Is it really him?' Mustafa Bey asked.

'It's him.' Ibrahim Ibo was wearing breeches and a navy-blue jacket over a white shirt. An Antep sash was wound about his waist and a kerchief tied at his neck. His boots were polished bright, his mustaches set in a stiff crescent. Over his right hip hung a silver-nielloed, gold-handled Circassian dagger.

Mustafa Bey did not move. His eyes followed the galloping rider until he was lost to sight.

'If only we'd set an ambush!' Ibrahim Ibo complained. 'We'd have got him. He'll come this way every day.'

'He won't tomorrow,' Mustafa Bey said. Ibrahim Ibo did not reply.

Mustafa Bey turned away, only to come face to face with his mother. Her eyes were fixed on his, questioning, sorrow-stricken. 'We'll ambush him tomorrow,' he stated. 'Or even today. He may return.'

He had barely spoken when Ibrahim Ibo shouted out: 'Look, Bey, he's coming!'

The Lady Karakiz clutched at the balustrade, craning her neck like a bird of prey ready to pounce on its victim.

'Bey, let's lie in wait for him down by the ditch behind the reeds . . .'

His mother's eyes were on him, the eyes of a wounded impotent tiger. He fled back to his room and banging the door threw himself on to his bed.

A large plane tree grew outside his window with bird-nests on every branch and twig. No bird-nest is quite like another. This Mustafa Bey knew very well, having carefully observed them for years from his window. The newly-hatched yellow chicks with their screeching wide-open beaks, they too seem alike, but each is different from the other, and so are the flowing streams, the flowers in a garden, the yellow narcissus that bloom in profusion all around Akchasaz swamp, the water-lilies in the pools, insects, ants, clouds, every object, every creature has its own individuality, some distinguishing trait. What was it the Kurdish Physician had said, that taciturn wise old man who was conversant with all the creatures and plants of this world, familiar with their every property? Look at this stream, he had said. It flows to the sea like all other streams. On and on it flows, for ever. And a little further away, over this very same earth another stream runs its course, and it will seem to us that they have sprung from similar sources, and run through similar rocks, but we will be mistaken. If we live with them from the start we will see how different they are. And the long-legged horse-ants . . . They seem all alike to you? Well, no two are alike! See them gliding in long columns, skimming through the green grass, over the dusty roads, their long thin legs, their red, flaming trunks, each shining with a separate beauty . . .

Yet all the Sarioglus are alike . . . This one now, riding by every day at the same time, on the same horse . . . All their horses are bays. The Sarioglus all talk too much, every man of them. They are all cowards and their women are nympho-maniacs. The Sarioglus all dress the same. And they are all bloodthirsty, crafty cowards who hit a man in the back . . . In the back and in his sleep too . . .

Who had killed the most, they or us? Surely us in the last years, because we are made of sterner stuff, we don't talk all the time as they do, bragging impotently. All this fuss about noble ancestry . . . As if there was such a thing on earth! He was mocking me, that cursed Kurdish Physician, when he said I was of nobler stock than anyone else. He doesn't believe there is such a thing as blue blood. And why should he? The Arab steed is swifter, but less resistant than the Chukurova packhorse. So, tell me, with its short sturdy legs, its devil's speed, isn't the Chukurova packhorse the nobler one? If my father had heard me say such a thing he'd never have looked me in the face again . . . Yet nobility is a kind of decadence. Look at the first Ottoman Sultan and then at Sultan Reshat and the last one, each bearing some infirmity or other, and this in spite of the fresh blood brought by the women who married into the dynasty . . . Nobility is just a degeneration of mankind. It's artificial. There can be no separation between noble and common. Then what are we fighting each other for, Dervish and I? Why didn't he spare Murtaza, who fled the country to avoid death? If he hadn't hounded him to death, there would have been an end to this blood feud. We might even have been friends, the best of brothers, united against these upstart money-makers . . .

'Bey, Bey, Bey!' came a shout from the stairs. He rushed out and there was the streaking bay, its mane rolled up like a flute, its tail sailing smoothly in the wind and Dervish on the saddle, straight as a ramrod. His hand went to his gun. He drew it out and took aim. But Dervish was already out of range. Slowly he replaced the gun and turning saw his mother, shrivelled stiff, her eyes still on the fast-vanishing rider.

'Ibrahim Ibo! Tomorrow we'll wait for him in that hollow reed-bed. But will he come again, d'you think?'

'He will,' Ibrahim Ibo replied quickly. 'He's gone crazy, sweating, cooped up in that room of his. It's made him sick of life. He wants us to kill him.'

'Shall we kill him then?'

'No,' Mestan interposed. 'Not yet, Bey.'

The Lady Karakiz started forward with a rending scream: 'Kill him, my Mustafa!' she said grasping his hand. 'Don't listen to these people. Kill him and bring me back his heart. To me . . . To your mother . . . His heart and a jugful of his blood . . .'

Dully, as though nothing had happened, Mustafa Bey descended the stairs. Memet Ali was just preparing to drive one of the tractors into the fields. It was a bright blue one and it stood there in the middle of the yard like a huge freshly-blown flower. Like a fabulous blue insect . . .

27

'I'm telling you, Kaymakam Bey, this country will never take a step forward as long as these people are not plucked out root and branch. They are like cancerous growths in our midst. Imagine, Kaymakam Bey, the whole land bordering Akchasaz swamp is one big graveyard filled with countless poor devils they have killed. These feudal lords occupy vast tracts of land and not only do they not farm it themselves, but they also refuse to let us do so. Why, only a week ago Mustafa Akyollu slaughtered five men who were travelling on the Anavarza road. He buried them deep in the swamp and took their horses and money. Isn't it the Government's duty to protect the lives and property of its citizens? To prevent all this inhuman killing? Take the case of that Kurd, Mahmut, the son of poor parents who emigrated from Van, but soon perished in the heat and fever of the Chukurova. Who knows how young he was when Dervish took him into his house and raised him as his man-at-arms? He'd already killed countless times before murdering Murtaza Bey. And there are others like Mahmut who all worship the ground Dervish walks upon. They'll do anything for him. Mahmut is a fugitive now, defying the law and the state, but nobody can catch him because people like Dervish and Mustafa are the law and the state around here, and have been for the past hundred years. So long as their influence isn't broken . . .'

'We will break it!' the Kaymakam shouted, his scraggy neck stretched taut, his tobacco-stained fingers shaking. 'Our Government is all-powerful. We can wipe out these reactionary lords in one day if we wish to . . . I can set out one early morning with a detachment of gendarmes and round up all these Beys one by one, yes all of them, from all over the land . . . And then I can empty one of these towns and pack them all in there with a handful of sentinels to see they don't get away. It's as simple as that! As if our young republic couldn't deal with a couple of old feudal fossils when we kept whole armies at bay during the War of Independence . . .'

At that moment a group of town notables with the Mufti at their head entered the room. The Kaymakam rose and met them at the door, still talking, carried away by his own words, whipping himself into a passion, the veins in his neck swelling as he paced the room, shouting and stamping his foot irefully. 'Yeees! You are too quick to take alarm, gentlemen, much too quick. Just because a couple of old feudal relics are killing each other! Our Government can pick them up any day like so many pears. Yeees in-deed . . . If we want to . . . Haven't we already abolished the feudal system in this country? What power have these people left save that of killing each other? And that they will lose very soon, and also the vast lands they are sitting upon. This nation, this Government is irrevocably pledged to attain the level of Europe under the guidance of our great leader, the Grey Wolf who showed us the way. Let no one have any doubt about this. No one!' he repeated, stamping his foot so fiercely that the wooden floorboards and walls shook and rattled.

The Kaymakam had taken up office in the town ten days ago, but this was the first time he was holding an audience with the notables.

Mahir Kabakchioglu had arrived before the others. He had begun by introducing himself, negligently dropping a hint about his studies in Vienna and his knowledge of German, and of the many high government posts, even ministries, that he had turned down in order to devote himself to his country, and confessing that this was the reason why he had remained in this little town. Then he had gone on to give the new Kaymakam an account of the state of affairs in the district, dwelling particularly on the activities of those bloodthirsty feudal lords. And when the other notables had filed in . . .

'Very true, Kaymakam Bey,' Süleyman Sami said. 'An army like ours that has triumphed over the Big Powers and put their armies to rout can soon make dust of a couple of feudal fossils.'

'Dust indeed!' the notables echoed as they settled themselves on the creaky old chairs and sofas. 'There's no power on earth that can stand up against our great army at this moment.'

'At this very moment,' Süleyman Sami pursued, 'the Big

Powers are still digesting the blow they received from us. They won't launch another such crusade against us in a hurry! And these feudal fossils must recognize our power too and stop troubling the peace. As if it isn't enough that hand in glove with the enemy they tried to dismember this native soil . . .'

'As if it isn't enough . . .' the others mumbled.

'And if they hadn't killed so many of our native sons, the Big Powers could never even have cast a look over our frontiers, nor a hundred Big Powers, let alone give battle on our native soil. Ah, if it weren't for these feudal lords . . . They're always there to hinder every new reform we wish to bring. But we won't let them, gentlemen, oh no we won't.'

'We won't!' they all agreed as they sipped the coffee the servant, Dursun, had brought in and smoked the cigarettes offered by the Kaymakam.

'While we were up in the mountains fighting the enemy, carrying our shrouds round our necks, so to speak, these feudal lords were popping champagne with the French in Adana.' This was a particularly good touch, popping champagne . . . 'Yes,' Süleyman Sami repeated with emphasis, 'yeees, popping champagne, bottle after bottle!'

'Champagne!' Mahir Kabakchioglu exploded. 'That shows how vigilant we must be. We can't allow those feudal lords to play havoc with our fatherland.'

The Kaymakam bristled. 'What's that, what's that?' he cried. 'Who would dare raise a hand against our fatherland? We'll round them all up, those feudal lords, and very soon too.'

The audience lasted for some time, each notable airing his grievances against the feudal lords and explaining to the Kaymakam how harmful they had become in the district.

Two days later the news burst upon the town and travelled from mouth to mouth even reaching the ears of Dervish and Mustafa. At once the town was split into two camps.

'The Government's right,' was one opinion. 'These feudal lords have done nothing but spill the blood of poor innocent people, besides killing each other too. It was they who destroyed the all-powerful empire of the Ottomans. And now they want to destroy our republic as well. The Government's perfectly right . . .'

The Government, the news ran, was going to arrest all the feudal lords one morning and herd them on to a desert island. Then they would bring in the two warships, the *Yavuz* and the *Midilli*, and turning their cannons towards the island would pound away, volley after volley, until not a single living thing was left on it.

'It's a shame,' was the conflicting trend. 'A great shame. Aren't these feudal lords you are denouncing now the same you once looked up to with veneration? Who was it fought the enemy like tigers during the War of Independence? Wasn't it Dervish Bey and Mustafa Bey? And haven't they got red ribbons with gold medals attached to show for it? We've heard rumours like this before, but our Government will never touch a hair of their heads. They are the flower of this country, the foundation of our wealth.'

'But the Kaymakam said . . .'

'What did he say? What?'

'I've come here, he said, with full authority either to put an end to these feuds or to banish the Beys, family, children and all. He said they were cancer growths in our country and that he was going to root them out.'

'Mark my words, they'll be sending a whole army in a couple of days with Marshal Fevzi Chakmak* at their head . . .'

'God forbid! Not him . . .'

'Why not? What have you got against him?'

'He'd set the whole Chukurova on fire, stones and all. He's a hard man.'

'No such thing. He's good and pious, and kind-hearted too . . .'

'Listen to that! Is the man mad or what? Remember what happened to Nejati, the Minister of Education when he said, God doesn't exist, but the State does? Remember what Fevzi Pasha said? If God doesn't exist, Nejati, he said, you don't exist either. And then . . .'

'And then he pulled out his gun. Open your mouth, Nejati, he said.'

*Marshal Fevzi Chakmak: a hero of the War of Independence.

'What coud Nejati do? He had to obey.'

'And bang bang bang . . . The Marshal emptied the gun into his mouth . . .'

'And Gazi Mustafa Kemal heard of the affair. He loved Nejati, you know. Pasha, he said to the Marshal, would that you'd cut off an arm or an eye of mine, or killed fifty of my army generals, but spared my Nejati . . .'

'Yes, and they say he wept over Nejati's bloody corpse . . .'

'And Fevzi Pasha stalked off angrily, but he could not say a thing.'

'And now this same Fevzi Pasha is coming to the Chukurova with his soldiers, young tigers every one of them. And he's vowed to have the heads of the feudal lords.'

'The whole world . . . The Big Powers . . . Huge armies weren't able to stand up against him . . . Why, he'll pick these Chukurova Beys up by the ears . . .'

'They say he carries a full kilo of gold on his epaulets . . .'

The town was startled and troubled at the news.

Dervish Bey smiled and said nothing, but he felt curious. There must be some fire to all this smoke.

Mustafa Bey's reaction was stronger. 'But I was in Ankara at the time!' he shouted. 'I know, and so does everyone else that Nejati died a perfectly natural death. Who could be making up such cock-and-bull stories? And why? If Fevzi Pasha would deign to come to the Chukurova just for us, he's welcome, I'm sure. He'd be paying us a great honour . . .'

Finally, Dervish Bey ferreted an account of the meeting in the Kaymakam's office out of Süleyman Sami. 'Scoundrels, wretches!' he fumed. Then he smiled. 'As for that scum, Mahir Kabakchioglu . . .'

28

'There!' Süleyman Sami said. 'I knew this would happen! Let's see how Dervish'll get out of this one ... We warned him, we begged him, we told him such things aren't done in this age. But he wouldn't listen, gentlemen, no, he just wouldn't!'

'What on earth are you talking about, Sami?' Gambler Riza inquired.

Süleyman Sami ignored him. 'They wouldn't listen to me, though I went to them with a delegation of the most important notables in the district. And now it's too late. This means the end of two great and noble families. Alas, poor Dervish Bey!'

'Go on!' Gambler Riza scoffed. 'What d'you find to pity in those people?'

'Poor Dervish Bey!' Süleyman Sami pursued. 'What will he do now? Akyollu is avenging all his ancestors at one stroke by not deigning to kill Dervish. And now they've both disappeared. Nobody knows where they are.'

'Let's hope they've finished each other off,' Mahir Kabakchioglu said. 'It would serve them right.'

'But we all know what Akyollu is doing to Dervish Bey,' Ahmet the blacksmith said. 'We have to save him from that monster's clutches. It's only human. They say Akyollu is torturing him with tortures unheard-of in history. They say ...'

A cunning man, this Mustafa Akyollu. They say he's set an ambush in some reed-bed and, together with his men, has not stirred from there for the past six months. Dervish goes riding every day, though never by the same route, and Mustafa reckons he'll be bound to come his way some time, absolutely bound to. And so he waits there like a poisonous spider in its web, and with the patience of a cat too ...

That day I was lying in a covert watching for foxes. I had already killed three. They would come towards me, unsuspecting, waving their brushes, and I bagged them at one shot. Strange things happened that day. A flight of eagles alighted near me. Then that rider appeared. The horse was galloping so fast that its belly razed the ground. Suddenly three shots rang out. The horse reared and fell and its rider began to run towards the swamp. Five men emerged from the reeds and gave him the chase. He was coming in my direction. I could hear him panting hard and his pursuers were firing at him all the time. They all disappeared into the swamp. The shooting went on till dawn. Then a long scream rang out and a frantic neighing of horses . . .

The eagle was huge and tawny, with feathers that glistened like burnished copper. Mustafa Akyollu would put a sheep in a certain spot and at his sign the eagle would rise in the air with taut widespread wings and slowly circle over the sheep, lower and lower, the tips of its wings trembling, the trembling spreading gradually along the wings to the body, a hovering quivering mass above the sheep . . . Suddenly it would gather itself into a ball and surge upwards, only to pitch down like a thunderbolt, picking out one of the sheep's eyes and soaring up with it almost at once. After a while it would come down again, tremblingly circling its prey, rise high and, pouncing down, snap up some other part of the sheep.

Mustafa Akyollu had trained this eagle especially for Dervish Bey. They say he had trained four just like this one over the years. And finally he had run down his foe in the Akchasaz swamp. Treating him with courtesy as though the feud had never existed, he had taken him up into the Anavarza crags and there he had strapped him securely to a rock. His eagles were ready. They had gone hungry for three days. Ah, but before tying him up, Akyollu had stripped Dervish naked and thrown a sheepskin over his shoulders. Then he had flown the first eagle. And the eagle had hovered in the air, its wings quivering, it had soared up into the sky and swift as lightning it had swooped down on Dervish with a loud swish and plucked out his eye.

They say that Akyollu's five trained eagles have been eating up Dervish bit by bit for days now . . .

* * *

Such bitter rancour was never seen or heard of before on this earth . . . It was raining, a yellow drizzly rain, and the mauve crags, the green trees, earth and sky, streams, houses, villages, towns, everything had turned yellow. Mustafa Akyollu too had taken on a deep yellow hue. Birds, ants, the whole world was yellow, when suddenly Mustafa Akyollu vanished into thin air. Dervish Bey at once made inquiries after his arch-enemy. He searched for him everywhere, but found not the slightest trace of him. He was afraid, Dervish Bey, that Akyollu would spring upon him one day when he least expected it, for he was not a man to give up or be put to flight. But time passed and Dervish Bey's fears waned and soon he abandoned caution, that best friend of man . . .

So that one day Mustafa Bey came upon him unawares and before he knew it the horse he was riding had dropped stone dead, without even a tremor. He made a dash for the Akchasaz brake, but Mustafa Bey and six men were hard on his heels and he was forced up into the Anavarza crags, panting hard, his hands and knees torn and bleeding, and the yellow rain lashing at him, razor-like, searing as though each drop were aflame.

At last he dropped down at the foot of a rock. He was bleeding. He tried to rise, swayed, and Mustafa Bey was at his side holding him up. 'Too bad,' he said. Then, as Dervish never spoke a word: 'Dig me a pit here,' he ordered his men.

There and then, the pit was dug, man-deep. Dervish was stripped naked and sunk into it. And still the razor-sharp yellow rain lashed down, hard as steel wire.

And when the sun came out it was so hot that the very rocks cracked.

Two days passed before Dervish spoke. His whole body was buried in the ground. Only his head emerged. Green flies and bees were swarming about his eyes, ears, nose and mouth. 'Water, water, water . . .' he croaked in an expiring voice.

'So, Dervish,' Mustafa said, 'you've lowered yourself so far as to beg from me? So it's water you want? All right, you'll get it.'

Ibrahim Ibo filled the pail from the cask and threw in large blocks of ice. The pail sweated and misted over. He put it down two paces away from Dervish's head. Dervish's eyes dilated, his lips moved.

'Wretched man, I'll give you water,' Mustafa Bey said. The noon-heat was upon them, melting the earth and rocks. Ibrahim Ibo put some salt into another pail and poured water over it . . . Dervish's tongue was hanging out.

'Water, water, water . . .'

'Here's water for you . . .' And Ibrahim Ibo held the salty water to Dervish Bey's lips. He drank and drank. He drained it all. Then his eyes bulged, bloodshot, straining from their sockets as though about to leap over to the ice-filled pail that still stood only two paces away. Mustafa Bey moved the pail. It was now under Dervish's very nose. His tongue stretched and strained. It spun out thin, but could not reach the pail.

And the yellow, razor-like rain began to fall again.

Mustafa Bey's ear caught a low dull moan . . .

'Come here,' Mustafa Akyollu said. 'Come, come, Dervish. It's years I've been waiting for this day, this beautiful day. I'm going to tie you to the tail of this horse. It'll drag you along, drag you until . . . No, that won't do! It should be a slow death, very slow . . . If you like I'll cast you into an empty room . . . With no other food but one chicken a day . . . A putrid chicken, all infested with worms . . . No, that won't do . . . No, Dervish . . .'

Yellow ants are crawling all over Dervish's body. Very tiny . . . Little by little, almost imperceptibly, they are nibbling Dervish up . . .

In the market-place under the plane trees the blacksmith was shoeing a grey horse with the help of an apprentice, while two others were busy beating shoes. The horse's owner was holding the bridle. Then from the other end of the market came the clattering of a galloping horse. Even before the blacksmith had time to raise his head, the rider had stopped at the smithy and was dismounting.

'Hey, Master Blacksmith!' he cried in buoyant tones. 'Could you shoe my horse immediately?'

The blacksmith was struck dumb. 'Bey, Bey . . .' he mumbled, his tongue stuck to his palate. 'Bey . . .' Then he collected himself. 'I've just this one hoof left,' he said and smiled in wonder. 'Bey, we all thought that you . . .'

Dervish Bey laughed.

Yellow ants, the blacksmith was going to say. Millions and millions of them . . . And Dervish trussed up hand and foot, his body smeared with honey, and the yellow ants swarming all over him . . . And three days later, when Mustafa comes, only a skeleton, the white bones picked clean, is lying there in the position of a man asleep. 'Oh dear!' Mustafa Bey cries. 'Oh dear, that's not what I wanted . . .'

'Bey, Bey, and to think we . . . We were afraid . . .'

Buried to his neck in the ground . . . A pump in his mouth. They are blowing into it and blood is spirting out of his mouth and nose.

'Bey, we believed that . . .'

Dervish Bey was still smiling. 'I've got a short matter to attend to.' The apprentices were gaping at him, round-eyed, as at some strange creature. 'You'll have finished the job by the time I'm back.' He walked off through the market-place with his springy gait, attended by wondering stares on all sides.

The beat of the hammer fell drop by drop on the baffled heat of the market-place. And the trunk of the old tree near the smithy was seething with yellow ants. The tree was quite yellow, dotted with millions of darkly glittering eyes and millions of pin-point flaming heads . . . They swarmed over the market-place, invading the shops and streets and houses, and the townspeople turned yellow. The roads, the whole town, even the flowing streams were yellow. And a yellow rain fell over the town, razor-sharp.

29

'It's all decided, Ibrahim Ibo,' Mustafa Bey said. 'A hideout in a brake on the edge of Akchasaz swamp, impenetrable even for a snake ... That's where we are going to live for a time, so get everything necessary to make it snug as a house. We'll go there every day before sunrise and return when it's dark.'

'But where?' Ibrahim Ibo asked. 'We must choose a spot where he's more likely to go.'

'There's no such thing. He'll go anywhere. We have to fix ourselves in one place and wait, just wait there until the day he comes galloping right upon us.'

'You're right,' Ibrahim Ibo said. 'There's no other way.'

'Bring out the horses.'

'They're ready,' Hamdi said.

'Has Whirlwind Veli come back?' Mustafa Bey asked.

'No counting on him!' Hamdi said. 'He's running away, on the move all the time. Can't sleep two nights in one place. He seems to have cracked up after Hüseyin's death. I heard him. Death is after me, he kept muttering, death is hounding me ... So there he is, tearing all over the Chukurova, up into the mountains, down to the sea ...'

'He'll get over it when we catch Dervish,' Mustafa Bey said.

The Lady Karakiz watched them go down the stairs, her hands lifted in prayer, her lips moving silently. Then she went to the balcony and took up her accustomed place, her right arm hugging one of the balcony posts, her neck craning after the galloping riders. They had long vanished into the shadows of the Akchasaz brakes, but still she remained there, motionless, silent. Suddenly she started up. There in the distance, riding hard along the cluster of elm trees, was Dervish on a glossy black horse with its silver-inlaid harnessing flashing brightly in the sun.

The Lady Karakiz let out a moan. 'Aaah, will I live long enough to see you dead, Fiend?' She fell to praying again.

Please Allah, let him come Mustafa's way now! Please please, now that he's all by himself and they're four in the ambush, before he has time to draw his gun . . . Come, Dervish, come, come come . . . He's coming, my Mustafa, coming towards you. Catch him, catch him! Tie him to the horse . . . Drag him on and on until there's a piece of him left on every bush . . .

'This is a good place, isn't it?' Mustafa Bey said, pointing to a thick-growing brake that loomed darkly off the edge of the swamp like an island on the plain. 'And quite near the road too. He's sure to come this way sooner or later. We'll wait. A month, a year, as long as is necessary.'

They tethered their horses to a bush on the edge of the brake and penetrated into the undergrowth.

'Here, Ibrahim Ibo, you'll hack out a clearing in front of this clump of reeds, the space of a small room. You'll bring rugs from the house, and cushions and a coffee-set. Whatever's needed to make us comfortable.'

'I'll have it all ready by tomorrow morning, Bey, I promise you!'

They left the brake and started back, Mustafa Bey in front, followed by Ibrahim Ibo and Mestan. Hamdi was lagging in the rear, lost in thought, frowning darkly. Suddenly his face cleared. 'I've got it, Bey!' he shouted. 'I've got it!' He spurred his horse and rode up alongside Mustafa Bey. 'I've just remembered about Black Bekir who was in prison with me . . .'

'Well?' Mustafa Bey said without interest.

Hamdi was trembling with excitement. 'Well, this Black Bekir had killed a twenty-year-old youth. But how, that's the question!'

'Well, how then?'

'The best, the most perfect way you can imagine, Bey. Why, oh why didn't I think of it before? It was during my third year that they brought him in, a dark dried-up man, half Arab obviously, with huge black eyes. And as soon as greetings had been exchanged he announced he was tired. Yes, friends, he said, very very tired, but I can't leave you in suspense. I must tell you my story, for they're going to hang me. I'm not really guilty, but that's how it is. And anyway is it so bad to be

205

hanged? It was past midnight when he finished his story. But the next morning he began telling it all over again the minute he was awake. And so it went on for a month, a whole year. Every goddamn day Bekir would repeat his story, until everyone was sick and tired of listening to him and fled at his approach. In the end he found Lütfi . . .'

'Well?' Mustafa Bey said.

'He paid Lütfi one lira a day to listen! And when a new prisoner was brought in, Black Bekir would lick his lips and purr like a cat. Every prisoner tells his own tale, Bey, but always embroidering on it a thousand times. The thing is that Black Bekir wasn't like that. He never added anything, not once. He lived through it all, sweating where he had sweated in the first telling, laughing, cursing, frightened, angry all at the same places. He never varied once from the first day.'

'Well?' Mustafa Bey said again.

'He'd make the most beautiful necklaces and prayer-beads you ever saw, Bey, this Black Bekir, out of wood and fruit-shells and stones . . .'

'Well?'

'He hardly ever slept, always muttering to himself he was, and pacing up and down the ward . . .'

'Well?'

'And before he'd served his first year, his wife had got a divorce and was married again to Hassan's cousin. That was when he really went off his rocker.'

'Well? Who was Hassan?'

When Black Bekir came home that evening his wife told him everything, just as it had happened. I had just finished washing the clothes at the stream, she said, and was spreading them to dry when I heard a sound right behind me, and who should I see! Hassan, a naked dagger in his hand. He laughed and fell upon me. It was still early morning, but he never let me go till nightfall . . . Enough woman, Bekir bellowed, stop stop stop . . . He could say nothing else. She was a young woman and he, Bekir, was much older. He procured a gun from somewhere, a long slim brand-new revolver, and after oiling and polishing it he went out into the village. For days he searched high and low in every nook and cranny, in the fields, up in the mountains, but Hassan was nowhere to be found. The whole village knew of the affair. It had been one of long standing and that last day by the stream five little boys chasing after butterflies had actually seen the lovers behind the bushes. Bekir's wife had been seized with fear for this time Bekir would be sure to hear of it. So she had spoken first . . . Bekir was a patient man. Doggedly he kept up the search. Day and night he roamed the countryside like a sleepwalker. It was as if he had nothing else left to do in life. One morning it was raining very hard. The sun had barely shown a fiery red tip over the mountains only to be swallowed up again into the smoking clouds and the rain was lashing down on Black Bekir's back like hail. Sharp flinty rocks glinted all about him, red, mauve, yellowish, as though stuffed with splinters of broken glass . . . Stop, Hassan, he called out. Hassan halted, his eyes starting from their sockets as he saw the pointed gun. He stood there, trembling all over, white as a sheet, waiting for Bekir to press the trigger. But nothing happened. Bekir was looking intently at Hassan's pleading eyes, frozen wide, and growing wider and wider. After a while the blood rushed back to Hassan's face. Then he saw Bekir close his eyes and make ready to shoot. He went pale again, a sick vomiting feeling rising in him. And again nothing happened. For a long time they stood facing each other. Then Bekir heard a dying moan. Don't kill me . . . He was startled. The sound had not come from Hassan. He could not place it, and it did not stop, but rose louder and louder, vibrant, urgent. Don't kill me, don't don't don't kill me . . . Hassan's face too was changing, brighter now, alive again. Black Bekir suddenly collected himself, lifted the gun and closed his eyes. When he opened them Hassan's face was chalky, cadaverous and a terrible scream rang out raising long echoes from the crags, the valley, the whole forest. Kill me, kill me! Kill me! But the voice never came from Hassan . . .

'Well?' Mustafa Bey said. 'And then?'
    'Then, Bey . . . Black Bekir . . .'
    'All right, all right,' Mustafa Bey stopped him. 'I know. It's

old as the hills this method of killing, but it's good. The Germans used it for enemies they particularly hated. It's good, very good.'

Hamdi was gratified. 'The other prisoners were disgusted by Black Bekir. Hardened murderers they were, more than half of them, but still they loathed him because of this . . . In the end nobody would speak to him.'

'The Germans,' Akyollu pursued, 'would hold a gun to a man's head like that, for an hour, two hours, three . . . Sometimes for a day, even two days . . . And often, the man would be unable to bear it. He would drop down stone dead on the spot. It was in the newspapers.'

'But Dervish Bey wouldn't die that quick, would he, Bey?' Hamdi asked.

'God forbid!' Mustafa Bey exclaimed. 'This is not a bad method at all. Let's hope he'll hold on a week, maybe a whole fortnight. Just imagine him, a gun jammed at his temple, now sweating hot, now ice-cold . . .'

'Long live the Germans!' Hamdi shouted. 'They're even better than Black Bekir.'

'The Germans are our brothers,' Ibrahim Ibo said, 'our companions in war. They've got tons of good sense.'

'Aaah,' Hamdi said, 'if only their great leader, Hitler Pasha, hadn't died.'

'A brave man,' Ibrahim Ibo said, 'but simple like all brave men. His enemies took advantage of this and killed him. And when they opened his heart afterwards they found four hearts in place of one . . .'

'Four hearts!' Hamdi echoed. He was very pleased with himself. 'I knew I'd find the best way to kill him. It's that my brain works like a German's brain.'

The Lady Karakiz was on the balcony clinging to the post as they set out next day before dawn. They had told her about Black Bekir and the Germans and she had approved. 'There couldn't be a better death for him than this,' she'd said. 'He wouldn't drop down lifeless in three days, not he! He's a Sarioglu, that cursed race. He'll hold on, he'll suffer, yes . . .'

She remained there, stuck to the post, till long past noon.

Suddenly she gave a start. Way in the distance a horseman was streaking towards Anavarza. 'He's going, he's going, he's going!' she cried, clapping her hands in glee. 'Right where Mustafa's waiting for him . . . Here he comes, my Mustafa! Catch him, catch him! Thrust your gun to his head and keep it there. Don't, for God's sake don't press the trigger by mistake. For God's sake . . .'

30

With one thought ever-present in her mind, she sat there by the balcony post, on the same wooden chair, cracked but solid, beside the blackened box with the dusty-leaved single marigold, never once turning back, dreading to look to where beyond the open door of the drawing-room, on the wall exactly opposite, hung the portrait of her husband in a flashy gilt frame, the long mustaches, the grim stern countenance, frowning brows over large hazel eyes etched out with a black pencil to make them look still larger. The servants, the children, her daughter-in-law, guests in the house would tiptoe by, silent gliding shadows, filled with reverent awe, fearful of waking some slumbering unknown. Those hands, fused to the railing, emaciated, spotted, the veins so swollen the blue was no longer visible . . . Those eyes turned towards that one spot, the Akchasaz swamp . . . The narrow pointed wilful chin, the wizened trembling mouth, the tense shrivelled neck, white as though the skin had peeled, the veins sticking out, green, almost alien . . . That face, burnt by the sun . . . Those long gnarled fingers, yellow, lifeless . . . And that ever-burning cigarette. Lighting the new one as soon as she had extinguished the other. Extracting it delicately with two long fingers from the gold case she always kept in the silk sash at her waist, shakily lifting it to her trembling lips, then placing the tinder over the stone with fluttering hands and striking the flint and steel on the scarred stone until the sparks shot out and the tinder kindled, then finding the cigarette in her mouth soggy, selecting a fresh one and holding the smoking tinder to it . . . And settling herself more comfortably with one leg tucked beneath her, inhaling deeply and sending out a cloud of smoke, blue and silvery under the blazing sun . . . Like a relief against the opaque shimmering heat-haze . . . And that long grieving lament, muffled, coming from nowhere . . . As the Lady Karakiz swayed back and forth, the cigarette forgotten, its glow smothered by ash, lost under the sun, burning her fingers . . .

Her eyes fixed on Akchasaz swamp . . . Seeing horsemen
streaking through the plain, flickering dots, swift as skimming
birds . . . And all of them stumbling into that darkly looming
brake on the edge of the swamp, scattering fleeing . . . And the
taut-spun layer of heat shattered by shots, quivering . . . And
the Lady Karakiz crazed with waiting, winging over the plain,
cleaving the glaring heat, gliding into the fresh humid shadow
of the brake . . . To where, hawk-eyed, drawing out his long
dagger he leaps at the oncoming horsemen . . . 'Wait, damn you,
wait! Don't make a noise . . . Wait and see how he'll come
bringing Sarioglu's heart . . . Still warm . . . Beat-a-beat-a-beat,
beating madly in my Mustafa's hand . . . Wait and see Sarioglu's
head! The lips still pleading, the tears still flowing and mingling
with the blood of his severed neck. Wait, wait, wait!'

A figure of passionate hope, there beside the single marigold
and the rows of boxes planted with blue-flowering sweet basil,
immobile, graven into the heat, waiting, forever waiting,
wizened with waiting, like a very aged greyhound, her face
drawn thin, her cheeks sunken, her emaciated body worn to a
shadow.

> He was one of the many slain
> Murtaza the Bey
> The Bey . . .

And rising gently, dissolving in the air the smoke from that
cigarette, never fully tasted . . .

> All of tiger-skin was his saddle
> Of tiger-skin
> Of tiger-skin . . .

Sung for how many centuries? Running in the veins of how
many generations?

> I have seen in the hands of his foe
> The half of his dear heart
> Dear heart . . .

That slimy yellow rain, and the yellow face, the staring eyes, the
white teeth, full of life . . . They have laid him down naked
under the rain. How long his body! His hands, his feet . . .
Twice as long as when he was alive . . .

And there it still stands, the enemy's accursed mansion . . .
May it be dashed to the ground! And flames flare up into the

sky . . . And the Lady Karakiz, clutching the balcony railing, is swelling, growing taller together with the billowing, blustering flames. 'Burn!' she cries. 'Burn down to ashes.' She rises and takes a few dancing steps on the balcony, and the crops are on fire, one huge blaze right up to the Anavarza crags. 'Burn, burn, burn!'

For how many days, perhaps a whole month—the days are all alike, no night no day, timeless—Mustafa Bey has been rising before dawn, creeping from his room without even stopping to wash his face and hands, shuddering at the thought of meeting his mother, and each time coming face to face with her waiting for him at the top of the stairs, waiting, and he waiting too until, as the first light touches the marigold on the balcony and lengthens and spreads, he slips past, sullen, bitter, slowly down the stairs and on to his horse, Mestan, Hamdi and Ibrahim Ibo following him. But not Big Hassan. He stands there in the yard beside Memet Ali, arms akimbo, old and bent now, looking after them.

'How many days, Ibo? Hamdi, Mestan, how many? No one's come this way, neither on foot nor on horseback. What's happened? Where can he be, this Dervish who would ride all over the place every day?'

'He'll come,' Ibrahim Ibo said.

'Yes, he'll come,' Hamdi said.

'Sooner or later, Bey,' Mestan said. 'They say he's shut himself up in his house again. But he'll come out, never fear, and pass by this road too, sooner or later.'

But Mustafa Bey was not listening. 'How many days, how many? Tell me that!'

'We'll wait a year if we have to, five years. He's sure to come in the end.'

Mestan will be the first to see him, Mestan whose piercing eye can spot a sparrow a mile away. He is posted outside the brake, crouched behind a mauve-flowering agnus castus bush, his gun in his hand, his inseparable clay-pipe in his mouth, shrewd as an old fox, not giving a damn, having learnt to take things as they come, settling for whatever the new day will bring. And concealed among the tall, purple-tufted thick-set reeds are Mustafa Bey, Hamdi and Ibrahim Ibo, and the pawing sweating horses ... And the steaming bubbling samovar a little further off, in the shade, the blood-red tea in long slim glasses ...

'Mestan, isn't there anyone in sight?'

'No, Bey.'

'Come and drink some tea.'

'Ibo, will you bring it here? I can't risk missing him if he comes now, just for the sake of a glass of tea.'

The dull sheen of the brass samovar ... The clammy heat of the reed-bed ... The horses, stamping, snorting, crunching, swishing at the flies ... It's hard to wait like this ... To wait with nothing else to do but drink tea until your belly is like a drum, and watch the horses pissing long and hard on the ground ... It's hard to bear the torrid dampness of the swamp, fraught with fever and sickness, and never a breath of wind ... But how to go back, to see her there, hunched over the balcony railing, frozen numb, how to meet those eyes starting from their sockets with waiting? To have her stand before him every day without a word, without a question, her bones wasting with revenge ...

'What shall I do, Mestan, what? Again he hasn't come! How can I go home, Mestan, how? She's there waiting, stuck to the balcony, craning her neck, straining her eyes, waiting, Mestan, waiting ...'

It was the same day after day. As evening came Mustafa Bey would emerge from the reed-bed, fretting and fussing, and Mestan would say: 'Well don't let's go then. We can stay the night here, in the reed-bed.' But there were the mosquitoes to reckon with. Even during the day they gave them no quarter, stinging the horses until their backs were red with blood. And anyway, how could Mustafa chase from his thoughts the craning straining face of his mother? He had no choice.

That evening on entering the yard he saw a great crowd in the gloom, men and women, old and young, He started back at first, then recognized them. They stood about without making a sound, and only the rumbling of the distant swamp could be heard in the deathly silence.

'What is it? What's the matter?' Mustafa Bey asked, as he dismounted and advanced to the centre of the crowd. 'Speak!

You, Hassan,' he tackled an old man, 'has something happened?'

'How can you ask, Bey?' the old man said. 'Where are we to go now? How can we leave our houses, the homes of our fathers, the age-old winter-quarters of our tribe? Tell us, Bey, where can we go? Who will accept us?'

'But why should you go?' Mustafa Bey exclaimed. 'What's happened?'

'Don't you know then?' Hassan said brightening. 'Yes, we thought so. We talked it over and everyone said you wouldn't do such a thing to us. Everyone . . .'

'Do what?'

'I'll tell you, Bey,' Hassan said, his voice firm now. The crowd stirred.

Mustafa Bey cast a look at the balcony. The Lady Karakiz was there like the shadow of a bird, wings outspread, ready to pounce upon the crowd. Suddenly he had an impulse to leave it all, to jump on to his horse and ride away from here, anything rather than to see his mother like that every single day . . .

'Your son, Memet Ali Bey, has ordered us off your farm. He gave us one month to put our things together and pull down our huts and leave. "But where shall we go, Memet Ali Bey," we said. "Wherever you like," he replied. "The Republic of Turkey is a big country. You've occupied this land of ours long enough." "But Bey," we said, "it's your land, we know that, but the people of your tribe have always wintered here, haven't they? Ever since before the settlement." "That's neither here nor there," he said. "You're to go." So we came to you, our Bey. What do you say?'

The crowd swayed and quickened. 'What do you say, Bey?' another voice cried.

What could he say? After Murtaza's death he had had no time to deal with the business of the farm and had left it all to Memet Ali.

They were all speaking now, one after the other, and Mustafa Bey, dreading to go into the house to his waiting mother, did his best to keep them talking. With every outward show of respect they voiced their grievances about Memet Ali. Mustafa Bey understood perfectly what lay behind all their roundabout phrases. Memet Ali, they were saying, has become just like

214

those new Aghas, mean and ill-natured and so proud he won't talk to us or even greet us any more. In his eyes, we're no better than dogs. He's not a Bey any more. God protect us if we're left to him, we'd be much better off dead, or even away from the land of our fathers . . .

Darkness had fallen when Mustafa Bey spoke at last. 'I'll talk to Memet Ali,' he promised. 'We'll see what he wants.'

He mounted the stairs, his feet dragging him backwards and slipped rapidly past his mother without looking at her. Safe at last, he entered his room, a weight lifted from his heart, to find his wife waiting for him. Tall and slim, with large eyes and the pointed chin and high cheekbones of the Turcoman women, Seher Hanum had an air of good sense about her. She looked pale now.

'You've heard,' she said, 'what Memet Ali has done.'

'I've heard,' he said. 'How was my mother today?'

'How would she be?' Seher Hanum sighed. 'She doesn't eat, she doesn't drink. It was all I could do to make her swallow a glass of tea. She just sits there on the balcony all day long with her eyes fixed on where you have gone. She didn't even smoke today.'

'What can I do?' Mustafa Bey said. 'I just can't get hold of him. It's not easy to kill a man like Dervish . . . Mother's right, this business shouldn't have taken so long . . . Aaah, I know it shouldn't, but . . .' He raised his voice so that it rang through the whole house. 'But I'll catch him sooner or later. Mother needn't worry. It won't be long now.' She can hear me, he thought with joy. 'No, it won't be long now, please God, before I drag him here to Mother with a rope around his neck. Yes, soon, very soon, he will fall into our ambush . . .'

'Yes,' Seher Hanum said. 'But what about this business of Memet Ali's?'

'Where is he? Go and call him, Hanum.'

She went to Memet Ali's room. He was waiting. 'Your father wants you,' she said. 'Let's see what you have to say for yourself. Doing this to those poor people, like any spoilt new-rich Agha. Shame on you.'

'You wouldn't understand, mother,' Memet Ali said, adding softly: 'Neither would father . . .' And as he made his way to

215

his father's room he kept muttering: 'I'll never be able to make him understand, never . . . He just can't, they both can't . . .'

Mustafa Bey greeted his son very sternly. 'What's this you're doing, Memet Ali?' he said. 'What do you want from my men, my tribe?'

Memet Ali looked defiant. 'Nothing, father,' he said. 'I want absolutely nothing from them.'

'Then why are you doing this?'

'I have no choice. We have to, or we'll all be ruined and this farm will go to the dogs.'

'But why?'

'Look, father . . . The day's long past when farming was done with wooden ploughs and horses and oxen. And as for share-croppers . . . There are tractors now. One tractor is worth a thousand men, one harvester, ten thousand . . .'

'But, my son, these are our people, our tribe. We've been together, we the Akyollus, soldered to each other with these people like flesh and bone. Where would they go? What would they do? This land is theirs as much as it's ours. It's the age-old wintering place of our tribe.'

'Who's got the title-deeds?'

'We have, but . . .'

'This system of sharecropping is finished, father. How will we be able to feed all these people? Father, father, please understand that at this rate we'll all go down together. Let's take steps while there's time . . .'

'But they could stay in the village. Anyway, we can't evict them.'

'For God's sake, father, don't let them know it!'

'All right,' Mustafa Bey yielded wearily. He had been ex-pecting this for a long time now. Sharecropping was fast dis-appearing and the plain was full of landless peasants seeking work from farm to farm, from village to village.

Suddenly, the door was flung open. It banged against the wall and the Lady Karakiz appeared like a fury. Her blue skirt with the three loose panels embroidered in stripes of yellow, red and mauve, reached to her ankles. A yellow sash of Indian silk was wrapped around her waist, the tassels hanging down to her knees. Over her hennaed hair she wore a little fez ornamented

216

with several rows of gold coins and draped with crapes of many colours. Her waist was so narrow it seemed as if it would snap in two. Like a thin-bellied yellow bee she was, whose honeycomb has dried away under the sun.

'Heathens!' she cried, quivering. 'Have you no fear of God? What else have we left, what, but our tribe? And that too you want to destroy! That's all you're capable of doing, driving a handful of poor beggars from their homes. What will happen to them, where will they go? And we, what shall we do without our tribe, our people? How can we live without them, Mustafa? You would let this young greenhorn lead you by the nose. You would sacrifice my people . . . When you've better work to do . . . Yes, much better . . .' She raised her arms, clenching her fists, then went on with railing poisonous vehemence. 'Eh, my brave ones, if you're so brave you'd much better deal with your enemy who goes galloping past our door every single day on his bay horse.' Her arms fell and she turned towards the door, tired, her back bent, a tiny spent figure. Then on the threshold she swirled back with unexpected vigour. 'And so long as I'm alive you won't touch a hair of my people's heads, Mustafa,' she said. 'Neither you nor this snivelling son of yours.' She cast a scornful glance at Memet Ali and screwed up her mouth and nose as though she had just caught a foul smell. 'So long as I'm alive . . . And don't forget that this farm . . . You understand? If you do anything to them, I'll . . . I'll . . .' Her breath failed her. She flounced out of the room banging the door and resumed her place on the balcony, her hands grasping the railing, the palms sweating. They had been sweating for days now, the sweat seeping into the woodwork.

'Heathens,' she muttered to herself. 'If you had a spark of manhood left in you you'd have killed Sarioglu long ago. In your place, if his brother had been killed Dervish would have mowed down the lot of you . . . The lot of you . . .' On and on she mumbled, until suddenly she was filled with remorse. 'I shouldn't have said that,' she said. 'No, I shouldn't! I was too hard on my Mustafa. It must have cut him to the heart, what I said. All because I was angry with that wretched milksop of a Memet Ali, that gypsy Seher's son, would that she had given birth to a stone instead! Poor Mustafa who's been trying so

217

hard to kill that monster . . . What can I do to make him forgive me?'

The moon was near to setting. It would soon be dawn, but still she sat there, crouched on her chair, eating her heart out.

Mustafa Bey was awake too, brooding over his mother's virulent words. Never before had she let herself go as to humiliate him in this way. 'But you'll see, my Lady Karakiz, you'll see,' he was thinking. 'You'll be shamed to the bottom of the earth when I bring you Dervish's severed head, his ear, his nose . . . Just you wait . . .'

Suddenly his heart jumped with fear. What if something had happened to her after this fit of anger? He rushed to the balcony. Her tiny shadow was there, motionless beside the post. The warm pervasive smell of sweet basil hung in the air.

'Mother! Aren't you sleepy, mother?'

She straightened up at once. 'Yes, my child,' she said in her softest voice. 'You're right. I must go to bed.' She rose and took her son's arm. Together they walked into the house. 'I'm sorry I spoke like that,' she said, 'but so long as I live you must not drive away the tribespeople. After I'm dead . . . A man can give up every single thing in this world, all things pass away and become vain. Only one thing remains. Your people, your tribe. So don't ever break away from your tribe, my son. Go hungry, and thirsty, beg even, but don't forsake your own people. Don't kill Sarioglu if you can't, but one thing you must do: stand by your people. I shall never forgive you if you don't. Don't ever part from them.'

'I won't, mother,' Mustafa Bey said fervently.

31

It was hot. In the samovar the water boiled and bubbled. The swamp too was aboil with deep earth-shaking rumblings. Mustafa Bey had got used to all this. He no longer saw the gleaming blood-red tea in the slim glasses, nor heard the hollow boomings, the panting turmoil of the swamp. His heart constricting, beating a devil's tattoo in an agony of waiting, he kept turning over in his mind his bungling efforts, his enemy still alive, rock-like, his having to face his mother's damning grief, having to see that hunched wizened figure, vengeful, angry, with no more than a breath of life left in her. Her every attitude, her every look spelt humiliation to him now. He could not bear to see her reduced to this. How full of life she had been before Murtaza's death, how bright her eyes, tolerant even of Memet Ali and his newfangled ways, his love of money and tractors, his indifference to the feud with the Sarioglus. Even when she had accompanied Murtaza in exile, sharing his fear of being killed every day, every minute, feeling with him in the core of her heart the desperate inevitability of death, still she had kept her spirits high . . . But after his death she had shut herself up in her room for a whole month, and when she had emerged she was no more but a shadow of what she had been, a bent shrivelled figure, wasting away day by day.

'She's holding on,' Mustafa Bey said. 'Waiting.'

'She won't die,' Mestan said. 'If it takes us fifty years to kill Dervish, she'll still be waiting there on that balcony, her eyes on the road. But the very night of the day we kill him, she'll snuff out like a candle.'

They had been thinking and saying these same things for days now, sitting low in the sticky heat of the reed-bed beside that boiling samovar.

'Any news of Whirlwind Veli?'

'We'll be hearing from him soon, Bey.'

An excited yell came from Hamdi who was posted outs ide

He crashed in through the reeds. 'He's coming, Bey! On a black horse, galloping like mad . . .'

They all rushed out to look, but there was no one in sight.

'He's gone down the river-bank. I knew it was Dervish by the horse's shining harness. He'll come up in a minute.'

Instead of being elated, Mustafa Bey was struck with un-easiness. It was too sudden, almost unexpected. What should he do now?

'There he is!' Hamdi cried triumphantly. 'I told you so. And he's coming right our way. What shall we do, Bey?'

'Shall we aim at the horse or at him?' Ibrahim Ibo asked.

Mustafa Bey walked towards a clump of bushes, weary, unable to understand this sudden apathy that had come over him. He crouched down behind the bushes, emptied out the chamber of his gun, then filled it up again. The odour of Mauser grease filled the air. The others joined him and also checked their rifles.

'Shall we aim at the horse, or . . . ?'

'At him, all four of us,' Mustafa Bey said.

'Good,' Mestan said.

'Good,' Ibrahim Ibo said. 'Right at his heart.'

'At his heart,' Hamdi said. 'We've waited long enough for this day.'

The black horse was drawing nearer, galloping with ease over the rough country road, its tail flying in the wind. They held their breaths and aimed. Surely this was Dervish and in another minute he would be lying at his horse's feet with four bullets in his heart. On and on he came, and suddenly Mestan uttered a cry. 'Stop! Stop!' He clapped his hand over Mustafa Bey's gun, trembling, choking. 'Look, look, who's this? Who were we going to kill?'

'My God!' Mustafa Bey gasped, paling. 'It's Kurtboga's son!'

The rider was galloping along the road, a hundred and fifty metres off. He was a very young man with longish hair, of a stronger build than Dervish and dressed in sports clothes.

'To think we nearly . . .' Mestan was slowly recovering.

'Yes, Mestan,' Mustafa Bey said, extracting a cigarette from the pack with difficulty. 'But for you, we'd have been in a fine mess.' The cigarette trembled perilously on his lips. Ibrahim

Ibo lit it for him, saying: 'I never had a greater scare in my life.'

Mustafa Bey rose, picked up his gun and made his way back into the reed-bed to the samovar under the shade of the fig tree. There he lay down on the rug, rested his head on a saddlebag and drew up his knees. An orange butterfly, large as a hand, was flitting rapidly above the reeds from spikelet to spikelet. It came to rest on the mauve flower of an agnus castus bush and began to rub its head and huge eyes with its legs. Its wide quivering wings folded up and opened again, and Mustafa Bey noticed the blue rings in the orange, then the black, and inside the black, white and red blobs specked with tiny bright spangles. Two more butterflies came fluttering into the reed-bed, now dipping to the ground, grazing the grass, now zigzagging high into the ashen sultry sky. They were large and blue, flecked with tiny white dots. More and more butterflies drifted in, while the orange butterfly, wings folded now, not even quivering, remained on its agnus castus flower, deathly still, deaf to the flickering turmoil of colour around it.

Mustafa Bey was feeling better. 'Give me some tea, Hamdi,' he said. 'And you, Ibrahim Ibo, it's your turn to keep watch. Take care. I've a feeling that Fiend will be coming soon, very soon.' Then as Ibrahim Ibo was getting up, sullen-faced. 'Have some tea before you go,' he added, and Ibo quickly squatted down again, his rifle on his lap. Hamdi brought the tea. Ibrahim Ibo sipped his glass noisily. After he had drunk three glasses he rose at last. 'I've a feeling he may come today,' he said.

'He'll come,' Mestan said. 'But it's a good thing I recognized Kurtboga's son. He's the one who's studying in Switzerland, the one who says there's no God. And he's right too. If there was a God would He have allowed his father to do all those dirty things?'

'Be quiet! Don't go blaspheming like any heathen,' Mustafa Bey said, laughing for the first time. 'What of Whirlwind Veli, that's the question. He was going to bring us news.'

'Count him dead!' Mestan said angrily. 'That coward was dead even before we sent him to keep a watch on Dervish. If we have to rely on him . . .'

'Veli knows his business,' Hamdi said. 'Even dead he'll do what he has to do. You'll see.'

Mestan was incensed. 'Bey, tell this dog to shut up!' he cried. 'Why, you miserable wretch, if it wasn't for me you'd have killed Kurtboga's son. You'd have been done for. Kurtboga would've made mincemeat of you!'

'Shut up, both of you,' Mustafa Bey said, irritated. 'And let's be more careful in the future and not come to within an inch of killing any stranger who happens to come this way.'

'We won't,' Mestan said. 'Not while these eyes of mine can spy out a bee a day's journey off.'

'There he goes again,' Hamdi scoffed. 'We've heard all that before. You're just like Whirlwind Veli. He can cover a day's journey in the twinkling of an eye and you can see the veins on a bee's wings, and whether they're red or green or . . .'

'Hold your tongue, you dog!' Mestan said. 'Who was it spotted Kurtboga's son?'

'Thank you, Mestan,' Mustafa Bey said. 'But for you, we'd have been burying him in the swamp this very minute . . . And maybe it wouldn't have been such a bad thing either. After all they say he's turned into one of those godless leftists in that Switzerland where he's studying . . .'

'He'll be riding back this way,' Hamdi said. 'We can always kill him if you like, Bey.'

'Yes, let's kill him,' Mestan said. 'Who'll ever know we did it? And anyway, aren't they all our enemies, Kurtboga as much as Dervish?'

Mustafa Bey was lost in thought. Then he looked straight into Mestan's eyes. 'D'you think we'll ever be able to carry this business through?' he asked.

Mestan avoided his gaze. 'We will, Bey,' he mumbled with embarrassment. 'We'll get that Dervish in the end.' But Mustafa Bey's eyes were still on him, insistent. Mestan's greying beard trembled, his sunburnt deeply lined face twitched as if in pain.

'And what if Veli's dead?' Mustafa Bey pursued. 'What if Dervish has killed him?' His face was sombre, worried, his hands trembled slightly.

No one answered. They did not like the look of their Bey. It was growing hotter too. Mustafa Bey drank some more tea. He rose, sat down again, then went out into the open to where

222

Ibrahim Ibo was lying low, well hidden in an agnus castus bush, his carbine on his lap, his head turned to the far end of the road leading to the Sarioglu mansion. After a while he turned back into the reeds, but something drew him out again. He bent down, picked at a stalk and chewed it, his eyes on the mansion. Then he spat it out and walked round the reed-bed to the swampy brake that throbbed with the monotonous hum of bees, and back again to where he could see the Sarioglu mansion, newly-repaired, its windowpanes shining in the sun. How to learn about Whirlwind Veli, how? If they'd killed him, why hadn't they brought his corpse and hung it up on the big plane tree before the house, like Black Hüseyin's? Everyone envied him Whirlwind Veli, everyone, all the Aghas and Beys, the government people, even the military, and who wouldn't? He was so clever, so skilful, a real genius. I myself am jealous of Whirlwind Veli . . . Of Mestan too . . . If it weren't for him, Kurtboga's son . . . And then, oh my God, we'd have had Kurtboga to deal with, and his twenty-eight sons . . . He's someone to reckon with, though he seems to be always laughing and joking.

On and on he roamed through the brake and the reeds. A belated tortoise scrambled out of the brake in pursuit of its female. A long-legged pink heron flapped its wings three times, gave a few hops and flew off. A fox thrust its pointed head out of a blackberry bush and quickly drew it back, leaving the impression of two flashing beams in Mustafa Bey's eyes. A black serpent slithered on at a leisured pace, lifting its head from time to time to inspect its surroundings, and slid into the blackthorn scrub.

It was already afternoon when he returned to the hide-out, soaked in sweat. Ibrahim Ibo was still crouching in the agnus castus bush, asleep, his head nodding. He made no attempt to rouse him. The others too were sleeping in the reed-bed and so were the butterflies lolling on the blue-flowering, heavy-scented agnus castus branches that swayed in the barely perceptible breeze. The orange butterfly was there on a tall flower, motionless, wings folded up straight, its large protruding eyes perfectly still. A few butterflies floated languidly from flower to flower, alighting delicately, as though afraid to hurt them, on the yellow, white, blue and mauve blossoms and then flying up again.

Suddenly one of the horses neighed, the others followed suit and all the butterflies started up from the bushes and scattered into the sky, a spangled sparkling shining mass. Then the orange butterfly stirred and flew straight up, unswerving, until it vanished from sight.

The horses neighed persistently and the sleeping men sat up, grabbing their rifles.

32

Whirlwind Veli went first to Adana and stayed for three days at an inn called the Ashiret Han. There was a pump in the yard, but he could not even bring himself to look at it, let alone come near to wash his face. For three days, dirty and unkempt, he roamed the Adana streets, sucking gilded mauve candy sticks like the children. He was a knife-like man with a pointed face, a spiky beard and tapering oval eyes. His feet and hands were narrow and very long, and he reminded one of nothing more than a pink heron. One whole day he spent planted before the clock-tower, following the movements of the hands. Then panic fear seized him again and he found himself speeding along the road to Mersin as though he had wings on his feet. At this rate he would reach Mersin city before sundown. Labourers were at work in the fields, dark with sweat in the yellow heat, their necks straining, their eyes bulging. Whirlwind Veli had never been able to look on such scenes. It wrung his heart to see men made to work themselves to death in this way.

In the distance a tall man was bending and straightening up in the middle of a cotton field. Whirlwind Veli saw something flash in his hand and his heart jumped. There, he said, it's Dervish Bey's man! He's tracked me down, he's watching out for me . . . Quickly he swerved to the left into the fields and started to run in the direction of the Mediterranean. But he knew that the long shadow was behind him, following him. He dared not look back, and he was afraid, too, of having to pass through Tarsus. It was for him a city of magic spells, a place of dread, to be avoided at all costs, where the Cave of the Seven Sleepers was, where Lokman the Physician had found the remedy for death, where dwelt Shahmerdan, king of the serpents. He would have to by-pass the city.

At last, as he was entering an orange grove, he looked behind him. There was no one. Relief lent him a fresh impetus . . . Eh, Dervish, he gloated, it's me you have to deal with, me! Whirl-

wind Veli they've named me! See how I've ditched your man?
But just as he was thinking this, a man appeared before him,
holding a scythe. Veli swung around and fled for his life. My
God, he nearly got me this time, almost mowed me in two! No,
no, come now, Veli, my man, you're just letting your imagination run away with you, seeing Dervish in every creeping ant
and flying bird! As if Dervish Bey had nothing better to do
than to have you chased all over the country! Is that not so?
But what about his eyes? That murderous look . . . And anyway
what would anyone be doing with a scythe in an orange grove,
tell me that, you fool! Ah, Veli, God's granted you the power to
run like the wind, but never a grain of sense! What if you'd
taken him for the keeper and he'd come upon you unawares
and mowed you down? He spurted on, and the faster he went
the more his fears grew. Bodies swam before his eyes, slashed in
two, in a flood of blood. Not once did he look back. That long
man was coming after him with his scythe. He had a revolver
at his waist too. His keeper's outfit was just a disguise to catch
Veli when he least suspected it, to gouge his eyes out, to skin
him alive, cut his tongue, kill him by burying him to the neck
in the earth, by the torment of thirst . . .

Vicious monsters they were, these Beys, to inflict such tortures
on human beings. Hüseyin's dead bloody body rose before his
eyes. He was stooping over the spring . . . Don't, Hüseyin!
Come away, don't! Let's hide, you'll drink later. Oh, oh, oh,
Hüseyin! Come. Don't you hear the sound of shots? For God's
sake, Hüseyin . . . Black Hüseyin . . . Hüseyin's head plunged
in the spring . . . And bullets rending the hot air . . . And the
blood spreading through the water, overflowing . . . Whizz,
whizz, tearing endlessly through the heat . . . He's writhing,
Hüseyin, tossing and turning. Whizz, Hüseyin, whizz! Oh,
Hüseyin's rushing to the spring, bending down . . . Oh, his
head, drinking, buried in the water . . . Come, Hüseyin, come,
let's run . . . Hüseyin's long long legs, trembling, then rigid.
'There was another one. Whizz, whizz, whizz! Another one,
another. Whirlwind Veli! Quick, let's find him. Let's gouge his
eyes out, let's skin him alive.' Run, Whirlwind Veli! Bey, Bey,
Mustafa Bey, run! They're coming. Look, look at those yellowing feet, limp, his face amber yellow, his head sagging, his

tongue sticking out, long, oh so long! And his eyes bulging, long . . . Long long, oh so long! Bey, Bey, Mustafa Bey, run! Look, look they're after me. I'm going. You get away too, run! Where, Whirlwind Veli, where, where? Anywhere . . . To where Dervish and death will not find me. No, no, there's no such place, no place where death cannot track you down. Put no trust in your fleet feet, Whirlwind Veli, there's no place, no place where death will not find you. But there must be, there must!

Everyone heard the cry, the whole of the Chukurova. There must be, there must! The Anavarza crags sounded and re-sounded, the Chukurova earth, Jeyhan River, Yilankalé, Mount Nurhak, Büyükleché, Küchükleché, the Gavur Mountains, all returned the cry. There must be, there must, there must!

Ah, wouldn't Murtaza Bey have found it, if such a place existed! He came back, back to cast himself into death's arms . . . The hornets over the mullein flowers . . . That flashing wasp, now green, now black, madly buzzing. Whirling, spinning . . . Turn around, look behind you, Veli!

But Veli can't. He rushes past Tarsus city, veering south, arrow-like. The sun is at its zenith, a smouldering smoky mass. Whirlwind Veli is parched, desiccated. And Hüseyin's tongue is longer and longer, reaching to the ground, to the dust and the earth. And his body is swinging there from the tree. A cool wind blows, whipping up the dust, driving tall dust-devils before it, and the rain begins, yellow, large, slow drops, plop plop plop, like amber beads. Look into one and see your clear reflection, plop plop plop. Hüseyin's dead body in a drop of rain . . . Swung this way and that by the showery gusts, soaking wet, longer and longer . . .

Mersin! The city bright and streaming with lights. The sea, a leaping radiance of blue. And the yellow rain falling over the lights and the water. The shops, the well-dressed passers-by. And floating on the orange-lined blue sea, suspended in the air, the ships, black, illuminated from below, tossed to and fro by gusts of rain. He looked back and held his breath. A large automobile had stopped beside him, very black, its headlights ablaze even in the daylight. And above him, very low, an air-plane swooshed past with a deafening roar, almost licking the masts of the hanging ships. In the car was a slim young girl with large eyes and dusty lashes, and beside her a middle-aged man holding her hand, rapt. He had fat folds in his throat and soot-black pouches under his eyes. Obviously he had got the girl for a price. Her laughter was forced. The buckle of her bluejeans belt, a large shiny brass anchor, shook indecently over her tummy while she laughed and laughed as though someone was tickling her. She got out into the yellow rain and the dust on her lashes was washed down her cheeks. Yellow . . .

Whirlwind Veli dashed through the crowds which flowed in hurrying weary columns this way and that. A train was puffing smoke. And now the tracks were empty, stretching away into the distance. Trellised honeysuckle lined the road, their heady fragrance weighed down by the heat. And behind the shimmer of the rails a shadowy figure loomed into view, a revolver in his hand, or perhaps a sword, or a dagger, or . . . It flashed and was lost in the brilliance of the shining rails. But the figure came bearing down upon him. Whirlwind Veli turned and fled in blind terror. When he came to himself he was by the seashore. The suspended ships had lowered themselves on to the water now and the yellow rain had stopped. He sat down on the shingle and, breaking open a dappled watermelon, ate it with some bread. Suddenly, he raised his head and there, right beside him, was the man with the scythe, longer now, more awesome. He got up and walked straight into the sea, his head whirling. All the ships rose into the air again. On and on he pressed and when the water reached to his neck the sea began to ebb away, until it dried up completely and the sea bottom cracked open, shrivelled and furrowed, like a spider's web. And the ships melted into the vaporous sea, a vast expanse of blue, but dry and crinkled, the vapours closing and opening again.

And as the east began to pale, as his feet sunk into the soft earth of a field of bursting cotton, as the distant strains of a slow song floated through the air, as a pink heron, long-necked and powerful-beaked, paced on its tenuous legs, its wings mantled in the slowly spreading light, making ready to fly, springing up into the air, settling again, then winging off, from behind the blackberry bushes a man surged up and Veli fled for his life. My God, it was Dervish! Dervish himself! He tore along a dusty path, sinking to his knees in the dust, falling, scrambling up and running again, and behind him, snorting, its breath burning his nape, its bit and rump foaming with lather, its teeth bared, its ruby-red eyes glaring, came the horse that would grab and kill him by dashing him again and again on the ground. And riding the horse was Dervish Bey. Yes, yes Dervish of course! Who else would ride like that? Veli veered into a brake, then on into a swamp, but still the horse's hot breath was on his neck. He came to a mighty torrent, turbid, white foamed, and cast himself into its warm waters which swept him along, sinking and surfacing, down to a narrow gully between steep rocks where the water turned into a cataract. And still the pounding hoofs beat in his ears and echoed from the rocks. He closed his eyes.

The Aynzelha pool in Urfa . . . Its sacred fish, swarming, teeming . . . That huge fire, tall as a mountain, eternally blazing, visible from the far end of the plain, from the deserts of Arabia . . . And the tall slim, large-eyed youth with the curly ebony beard, the long white cape, holding a long mauve-flowering thistle, very thorny and aflame . . . He who was suckled and reared in a cave by a gazelle . . . Long-legged, fleeing with a thousand gazelles over the vast Mesopotamian desert, singing those long laments, the songs of the gazelles . . . The Lord Halil Ibrahim*, son of the gazelles, and after him, chasing him, a horde of men, the sound of hoofbeats . . . Naked swords slashing through the air, sprouting from the desert soil . . . But no man, no sword, no horse can catch up with Halil Ibrahim, son of the gazelles. Of his own free will he gives himself up, weary of flight and revolt, resigned, his hazel eyes clouded and dewy. And from the engine on top of the hill they have catapulted him into that blazing roaring fire . . . And lo, the fire is turned into a pool, the logs into fish . . . A beautiful garden, tall leafy trees, a cool shade . . . And Halil Ibrahim in the midst of it all! He whose cradle was rocked by gazelles, who was nursed by them and saved from death . . . That shadowy figure, that naked

*Halil Ibrahim: The Patriarch Abraham, an important figure in Islam. Urfa has a traditional story of the life of Abraham which does not agree with that given in the Bible, but can be found in the Talmud.

sword, lifted, about to smite at the cradle . . . But the gazelles have snatched the baby away and have sprinted off into the desert. Then the child grows into a tall youth with a dark curly beard, large hazel eyes and smiling face, he is long-legged like the gazelles, of the same race . . . The source of maturing brightness in this world, of the seed pushing up under the earth, of plenty of exuberant bloom and lush greenness. The Lord Halil Ibrahim . . . The earth he steps on, the running water, the very air he touches gush forth with strengthened vigour. Yet always over his head that flashing sword, naked, ready to smite . . .

Whirlwind Veli was worn down to skin and bone, exhausted, utterly spent. In his ears the persistent beat of a horse's hooves, on his lips, over and over again, Halil Ibrahim has surrendered, surrendered . . . Halil Ibrahim is defying Nimrod, defying him . . . He pressed on, never looking back at the shadowy figure behind him. Scaling the mountains he came to Marash. The shadow was after him, that flashing sword in his hand, ready to smite. He never stopped. In two days he had covered the distance to the Akyollu farm. It was midnight when he woke up Mustafa Bey.

'Look, look!' he whispered. 'See that flashing sword? They wanted to kill our Lord Halil Ibrahim. A wee babe he was, and his mother laid him in a wooden cradle, all carved and chased with blue. They had said to Nimrod, your death will be at the hand of a male child born this year. And he said, that will never be, for there's an easy way to prevent it. And he ordered all the male infants born that year to be killed on the spot. But the mother laid her baby in the blue-chased cradle, wrapped him up warmly and set the cradle to float on the stream. On and on it drifted until it was caught in a clump of tamarisks at the mouth of a cave and swept into its dark depths where a gazelle had just given birth. And when the gazelle saw the infant in its cradle she suckled him too with her young. And it grew into a gazelle-like youth. But when Nimrod heard of it, when they told him the youth was the only male child who had escaped that year . . . That's how it is, Bey. But I'll spy him out, that Dervish, I will. First let me eat my fill and then I'll go, and as soon as he sets foot outside his house I'll bring you word of it. Look, look!

See this man following me? There's no getting away from him. We have to kill him, it's the only way.'

'I'm waiting,' Mustafa Bey said. 'In the reed-bed . . . Patience, patience . . . Patience will flatten down mountains . . . It's so hot in that reed-bed. I'm getting sick of it. But patience, patience . . . I'm glad to see you. We feared you were dead. You know about Black Hüseyin . . . But patience, patience . . . He's bound to come riding my way some time . . . Before my mother dies . . . And she won't die anyway until . . . Where have you been all this time?'

'Our Lord Halil Ibrahim fell right into the flames. And all those swords ready to slash him to pieces . . . But I won't come back here without smoking him out of that mansion, I won't. He'll kill me . . .'

'Here's some money, Veli,' Mustafa Bey said. 'You'll be needing it. And take one of the horses too.'

Whirlwind Veli laughed. The white teeth, the pointed beard, the salient cheekbones, the narrow grey-blue eyes all laughed together. 'What would I do with a horse? I can run just as fast as any horse. You give me a gun.'

'Here you are,' Mustafa Bey said, and he produced a squat short-muzzled revolver from under his pillow. 'It's a good one. It belonged to Murtaza. Take it, for whatever use it'll be to you . . . I'll be in the reed-bed before dawn. I've a feeling he'll come today. Yes, he'll meet his doom today, Dervish. I saw it in my mother's eyes. He'll die today, today, that's what her eyes were saying . . . Go now, and if you bring us news, whistle your moon-whistle and I'll come out and meet you.'

33

From their holes at the foot of the agnus castus bush large well-fed black ants were wending their way round the bubbling samovar along the path they had made through the reeds to the threshing place beyond the brake, and dragging back full red grains of wheat, slightly faded by sun and rain, slowly, laboriously, their thin legs struggling to keep a hold on the ground, slipping, laying their heads down before a wheat-grain twice their size, pulling, stretching, unable to move its weight, tightening their jaws, never letting go, their legs obstinately scooping the earth, raising a whirl of dust, their bulging glassy eyes, their tough black heads, slightly downy, smothered in the dust, moiling in hundreds and thousands, stopping to snuff at each other, then a second ant grabbing at the grain, the two ants straining and striving and moving the grain at last, their thin legs quivering with joy, scrambling over huge clods of earth, down precipices, the grain at the entrance to their nest now, delectable, and every ant emerging from the hole sniffing at it once, then rubbing antennae with the two triumphant ants and going on their way.

Gritty black earth had been piled all around the mouth of the hole like a rampart and strewn over this earth were dead beetles, their hard shells glistening, bright with colour, their legs stiff and dry, and also greenish-yellow insect legs, long and thin and crooked, and wheat-grains and flower-seeds, all swarming with busy ants.

Mustafa Bey was lying prone on the ground, his eyes on the hole, watching this moiling swarm. A tiny red ant had found a dead beetle, at least fifteen times its size, and had been struggling with it for the past two days, only managing to drag it the length of an index finger. And now, this morning, the beetle had slipped into a hollow and here the little red ant had come to grief. Its thin legs straining and scraping at the earth, it strove and strove. In vain. The beetle was like a rock. At intervals the little red ant let go, rubbed its head and antennae and dusty eyes with its legs, circled the beetle, sniffing, questing, then grabbed it again from a more likely position, and pulled and pulled, never giving up, its tenuous neck stretched to breaking point, stopping awhile with locked jaws, stock-still, riveted to the beetle, feet sinking into the earth, as dead as the dead insect.

Suddenly it let go, wiping its eyes and antennae as though it were sweating. Its body, marked by faintly reddish rings down to its tail, had taken on a dullish hue. It began to circle the beetle again, eyeing its hard bright-coloured glistening shell intently, as if it had never seen it before. It raised its head sniffing the air, its antennae closing and unclosing. Its puny nodulous forelegs quivering, it made a sound like the buzzing of a bee. Or perhaps it didn't? Like a defeated captain now, with bowed head, it turned away, limping slightly and, emerging from the beetle's shadow that had lengthened to the east, crept wearily out of the hollow. At the top it pulled up, then quickly turning, hurried back to the beetle and fastened upon it once more. It was obviously now a question of do or die for the little red ant. Up above, on the edge of the hollow, scurrying ants paused to look, sniffed, and went their way, indifferent, not even making a motion to help, laughing, perhaps, at the little ant's efforts, large double-sized seasoned old ants, well-fed, dark with age, they left the little ant alone in its struggle unto death and went on to hunt for easier and lighter prey.

How would it end? Mustafa Bey, drinking his tea, kept watching the little red ant's efforts, He was bursting with curiosity.

And out under the torrid sun, in the agnus castus bush, beside a huge mauve globe-thistle, Mestan, half awake, half asleep, was on the watch. He was dreaming. Twenty years, he thought, a full twenty years! Brawling, fighting, killing, bullying, toadying . . . And the end? The end, a mere patch of earth to be buried in, and the same for your children. Well? Well then, when this business is over I'll speak to Mustafa Bey. I've had enough, Bey, I'll say. Think, Bey, just think of all I've done for you, how many people I've killed for you . . . And now Dervish is gone too. Look, don't leave me at the mercy of Memet Ali. He'll let me die of hunger . . . Set me free, make

provision for me and let me go. I'm too old for all this now . . .
Bey, if you leave me to Memet Ali, he'll treat me like he treated
your tribe. Haven't you heard, Bey, what happened to them?
No, you wouldn't, my noble Bey! It's not in your interest to
know! Beys and Pashas have always been deaf to the sufferings
of the poor . . . The farm's empty, Bey! Half the sharecroppers
are gone. They didn't appeal to you again. They knew too well
there was nothing you could do, nor the Lady Karakiz either.
It's Memet Ali, that money-grabbing Memet Ali, who calls the
tune now. You're nothing, zero. Memet Ali harried and heckled
the villagers, he made their life such a hell that in the end they
threw themselves at his feet. We were wrong, they cried, but
please don't punish us any more. We're leaving at once. Don't
tell your father! Don't let the Lady Karakiz hear of it or they'll
try to stop us . . . So they left, Mustafa Bey, of their own free
will! Heh-heh! So you were going to protect them, eh? Hah hah
hah . . . And if you think you'll do the same by me, well there
are five bullets in this pistol here. Two for each one of your
eyes and one right for the centre of your forehead. Wasn't it
you made gunmen of us? If you drive me away what else can I
do but use a gun? I never learnt to do anything else . . .

Mestan rose and sat down again. His bones creaked. They
had been creaking like this for some years now.

Three of my sons died for you . . . Dervish had them killed,
the three of them, just because they were Mestan's sons . . . And
still I was faithful to you, loyal because you were our Bey, for
whom we would give our lives and all. But I know better now.
Aah, too late . . . I saw those villagers pleading with Memet Ali,
and he looking down upon them from that orange tractor of his,
scornful, mocking, those eagle men begging like slaves from
that money-grubber, people who would have given up everything in the old days for their Bey . . . Ah, my eyes are opened
now, but too late. A whole life spent in vain . . . Three sons lost,
all for nothing. The Lady Karakiz, she was the last one, that
daughter of noble Beys. How she rode her Arab mare, like a
man, upright, a pistol at her waist! Like a tigress she was . . .
And look at this weakling! Scared to death, crazy, drinking tea
from morning to night in that reed-bed, watching the ants,
setting those poor dumb creatures to fight against each other . . .

He's a monster, not a human being, a savage monster . . . After we've killed Dervish Bey I'll ask for land, a hundred *dönüms* with the title-deeds. That's one, and I'll ask for money, ten thousand liras, that's two. And I want an IOU for the schooling of my last two sons. I want them to be educated like his own sons and daughters. That's three. And four, I want a good revolver and a navy-blue suit . . . And if you refuse I'll shoot you, yes, and set fire to your house too. As for your Memet Ali, I'll hang him on that same plane tree where they hung Hüseyin. You know me, Mustafa Bey, if no one else does. Remember the fright you had when my sons were killed? Quaking you were, terrified that I'd go crazy and do something to you. You shut yourself up in your room for three days, not seeing anyone, pretending to be overcome with grief. How taken aback you were, struck dumb, when at last you had me in and I acted unconcerned. My five sons, Bey, I said, are yours to die for you . . .

And do you know about old Corporal Hassan Hüseyin? How he begged Memet Ali? 'I've no one, no family,' he said, his thin beard trembling, wet with tears. 'Where shall I go, what shall I do?'

'How should I know? Do anything you like.'

Old Corporal Hassan Hüseyin, bent with age, his eyesight dim now. Eighty years old, ninety? Nine years at the Yemen wars. His brother killed in defence of Akyollu's older brother. All his life in the Bey's service . . . 'Where am I to go, Memet Ali Bey?'

'How should I know? Anywhere . . .' And adding with that shameless, odious, insolent, underhand sneer: 'Go to the Yemen again. Since you're always bragging about the bullets you got there! To the Yemen, yes, to the Yemen.'

'I gave you seventy years, I gave you my brother, my whole life . . . How . . . How? To the Yemen, ah me to the Yemen . . . So it's like that?' Straightening his bent back, he turned away with jerky dancing steps, chanting, repeating, to the Yemen, ah me to the Yemen, ah me to the Yemen, whirling dervish-like through the cotton field, away towards Akchasaz swamp, to the Yemen. Ah me to the Yemen, his voice swelled to a scream and echoed from the Anavarza crags as he whirled and whirled in the night, the scream prolonged into the dawn only dying out, silenced, with the break of day. 'To the Yemen, ah me the Yemen, ah the Yemen . . .'

> To the Yemen, to the desert
> To the Yemen he is gone
> Where the sands do burn and churn
> And the poor untrained soldier
> Stands lost and crazed with dread
> To the Yemen, to the desert
> My own Memet is gone
> Maybe he's rotting in the sun
> And ants are gnawing his dear eyes
> Hot is the Yemen, early sounds the bugle
> So young, my love, you'll not endure
> And when your baby starts to talk
> Father, he'll say, ah, but to whom?
> To the Yemen, to the desert . . .

Yes, to the Yemen again, Corporal Hassan Hüseyin, you who were like an eagle . . . Whirling round and round, with lifted arms, in a trance, agonizing, lost, never to return, only one long, mad scream . . . Bemoaning all those years spent under the yellow heat, behind the deep-shearing, gleaming plough . . . Parched and bent now, with sunken cheeks and thin sagging legs, the large hardened soles of his feet frayed . . . An eagle that has forgotten how to fly, one wing trailing . . . Whirling on towards the rumbling surging swamp, on the edge of the bubbling, smelly mire, cleaving its dark depths in a blaze of light . . . Corporal Hassan Hüseyin who was like a tiger, a mortal wound in his breast, slowly sinking, sucked into the mire, still whirling, only a hollow in the mud, a few bubbles, and the dark thick water closing over him, no longer wrinkled, smooth . . . Gone Corporal Hassan Hüseyin, leaving not a trace . . . To the Yemen, to the desert . . . Not a trace, not even a grave . . .

I'll kill this Memet Ali. I'll kill him! And as for you . . . Just let's get this business of Dervish done with . . . They're afraid, that's the truth of it. That's why they keep outbraving each other and talking of courage and valour all the time. In reality they're scared of their own shadows.

'Cowards all of them, craven cowards,' he muttered aloud.

Mustafa Bey cocked an ear. 'What's that, Mestan?' he asked.

'Nothing,' Mestan said. 'I was just wondering what the little red ant's done with that beetle . . .'

'Still trying,' Mustafa Bey said. 'It hasn't even moved it yet.'

I'll kill him, Mestan thought. His eyes were two narrow slits in a maze of wrinkles. His hands gripped his gun tightly. 'The little ant will get the beetle out of that hole today,' he said aloud.

'And Dervish too will come today,' Mustafa Bey said. He rose and walked out of the reed-bed. Dust was rising over the road though it was quite empty and there was not a breath of wind. A filmy haze hung above the swamp, spreading like blue gauze over the fields. A pink heron passed over him flapping its wide wings lazily.

After a while he turned back. The samovar was bubbling. He felt hungry. 'Come, lads,' he said, 'let's have a bite.' He opened the old food-box of engraved tinned copper, while Mestan spread an embroidered cloth on the ground. There were two roast chickens and a pile of pilaff. He dealt out the flat *yufka* bread, then disjoining the fowls with practised hands, he laid each one's share over the bread and licked his fingers. They began to spoon the pilaff from the large copper basin. They had cold water in a big Thermos flask and cucumbers and tomatoes on the side. This was their usual fare every day, spooning the pilaff, tearing the meat with their fingers and folding it into the *yufka* bread. Then they would retire into the heavy shade of the blackberry bushes, licking their fingers like cats cleaning themselves, and wash down their meal with glasses of tea.

'Whose turn is it to keep watch?' Mustafa Bey asked when they had finished.

'Mine,' Hamdi said.

'Take your tea then and go. Dervish is sure to come today. We mustn't miss him.'

Mestan glared at Mustafa Bey. Damn bastard, he cursed silently. Taking it out on those poor ants, are you? What the hell d'you want, tell me, you heathen wretch, from those tiny dumb creatures? Look, for heaven's sake just look at that great ass of a man! A baby wouldn't do what he's doing . . . And he calls himself a Bey! Thinks he can kill Dervish Bey too . . . I wonder if Dervish will come today . . . But there's no news from

Whirlwind Veli. Could he have run away? He's that kind, never one to stay in one place for long. Fleeing from death, as though death won't catch up with him in the end! Fleeing before a fiery-eyed flaming-tongued beast, never looking back . . . Could the monster of death have caught up with him, and in Dervish Bey's house too? Could he have betrayed us to Dervish? And then himself fallen victim to Hidayet's bullets? What d'you say to that, Mustafa, you son-of-a-bitch? Why hasn't Dervish come this way even once since we set this ambush, when he used to ride along here almost every day, even passing close to your house? Why don't you bend your mind to that instead of tormenting those poor ants? Oh, I know he'll come in the end, yes, riding that bay horse of his . . . And then . . . And then . . . Dervish at his horse's feet, struggling in a pool of blood. Four bullets have pierced his breast and blood is gushing out as from four separate founts. He writhes and claws at the ground, clutches at his horse's leg, biting into its hoof, and the horse kicks out at him. And we'll be standing there watching, feasting our eyes, praying that he'll not die too soon. That was how we'd killed Goldtooth Veli from Marash. We'd shot him down and he'd got his teeth clamped into his horse's foot and wouldn't let go though the horse went mad and plunged and tossed and turned. Bey, I said, finish him off. It's not so much Veli but the horse . . . No, he said, even if it takes three days Veli must die like this, his teeth clamped to his horse's hoof. What had Veli done? Who knows, I've forgotten, but it must have been a very bad thing to merit this, something to do with the Sarioglu feud, I suppose. Bey, I begged . . . I couldn't bear it any longer. Then the horse reared and freed itself. It flung Veli sprawling among some blue mountain tulips and dashed away. But Mustafa Bey was ready, this dog you see here playing with ants! Three bullets he fired and the horse stumbled once, twice, then pitched to the ground. Dirty low-down wretch! I still feel my heart burn for that horse. And now he's at those poor little ants.

Mestan couldn't bear to look at him any longer. He turned his back and fixed his eyes on the roots of the blackberry bushes in the moist heavy shade.

Mustafa Bey's eyes, eager, hawk-like, were scanning the scurrying ant columns, searching for a really large one. He

238

found it, a mature black ant, its antennae sharply noded, its downy body fat and ringed with red, its eyes gleaming under the film of dust. Then he looked for another equally strong ant and caught one just as it was entering its hole. He was overjoyed at having found two ants of the same size. The first ant opened wide its antennae. Quickly, he held the second one between them and slightly squeezed the first ant's body. The antennae closed on the narrow neck of the second ant. Mustafa Bey put them down and watched. They remained there unmoving, one on top of the other, their eyes bulging. Then the first ant for some reason loosed its grasp and scuttled off. The second ant too was making away when Mustafa Bey's long thin aristocratic fingers clamped down on them like so many demons. This time it was the second ant's antennae that seized at the other ant's neck. He put them down, but they separated again. With infinite patience he repeated the operation again and again until he knew that at last, stirred to anger, the two ants would remain locked for days. Sometimes he would hit on a particularly fierce ant that would fasten on its opponent at the first go, never once relaxing its hold, sometimes it would take two, three, four attempts. Then the ant would cling on obstinately, squeezing tight until the other ant's neck would snap.

The ground around the ant-hole was strewn with struggling ants, coupled together, antenna to antenna. It was like a battleground. The ants fought desperately, and if any two of them stopped out of sheer weariness, Mustafa Bey would notice it at once and quickly set them going again. Some ants would resist and stubbornly refuse to fight. But Mustafa Bey was stubborn too, and sometimes two small ants would occupy him from morning to night. He would get angrier and angrier as the ants balked at his efforts to set them fighting. He would squeeze them till it hurt, and even pull off a leg or two, but nothing would make the peace-loving ants fight, so in the end, as evening fell and it was time to go home, in a fit of helpless rage he would tear off the two ants' heads. But these peace-loving ants were not many.

Today he was satisfied with the result of his efforts, hundreds of ants locked into each other, struggling, fighting, tearing each others' heads off. He felt like a triumphant general on the battlefield. He felt too that Dervish Bey would come today. He would have liked to catch him alive, to kill him with a thousand tortures, but he dared not risk missing him once again. His mother was waiting, fervently holding on, determined not to die before seeing her son's murderer dead.

'Where are you going, you cowards?' he shouted out loud. Mestan started in alarm, then realized that the Bey was scolding the ants . . . Dog! he hissed, and returned to his thoughts.

Mustafa Bey had caught two recalcitrant ants and, with sweating slippery fingers, was trying to set them at each other.

I was sitting on a white slabstone. The Anavarza crags rose behind me, flaming red, right up into the sky, no, no, into infinity, for there was no sky, neither colour, nor light, nor darkness, nothing at all . . . Only a flowing something with ants swarming beneath it. The stone was the inscribed granite white stone at the foot of Anavarza. Suddenly, the sea was splashing at my feet and the next moment it was washing the red rocks above, changing from blue to green to mauve, then paling away. And before me a host of lizards, with scaly backs and lolling tongues, very old, coral-eyed lizards. Then it was night, a dark moonless starless night. And on the hill opposite, thousands of tiny pinpoints of light, coral-eyed, ant-like. A giant ant was scouring the lights, devouring them at lightning speed, but the lights kept reappearing, coral-red sparks, millions of them spangling the sky. Then everything was wiped out. A great void, a nothingness . . . The white stone I was sitting on was sliding, slipping under me. And in the void I saw Dervish riding his bay horse. The horse was turning somersaults and Dervish was clinging to its neck. Then from the horse's hooves who should appear but Whirlwind Veli, also spinning like a top, and from somewhere there floated into his hand a long narrow grooved knife, very black. It pierced Dervish's eye and the eye came out. Then the other eye . . . And back to the first eye that was in its socket again, on and on, shuttling back and forth from one eye to the other, until suddenly a rending scream filled the void . . . And all the horses neighed. Enough! Enough! Enough, Mustafa! Take that knife away! Call Veli back, call him! Don't do this to my eyes. Anything, anything but this . . .

'Dervish will come today,' Mustafa Bey said aloud. 'I'm sure of it.'

'He'll come,' Mestan agreed sleepily. 'A white stone spells death . . .'

'He'll come today,' came Hamdi's confident voice from outside the brake. 'Soon now . . .'

'Soon,' Ibrahim Ibo said. 'All this waiting . . .'

'Yes,' Mustafa Bey pursued. 'But what's happened to Whirlwind Veli? I shouldn't have sent him. He's getting on in years. Why, Whirlwind Veli should have found a thousand tricks by now to lure Dervish out of his house. He's grown old, poor fellow, too old . . . I'll be really sorry if they've killed him.'

'So will I,' Mestan said. 'There's no one in the world so afraid of death as Veli.'

'Yes there is,' Mustafa Bey said. 'Dervish.'

And you too, Mestan wanted to say. And if after we've killed Dervish you don't give me what I want . . . Then you too . . . You'll know that fear too, my lion. You people who play the game of death are the most cowardly of all.

In the hollow, the little red ant was still crawling about the beetle. Suddenly it grabbed it once more and began to pull.

The sun was setting, the evening shadows slowly melting into darkness. Mustafa Bey rose, swinging on his long legs, and looked at the sun sinking over the roseate crags of Anavarza. 'He won't come now,' he said dully. 'It's too late. Tomorrow. He'll come tomorrow.'

'Yes, tomorrow . . .' Mestan said.

They emerged from the reed-bed. The horses had plunged their heads into their feeding sacks and were munching away noisily.

34

Haji Kurtboga woke up at his customary rising time though he had spent a wakeful night thinking and laying plans. He was about to give a difficult battle. All his life he had worked hard and had seen his efforts crowned with success. Looking backwards he was proud of himself, especially when he recalled his childhood, his mother dying of malaria in the throes of terrible convulsions, his father gone to the Yemen wars, never to return, his eight brothers all falling prey one after the other to the same sickness, the deadly blackwater fever which took such a heavy toll of children on the Anavarza plain. But clearer than all, the image of Ibrahim would rise before his eyes, his favourite brother, tall, slender, handsome. He saw again the long skilful fingers, the reed-pipes he made, so beautifully trimmed, the little camels and carts carved from willow branches, the devil's houses of leaves and flowers. He felt again burning his throat the tart pungent taste of the honey Ibrahim would extract from dry asphodels, the dizzying fragrance that would make one's breath smell of flowers. When other children could only find a dozen honey-filled asphodels, Ibrahim would gather a whole armful on the wind-scoured thyme-scented terraced slopes of Anavarza. Then he would sit on a sun-warmed stone, handling the asphodels with almost reverent rapture, opening them carefully one by one, discovering the honey that lay deep in the green, gleaming hollow stalks no thicker than ten wheat-grains. He'd lick his fingers, scoop up half of the honey with a twig, hand it to Haji, and lap up the other half, turning it over and over on his tongue until the savour had quite dissolved . . .

Haji Kurtboga would never forget that hot sizzling summer day when Ibrahim suddenly started to writhe in the ankle-deep dust under the mulberry tree. I'm freezing, he moaned, freezing, freezing . . . His teeth rattling, doubling over, unfolding and folding up again, tensing his hands and feet to breaking point . . . And then, I'm hot, burning, burning . . . And so it went on, and after a while his teeth stopped rattling, his body was quite still except for a slow continuous trembling. His face turned yellow, then green and his mouth began to foam. He's got it badly, the neighbours who had gathered about him said. He'll never pull through. Old Hüsné woman hobbled up, her hunched body leaning heavily on a stick, her moss-green eyes sad. Poor Ibrahim, she muttered. Always I've feared for children like this one, the quiet ones, who keep to themselves and brood from morning to night. They never live long. Alas, what a lovely boy he was with those huge hazel eyes . . . Poor Ibrahim . . . Quick, she said aloud, get a saddle. We must have faith in God. An old pack saddle was found, worn and dirty, its grass stuffing spilling out. They placed it upside down on the dust and laid Ibrahim in it. He was too big and his legs and feet jutted out, bare and yellow, quivering and jerking spasmodically. Strange moaning sounds came out of him. A woman leaned over to wipe the foam from his mouth. The circle of women and children about him grew larger, there under the winged branches of the dust-smothered mulberry tree, and slowly the trembling abated. Only a few weak tremors shook him now and the beads of sweat on his forehead began to dry. Some of the women wept, especially those who had seen their own children die just like this . . . A woman was rushing up, weeping, screaming in a voice like a razor that echoed against the crags. Her arms flapping her sides like a bird's wings she circled the group of women, then broke through. At the sight of Ibrahim her screams redoubled. Round and round the saddle she went, then stopped suddenly, still, rigid, her eyes huge, unblinking, her lips blue and chapped, her hair in a tangle. She was quite a young woman. It's his aunt, the murmur ran through the crowd. She brought him up. She has no children of her own.

Suddenly, Ibrahim sat up, his eyes blank, unseeing, then he fell back, rigid and lifeless. The crowd stirred and broke into a lament. Quietly Haji turned away. Once out of the village he began to run, and ran on until he reached the river-bank. There he found a sheltered nook and crouched down to cry. The sun set and still he wept. Weeping he fell asleep and when he woke up it was past midnight. He went back and crept into his pallet on top of the *chardak*. Mosquitoes whirred about him in clouds, deafening, tearing at his flesh. The poisonous fever, someone was saying . . . Deadly . . . But doctors have an injection against it now . . . Poor Ibrahim . . . Curse this Chukurova. No child can survive in this morass . . . He listened in a daze, his whole body swollen with mosquito bites that turned to sores as he scratched away. The day was already suffocatingly hot when he came down the *chardak* ladder. His aunt had tied a black head-band across her forehead. He could not bear to look at her sorrow-filled face.

'Sit down and eat something. You're the only one that's left . . .'

He walked unseeingly as though groping in the dark. A vague memory he still had of a dusty road burning into his feet like red-hot iron. And then he was in a town, in a house, kneeling before a turbaned figure, trying to learn something by heart and scrawling strange signs on a slate. How had he come here, who had brought him to this house, how long had he been with this Imam repeating unfamiliar guttural sounds like words? He had no recollection of this part of his life, not even as a dream.

He washed his face and hands and sat down cross-legged to eat his breakfast which was ready for him as usual on a tinned copper tray, a freshly churned pat of butter, the fingermarks still on it, a comb of honey come straight from Chichekli valley, and a slab of cheese, porous, just like the honeycomb. First he rubbed his hands over his white beard which was trimmed short and round. He did not approve of long beards. Then, with a wooden spoon he scooped up a lump of butter and put it in the middle of a slice of *yufka* bread. He plunged the same spoon into the honey and emptied it over the butter, deftly, with practised hands. Folding the bread into a roll, he closed his eyes and bit into it. From the bottom of the roll a few drops of honey mixed with butter trickled down his palm and on to the rest of the *yufka* bread piled in front of him. And even as he was chewing that first mouthful someone handed him a steaming glass of tea from the samovar on the boil at his side. This would always come as a surprise to Haji Kurtboga and afford him infinite pleasure . . . His next roll would be cheese and he would finish with another one of butter and honey, standing up already, or even on his horse or in the car.

The east was only just lighting up and in the village the butter was being churned with deep booming sounds. The first butter to be scraped out of the swinging churn would always be brought to Haji Kurtboga, smelling of pinewood, because of the red pine-bark that was rubbed into the churn, which was made of the hide of a large goat, the hairs plucked off, salted and treated with extracts from a thousand and one plants and trees, thus ridding it of its natural odours, then filled with water and left to stand a few days. Only then would the yogurt be poured into it, and after the churning was over, the hide would be laid over a red pinewood bark pounded into flakes which lent the churn a reddish hue. This was the ancient Turcoman way of churning. Those long barrel-like churns made of pinewood had newly made their appearance, but Haji would not dream of using them. It would never do.

'Call the chauffeur.'

His car was a long black Ford, bought less than a year ago. In the old times he would go riding on an Arab steed, the most handsome in the countryside, for that had a great effect on people. Afterwards, he was the first to drive a phaeton, brand-new, spick-and-span, drawn by a splendid white pair. It was even more impressive than the Arab steed and he cut a dashing figure, sitting in it negligently smoking a cigarette. But the age of the phaeton was soon past to be replaced by the motor car. Haji Kurtboga's car must be the best in all the Chukurova. It must make that crony of Mustafa Kemal Pasha's, Ali Saip Bey, green with envy, and also Mad Memet and those Ramazanoglu Beys, all of them, the Antep Beys, the fierce Beys of Marash . . . Horses were all right, but there's an age for everything and the age of horses was over and done with. In the whole plain only that stiff-necked, stuck-up Dervish, who thought he was Allah's own son, the Prophet's vicar, the descendant of Jenghiz Khan, still persisted in riding horseback, to be worthy of his noble ancestors no doubt, damn them . . . Well, let him! Let him go riding horseback and see how his noble race will prosper!

'Good morning, Haji Agha. Good morning, my dear friend. We've all been straining our eyes for you.' The car had stopped at the door of the town club under the tall plane tree and Mahir

Kabakchioglu was holding the door open for him. 'Welcome!'

Haji Kurtboga extended a stiff reluctant hand. He did not approve of this newfangled greeting, a heathen invention no doubt. But Mahir Bey was a cultivated man, a gentleman, who had studied in Vienna and seen the world. He had even been invited to eat at Ismet Pasha's table. There was nothing he did not know. He could hoodwink the Devil himself. Witness how he had wangled Abdülhalik Effendi, the registrar, into turning over to him the title-deeds of all those lands left by the Armenians . . .

'They're waiting for you upstairs. The schoolmaster, Rüstem Bey, has come too. And Süleyman Aslansoypenché, Jafer Özpolat, Zalimoglu . . .'

'Good, good,' Haji Kurtboga said and walked in, his full striped shalvar-trousers flapping round his legs. His jacket was fitted at the waist and under the slits at the back could be seen a white waistband. He wore patent leather shoes that shone dully under a film of dust. His large moss-green eyes flashed from under bushy brows. At a first glance people would be struck by those shaggy reddish brows and also by the long drooping mustache. It would seem as though he had no beard at all. Haji was a tall man, measuring one metre ninety. He had broad shoulders and held himself very straight. On his right cheek a large mark left by the Antep boil would often be seen to redden. His wide forehead was heavily furrowed, His huge hands and feet, his mustache would precede him when he entered a room and then his majestic form would follow.

They all sprang to their feet with a respectful humming as he came in.

'Selamünaleyküm,' Kurtboga said with a smile, his large hand, suddenly small, on his breast, his eyes taking stock of the assistance.

'Aleyküm selam,' they cried all together. He had obviously inspired everyone with respectful awe. As they sat down, cigarette cases were held out to him on all sides.

'If you don't mind,' he said shaking his head, 'I'd rather have mine.' He produced a gold case and slowly rolled himself a cigarette which someone hastened to light for him. 'Well, Effendis, well, Aghas, so that man who calls himself a Public

246

Prosecutor is making a stand again? Eh, let him! Let's see him cross us, just let's see him!'

'Let's see him,' Mahir Kabakchioglu said.

'Just let's see him,' the others murmured obsequiously.

The Public Prosecutor in question was Izzettin Fahrettin Bey. Nobody knew exactly when he had been appointed in the district. Several gold chains swung over his large paunch, of twenty-four-carat solid gold too, and his frayed red necktie was held by a gold pin with a diamond. One of his grandfathers had been a Grand Vizir, but had been beheaded by the Sultan. Who this Grand Vizir was and which Sultan had beheaded him, nobody knew. The Prosecutor himself either did not know or wouldn't say. He was not one for boasting of his descent, and had turned his back on his old life, retiring into this little town, like a strange lonely bird, or rather dropping anchor here, away from the blustering storms in this shallow bay, never to sail again, letting the bark of his life quietly rot away. And rotting away it was. Every evening would find him in Injejikoglu Restaurant with a few other civil servants around a *raki* table, reciting to them, whether they understood him or not, the Rubaiyat of Omar Khayyam and verses from such classical eastern poets as Fuzuli, Nedim, Naili, Nabi, Nizami and Örfi. Some there were who had heard him declaiming like this at this table for twenty years. The usual *raki* table talk, the toasts and mutual courtesies would end at ten o'clock and at exactly quarter past ten the jolly compeers would repair to the town club where their tables were ready for them. And the gambling would begin, lasting to well after midnight, poker, blind poker, rummy, roulette, all the most hazardous games of fortune . . . At the gaming table the Public Prosecutor changes. He becomes an entirely different man, flying into a rage when losing, belligerent, a veritable fiend. And when he has no money left to lose, he will buttonhole anyone, acquaintance or not, for a loan. First he'll ask for ten liras and if he gets it, like as not will gamble it away and return for more, twenty liras, fifty, one hundred, sometimes as much as a thousand, depending on the turn of his luck. And many's the time when, having touched everyone in the club and despairing of getting more, he has gone knocking on any door in town in the small hours of the morning, rousing the alarmed household with his yells. 'Help! They've robbed me! They've sponged me dry, me, the grandson of a great Vizir! Lend me a hundred liras so I can make good my losses or I'll have to go hungry tomorrow . . .' There were nights when he would go banging like this on more than a dozen doors. And these were the nights chosen by people who had business with the Public Prosecutor. The next morning his office would be the scene of angry wrangling, as he would have no recollection, most of the time, from whom he had borrowed or whose house he had gone to. Moreover he was not a man to be suborned and he would generally do absolutely nothing in return for the money he had received. But there were some people he feared and dared not turn away. One of these was Haji Kurtboga.

'I gave you ten thousand liras last night.'

'Sir? Who are you? Forgive me, but I'm afraid I can't place you. What ten thousand liras? Has somebody despoiled you of this sum?' Polite, courteous, Izzettin Fahrettin Bey was rubbing his hands in unfeigned bewilderment. 'Too bad, too bad, sir! Ten thousand liras you say? . . .'

'Why, you double-crossing rascal, you knew me well enough yesterday to gamble away my ten thousand liras! And today you . . . I'll show you! I'll show your famous Vizir granddad . . . I'll . . .'

'Calm yourself, calm yourself, sir . . .' Suddenly a gun flashed green, the barrel pointed straight at the prosecutor's forehead. 'Please, please, sir . . . Control yourself and tell me who you are.'

'My name's Haji Kurtboga. I'm the one who killed Rejep Jümbüsh. It was just an accident. There's another ten thousand for you if you get me out of this mess. I don't care how you do it, but do it.'

The prosecutor wiped the sweat off his brow. Slowly the blood flowed back to his face. 'Sir,' he said with dignity, 'this is a government office. Put that gun away and don't get excited. I recognize you very well now. Tell me when you'll be able to procure that ten thousand for me. I need the money badly. And as you're an old friend I'll see to this business of yours. But you must help me.'

'I will. As for the money, it's ready.'

'You've been sentenced for murder and your sentence has been ratified by the High Court. Twenty-four years, wasn't it?'

'Right.'

'Well then, find me another Haji Kurtboga. And also pledge me two thousand five hundred liras for each of these twenty-four years.'

'The money part's easy, but where am I to find another Haji Kurtboga?'

'Go to the Registry of Births, sir. Find somebody who's not registered.'

'Why, who'd ever think of that! You're a genius, prosecutor. Good for you . . . I'll bring you one of those gypsies . . . Will that be all right?'

'A good gypsy can make a good Haji Kurtboga. I'll send him to Diyarbekir. And even if he has second thoughts later and swears himself blue saying, I'm not Haji Kurtboga, I'm the gypsy, Rejep Zobi, no one will believe him. He'll go on being Haji Kurtboga till the next amnesty.'

'Well, bully for you, Prosecutor! Where on earth did you hear of Rejep the gypsy? How did you think of him?' And he roared with laughter. The Public Prosecutor burst out laughing too and for a long while the room was filled with gusts of laughter as the two men sat there, paunches shaking, mustaches wobbling, hands slapping their knees.

And so Rejep the gypsy became Haji Kurtboga, and remains so to this day, though he has long been released from prison. It suits him to be known as Haji Kurtboga, but not, of course, before Kurtboga himself who would raise hell if he knew of it.

'Shall we call him here?' Mahir Kabakchioglu asked.

Haji Kurtboga thrust his large strong fingers into his beard, scratched his chin and thought, while they all waited holding their breath. His fingers strayed to his mustache then to his nose. 'No,' he said at last, taking the cup of coffee that had been waiting before him some time. 'He's not our servant. He's the estimable, conscientious representative of our great Government. Even if you have no consideration for him, I have, more than I can say, you've got to treat him with the respect we owe

249

our Government. We can't summon him just like that. We'll form a delegation and go ourselves to our brother Izzettin Fahrettin Bey, the descendant of Grand Vizirs.'

'Nothing could be more proper,' Mahir Bey approved.

'I'll go, and you. And . . . And . . .' Kurtboga surveyed the group sternly. 'Schoolmaster! You can make a third. You've got the gift of the gab. Süleyman Agha, you come too.'

'Very good,' they all said. 'Just the thing.'

Yes, my friends, just as I tell you . . . They are parcelling out the Akchasaz swamp. But where have those Yörük nomads sprung from? And what about the villagers, what's got into them?

The Yörüks settled on Boga knoll and occupied ten thousand *dönüms* all around it. They laid aside their tents and made huts for themselves. This is our very own land, they asserted. It was our wintering place since the time of our forefathers and after the settlement Dervish Pasha himself gave it to us for a home. What a Pasha he was, his epaulettes shining like the sun, a lion on the saddle, so big and strong the horse's belly would sag to the ground under him . . . That's what they were saying now. But, while at that time those foolish Yörüks refused to be fixed and fled from the land they called their ancestral winter home, Dervish Pasha was busy staking whole areas for himself from Islahiyé to Hassa, right down to Aleppo. And now, when it was too late, they were hankering after land that was no longer theirs. Yes, my friends, just as I tell you . . . But careful, there's no telling what these Yörüks may do. Like a shot they may spring on you with a hundred armed men, each one a fierce, hawk-like warrior. So how to uproot them from Akchasaz swamp?

Yes, my friends, just as I tell you . . . And those villagers, marooned in the middle of Akchasaz on that small patch of dry land? Are they not citizens too? Are they not our brothers? I have witnessed their tragic adventure, with these two eyes, and may they drop before me if there is one false word in what I tell. They will never allow these villagers to remain there, never leave them this land, every fistful of which is worth its weight in gold. Never! I can swear to that on the Koran. My heart burns for them. Yes, my friends, just as I tell you. My heart burns for them and there is nothing I can do about it.

They came from the mountains. On their feet rawhide sandals, red buskins, yellow calfskin boots . . . Their thick handwoven woollen shalvars were dyed with pomegranate rind and walnut shell, their shirts were of striped Marash cloth with embroidered collars. The women in red aprons trimmed with silver thread, the older ones in simple blue skirts and white headkerchiefs, the young girls and brides with little silver-filigreed fezzes topped by a silver coronet. They came with their quivers, their double-barrelled flintlock pistols, their bagpipes and drums and pipes, their *sazes* and gourd citterns. On their lips the songs and laments that had come down to them through the ages. Some were from the farther reaches of the Taurus Mountains and spoke only Kurdish. They danced the *semah** and lit great fires at the foot of the rocks. And kneeling on the ground, their right knee touching the eternal earth, in a trance, forgetting everything else, they paid worship to man and fire and the good word, to all of creation, to all things beautiful, to the flowers, to the sky that spread above them like a huge blue flower in bloom, to the brightly flowing streams . . . Forsaking their homes and villages they came trekking down the steep slopes of the lofty Taurus Mountains among the pines, cherry trees and flowering wild rose, their numbers decimated, victims of centuries-long oppression, felling the trees of the forest, uprooting bushes and briars, toiling three years, five years to clear a half-acre patch, a labour of blood, each inch of the land watered by the sweat of their brow, sowing it one year, only to see the rains sweep away the earth the second year, leaving sharp rocks and stones in its place. The woods and forests of the Taurus wasted away, the flowers and grasses, the bees and birds and earth dwindled, and the migration started again, down from the mountains into the plain, a trickle at first, then in swarms, only to fall prey to mosquitoes and malaria, the survivors to work as sharecroppers or retainers in the big farms.

The Lady of Gözükara was filled with alarm. She had lots of

Semah: a kind of whirling religious dance.

land on the Anavarza plain and a great number of sharecroppers working for her, and now word was being spread that the Government intended to give these sharecroppers the land they were cultivating . . . Without waiting a minute she summoned them all. It's not my fault but the Government's, she told them. They've had this idea of distributing my land to you. So you must all leave by tomorrow . . . Don't do this to us, Lady, they said. We love our homes, we love you. Remember how many of us died before we got used to this land. You've been good to us and taken us on as sharecroppers. We wouldn't want your land, we wouldn't bite the hand that feeds us . . . I know, she said, you wouldn't want my land, but the Government would force you to take it . . . We'd never take it, not even by force, they wailed . . . I know what the Government is, she said. You'll refuse and they'll harass and torment you and if you still won't heed them they'll kill you. I know you'd never take my land. I know you wouldn't bite the hand that feeds you, but there's no escaping it, one can't get the better of the Government . . . And there was nothing more to be said. That night they packed up their belongings and at dawn they left the Lady of Gözükara's village. At the foot of the Anavarza crags they stopped and lit a big fire. For a whole day and night they prayed and worshipped and danced the *semah* around the fire. And the next morning what should they see! The vast plain around them up to the borders of Akchasaz swamp was teeming with villagers like themselves thrown out of their homes, with nowhere to go to.

It was on the noon of a hot sizzling day. A voice rang out through the heat: Villagers of Gözükara! Villagers of Gözükara! They huddled up under a tree, nothing but skin and bone now, their lips cracked with fever. The children were dying one after the other. Like thieves in the night they would take their dead back to Gözükara village and bury them there in secret. Among the villagers was one Long Ali Riza, an old man, wise to the ways of this world, upright and honest, and he was calling to them now. Neighbours, he said, this can't go on. For months we've been wandering, sick and dying, all over the Chukurova plain. We've found nothing. Now, I've got a plan, not an easy one, a fifty-fifty chance between life and death. I'll explain, and then whoever chooses will come with me . . . Tell us what to do and save us from this calamity, they said . . . All right, he said. Long Ali Riza he was named, because of his very tall rugged stature. And he began. His voice was like a whistle, lengthening and shortening, now low, now loud and strong. Do you see that swamp, he said, those reed-beds and brakes, the thickets, the blackthorns, the eddies and whirlpools? What really lies there is something like between a hundred and two hundred *dönüms* of land. And what land! Sow a man in it and he will take root and put forth shoots. While you were searching the Chukurova for a place to settle, I've been inspecting this swamp inch by inch. Right in the middle there's a dry mound, as dry as this ground here. Its length is one thousand three hundred and forty-six paces, its breadth eighteen paces in some places and twenty-three or twelve and a half in others . . . That is where I intend to settle. The water around this mound is quite shallow. We can build ditches and canals to drain it away and gain still more land for ourselves . . . Let's go, they all cried. Long Ali Riza stood silent for a while, cracking his knuckles. Then he sighed. It's not going to be easy, he said. This place is hemmed in with reeds and rushes and sedge so tall and thick you can't even see the sky. The heat's deadly, not a breath of wind seeps through, the air steamy, poisonous, infested with mosquitoes as large as this finger of mine. As for snakes and other vermin you'd think that mound was their meeting place. I saw one snake that stretched from here to there, a dragon, not a snake. Its tongue flickered out when it saw me, a forked tongue as big as my hand. If we decide to make a home there, we must know that at least three-quarters of us will die, and above all the children . . . At this, nobody said a word. Slowly, one by one they turned away, their heads hanging. Yes, my friends, just as I tell you . . . Such are the bare facts of our existence. Just as I tell you, yes! Like a man turned to stone, his tall figure very straight, Long Ali Riza waited there till nightfall. Then he vanished into the darkness.

It was not till many months later that the villagers heard from him and soon his story spread all through the Anavarza plain. He had built himself a raft of willow branches and on this raft he had transported his wife and six children, his two cows and three heifers, his horse and donkey and chickens to the mound in the middle of the swamp. There he had built himself a hut and a *chardak*, drained a two-*dönüm* patch of land and sown it with watermelon. And what a crop he'd got! Each watermelon reaching up to your knee and almost too good to eat. But, alas, his youngest son, only six years old, had died of the fever.

When they heard the news the villagers crowded up to Akchasaz. Unable to tear themselves away, yet not daring to penetrate through to the mound, they straggled about on the fringe of the swamp, not even noticing the fragrant narcissus in bloom, each one as large as a rose . . . It was Beardless Duran who said at last: 'We have no choice. Earth and sky have shut us out. If it's death we're afraid of, well, we're dying here anyway. I've lost two children wandering round and round like this, while Ali Riza's lost only one. I'm going to him . . .' When he came to the mound Ali Riza greeted him warmly and helped him to build a hut and *chardak* and to open up a field for sowing. Then, in ones and twos the other villagers followed suit and before the month was up they were labouring, tooth and nail, putting all their efforts in common, to clear land for themselves. Two years later they had reclaimed a thousand and two hundred *dönüms* of wonderfully fertile land. But their children died, all of them, and their old people too, succumbing to the lethal marsh-fever. They called their new village Jankurtaran, the Life-Saver. Yet still they had no cemetery and would cross the swamp to bury their dead secretly at their old place in Gözükara.

Yes, my friends, just as I tell you, and a hundred times yes . . . And what is it that those Aghas are claiming? If we hadn't sown rice, they say, and deflected the flow of Savrun River for a whole six months, would the Akchasaz swamp be going dry? Therefore, they say, all that new land is ours by right and no force in the world can wrest it from us. We will evict those villagers, we will kick out Long Ali Riza. Not the Government, the whole world won't prevent us from throwing them all out. Akchasaz shall be ours . . . And what about those other villagers, from Vayvayli? Like famished wolves they've fallen upon the swamp! Damn you, your village boundary's right here, by this ditch. That's where it was before the waters receded. And now?

254

Now you're five kilometres way beyond the ditch! What are you going to do with so much land? As though it was your father's own property! This land belongs to whoever reclaimed it, to us, the Aghas, understand? And if you won't understand, a knock on your heads with a rifle butt will soon bring you to your senses . . . The Kaymakam? Is *he* backing you up? Who cares about a mere Kaymakam! We can have him removed any day and appointed to some god-forsaken town in the east like Kagizman or Shemdinli or Muradiye on the Russian frontier. The generals, yes the Pashas are on our side. Long live the generals! Our generals . . . And you, Rüstemoglu, you bare-footed nobody from Darendé, so you would talk that fool of a Dervish Bey into selling you seven hundred *dönüms* off the edge of Akchasaz and then help yourself to many thousands more next to it? You'll see, you'll see, both of you . . . And where have you sprung from, Altigözoglu? Who are you, what are you? Where did you get those title-deeds from? Damn you, was it your grandfather bought this swamp? What! He bought the Anavarza crags as well? What the hell was he going to do with those crags? Must have been a funny chap, your grandfather! And what about all those factories, eh, Altigözoglu? A ginning factory in Tarsus, a textile plant in Adana, a rice mill in Jeyhan . . . What a grandfather! Now tell us, for the love of God, how did you trump up those title-deeds? A holy secret, is it? Well, we're the ones who dried that swamp up and we have the Government supporting us, and the political parties, and . . . and . . .

Yes, my friends, just as I tell you . . .

Schoolmaster! Schoolmaster Rüstem Bey! You with the clear blue eyes! All the children in this town have passed under your ferule, all these eagle-like Aghas. It's you who put these ingenuous ideas, these tricks into their heads. You came to this town without a stitch on your back. And when the Armenians fled you possessed yourself of the most beautiful of their houses, the one that belonged to Artin Külekyan, and you established your school in the mansion of that other Armenian, Kendirli. To all your friends, to the nomad Turcoman Beys you distributed the rest of the Armenian houses. It is with the sons of these very same Beys that you are plotting now to parcel out

Akchasaz. And how did you acquire the title-deeds to the estate of Hayk Topuzyan, that priceless land, eh, Schoolmaster, tell me that! And that donkey driver, Rahmet Effendi, where would he have got the idea of buying a farm if you hadn't prompted him? Out of the blue you cornered him in the market-place and asked him how much money he had. Weren't you pleased when he replied quite frankly that he had nothing? In one day you made him the owner of the six-thousand-*dönüm* lands deserted by another Armenian, Vartan Begyan. Now why did you do it? What was Rahmet to you? You're not even compatriots. He comes from Malatya and you from Rumeli*. What did you like so much about him? He had a sister, a slim black-eyed beauty, only seventeen. You were forty at the time. What was it passed between you? He's a rich man now, this Rahmet. People address him as Rahmet Agha, and even Bey. He's grabbed a piece of Akchasaz too, two thousand *dönüms*. Don't tell me he reclaimed it! Your daughters are elegant and cultivated. Your sons-in-law come from the oldest Turcoman families . . . And it was you who first thought of draining this swamp, together with Fani Bey. You had collected a great deal of money from the villagers, by force of course, when the First World War broke out. Where did all this money go to, Rüstem Bey? Yes, it's your due, Rüstem Bey, to add as much ground from the swamp as you want to your lands. You're everyone's teacher in this town, everyone's father. If it were not for your wisdom, your foresight, your guidance, who would have thought of settling in the houses left by the Armenians? Who would have troubled to get the title-deeds to their lands, and spending all that money on transfer charges too? Who would have bothered about Abdülhalik Effendi, the land registrar, and scoured the highlands for the rarest, most luscious white-combed honey to offer him? Who could have known, who, that in the years to come this land would be worth its weight in gold? Who but you, Rüstem Bey, who? Whatever you want of Akchasaz, you've deserved it. You've made us all . . .

Yes, my friends, just as I tell you . . . All these trials and tribulations, blood and death, the mosquitoes, the fever, this

---

*Rumeli: the European part of Turkey.

level plain covered from end to end with jilpirti bushes, black-thorns, briars, brakes and forests . . . Who could have imagined . . . Who could have known that those forests, those tangles of bushes would be cleared and the land sown? That those swamps would be drained? Who could have predicted that this town's population would rise from two thousand to ten thousand? And then to thirty thousand and forty thousand? That more and more country people would come crowding ant-like into the town? Who could have known, who, who but our teacher, our father whom God sent us as a guide? Whose eyes but his, piercing the darkness like two headlights, could have seen all that was to come?

Yes, my friends, just as I tell you and a hundred thousand times yes, and even more so!

Like a great eagle he swooped down from the mountains, a wide-winged majestic copper-coloured eagle. His hair was flaming red, bristling like a hedgehog's spines. So was his mustache, and from his nostrils too the red hairs stuck out thick as spines. His powerful chin was forked, his cheekbones salient. He had slanting greenish-grey eyes, a poisonous green, with bloodshot whites. His legs were long, his waist short. From his sloping shoulders hung a pair of very long arms with broad hands. His head was large and the veins of his forehead stuck out like fingers. He would clasp his big hands behind his back right over his buttocks and walk with his body leaning backwards, his head in the air, never looking at the ground he stepped on.

He came from the mountains, but his fame preceded him. Long long before he arrived the whole of the Chukurova had heard of him. He it was who, on the bridge near Hachin, swooped like an eagle in the night on the fleeing Armenians and slashing them all to pieces cast them into the river, then took their sacks of gold and gave them to the Adana Pasha, and went on hounding out Armenians in every nook and cranny all over the Taurus Mountains. He it was who in a cave near Koz, together with his band of followers raped fifteen young girls and made them belly-dance for days on end on large salvers, then declaring that such defiled girls were no good for mankind, killed them all, one by one. He it was who, when encircled by the dread bandit Captain Sultan, threw himself down a precipice deep as ten minarets, yet saved his neck by catching on to the branch of a pine tree, breaking only his rifle. He it was who by sleight of hand managed to bring back from the stables of the Arab and Kurdish Beys of Urfa a hundred and forty-six noble Arab steeds, earning the open-mouthed admiration of all the Chukurova. He it was who sired nineteen sons by his four wives, declaring that the stoutest tree needs its many branches to roar. He it is who when he strikes up a tune will make the whole town ring, who when it takes his fancy will gallop through the market-place shooting to right and left, who once rode up the steps of Government House in Adana on his Arab horse to visit the Vali. He it is who wears accordion boots, a Tripoli sash round his waist, a silver-embroidered cloak over his shoulders, who winds a silk turban about his head and has the pockets of his shalvar-trousers trimmed with gold thread. And when the law obliging everyone to have a family name was promulgated, he it was who for months went taking counsel all over the country to find a family name worthy of his fame and prowess, deciding on one, then discarding it a week later, unable to make up his mind. Who was it ordered the Turks to have a family name? Our great Mustafa Kemal Pasha. And what name did he choose for himself? Atatürk! Father of the Turks . . . Good, very suitable, the proper name for him. Now, something like that would be right. What about Ulutürk, Great Turk? He repeated the name over and over again, then after a week he gave it up. He made it his business to go deep into the reasons for this new law and discovered that in Europe everyone had a family name that they put after their own name. Well, in Turkey too, people had patronymics, but incongruous, un-dignified ones, and furthermore these patronymics were used before the name. Vulgar patronymics like Earless Memet, Hard-Times Hassan, Farting Juma . . . And so on and so forth, all dirty, disgusting names. But compare the family names that came from Europe! Steelstar, Thunderhawk, Falcon-Winged, Lofty-Cloud, Steelclaws, Brightstar, Swordheart . . . He must choose among these, the one that rang best, that suited him most. Süleyman Lionhearted! This was good . . . But three days

later it already sounded jaded, and Pureturkishironstock, which
he tried next, lasted only one day. For three days he wandered
disconsolately about the market-place, still without a family
name. Then he hit on Greatbraveinarms, and was highly
pleased with himself, asking everyone he came across: Isn't it
good? Doesn't it suit me? In the end he got tired of this one too
and fixed upon Aslansoypenché, Noblelionclutch. He'd had his
fill of glorious names and Noblelionclutch was really the best
of all.

Yes, he came from the mountains, swooping like a mighty
eagle upon the town . . . One of the most imposing of the old
Armenian houses, the famous Panosyan mansion, whitewashed, boasting fourteen rooms on two floors, studded with
numberless windows and with a tall turret at the top, had been
allotted to a certain Mustafa Agha from Chatalhüyük. Süleyman
Aslansoypenché knocked at his door one fine day at noon,
accompanied by nine armed men.

'You have to evacuate this house,' he said. 'I'm Panosyan's
heir. Not because I'm his son or anything, but because I'm the
one who sent him packing. That's why all his property, his
house, land, farm, shops, everything has been left to me.' He
produced a sheet of paper from his pocket. 'And here's the
proof.'

Mustafa Agha did not even wait to examine the document.
'Just allow me a few minutes, Süleyman Agha,' he said and
called to his wife. 'Lady, quick, take the children. We're going
back to the village. Didn't I tell you that no good would come
of settling in this Armenian house? Quick now . . . We'll send
for our things later.'

And so Süleyman Aslansoypenché established residence in
Panosyan's mansion and took possession of his whole estate. He
had all the valid documents drawn up to show for it too. Yes,
by the strength of his fist, by his powerful wits he won his way.
Such lions, such zealous patriots deserve not just Panosyan's
estate but every stick and stone in the Chukurova. The name
of his village has to be changed too. Köstüköy . . . Mole Village!
Nothing better than wild rats village! Is that a name worthy of
the noble Turkish fatherland? From now on it shall be named
Ishiklar, Village of the Lights. Even this falls short for a village

that has produced such a hero. But he's modest, our Aslansoy-penché Agha, he could have called it Rising Sun, but he didn't. His nineteen sons he named after the famous leaders of the day, the first-born Kemal, the second Ismet, the third Fevzi, the fourth Kazim, and so on . . . Whatever he did was well done. He joined the People's Party and rose to be president of the local branch. Then when the Democrat Party's star began to rise he made it his business to introduce the leaders, Celal Bayar and Adnan Menderes to the town. He was the first to sacrifice a camel at Menderes's election as Prime Minister, and six valuable bulls all along his path when he visited Adana. Yes, whatever he did was well done, but for one thing. How did his son evade punishment when he killed Hassan Kimsesiz with seven shots in broad daylight in the middle of the market-place? Who was it drove the Chief Justice Hurshit Bey to die of shame? Who hounded the judge Mazlum Bey out of the town and had him shot dead right inside the Criminal Court at Antep? Yes, whatever he does is well done, but . . . Was it worthy of him to go to the Chief Justice, saying: This is my son's first hunt? Don't sentence him or he'll turn into a timorous milksop, of no use to his country at all . . . What harm would it have done the lad to spend a couple of days in prison? For that's what it would have amounted to, only a couple of days . . . Was it right to trifle with the honour of a great Court of Justice for just a couple of days? And that's not all. What about the man his second son killed? For years afterwards the judges who acquitted him could not lift their heads and look anyone in the face. And the Public Prosecutor, Izzettin Fahrettin Tugsalur, a great Government official, was it right to go bribing him in the market-place in full view of all the town, branding him with venality for ever?

Let him take as much land from Akchasaz swamp as he wants, let him . . . And if he can lay hands on the estates of Mustafa Akyollu and Dervish Sarioglu, all the better . . . Have them exiled? Certainly, now he's got a chance. After all, he has nineteen sons to think of and the lands of those estates will be only just enough for them. But he can't draw a gun at those two Beys. Why? Because they've got guns as well . . . He can't set the Government at them. Why? Because they've got their men in the Government too. Well, now's his great chance. See how he'll destroy their houses, Aslansoypenché, how he'll raze them to the ground . . .

Yes, like a copper-coloured eagle he descended from the mountains into the plain . . . And made of Panosyan's estate his home, that Panosyan whom he had forced into exile, put well out of the way, killed perhaps . . . And many other undertakings he was engaged in . . . Now he is founding a factory . . .

Yes, my friends, just as I tell you and a hundred thousand times yes, and even more so! Such are the barc facts of our existence . . . Akchasaz swamp is a bowl of honey, the Aghas and villagers so many bees and flies that have set upon it . . . To the spoil, to the loot . . . Quickly, grab as much as you can . . . Woe to the underdog . . . All for the strong . . .

These are the people of the Chayanli tribe that in the old days used to number a thousand tents, perhaps two thousand. From Khorassan they came, from the land of Harzem* between two great rivers, moving on and on for years over the boundless limitless expanse of the steppes. And now they do not even know from which line of the Turcomans they stem. They have seen the destruction of Harzem, razed to the ground by those slant-eyed people who came swarming upon the land on their tiny horses, sweeping everything before them like a hurricane, casting them all, young and old, up hill and down vale, through great deserts, from land to land. They were among those who fought at Jaber Fort.** Diyarbekir town they laid siege to for one whole winter, pitching their tents around its walls, a teeming horde of Turcomans. But the gates of the town were not opened to them, its bastions did not fall, and at the approach of spring they retired into the hills, leaving behind only the trace of their hearths, black patches over the plain, and the holes bored by their tent poles. And also the folds of their sheep and cattle, a brighter green on the green of the plain. They were also

---

*Harzem: an ancient region in Turkestan, which incorporated the cities of Samarkand and Bukhara.
**Jaber Fort: an old fortress in Syria.

present at the sieges of Malatya and Kayseri, and in the course of the Baba Ishak* uprisings they lost many lives, almost half of them were slaughtered. Their foes made no distinction of old or young, women or children. All the ancient Turcoman traditions of human mercy were trampled underfoot in this cruel battle. The followers of Baba Ishak had only their naked swords to fight with and they were vanquished, mown down like grass, but this, the worst defeat in their history, was also the first revolt of the Turcomans against their Beys, and for long years, like a great epic, like a sacred trust, they kept alive the memory of Baba Ishak and his holy war, and rose up again and again to fight for the way he had shown them.

This same Chayanli tribe, now reduced to some hundred and fifty tents, summering in the highlands of the Taurus, wintering in the Chukurova plain, were in the end forcibly settled by the Ottomans on the banks of the Savrun where the river makes a deeply eddying bend. They formed a village as others of the tribe who had broken away had done in various parts of Anatolia, and learned to live in the heat of the Chukurova, to sow and reap, these people who for centuries had roamed the steppes freely with their flocks. Their names passed into the Government records, and all their fears at being settled were justified. Impossible taxes were imposed on them. They were enrolled in the army for an unspecified number of years, five, ten, sometimes fifteen years. Not easily could a soldier return to his village and many were the brides and betrothed who grew old with waiting. 'Go not to the Yemen desert,' they mourned, 'to be lost in its churning sands . . . Send me a letter, oh my brother, set your sister's mind at rest . . .' The Yemen desert was ever in their thoughts, their dear ones gone never to return, the desert sands their only grave. 'And maybe rotting in the sun . . . And ants a-gnawing his dear eyes . . . Go not to the Yemen, to the Yemen where the poor untrained soldier stands lost and crazed with dread . . .' Most of the men were deserters. What else could they do? To go to the Yemen wars meant certain

---

*Baba Ishak: a thirteenth-century Turcoman Sheikh who led a series of revolts against the Seljukide empire. These uprisings went on long after he was killed.

death. For the Turcoman women, war or conscription spelled the Yemen desert and even when the men were drafted to Istanbul or Thrace, the Balkans or the snow-capped mountains of the east, their songs and laments for the departed were all on that accursed land of Yemen . . .

But the worst had still to come. Some ten years before the great mobilization the gendarmes surrounded the village one night towards dawn and took away all the male population from seven to seventy. The fugitives in the mountains were caught as well. Not a single man was left in Chayanli village. A few days later a stranger appeared, a tall broad-shouldered handsome young man . . . His name was Haji. He began by lending a hand here and there, helping one woman to plough her field and another to gather the harvest, tending to the sick and the maimed and befriending the lonely. He could recite the Koran beautifully for the dead and the sick, as well as on Fridays and on ceremonial occasions. The fervour of his voice would make many a woman cry . . . Then one day the grievous news was spread that all those who had gone to the Yemen had died. Lists of the dead had been posted in the town. A storm of lamentation swept the village. The women never thought to go and check. Such news, such lists had ever been their accustomed lot . . . Not many days later, even before the period of mourning was over, it was learnt that Haji had quietly taken to wife the beautiful young widow, Fatmali. He had performed the ceremony himself, and after all why not? Wasn't he an Imam? Hadn't he told them that the Government had dispensed him from military service because of this? And an Imam has the right to marry himself where there is no other Imam to do so . . . Anyway, Fatmali was happy and so was Haji. So was everyone else because Haji, though married, continued to help the other women in their daily tasks. He was a father to the whole village.

At the time of the settlement every family had been allotted some land and these lands had been registered with title-deeds . . . The minute he was married, Haji rushed Fatmali to the town and had all her land transferred in his name. And only a few days afterwards he pronounced his divorce by repeating to her three times the ritual formula, 'I repudiate you'. Fatmali was astounded, but there was nothing she could do about it, especially as not many days passed before Haji married again. His new wife's land too he proceeded to register in his name and then promptly divorced her. After the fourth wife the village women got the idea and decided to try their luck. That is how in the space of five years Haji had married and divorced every single Chayanli woman and many from the outlying villages too. Some there were who could not bear to be put away. The young widow Hürü threw herself into the swamp and died for the love of Haji. And Zala who was only seventeen was found hanging on the plane tree near the river. Only one of his wives remained married to him for a full year and a half, the daughter of the Bey of Sumbas, a large strapping girl who, every time Haji attempted to pronounce the ritual words of divorce, interrupted him threateningly: 'Careful, Haji, or I'm going to kill you . . .' In the end it was she who left him.

Yes, that Haji is this very same Haji Kurtboga who after the proclamation of the Republic grew to power, entered the People's Party, was elected to the Provincial Council and even served as mayor of the town for a few years. He was the intimate friend of the Governor, the Prosecutor-General, the judges, the commandant of the gendarmerie and the Kaymakam. All these officials were kept well provided with milk and butter, yogurt, meat, bulgur, honey, cream and other dainties by Haji Kurtboga, and as he was a respected leader of the party such gifts from him could not be regarded as bribes . . . And one day, at the summit of power and sure of his high repute with the authorities, he decided to evict from Chayanli village all his former wives, who in the meantime had been reduced to dire poverty, and their children too. How many were his, he himself did not know . . . Haji had suffered poverty, great poverty, and for that reason poverty disgusted him. It drove him mad to see a person in rags. Of what use were paupers in this world? What difference did it make if they lived or died? Better kill them off, all of them and leave this noble fatherland to the well-to-do. Yes, Haji had known poverty, dire poverty, and for that reason he hated the sight of it . . .

First, he dispatched the village watchman, Dursun, to cry his orders. Dursun was over seventy, the only man to have returned from the Yemen wars to tell of how all the rest had been decimated like flies in the desert sands.

'Hark ye, villagers,' he went calling through the village in his falsetto girl's voice. 'Hark ye, women, attend to my words and don't say you haven't heard! Everyone is to get out of this village, our Agha's village, within three days . . . Government's orders! You can go wherever you like . . . No kicking and whimpering. There's a squad of gendarmes posted here already, waiting for a sign from our Agha to kill you all. Hark ye, women, don't say you haven't heard!'

A shrill clamour broke out. The women's screams rose to the skies as they all rushed to the Agha's house. 'Where shall we go? Where, where? What are we to do?' they wept. For three days they begged and cried. Then they fell silent and just stood there like so many stones before the Agha's gate. The sight of this ragged, miserable crowd was too much for Haji Kurtboga. 'Gendarmes,' he shouted, 'throw these creatures out of my lands, these enemies of the people who want to destroy this last Turkish state, our fatherland!'

And the gendarme commander gave the order: 'Fix your bayonets!'

With cries of terror Haji Kurtboga's former wives and children fled before the onslaught. Those the gendarmes could smite with their bayonets they threw on to the dung-heaped village square. By evening they had bayoneted and wounded at least half of them, and all through the night moans rose from the huts, from beneath the tall plane trees and from outside the village. At dawn the battle between the women and the gendarmes started again. One elderly gendarme suddenly placed his Mauser rifle upside down, the mouth against his brow, and pressing the trigger with his right foot blew out his own brains. At nightfall a truce was called and the gendarmes went to the Agha's house to be treated to roast lamb that had been cooked especially for them. That night the few moans to be heard at all came from outside the village.

Morning came, may happy mornings dawn on us all, and the gendarmes launched one last attack on the remnants of women still clustering on the outskirts of the village. Their bayonets pierced and struck. Haji Kurtboga clutched at the commandant's hands. 'I can't bear it!' he cried. 'I can't bear all this screaming and moaning. It's too much, too much, what I've had to suffer at the hands of these enemies of the fatherland! Look, Commandant, look how they're still putting up a stand! Defying the army, that's what it is, for gendarmes are every bit a part of the army, and the best at that! They're revolting against our great army, these women! Imagine if their men had been here too, if they'd come back from the Yemen! There's trouble for you, there's a real uprising in good and due form . . . No, no, I can't bear it! It goes against the grain to see a group of women keeping the great Turkish army at bay . . .'

By noon the cries had died down. That evening Kurtboga held a drinking bout for the commandant, and when they woke up the next morning there was not a sound in the village. Arm in arm they inspected the whole place like two victorious generals. The doors were open and only a few frightened dogs and cats could be seen crouching inside the huts among the disarray of old household items. There were traces of blood everywhere.

Yes, that Haji Agha is this very same Haji Kurtboga we see now . . . And he bears a violent grudge against Dervish Bey. 'Why you old whoremonger, was it for you to champion those women? Aren't they all former wives of mine? These lands are mine by right, by the sweat of my brow. You throw your share-croppers out of your land when you want to, don't you? Well, I've thrown out of my village this lot of good-for-nothing women. After all my farm's not a poorhouse! Why don't you stop meddling in my affairs, man? What harm have I ever done you? But I'll get even with you sooner or later. I'll teach you to stir up my old wives against me . . . What's it to you if they're dying of want or what not? Must you go and bother a great Vali about this, wretched man? Aah, not even the Republic has been able to root out such bloodthirsty feudal lords as you . . . But you just wait, we'll root you out, we Aghas will! Why, just to spite us you go and sell some of your best land to that Rüste-moglu, that nobody from Darendé! And right on the edge of Akchasaz too, with my own land bordering it on the other side! Barring my access to the swamp, that's what you've done, when I begged you for only a few *dönüms*, a narrow passage to this land that's worth its weight in gold, this land that perfect

strangers are splitting up between them . . . Well, you just wait
. . . You've fallen into my hands. There's no escape for you . . .'

They sat around in the town club, talking of this and that until
sundown.

'Well it's time,' Haji Kurtboga said. 'Have you got enough of
the ready? It mustn't be a paltry sum. First of all I'm concerned.
And second, it's no small-fry Kaymakam we have to deal with,
but an eminent Prosecutor-General of the Criminal Court. And
no common man either, but the grandson of a prestigious nine-
plumed Grand Vizir.'

'God forbid,' Süleyman Aslansoypenché said. 'Of course it'll
be worthy of the scion of a Grand Vizir!'

'Yes indeed, it should be,' Schoolmaster Rüstem Bey said. He
had plastered his hair very slickly about his large face and his
brown trousers with red pin-stripes were immaculately pressed.
'But I don't know anything about it.'

'Neither do I,' Mahir Bey said. 'Süleyman Agha was going to
see to it.'

'With God's help,' Süleyman Aslansoypenché said, 'and your
good services, I've seen to everything. Don't you worry. I'll
slip it into his pocket in a twinkling.'

They all rose. Haji Kurtboga went in front followed by
Süleyman Aslansoypenché, then Mahir Kabakchioglu, and
lastly, with slow dignified steps, came Rüstem Bey. Everyone in
the club rose to see them off. At the door, Kurtboga stopped and
stood aside. 'I won't take a step out before my master, the
master of us all,' he said. 'Our master who brought us all up,
who taught all the young people in this town.' He turned to the
company and put his hand on his breast. 'We can deny all
claims of father and mother, even of country, but never can we
deny the claim our master has on us!'

'Never, never!' they chorused.

Rüstem Bey blushed crimson. 'Not at all, not at all,' he
murmured. 'I've done nothing, nothing but my duty . . . A man's
duty is a sacred call . . .'

Kurtboga overrode his feeble protests. 'If it weren't for our
master,' he said striking a pose, his head thrown back, his
mustache twitching, 'if it weren't for him, we would all have

been bandits in the mountains. We ... All of us ... He it is who taught us the human virtues of this world. Without him we'd have gone through life like dumb fools.' He raised his hand from his breast and waved it towards Rüstem Bey: 'After you, my master.'

The Schoolmaster, his ears burning, proceeded to pass under the extended arm and together they got into the car, with again the same ceremony and a few well-placed words by Kurtboga. As soon as the car had started Kurtboga leaned over to Rüstem Bey's ear. 'That was well said, wasn't it, master?' he inquired. 'Let them understand, those rascals, who's who in this world. I did it on purpose so they'd know once and for all that there's no one greater in this land than our master.'

'Thank you, thank you,' Rüstem Bey kept repeating with diffident dignity.

The Prosecutor-General greeted them at the door of his house. He was in high good humour, but a little anxious too. 'Come in, come in, welcome, welcome ...' He led the way up a creaking flight of stairs and ushered them into one of the large rooms of the old Armenian mansion. A young girl appeared at once with coffee in gold-sheathed cups, while the Prosecutor went round offering cigarettes.

'Come and sit down, Fahrettin Bey, brother,' Haji Kurtboga said. 'You know why we're here and the important request we've come to make to you. And we know of your high ancestry, dating back to ... Way back to ...' He looked at the others. No one proffered a word. 'Your noble ancestry, dating back to ...' Again he found nothing. 'Dating back to who knows when.'

'Right back to the Pashas of Evrenoz,' Mahir Bey rectified.

Izzettin Fahrettin Bey felt slightly ashamed. 'Thank you, Agha,' he said.

Kurtboga slapped the Prosecutor's knee with a resounding whack. 'No need to thank me,' he said. 'The whole world knows of your aristocratic origins. Only Allah will have no ups and downs ... And when a diamond falls to the ground it doesn't lose its value for that ...' He looked round proudly for approval.

'It doesn't. It can't,' Süleyman Aslansoypenché concurred. 'And the noble man strays not from the right path ...'

Haji Agha shot him a black look. He did not like being

interrupted. 'Noble men,' he pursued, 'are the safeguard of this country . . .' While he was speaking Süleyman Agha drew the Prosecutor's attention to the envelope he was holding and smilingly slipped it into his pocket. '. . . And I trust you as a brother, you the noble descendant of Grand Vizirs . . . You know what we've come to you about. Those Beys are turning out to be a nuisance for the whole countryside. At this rate they'll take us back to the age of cavemen, killing each other all the time. And if it was only each other they killed that wouldn't be so bad, on the contrary! They'd be wiped out all the more quickly. But they also incite our pure innocent brave young men to kill each other. This plain's very poor, and as you well know, a man will kill for just five hundred liras, and for three thousand he'll risk a twenty-year sentence. These Beys own limitless lands because their fathers just rode and said, the land my horse steps on is mine, and indeed they appropriated the whole of the Chukurova plain. They're very rich too, and maintain gunmen. This has gone on for a hundred, two hundred years. It's up to you, Prosecutor, to put an end to all their killing. Just think, Fahrettin Bey, brother, just figure out how many potential soldiers are exterminated by those monsters! At this rate if there's a war we risk being defeated by Syria or Greece, or even our old territory of Lebanon . . . Isn't that so, Schoolmaster?'

Rüstem Bey, who had let his thoughts wander, jumped. 'Yes, yes yes,' he said, 'even our old territory of Lebanon. We . . .'

'Wait, master, I haven't yet finished. You'll speak afterwards. Fahrettin Bey, brother, you've got to have those two nuisances, Dervish Sarioglu and Mustafa Akyollu, exiled from this town to some place five hundred, a thousand miles away. The father-land expects this of you. They'll have to sell their lands and property and go to where they've been ordered. And then I'll go to Ankara and have you promoted to the High Court there. That's a promise! Word of honour! My word . . .' He rose and sat down and rose again. 'Have I ever been known not to keep my word, tell me?'

Izzettin Fahrettin rose too and put his hand on his breast. 'God forbid,' he said and sat down with great dignity.

'Well then, master, you can go on from here. Tell him about that law and how we see the problem.'

Rüstem Bey was well prepared. He spoke calmly, almost monotonously, without once raising his voice. 'According to Clause 3236 of the penal code those who kill each other because of a blood feud and make a custom of this, may be exiled to a place not less than five hundred kilometres away, provided the Prosecutor-General brings a charge and the Criminal Court passes the sentence. What we're asking of you is that you should do everything in your power to secure the banishment from this district of Dervish Sarioglu and Mustafa Akyollu, together with their families and all their relatives. Our town is an old centre of blood feuds and therefore comes under the scope of this law, together with a few more districts and provinces in the rest of Turkey. This we consider a blot on us all, a shame for us and for future generations. For that reason, Mr Prosecutor, we must, without wasting time, remove this cancer. We must get these two families out of here before more of our young people fall victim to their machinations . . . That's all I've got to say.'

The Prosecutor drew nearer. He frowned. 'As a man of the law, I could possibly ask that these two families be banished to other provinces. For instance, Kars . . .'

'Kars is good,' Süleyman Agha shouted.

'Very good,' Haji Agha approved. 'The other end of the earth. They could never come back.'

'Or, for instance, Edirne . . .'

'That's good too,' Süleyman Agha said. 'As far from here as hell . . .'

'Yes, gentlemen, I can do that. But the law gives me only the right to instigate proceedings. The rest is in the hands of the judges. I can get the dossier ready whenever you like and present it to the Court.'

'At once!' Haji Kurtboga said.

'All right. I've got so many documents on those two families, accumulated over the last fifty years . . . The Court would only have to glance at them to bring in a verdict of exile. Only, you know the Chief Judge of the Criminal Court, Tahsin Bey . . . He's not one to be moved by words or even bullets.'

'But it's quite legal,' Rüstem Bey said. 'The Chief Judge has no choice.'

'And what about the other two members of the Court?' Mahir

270

Bey said suddenly. 'If they're for us what can Tahsin Bey do?'

'Nothing, of course,' Rüstem Bey said.

'Tevfik Bey's our man. He'll do as we say.'

'Yes, but the other member-judge, Osman Alniachik, always casts his vote with the Chief Judge.'

'We'll see about that,' Süleyman Agha said angrily. 'Just let him defy us . . .'

'I'll have the dossier ready within a week,' the Prosecutor said, 'and hand it over myself to the Court. As a tribute to your magnanimity . . . But I would advise you not to neglect Tahsin Bey. The whole matter rests in his hands . . .'

'That's easy,' Haji Kurtboga said. 'If he won't see reason, by God he'll find himself in Kars too before he knows it!'

'With Allah's help,' Süleyman Agha said, 'and our great party, our Government . . . Ankara has never refused us anything.'

'Our Ankara,' Mahir Kabakchioglu said with a trace of irony in his voice.

35

The shutters of the shops were being thrown open with a loud clatter, one after the other, sometimes four or five at a time. It was not yet sunrise. Even before the east began to pale the baker had filled his oven with brushwood. It was a glowing mass of embers now and the odour of freshly-baked bread pervaded the market, warm, appetizing, delicious. The baker was a bandy-legged, wall-eyed man who wore his wide-vizored cap well down over his peering eyes. Boisterous, unrestrained in joy or grief, at home with children and adults alike, he was much loved in the town. With a last proud look at the well-browned loaves which had burnt his hands as he disposed them neatly on the counter and the surrounding shelves, he went out for a turn in the market as was his habit each day, before starting to serve his first customers. But this morning was different. The baker was seething and muttering oaths and imprecations under his breath. Sometimes his voice rose and was heard all over the market, ripping out curses at somebody he did not openly name.

The clatter of shutters had stopped now and the first rays of the sun shone over the market. Far in the distance, behind the unbroken line of pale blue hills that levelled out and merged into the greyish sky, Mount Düldül reared up in all its majesty, bathed in sunlight, as though it had just stepped from the hills into the plain, so clear it seemed one had only to stretch one's hand to touch it, its valleys and rocks and shadows clearly etched, very blue in places, reddish in others, sometimes very white. Mount Düldül is a feature inseparable from the plain. There it stands, snow-capped even in the summer, cool, gleaming with a copper glow in the afternoon when the south wind rises and sweeps the snow-white billowing clouds on to it and the clouds cast dark shadows over its flanks and swell out broader and broader, translucent over the mountain . . . But after mid-August Mount Düldül is bare, denuded, cloudless, the colour of an unfledged swallow.

The market was paved with large cobblestones, a man's head in size, stones that had been polished smooth through centuries of being rolled and dragged along the bottom of the stream. Perhaps he was tall and pleasant-faced, perhaps a little hunch-backed, with long fingers, but surely he had magic hands, the master-craftsman who thought of using these cobbles and weaving them with such infinite love and taste into the streets and sidewalks of the market, and beyond doubt, his eyes were black and melancholy and he would murmur a song as he disposed the white stones side by side, throwing in a red one here or a blue one there, and a pale mauve or a green one, making floral designs out of them, set in a white background. He laughed warmly, showing his pearly-white teeth, but surely also he was capable of furious anger if his work was spoilt.

But this too is certain, nobody in the town remembers him, no one remembers when he decorated this street, these sidewalks. If this master-craftsman had lived long, if he had trained apprentices to grow into masters like himself, good-natured yet mighty in anger, whole-hearted in laughter, then the market-places and squares and streets of all the towns would have been graced with stones like these, polished smooth, decorated with blue and red and moss-green. Too beautiful to step on. He would have found a way, this master-craftsman, of paving at least one more street like this with large milk-white cobbles, flecked with many colours, of wheedling the funds out of those vulgar, upstart mayors and out of the town's new-rich, those apes, no longer human, who are drowning the whole world and sky in ugly rigid cement, building colourless, featureless towns, stark warrens of bloodshed and death, those callous creatures who call themselves men and have forgotten how to feel, to think, to weep and laugh, who are stirred by nothing, who do not sing or read or write, or listen to music or even whistle a tune, whose sole aim is to pretend that they are something other than they are, denying their origins, hating all that is not concerned with themselves or their children. Yes, he would have found a way, I'd wager my life on it, even if he had to pay the cost himself. But he is dead and gone, this master-craftsman with the magic hands and he had no apprentices. And for this reason these towns are now dead . . . Stinking . . . Reptilian.

Cement-like. Hard. Apish . . . Graceless . . . Inhabited by money-grubbers who spend their whole lives squabbling with each other, gouging each other's eyes out, who deal destruction to all that spells beauty and hope, who corrupt and lie and kill, who brag endlessly and drink all night long in filthy restaurants and bully poor, forlorn, weary, nightclub girls, who are unfaithful to their wives and sweethearts, who spend their time gambling, and their wives and children as well . . . Those new-rich town Aghas, frenzied, alienated . . .

How can we expect them to cherish the memory of this master-craftsman, to honour his apprentices, to keep and safeguard and not to kill what is individual and talented and beautiful? This man who in all humility when he was told he had to have a family name, that it was the law, chose not a grandiose name such as Lionheartedturk, but Stonecutter, for, he said, we have always been stonecutters from father to son. Only for this they would have killed him, and perhaps they did kill him, these ferocious sanguinary creatures, these slimy maniac town Aghas, as they are killing and destroying everything human, everything beautiful around them. Nothing will stop them, not even the will of the people. They will kill music and love, laughter and tears, they will kill the joy of the heart, until only their money is left, and also the ugly ten-storey block buildings, as monstrous as themselves, that they have erected beside the town's lovely little stream. They will kill all that is human . . . They will tear out these stones in the market-place, this work of love by the forgotten master . . .

A fountain flowed at one end of the market-place and all around it rose tall plane trees, their wide-spreading branches shedding a generous shadow. The sidewalks were strewn with watermelon rinds alive with honey-bees and wasps. Slim, long-waisted, delicate-blue damsel-flies flitted very low, alighting on the white cobblestones, unalarmed by passers-by. From the plane trees came the loud, incessant, strident sound of crickets, lulled only by the noonday heat, and the pandemonium of twittering birds.

These plane trees too will be cut down, and by that lousy ignorant braggart, that aping toadeater son of Haji Kurtboga's, he will do it during his term as mayor before he becomes a

274

deputy. Yes indeed, he will have them felled, all of them . . .

A damsel-fly alighted on the baker's shoulder and swayed there like a long blue feather. On the further side of a plane tree, beside the stream, the wheelwright was hammering away. He grasped the red-hot iron with a huge pair of tongs and plunged it into the water that sizzled and steamed. He was old, the wheelwright, bald and ruddy-complexioned, with a long white beard and a thoughtful deeply-wrinkled face. His red waistband was carefully bound, as always, catching the eye from afar.

'It's happened,' the baker said. 'They've done it, as they said they would. Didn't I tell you, you old emigrant, that they would banish the Beys? The Prosecutor's agreed.'

'Really?' the wheelwright exclaimed, the iron still sizzling and steaming in the water. 'Who told you this?'

'Who? Everybody's talking about it.'

The wheelwright lifted his iron out of the water and laid it beside the anvil. All about him, strewn over the ashes and half-calcinated coals, were rusty frames and bolts, broken pieces of wheels, axles, headgears, harnesses, bellows, and a couple of derelict phaetons. Cleaving through a large heap of ashes was a burst of green with a prickly mauve flower in bloom.

'This town has really gone to the dogs now,' the wheelwright said, thrusting his hands into his waistband. 'We said Motherland and came here. And saw what! . . . A barbarous Motherland . . . Barbarian Aghas. It was not so in the old land . . . Here, everyone kills each other. All the time. They do nothing else. No work, nothing. They draw their pistols and bang bang bang. They don't fire in the air, nor at your feet, but shoot straight at your eyes! Our Motherland is very barbarous. Let them kill, let them banish . . . You bake bread, hot and crusty. Do not meddle. Or get killed, bang bang.' He picked up the iron, shoved it into the furnace and swung at the bellows.

'Man,' the baker cried, 'are you mad? They're sending our Beys into exile. We'll be left at the mercy of those new-rich Aghas. They'll make slaves of us all. What d'you mean, not meddle, bang bang!'

'They only understand, bang bang . . . Bang bang,' the wheelwright retorted. He drew the iron from the fire and placing it on the anvil began to hammer away. Sparks leaped up all around him and the sound of hammering echoed through the town. 'If I had known that this Motherland was so barbarous . . .'

The hunchbacked town-crier came rushing up. 'Have you heard?' he said. He was sobbing, dry, racking sobs. His tiny figure seemed to have shrunk and his hump stuck out more than ever. 'That low-down wretch . . . That scoundrel of a Kurtboga! I'm going to send telegrams to Ismet Pasha and Fevzi Pasha at once, and denounce him. I'll tell how he murdered his eighty wives and buried them all in the Akchasaz swamp. What if it *was* long ago? Is there anybody in this town who doesn't know? And what shall I do now? For the past twenty years I've lived on the flour Dervish Bey sends me from his mill and the butter from Mustafa Bey's farm. If I have to rely on the pittance I get here . . . Why, each time Dervish Bey comes to town he puts twenty-five lira into my pocket, and what do I do to earn it? Only run and hold his horse and take it to the *han**. And Mustafa Bey? Every *Kurban Bayram*** he sends a whole sheep to my house. And what do I do for him? Nothing but curse his enemies in public once in a while, that's all . . . No, no, I've got to denounce him . . .' His voice rose. 'How he killed his eighty wives . . .'

'Don't be crazy, town-crier,' the baker interrupted him apprehensively. 'Who said he killed his wives? He just had them thrown out and bayoneted by the gendarmes. Be quiet. Don't shout or you'll get us into trouble.'

'I don't care,' the other cried louder than ever. 'Just let them banish our Beys and I'll show them.' And he went from shop to shop repeating the same stories even more loudly and getting angrier every minute.

'Be quiet, brother!' the carpenter cautioned him, then the draper and shoemaker too. 'There's nothing those Aghas would stop at. Be quiet! You're risking your life.'

'What's my life worth anyway if the Beys go? I'll die of hunger! Tell me, you people, just tell me, has there ever been a town-crier like me, with a voice like King David's that would move a heart of stone, and make a Moslem of a confirmed

Han: an inn.
**Kurban Bayram:* famous Moslem feast.

unbeliever when chanting the *ezan*?* What's going to become of me? Two children I have studying in the high schools of Adana, so they should be educated people and not like me, dependent on Beys and Aghas. Tell me, saddlemaker, tell me, what's going to become of me?'

The saddlery faced some old Armenian ruin, alive with hundreds of swift-flitting swallows and shrill-voiced kestrels only slightly larger than the swallows, grey with black-tipped wings. A family of kestrels had nested in the roof of the saddler's tumble-down shop. He loved these little birds of prey.

'You're right, town-crier. Perfectly right. It'll be the end of this town if our Beys are exiled. We'll all be left at the mercy of the upstart Aghas, those money-grubbers for whom a man is worth nothing, who don't even ride any more . . .'

The saddler's grandfather had come from Marash. He made saddles for the Chukurova Beys, Turcoman saddles all worked in silver and gold, and nielloed Circassian ones too. One of his saddles still hung on a worm-eaten blackened board on the wall, shining like a bright star, and every morning the saddler would kneel beneath it and pray. And so it should be for every beautiful craft that has had its time, its last master should worship before the dying art. They are going, the saddler thought, the last of the Beys, who valued noble horses and silver-worked saddles and harnesses. Only those two are left, only those two . . . After they are gone I must hang up this knife, this hone, this needle, there beside that starry saddle and to my dying day worship them and return thanks to all those who in the past added beauty and grace to this world.

Beads of sweat trembled on the saddler's wide furrowed brow and his grey drooping mustache, his long neck, his hide-stained powerful gnarled hands sweated too. He seemed to be waking from a dream. 'They say,' he said, 'the whole matter rests with the Big Judge.'

'Yes,' the town-crier said. 'And he's married into the Savuran family who hate our Beys.'

'But I trust him,' the saddler rejoined. 'What can have got into those buggers, damn it? If the Beys kill, it's each other they

---

*Ezan: Moslem call to prayer.

kill, and they've been doing it for the past two hundred years. It's nobody's business but their own.'

'It's because of Akchasaz drying up,' the hunchback said. 'The Beys' farmland borders almost half the swamp. If they're exiled, the new Aghas can stake a claim to the reclaimed land and divide their present lands between themselves too . . . But me, what am I to do, what?' Two big tears welled in his eyes and he crumpled up on to the stool by the workbench.

'The last of our Beys . . .' the saddler sighed. 'Are they mad? Why don't they just end this feud?'

'They can't,' the town-crier said straightening himself up sharply. 'It's the old tradition. If a Bey has a feud he must carry it on to the bitter end. A man can't live without honour.'

'That's true,' the saddler said. 'You're quite right, brother.' He fell silent, lost in a dream, seeing the slim, keen-eared, noble horses of old brought over from Urfa and Arabia, too lovely to gaze upon as they streaked over the land, and the short-legged, broad-flanked crossbreed, that has graced the Chukurova since time out of mind, swift as the wind, wise as a human being, a friend to man. This saddle would remain there, shining on the wall, so long as the saddler lived, like a lush garden opening into Paradise, full of light and colour, and every morning before dawn, his right knee touching the ground, his right hand on his heart, he would pray for the soul of his ancestors who had plied this same craft with exquisite skill for more than a thousand years. And when he was dead his good-for-nothing son, riddled with gambling or drinking debts, would sell it to some young peasant who still retained a feeling for beauty in his breast or perhaps who had a mother who still wove colourful *kilims*. 'Take it,' he would say, poking it with his foot. 'It's yours for only fifty liras. Don't hesitate. It belonged to my saddler father. If he'd been alive he wouldn't have parted with it for five thousand liras. Not for ten thousand!'

How they would crowd before the saddlery, the Beys in those days, how they would beg the saddler and press him with pouches and pouches of gold coins . . . Whose horse was the most handsome? For him the saddler would fashion his most beautiful saddles and harnesses.

'Look, Master, look! This one's just come from Aleppo. Look,

278

d'you like him?'

'Yes, yes, I like him.'

'Then you'll make the trappings, won't you? In three months . . .'

'Not before six months.'

'But, Master . . . Master, didn't you like my horse?'

'He's a good horse, but I've a lot of work. If he wasn't such a handsome beast you wouldn't have got your saddle for another year yet.'

'Master, four months . . .'

'Impossible.'

'I'll give you as much gold as you wish. Please, Master . . . Five months. Can't you make it in five months? Come, Master, say yes . . .'

'All right then. Just for the sake of this lovely black horse . . . May he bring you luck.'

Gone are those mettlesome steeds that would gallop across the Chukurova plain, gone their proud riders, the last of them to be banished now by their former farmhands . . . Where are they, where, the Beys of Dulkadiroglu, Beyazit, Payaslioglu, Janpolat, Kozanoglu, Chapanoglu, Küchükalioglu, Jadioglu, Menemenjioglu, Mursaloglu? . . . What has become of all those who rode the horse, who girded the sword? Of the gazelles and tawny-eyed lions of the desert? . . . Their children are left, their children . . . Each one another Haji Kurtboga! Enemies of horses and friendship and the old tribal traditions, money-grubbers now like the upstart Aghas, worse than usurers . . . Lending money on interest, borrowing on interest, whoring, oppressing the poor . . .

The town-crier rose, chastened now, and walked out of the saddlery. The usurer was just opening his shop. He was a tall man and the first things that struck you in his bulky ungainly frame were the thick pendant horse-like lower lip and the bovine stare of his eyes. His neck was long and stiff as a pillar. At school he had been too dumb to learn even the alphabet and it was only much later, during his military service, that the rudiments of reading and writing were beaten into him. After serving his term he asked to stay on in the army and was assigned, with the rank of corporal, as head of a gendarmerie post in a mountain village of eastern Anatolia. His parents were extremely poor and he wanted nothing to do with them, so that his mother was left to die of starvation among strangers in the Chukurova. He remained only five years at his post, but that was more than enough to make his fortune, and when he moved to this Chukurova town he opened shop and began to buy and sell grain. He would boast endlessly of his exploits as a gendarme, of the beatings he had administered to the villagers, of how he would make them carry him on his back, men and women, from place to place, and how they would all press him with bribes, selling their only sheep or goat or hen, their *kilims* and rugs to do so. He found a way to ingratiate himself with the town notables, the Kaymakam, the chief of the gendarmes, the deputies and even of sitting at their evening *raki* table. He joined the opposition party, then on the rise, and it was at about this time that he began to lend money to the peasants at interest rates or on the strength of their future crops of wheat, oats or cotton. He would exact one thousand liras for the loan of three or five hundred, and the peasants and cultivators, always hardpressed for money, had no choice but to sell for one lira the kilo of cotton that would fetch three in the autumn. Yet even this threefold profit, realized in the space of only a few months, say between May to September, was too little for him, though his capital increased daily and the peasants fell more and more into his clutches. During the electoral campaign he was especially diligent. No peasant who had borrowed money from him could dare vote for another party. And when his party came to power his success was complete. He spent the night of 14 May, election day,* listening to the results on the radio, drinking and yelling himself hoarse: Long live democracy, long live freedom, down with the People's Party, down with the feudal lords! When on 18 May he went to Ankara to congratulate Menderes and Celal Bayar, his voice was only a whisper. Thank God, he croaked, the people are freed at last from this long tyranny . . . After this the former corporal could draw as much credit from the banks as he wished to. The number of villages he worked

*14 May 1950, when the Democratic Party overthrew the long rule of the Republican People's Party formed by Atatürk.

with rose from sixteen to thirty-nine and his circulating capital ran into millions. More often than not the peasants would find themselves unable to repay all the sum they had borrowed, because hail or some other natural disaster had befallen their crops. The debt would be postponed, but the corporal would then exact six times the earlier rate of interest. The next year it would be ten times more, until at last the peasant was insolvent. Now what could the corporal do against this? It was his money and he had every right to claim it. He had no faith in bills and law courts. His system was to maintain a few armed retainers. Woe to the villager who failed to pay his debt or rebelled in any way! That very night his house would go up in flames, his cattle would be butchered and if he had a young and beautiful daughter she would be abducted into the mountains and raped. The police, the Kaymakam, the courts, everyone knew who had done it, but no one lent an ear to the villager's complaints. On one occasion half the houses of a village were destroyed in this way. 'I'm really sorry for these villagers,' he had said afterwards, drinking *raki* with the Kaymakam and other notables. 'But what else could I do? I couldn't let myself go bankrupt! And anyway the whole burden of these villagers fell on me again. They came the very next day, pleading and weeping, and I simply couldn't resist. No, I've got a heart that beats here. So I advanced them some money and they showered blessings on me and went off to build new houses for themselves.'

'Ah,' the Kaymakam, the members of parliament and the judges would say, 'the corporal's got a heart of gold! And if they've paid you back now, both the new and old debts . . .'

A loud booming guffaw and the corporal's gold teeth would flash, his paunch would shake with laughter. 'If?! Of course they did! On the dot and to the last kurush, filing up at my door and kissing my hand to boot. The Turkish peasant is noble, heroic, devoted. He will never bite the hand that feeds him. He's rich too, the richest peasant in all the world. Never believe his cringing weeping protests, never! He's cunning, deceitful. You've got to beat the money out of him. He's like a sack of flour. The more you beat it, the more it flies up into the air. There's no end to it. Hah, hah, hah . . .'

The corporal had lost no time in grabbing a part of Ak-chasaz, five hundred *dönüms* that he had quickly planted with poplars. These would grow into a forest in ten years' time and bring him a million. He had also bought a farm from a destitute widow, on an instalment basis, and had entered into partnership for the establishment of a new private bank.

This morning he was seething, unable to keep still, tugging at his mustache, raging, stepping out of the shop every two minutes, on the watch . . .

The town-crier tried to slip past the door, but the corporal pounced on him like an eagle on its prey, seized him by the neck and dragged him inside. 'Now I've got you, you wretch! What's all that cursing and swearing at us you've been doing since morning? There, take this and this!' His huge hands came and went at the hunchback's tiny face. 'I'll kill you, kill you! I'll banish those precious Beys of yours, I will!' With a mighty shove he flung him down on to the hard cement floor and began to kick him. 'Dog! Misbegotten wretch! I've had enough from you!' Suddenly he realized that the hunchback was quite still. Not a sound, not a breath came out of him. Alarmed, he shook him and tried to find his pulse, but there was nothing. My God, he thought, here's a mess! After all this toil and trouble, just when I've made myself, I'm going to lose it all because of a miserable good-for-nothing hunchback! He sprinkled some water over the town-crier's face. 'Don't die, brother,' he pleaded tearfully. 'What did I do to you? Hardly even touched you . . . For heaven's sake, wake up! If you die here in the middle of the market . . . Everyone will bear witness . . . Don't die, please . . .' His face ashen, his hands flying, he lifted the hunchback's head on to his knee. 'Wake up, my lion, come, wake up! I'll sacrifice a huge bull for you if you don't die . . . And three sheep too, I swear to God I will! Why are you doing this to me?'

A crowd was gathering in front of the shop and a low murmur spreading through the market. On a sudden impulse the corporal jumped up. 'You've seen how it happened, all of you, haven't you?' he cried. 'He came into my shop and fell down just like that, jerking on the floor like a chicken you've just killed. I tried to revive him, threw water over his face . . .'

282

'I saw it all,' the saddler said. 'As God's my witness. You banged the poor fellow to the ground and killed him.'

'Now come, saddler, there's a God above. There's the Prophet . . .' Suddenly his face brightened. Even the dullest brain may start working under pressure. 'Yes, there's a God . . . And there's the doctor, the doctor . . .' He repeated this as though the needle had got stuck in a record. I could give him ten thousand, he thought, or a hundred thousand . . . Even half a million would be worth it. Who could resist that? He decided to brazen it out. 'Don't slander me,' he shouted, 'just because this hunchback's croaked in my shop . . .'

'I saw it too,' the old shoemaker said. 'You grabbed hold of him and carried him into this shop like a rabbit.'

'Slander! There's a God above . . . There's the doctor . . .'

'I saw it too,' the baker said.

This was too much for the corporal. He seized the town-crier by the arms, dragged him swiftly out of the shop and cast him on to a heap of watermelon rinds. 'Just look at this miserable fellow! Why should I kill him? Why? Have I no fear of God?' His mouth foamed, his lip hung down larger than ever.

Then the miracle happened. The hunchback sat up and a murmur of wonder ran through the crowd. As he stared dazedly about him, his eyes fell on the corporal and it all came back to him. He jumped up and sprinted through the crowd down the market-place, never looking back until he had reached the plane trees. There he dropped panting on to the blacksmith's bench.

Taken unawares, furious at having been deceived, the corporal drew out his gun and started after him. 'Wretch! Trickster! I'll kill you yet, you wait . . .' he howled trying to wrench himself from the grip of restraining hands. Then he gave it up. 'Nothing will prevent those Beys from being banished, nothing!' His voice rang through the market-place. He was pleased with himself now as he regained his shop. The Aghas, Jafer Özpolat, Süleyman Agha, all the others would hear of the stand he had taken for them. His credit would rise. But something, some little black spot was marring his pleasure. Why the hell had he vowed to sacrifice a bull and three sheep for this wretched hunchback? What matter if he *had* died? Would the

Aghas, his friends, have let him go to prison for that? Anyway, a vow made in such haste, and for a hunchback at that, couldn't be binding, could it? He'd just have to take it back. After all, it was all for the good of the party, wasn't it?

The town-crier had remained there on the blacksmith's bench, his tiny glabrous face clasped in his hands, thinking, and the more he thought the angrier he grew. He rose and quickly made his way to the sawmill under the willows by the stream. The sawyer, a doughty man as strong of spirit as of fist, was his friend.

'He's killed me,' he announced. 'That low-down money-lending corporal's killed me. And they're exiling Dervish Bey and Mustafa Bey. Think of all they've done for us, even inviting us to eat at their table, not like those Aghas who treat us like dirt. Can't we do anything for the sake of old times? Have we no feelings left at all?'

'We were all stricken by the news,' the sawyer said. 'But what can we do? It's the Government that's exiling them, the tribunal. The finger severed by the Sheriat* does not hurt.'

The hunchback flared up. 'Look at me then,' he cried jumping up and down. 'See what they've done to me. Twenty years I've been crying the news in this town . . . Do I deserve this treatment? Is it the Sheriat that's cut my finger or the corporal?' The scent of agnus castus and willow leaves pervaded the air, of marjoram weighed down by the heavy shade, of pine and cedar and sawdust . . . 'And it's not the finger the Sheriat is cutting now, it's the head, and that hurts . . . And you . . . You . . . Everyone fears you in this town, because you were a bandit once. Wasn't it you machine-gunned this town for three nights running, just because Jafer Özpolat asked you to? You're nothing but a dirty toadying wretch . . .'

The sawyer swallowed, but before he had a chance to speak the other was already limping off, bent almost in two, his hump twice as high. 'He doesn't understand,' the sawyer sighed. 'He doesn't see that I've had my day, and the Beys too. It's the Aghas who are the Government now . . . He's a good brave man, but he doesn't realize that they'll kill him, that his children

---

*Sheriat: Moslem Law.

284

will be orphaned. Aaah, he doesn't understand anything . . .'
And he stood there gazing after his friend as though after a
coffin.

It was the barber this time who waylaid the town-crier. He
was a short man, not much taller than the hunchback himself.
'See here, you crooked dog,' he growled, 'what business is it of
yours to protect those Beys who've been wrecking the country
for years? Of course they must be deported. And from here to
Fizan* too . . . Never to return, never! And don't you dare go
swearing at our Aghas, especially Haji Agha . . .' He snapped
open the razor he was holding. 'Or I'll slash your belly open
and let your guts pour out. Now get the hell out of my sight,
you mongrel cur! You don't know me yet.'

His lips blue now, dry and splitting, the hunchback was
creeping away when Haji Kurtboga's car appeared. It was
coming straight at the hunchback, and at full speed too. He had
only just time to cast himself out of the way into the shelter of
the plane trees.

'Stop!' a voice roared out and the hunchback stood arrested
in his flight. Bees were humming all about him, swift bumble-
bees, reddish wasps, all a-glitter, skimming over the white
cobblestones from one end of the market to the other, yellow-
flecked, their tails flashing bluely. And far in the distance,
behind the curtained rows of hills rose Mount Düldül, faint and
tinged with rose, three white clouds billowing gently at its foot.

The voice boomed out again, resounding through the market,
and all the shopkeepers ran to their doors. 'Stop, you humpback
dog, stop I say!' And he descended from the car and marched
upon the hunchback. But what was that? No, it couldn't be!
The hunchback was standing his ground, not running away, as
everyone had expected, before the formidable figure of Haji
Kurtboga! Well, I'll be damned . . . If Kurtboga could have
known this, he'd never have got out of the car, never have risked
getting into the same boat with this dirty hunchback . . . There
was no turning back now. He strode on majestically and still the
hunchback stood there facing this onslaught of wrath. Then,

*Fizan: a place in Arabia where people were exiled under the
Ottoman Empire.

285

just as Haji Kurtboga had lifted his huge hand to strike, the town-crier shouted out: 'Stop! *You* stop! If you strike me now, I'll kill you right here. There'll be your blood on this black earth in a minute.'

Kurtboga was dumbfounded. His arm remained arrested in the air. A crowd was gathering about them. 'Dog!' he stammered out at last, his arm sinking to his side like a deflated balloon.

'Dog yourself!' the hunchback retorted. His crier's voice rang out clarion-like.

'I'll kill you for this, damn you,' Kurtboga hissed, gritting his teeth.

'You can't do a thing to me,' the hunchback shouted at the top of his voice. 'Nor all your mucky family either . . .'

Kurtboga saw red. He whipped out his revolver. 'I'll show you who's muck . . .' he began to say, when the hunchback with lightning speed leaped forward and planted himself only two paces in front of him. He seemed suddenly taller, larger. Even his hump was no longer there.

'Shoot, you bloodthirsty monster,' he yelled, tearing his shirt open. 'Shoot if you're a man. It's easy to brandish a gun, but not so easy to use it, you braggart . . . If you don't shoot then you can go and hide your head in the pants of all those eighty wives of yours that you murdered. Shoot, you son-of-a-bitch. Here's my breast and there's that revolver in your hand. Shoot man, shoot . . .'

Kurtboga's face was yellow, his mouth dry, his head reeling. The yelling hunchback, the people, the plane trees, Mount Düldül, everything was spinning before his eyes in a dense haze. The revolver in his hand trembled convulsively, pointing this way and that, and even if he had tried to fire now he would not have been able to aim at the hunchback only two paces in front of him. He could see the bees, tiny yellow dots buzzing about him, and the dainty damsel-flies gliding along the ground with a silent whirring of gossamer-blue wings. He could hear the town-crier's sonorous voice, blaring on and on, but no longer grasped what he was saying. The hunchback's white teeth and a huge spider in its web on the plane tree were somehow tangled together, whirling round and round.

'Everyone knows how you sowed your rice and poisoned the

whole plain, killing hundreds of children every summer of the fever and mosquitoes . . . That's what's called treason . . . Shoot, man, shoot! Why did you draw your gun, you lily-livered wretch, if you won't shoot? So you thought I'd beg you for my life, eh? All you can do is marry poor widows, whose husbands died in the Yemen war, and divorce them, and rope them together and bury them alive in the swamp, and with the Government's help at that . . . Come on, you coward, shoot . . .'

Haji Kurtboga blinked at the crowd almost imploringly. His eyes focused on Jafer Özpolat who had been standing there, just as dumbfounded as his friend. On meeting Kurtboga's face, he collected himself and rushed up, his hand lifted to slap the hunchback's face. Instantly a flick-knife flicked open and flashed at him.

'Lay a finger on me and I'll tear you to pieces!'

With great presence of mind Jafer Özpolat turned away and, taking the ashen reeling Kurtboga by the arm, supported him back to the car. 'Drive on,' he ordered the chauffeur. Kurtboga had slumped into the seat, utterly spent, the revolver slipping from his hand, his eyes closed. 'For heaven's sake, Agha,' Jafer Özpolat admonished him, 'have you no sense? The idea of squabbling with that dirty hunchback, and in the middle of the market too!'

The Mercedes started up and the crowd made way to let it pass. The hunchback still stood there, his legs planted wide apart, the open flick-knife gleaming in his hand, as a murmur rose from the silent dazed crowd. He turned away and made for the blacksmith's bench under the plane trees. Tired now, beads of sweat shining on his brow, he folded back the knife, put it into his pocket and lit a cigarette. The whole market was in an uproar and people were gathering around him again.

'Kurtboga will never let you get away with this,' the round-faced shoemaker with the drooping mustache said, wiping his hands on his apron. 'He won't rest until he sheds your blood on these very stones. It's a bad business.'

The carpenter came up. He had long arms and was wearing a necktie. 'You did well, man! Let these people understand what paltry cowards these Aghas really are, not even men enough to shoot a gun. Good for you, brother! Baring your breast before that revolver! And you weak and infirm too . . . Like a fortress of steel you were! Bravo to you, and a hundred times bravo to the mother who gave you birth . . . To all your ancestors . . . The town will never forget this day.'

'Why, you dog,' the coffee-shop owner shouted, 'who are you to curse an Agha like that?' He wanted everyone to hear him.

'Good for you, brother!' the shoeshiner said. 'I'll shine your shoes for you to celebrate.' And he cast his kit down, placed the hunchback's foot firmly on the stand and lifted his brush with a smart flourish.

The ironmonger stroked his sleek mustache. 'Dirty hunchback!' he sniffed. 'You did it just to show off. You knew very well, you grovelling mongrel, that Kurtboga would never stain his hands with the blood of the likes of you . . .'

The ironsmith flew into a rage. 'Go fuck yourself, you coxcomb, you!' he cried. 'What's wrong with our town-crier? He's a lion of a man, worth a thousand Kurtbogas. Just let me lay a hand on you and you'll find yourself in Adana before you know it . . .' With his huge fist raised like a black sledge-hammer he advanced threateningly upon him. 'Get the hell away from here, quick, before . . .' The ironmonger lost no time in beating a retreat. The ironsmith marched up to the town-crier and kissed him on the brow. 'But they're going to kill you, those Aghas,' he said, 'and as soon as they can. We've got to do something to prevent it. Yes, my lion, my brave friend, the best thing is to disappear for a few days . . .'

Just then, Mad Haji appeared at the other end of the marketplace, howling, foaming at the mouth and brandishing a gun. 'Here I come, you son-of-a-bitch . . . You'll soon see what's what! So you think you can insult our Aghas, the lifeblood of our country? You think nobody will defend them? Here I come . . . I'll drink your blood . . . Your blood!' His tall figure towered over the crowd and he spotted the town-crier. 'Here,' he yelled, 'take this!' The gun exploded, but the ironsmith had seized his wrist just in time. Two leaves from the plane tree dropped over the crowd. The ironsmith wrenched the gun out of Haji's hold and hurled him far away to the grass by the stream. 'Bootlicker! You're just the toadying dog of the Aghas . . .'

Haji was obviously very drunk. 'Brother, brother, please,

288

please,' he croaked, his tongue too thick for his mouth, 'never, never, never again . . . I won't touch the hunchback, I swear it. He's my brother . . .'

At that moment the Chief Judge was passing through the market-place. He walked with slow prudent steps, his gold-knobbed amber cane tapping over the cobblestones. He was an old man, but of large build, with a big head and protruding eyes. His bulky paunch stuck out sharply under a mauve waist-coat across which dangled a thick gold watch-chain. He wore narrow striped trousers, a jacket cut like a dinner-coat and patent leather shoes. A very black hat was pulled well down over his balding head.

'So long as there's the Big Judge,' the ironsmith said loudly, hoping the judge would hear him, 'they'll never be able to exile the Beys.'

'Never!' more than half the crowd shouted.

'It's not for nothing they've called him Big Judge,' the baker said. 'He wouldn't bow to fate or any other power.'

'No, they can't have the Beys exiled,' the grocer said in his deep booming voice. He had waited a long time before making up his mind. Dervish Bey owed him thirty-six thousand liras . . . He was the grocer's best client, always buying on credit and in large amounts, and when he came into money he would just ask the grocer, 'how much', neither checking the account, nor looking at the grocer's little book, just that, 'how much?'

The Chief Judge was well aware of what was going on. He had heard, too, the remarks that were intended for his ears, but he gave no sign of it. Without a change in his customary stern countenance he walked on out of the market. Only once did he lift his head to look for an instant with sad moist eyes at the roseate bluish heights of Mount Düldül that seemed to tower right above the town now. It was his customary walk every day.

'No, they'll never be able to exile them!'

'But Kurtboga will kill the town-crier.'

'What shall we do?'

'Poor town-crier . . .'

'Let's collect money for him.'

'He's proud, he'd never take it.'

'We'll force him to . . .'

'Let him go away.'

'To Izmir . . .'

'That's a good idea.'

That night the saddler and the baker did not sleep. They went from house to house and soon they had collected quite a considerable sum for the town-crier, enough to enable him to live for three years away from his home town. Then, together with the ironsmith they went to him with the intention of spiriting him away to the train station in great secret that very night.

'You're good true friends, thank you,' the town-crier said, waving away the money with the back of his hand, 'but I can't take this money. Nor can I leave town. After having gone so far I can't have people think I'm running away.'

'But they're going to kill you . . .'

'I know they are.'

36

Whirlwind Veli was running. His long greyhound legs tense, his body strained forward, his cheeks sunken, he ran through fields of cotton, sesame, melons, chick-peas, lentils, onions, stubble, never looking back, but never never, terrified, and behind him rose that column of red dust, hot and dense as oven ash, starred with cinders, stifling, swirling cloud-like high into the sky, burning his heels . . And cleaving the fiery dust column came the shadow, a thing of terror, Dervish Bey himself on that long broad-flanked bay horse of his with rolling mane and streaming tail, his wolfhound racing alongside, tawny, black-streaked, with bared teeth . . . On and on he came, in and out of the red dust-cloud, at a gallop, brandishing his gun in his right hand like a whip. 'You are doomed doomed doomed, Whirlwind Veli. Doomed to die at my hand. You cannot escape. Though there was never a man like you, swift as the wind, the best tracker the world has seen, you have to die . . .' Whispering in his ear, vanishing into the fiery embers of the dust. 'I'll catch up with you, I'll kill you. There's no avoiding your fate.'

And the soothsayer spoke: Hark ye, Nimrod, know that your death will be at the hands of a man-child born this year. A single solitary star, the hidden moon and the sun at dawn have carried the portents . . . Is there no way to avoid the prophecy? Never, the soothsayer said, never! What will you say, soothsayer, if I do? The soothsayer laughed. Never, Nimrod, never can this prophecy be reversed. And the red dust swirled like a flame over Harran desert and up into the mountains of Urfa . . . This prophecy shall never come true, soothsayer. I will prevent it . . . It cannot be, the soothsayer said, his hair standing on end, his eyes red as coral . . . And Nimrod dispatched soldiers to the four corners of his land with orders to kill all the male children born or still to be born that year. And so it was . . . But one single woman, unknown to her husband, her children, her fellow-villagers, to the flying bird or the creeping ant, gave birth to a son by a lonely stream. She kissed and fondled him and gave him his first milk. Then she fashioned a cradle out of willow branches, with infinite care so that it should be as water-tight as a boat, and laying the baby in it, set the cradle to float on the stream, singing lullabies while her heart was breaking, singing to the flowing stream, the mountain flowers, the trees, the gazelles of the desert, her breasts swelling with milk, prostrating herself to the ground, her hair dishevelled, praying, imploring that her baby should not fall into human hands. And a golden cloud descended over the cradle and concealed it as it drifted down valleys and waterfalls, across plains, on its way out of Urfa to stop at the mouth of a cave, in the tangles of a weeping willow. The golden cloud lifted and moonlight lit up the cradle. And the gazelles drinking at the stream saw the baby sucking his thumb. Straightaway they drew the cradle into the cave where a doe suckled the baby to his fill. Every day as evening fell the gazelles returned to feed him, and so he grew up without ever seeing a human face, learning the language of the gazelles, loving them, roaming the desert in their wake. And so it was his eyes were like those of a gazelle, so handsome a youth with his shimmering curly black beard, too handsome for human eyes to gaze upon, tall, with flaming red lips . . . And one day he felt a shadow following him. Day and night it followed him, and he learnt about men, he learnt to speak their language, he knew what the shadow was . . . In broad daylight, together with thousands of gazelles he entered Urfa city. Hark ye, Nimrod, he said, I am tired of being hunted high and low. Here I am, do what you like with me . . . Nimrod rejoiced. Off with his head, he ordered. The executioners swung their swords, again and again, but not even a hair of his head could they sever. Strangle him, Nimrod said. But the knot would not tighten. They tried everything, and still they could not kill him. In the end they lit a great fire on the plain and from an engine on top of a hill they catapulted him into this fire. And lo, the fire turned into a pool, the half-burnt wood into fish, the ashes into a garden full of flowers . . . Gazelle-like he darted out of his garden and dealt Nimrod the death-blow. And so he became the Lord Halil Ibrahim, bestowing bounty on this earth to whoever invoked his name in harvest and vintage. And he married a girl who was like a gazelle too, and they had many sons, and hundreds of thousands of gazelles took refuge in his land and he protected them. And that is why it is forbidden to eat the meat of a gazelle, but good to drink its milk.

The moon rose, a full moon, bright yellow, shedding a glittering radiance over the countryside, bathing the night clean. Whirlwind Veli was roving about the mansion. For how many days he had been wandering like this, he himself did not know. Ibrahim, Dervish Bey's eldest son, a tall timid young man with sad black eyes, had seen him. 'Father,' he said, 'father, that man's here again, prowling about the house . . .' And Dervish Bey stuck his eye to the small watch-hole he had pierced in his window and saw Whirlwind Veli pelting round and round. Father and son did not sleep all night and in the morning the man had vanished like a cloud in the sky. Night after night he came again. Everyone saw him. They tried to catch him. They sent dogs after him, then swift riders, but he out-distanced them all.

Sometimes Whirlwind Veli would feel hungry. He would slip into the village and steal the yogurt that the peasants mixed in large bowls and kept on top of their *chardaks*. He would take it in turns, another house each night, and though they watched out for him, they could never catch him. He came like the wind, snatched away the yogurt and disappeared. During the day he would sleep up in a willow tree by a bend of the stream in the thick of a wood of plane trees. Some nights too he would remain up there in his tree.

It was on such a night of full moon, light as day, that he saw the woman coming out of the water. She was tall with full round hips, a slim waist, narrow shoulders and her breasts were firm and young. He could see every curve of her lovely provocative nakedness. Tightly he clasped at a bough beside him. The pebbles glistened and the blue-flowering marjoram grew thick as a field of wheat, waving in the breeze and wafting a strong heady scent that quickened the blood. The woman threw herself over the grass, rolling this way and that. Strange sounds came out of her, seductive, urgent, maddening. Whirlwind Veli clutched at the tree even more tightly. His hands, his whole body broke into a sweat. The woman rolled over to the thick grass under a plane tree and stopped there, her knees drawn up, her legs wide open, that strange maddening moaning more urgent now, like a song, like the call of a she-bird. And out of the agnus castus bush came a youth, also naked. He went and lay down beside her. She began rolling again, her moaning sharper, wilder, and he answered once with a sound just like hers. They rose and embraced, then fell back over the grass near some prickly burdocks and he came upon her. Whirlwind Veli closed his eyes and clung to the tree for his life. She was moaning softly now, soundlessly, but the man's breathing came loud and strong, like a racehorse when the race is over. Then all was silence and Whirlwind Veli opened his eyes. They were standing. The youth turned, making back for the bushes. 'Stay, don't go!' she cried. 'Don't go, don't!' But the youth walked on. He stopped by the bushes, picked up his clothes and slipping them on quickly stepped over the white pebbles to the other side of the stream.

The woman remained on the edge of the shingle gazing after him for maybe half an hour, an hour even, then she went back under the plane trees and kneeled over the grass, as though in some ancient ritual of worship, her breasts trembling, swinging uncannily, her voice faint and low. After a while she started crawling on all fours, circling the plane tree. Her buttocks were round and white in the moonlight. And out of the agnus castus bushes another youth appeared, naked too, so thin it seemed he would snap in two. He stood there, his hands over his groin, hunched, his head hanging. The woman's weird song grew louder and louder as she lay back, knees drawn up, legs parted again, and pulled the bashful young man to her. For a long time they were joined together. The youth's breathing seemed to have stopped, but the woman writhed madly under him and slithered through the grass carrying him along. Whirlwind Veli's eyes were riveted to the young man's jutting shoulderblades. Of the woman he saw only her very long hair spread wide over the ground. Suddenly, with a sobbing cry, the youth slipped to the ground, faint, utterly exhausted. She held his head on her lap and kissed it wildly, his neck and shoulders and breast, smothering his whole body with kisses. Then she kneeled down beside him like a worshipping idol, her breasts trembling, her arms lifted, uttering strange incantory sounds. The young man came to. He leapt to his feet and fled, grabbing his clothes as he ran. She remained kneeling, silent and still as a part of the earth.

And yet another man came, old and bent this one, with a long white beard that shimmered in the moonlight, and began to walk round and round the kneeling woman. 'Sabahat Hanum, Sabahat Hanum, I've come, I, old Corporal Müslüm. It's me, only me.' She made no sign at first that she had seen him. 'It's me, me, Corporal Müslüm,' he repeated. Suddenly, seizing his hand she pulled him down beside her and began kissing him, slowly, deliberately, until the man's breathing came loud and rasping. Then she drew him over her and for a while they remained like that, stuck together, without moving, until she started to slide and twist beneath him, very slowly, and he held his hands over her breasts, gently caressing, hardly touching them, feather-like . . . Finally, he raised her to her feet, kissed her and walked off with slow steps through the carpet of marjoram, his beard gleaming like silver.

She dropped to her knees and shuffled over to the stream. Then rising again, she stretched herself till her bones cracked. Arms raised, legs tense and wide apart she looked up at the willow tree. She had heard a sound. 'Who's there?' she called, her voice warm, inviting. 'Who are you?' And when she got no answer she turned and threw herself into the dark whirlpool of the gently purling stream. Splashing sounds came from the pool for a while . . .

'Father, father, father,' Ibrahim was shouting. 'Look, look! There he is again, that long long man . . . Oh, oh, oh, look how he's running! Like a greyhound . . . There! He's gone. Why didn't you look, father? I'm afraid of that man. He's going to kill me, father, I know!' Desperately he clutched at Dervish Bey. 'Save me, father, save me . . . Kill him. He passes so near the house, so near . . .'

'I'll kill him tonight, Ibrahim. I will, be he friend or foe. Just for you, Ibrahim.'

And the red dust swirled, and over the moonlit paling eastern sky, over the fragrant blue marjoram and mauve-flowering agnus castus a yellow rain began to fall. In the green light of dawn, gusts of yellow rain swept over the green paddies, bending the heavy bursting ears of the rice plants to the ground. And the oxen moved in the fields, their big hooves sinking into the slushy earth . . . And the smell of wet earth and myrtle leaves spread through the yellow curtain of rain . . .

And Halil Ibrahim saw that he would never avoid that stalking shadow. So he came to Nimrod with his thousands of gazelles and scaled the bastioned walls of Urfa city. Hail, Nimrod, he said, and the red dust-cloud behind him subsided, the gazelles mourned silently. Hail, Nimrod . . . He emerged from the blazing pyre and went straight to Nimrod's palace, his dagger drawn, and Nimrod recognized the hand of fate. He summoned the soothsayer and bent his head . . . And Ibrahim said: I am killing tyranny. There will be no more tyranny on earth after you are dead. And he planted his dagger into Nimrod's heart. But tyranny did not die. And Halil Ibrahim, son of the gazelles was confounded. Yet he never lost hope. Tyranny will die one day, he said. It must. And his testament to his children was this: I have given you in plenty of the good things of this earth. And now my last will to you is that you should put an end to tyranny in this world . . .

And so it shall be one day. There shall be an end to all tyranny.

And Whirlwind Veli rushed on, round and round the Sarioglu mansion. And behind him was the red dust-cloud, the yellow shadow . . .

'Father, father, come and see! There he is, running . . .'

'Stop!' Dervish Bey roared. 'Stop right where you are or I'll shoot.' And the long thin shadow pulled up as though suddenly nailed to the spot. 'Hidayet, go and see who it is.'

Hidayet advanced prudently in the dim light of dawn, his gun aimed at the shadowy figure standing motionless under the jujube tree that bloomed with thousands of red, yellow and pink flowers in spite of the huge prickly-pear cactus growing all over it. 'Throw down your gun,' he ordered. There was no answer.

'Throw it down or I'll shoot.' He hurled himself forward and pinioned the man, who offered no resistance whatsoever. Hidayet ran his hands over his body and found the gun. 'But you do have a gun then,' he commented. 'All right, come with me!' The man obeyed, still silent, moving like an automaton, and stopped at the stairs of the mansion. 'Come on, up you go . . .' In the big hall Whirlwind Veli stopped again, blinking at the bright *kilims* on the floor, the large-eyed, black-mustached portrait on the wall surrounded by old nacre-inlaid, carved firearms, the long embroidered sofas, the row of moss-grown pinewood jars at the head of the stairs, each one like an eagle poised for flight, oozing slightly over the floorboards.

'Who is it?' Dervish Bey called from his room.

'I don't know, Bey. He won't speak. He seems to be all in a daze.'

'Let's see him.'

And so Whirlwind Veli, still numb and rigid, like a sleep-walker, entered the room where Dervish Bey spent his life nowadays with a solid bulwark of sandbags in the window. The walls were painted pink and the furniture consisted of a glass-topped oak table, a chair with a feather cushion, and along the wall a divan spread with a Bitlis blanket. A small carpet covered the floor. Dervish Bey was standing. 'Who are you?' he snapped. 'Why have you been prowling about my house all these days?' Whirlwind Veli blinked several times as though he had just come out of the dark. His eyes had sunk into their sockets. His neck was scraggy and his head had grown huge, with every bone showing separately, and the skin and hair sticking to it like shrivelled parchment. His clothes hung down as a scarecrow's. 'Who are you? Speak! Are you mad or sane? What business have you to? . . .'

Without warning the petrified figure before him had suddenly slid to his knees at his feet. 'Don't kill me, Bey,' he breathed out in a moan. 'Please don't kill me. I'm too old to be killed and I've got a great deal to tell you. I can be very useful to you . . .'

'But who are you?'

Whirlwind Veli's blinking eyes rested fearfully on Hidayet. Dervish Bey understood. 'All right, Hidayet,' he said. 'You can go.'

297

With a curious glance at the kneeling man Hidayet left the room. Ibrahim had been waiting at the door in anxious trepidation. 'Who is it? Who, who, who? . . .'

'He didn't say,' Hidayet replied. 'Anyway he doesn't look to be in his right mind.'

Towards noon Dervish Bey's voice was heard calling from the room. 'This is my honoured guest,' he said. 'Take him to wash and tidy himself and give him a set of underclothes and also one of my navy-blue suits and some shoes . . . And tell the Hatun that I'm going to have my meal in this room with him.'

On the second day Dervish Bey rose at dawn in a blind rage. He drew on his boots, thrust his revolver into his sash and snatched up his whip made of a bull's member. Very rarely had he been seen so angry. His eyes were bloodshot. 'Call Kamil to me,' he ordered. 'At once!' And when Kamil came running up he shut himself up with him and Whirlwind Veli. They kept their voices low for a while, but then Dervish Bey was heard to explode. 'A man who can't control his own wife! That man must die. Is it for this we gave you Sabahat, our own sister? So you should drag the honour of the Sarioglus in the mud? You'll pay for this with your life . . .' He burst out of the room, his eyes starting from their sockets, his nostrils flaring like a horse's. 'Strip this dog naked,' he howled as he rushed down the stairs. 'Naked, naked . . .' He leaped on to his horse, as two men came dragging the half-fainting Kamil into the yard. 'To the black-thorns . . .'

The blackthorn scrub gleamed darkly brown, so thick-growing that only the sharp thin spines of the bushes were apparent. The two men stripped Kamil of all his clothes, leaving him quite naked, his hands over his groin, bent and tense as a bow, swaying with a shivering motion. Dervish Bey ground his teeth savagely and spurred his horse straight at him. In the twinkling of an eye the whip had slashed countless times at Kamil's back, leaving finger-size welts at each stroke. Round and round Dervish galloped, his rage mounting as he struck. Streaming with blood now, his feeble attempts to seize the whip unavailing, Kamil turned and fled into the blackthorns. This was what Dervish had been waiting for. He plunged after him, driving him mercilessly on and on into the lacerating thorns.

The villagers, young and old, men, women and children, huddled together on the edge of the scrub or on some elevation and watched the running falling scrambling man in the black-thorns and their Bey on the horse bending down to smite again and again. At every crack of the whip they flinched and trembled as though it had struck their own backs.

And so Dervish Bey whipped Kamil on into the very thick of the scrub. Not even from the hill could the villagers see him any more. Only his screams could be heard as the whip kept swishing down endlessly.

37

Ala Temir Yamakli had come to Bajak village at the age of
nineteen from one of those villages in the hills above Akarja
where every house is in a separate valley, at least an hour's
distance from the other and where the inhabitants communicate
by shouting from hill to hill. They sow patches of land only one
eighth of an acre that are cleared from the forest and that yield
forty to one the first year, but the second only fifteen and even
less the third year. In the fourth year the rains have carried
away all the earth, leaving only sharp purple rocks in its place,
and a new field must be cleared and it will take them many years
again before they have uprooted the trees and sown it, knowing
full well that it will inevitably be carried away in the end by the
mountain torrents. In Bajak village Ala Temir Yamakli was
hired as farmhand by a widow who owned a hundred and fifty
dönüms of rich fat land bordering the swamp and yielding thirty
or forty to one. His task was to till this land, sow it and gather
in the harvest, and soon his diligence was the talk of the village.
In the morning the widow would set before him a large bowl of
mirmirik soup, made of thin *bulgur** boiled in water with a dab
of butter, and he would scoop it all up with the wooden spoon
he had carved for himself back in the hills, together with a good
deal of toasted *yufka* bread. At noon he would break his bread
into diluted *ayran*** and eat it up accompanied by a single onion.
The evening meal would consist of *bulgur* pilaff with a whiff
of butter about it. It was the same every day. His shalvar-
trousers of coarse handwoven cotton were patched in a hundred
places. He wore them day and night, with a striped shirt and a
jacket also of striped cotton that the widow had sewn for him.
All the material for his clothes came from his home village,
woven with love and care by his mother's own hand. He had

Bulgur: crushed wheat.
**Ayran:* a cool drink made of yogurt and water.

always hated sandals. So instead he wore a pair of yellow-edged red boots, pointed at the toes and neatly tied up to the knees with leather laces. He would draw them on reverently and sit there for a while, his legs stretched out, contemplating them. He could never have enough of admiring his boots and would do his best to protect them from thorns and bushes, hardly stepping on the ground as he walked. Most of the time he would simply take them off when he was working or on a long journey over rocks and muddy roads. That is why his first pair, which he had bought in the Chukurova, lasted him eleven years.

His legs were short and stubby like tree-trunks, his shoulders and hips of exactly the same width. When he walked it was as if a log had been stood up vertically and was lumbering along. His tiny eyes were a yellowish green and every hair of his bleached yellow head bristled stiffly as though driven in with a hammer. He had hollow cheeks and jutting cheekbones. His lips were very thin. His beard, as spiky as his hair, spread all over his neck down to his chest and right up to his ears, even growing out of them.

The widow, whose name was Zöhré, was childless. After Ala Temir came to work for her the yield of her land increased rapidly and she soon found herself the wealthiest woman in the village with more money than she knew what to do with. 'Lady,' Ala Temir would say to her, 'lay up my share with yours. Let's store it up until we have a sackful.' In the sixth year the two decided to get married without ceremony or fuss. The villagers learnt of this long afterwards, and that only from the Imam, for Ala Temir never changed his way of life, working without stint, come wind come weather, still eating the same *mirmirik* soup in the morning, the bread soaked in thin *ayran* with the onion at noon and the *bulgur* pilaff in the evening, but with no butter at all in it now. He still wore those same patched shalvar-trousers and striped shirt and jacket and those long underpants tied with a cord at the waist that his mother would send him.

After a while Ala Temir started buying cows and bulls and, though Zöhré was torn with apprehension at first, this was soon allayed when she saw that after every purchase he would still slip a few coins into the little tin can that was concealed in a corner of the closet. They would sell all the produce of their farm, butter, grain, vegetables, chickens, eggs, and hoard up the money. Zöhré took to wearing the same coarse cotton shalvar-trousers and shirts as her husband's and the same men's boots too. Like him she would drive a hard bargain with Huge Hassan, the shoemaker in the town, then, slinging the new boots over her shoulder, she and Ala Temir would walk home and there they would put them on at last and, sitting down against the sunny wall of their house, would stretch out their legs and gaze at their new boots for hours on end, entranced.

In the first years of their marriage they had six sons born one after the other. These children never had a stitch of clothing to their backs until the age of seven and as soon as they were old enough they were set to work like galley-slaves. Meanwhile the tin can buried in the closet became two, then three and four. Soon they would have to replace it with a large oil can . . . And now the hundred and fifty *dönüms* of land fell far short of Ala Temir's needs. He bought some six hundred *dönüms* more from an eighty-year-old woman, who had been left alone in the world. He got it for a song, on an instalment basis too, and before he had paid off the whole the old woman died. Still, Ala Temir, an honest fair-dealing man, used the rest of the money he owed to pay for the woman's funeral and tombstone and to have *mevlut** prayers read for her. He even distributed grapes and sweets to the village children in her memory.

After this his income grew apace and he bought more and more land. His flair told him that there was a lot to be got out of Abdülhalik Effendi, the registrar. So one evening, with a comb of honey he had ordered from his mountain village and a pail of butter he had filled with his own hands, he knocked at the registrar's door and the minute he saw him, threw himself down to kiss his feet. Abdülhalik Effendi was highly flattered. He stroked Ala Temir's hair and drew him on to a sofa. His bleary eyes blinking behind a pair of metal-framed glasses, he gazed with surprise and affection at this strange red-booted man. 'What are those?' he asked, pointing to the pails Ala Temir had left by the door.

**Mevlut:* prayer for the dead.

Sitting bolt upright, stiff as a poker, sweating, his two hands stuck to his knees with the fingers wide open, his eyes looking straight before him at a fixed point, Ala Temir stirred a little. 'That one's butter,' he said. 'I churned it myself. Pure golden narcissus-scented butter. Our cows, you know, graze in the meadows near Akchasaz, which are full of narcissus, marjoram and wild rose. That's why there's no butter to compare with ours . . . So I said to myself, our honourable respected benefactor, Abdülhalik Effendi, has done so much for our village, he must taste of our special scented butter and go on doing even more for all of us . . .'

'And what's in the other pail?'

'It's honey, sir. I'm from the mountains and mountain honey is the best thing for one's health. The Hodja of Karatopak says it's a remedy for every ill.'

'Oh, so you've seen the Hodja?'

'Our kind can't ever see him. He's a great holy man, just like you, reverend sir, ripe for Paradise. We only hear of such saints and of their glorious deeds.'

Abdülhalik Effendi was delighted. 'Won't you seat yourself more comfortably?' he suggested.

Ala Temir sat up even straighter, his hands clutching his knees more tightly. 'This honey, respected sir, is a cure-all because of the heather that grows on our mountains. Lokman the Physician said that heather has properties to cure seventy-two ailments. It's good for bullet wounds, consumption, malaria, scurvy . . .' He stopped, eyeing Abdülhalik Effendi's pinched hooknose, his shrivelled neck, his mottled hands . . . 'Lokman the Physician said that it makes a man twenty years younger.'

At that moment Abdülhalik Effendi's young peasant wife came in, bearing coffee in little red-streaked golden-brimmed cups set on a tray lined with an embroidered white cloth. The two cups flashed like stars before Ala Temir's eyes. 'Please,' she said.

Slowly he lifted his right hand from his knee. The cup shook in his fingers, and the more it shook the tenser he grew, until his muscles ached as though his whole body were being squeezed in a vice. Beads of sweat studded his brow. He had never drunk coffee before, but he had watched others doing it. He raised the cup to his lips and took his first sip noisily as he had heard it done. Now everything was wiped out of his mind. He had forgotten where he was, why he had come. He could not see the relaxed figure of Abdülhalik Effendi waiting there at ease, smoking and sipping his coffee. Vaguely he wondered whether he should have accepted the proffered cigarette, but his chief concern was to finish his coffee and get it over with. At the fifth sip he realized with relief that the cup was drained to the dregs. Slowly his sweat began to cool, but now he was worrying what to do with the empty cup. The gilded brim danced before his eyes. A far-off voice came to his help: 'Let me take that cup.' He held it out quickly and at once clasped his hands to his knees again. He had leaned forward slightly as he drank the coffee. Now he sat up again straighter than ever.

'Let's see now, where d'you come from and what's your name?'

'I'm from Bajak village and they call me Ala Temir Yamakli . . .'

Abdülhalik Effendi was surprised, but did not show it. 'Oh, so you're the Ala Temir Agha, the one they all say is such a hard worker. Well! Bravo, bravo . . .'

Elated at being recognized and called Agha, Ala Temir relaxed just a little bit and smiled modestly. 'I've come to you, respected sir, knowing you never refuse help to people. My land borders the Jeyhan River and falls just below the village in the direction of the blackthorn scrub. I was wondering if you knew of any abandoned property in those parts, I mean that had belonged to our friends, the Armenians?'

Abdülhalik Effendi removed his glasses and polished them thoughtfully. Then he put them on again. 'Yes, Ala Temir Agha,' he said softly. 'I think I do. Kushoglu has also been inquiring about land in those parts and I looked it up only recently. Yes, indeed, my friend, there are plenty of fields near the blackthorn scrub . . . And then there's the scrub itself, six thousand three hundred *dönüms*, if I'm not mistaken. And from the scrub to Jeyhan River . . . Come to me next week and we'll see what we can do.' He rose and Ala Temir jumped up too, as though actioned by a spring. 'Yes, sir,' Abdülhalik Effendi continued as he walked to the door, 'next week we'll settle this matter. I have to look up the land records.' He turned and saw with surprise that Ala Temir was standing at attention in the middle of the room, stiff and upright, his arms pressed tightly down his sides, the fingers wide open. Puzzled, he went back to him, but there was no word or sign from Ala Temir. Then he understood. 'All right,' he said. 'You can bring me some more when you come. And other things too. They'll be most welcome.'

At these words Ala Temir flung himself down like a log and began to kiss the registrar's shoes and knees. Abdülhalik Effendi patted his head and drew him to his feet.

In the doorway Ala Temir stopped again. 'I need a lot of land, sir,' he blurted out, his eyes on the floor. 'A great great deal. I'll sell everything I own, I'll bring you all my produce. It's land I need, my very esteemed sir . . .'

Abdülhalik Effendi's eyes filled. Nobody had ever treated him like a human being before. He thought of all those he had made landowners, given them title-deeds without their having to pay a jot for the land . . . 'One day Turkey will be proud of you,' he declared, pressing Ala Temir's shoulder with fatherly affection. 'I'm sure of this as I'm alive. The Minister of Foreign Affairs, Dr Tevfik Rüshtü, is a close relation of mine. I'm going to write to him that Turkey is pregnant with a great and glorious future because she has now produced Aghas like Temir Agha, true Turks, pure-blooded, honest, industrious, Aghas who will carry on Atatürk's trust. And here he is, one of those Aghas, standing before me like a bastion of steel, at one with his nation and country, inseparable, immortal . . .'

Ala Temir had not understood a word of all this. What he had grasped was that Abdülhalik Effendi intended to write to Ankara about him and inform the Government that they had a solid supporter in this part of the country. He didn't care what he wrote so long as he procured lots of land for him and did not ask for too much money. His tiny sly yellowish-green eyes gleamed with satisfaction. 'I'll bring you everything I have,' he said again. 'I'll sell my cattle even . . . What I need is land, more land . . .' He kissed the registrar's hand and held it to his brow. Then he speeded back to Bajak village, singing as he went, repeating over and over again the one song he knew.

And so his business, his fortune, his land and his credit in the banks kept rising. Four of his six sons worked on the farm with him, while the other two were still at high school in Adana. All the boys were hard workers like their father and at least as thrifty. They had but one fault in his eyes. They insisted on wearing town clothes. Another horrifying novelty was that his eldest would kill a large chicken now and then, and have his wife cook it for him. And whenever he went to town he would bring back a cut of goat's meat from the butcher's. This would drive Ala Temir wild with frenzy. 'You're going to ruin me, ruin me!' he would howl, his voice ringing through the whole village, and everyone would know that meat had entered the Ala Temir house again. But Ala Temir could do nothing to prevent this dreadful extravagance, for his eldest son was a skilled technician, the best in the land, and ten times as hard-working as his father, endlessly repairing and driving harvesters and tractors and directing other workers, training them, sleeping in his machines, almost a part of them, always smeared in oil and dust, in the fields, in the workshop, never resting for a moment, sometimes absent from the house for months on end. The other boys were humble and worked diligently, never asking for anything. In looks they were all the exact replicas of their father.

As for Ala Temir he had not changed at all. He still wore those red boots, over which he would haggle for three days running with Huge Hassan, the shoemaker, and the handwoven cotton shalvar-trousers and striped shirt. His mother was long dead now, but his underclothes were always made in his village and brought over by relatives whom he would reward by giving them jobs on his farm. As always when he first put on his new boots he would lean against the sunny wall of his house and gaze at them for hours. In the morning he would scoop up his *mirmirik* soup until his belly swelled, and at noon break some bread into the same thin *ayran* and, smashing an onion with his fist, would gobble it up rapidly. The only change was the evening meal. The *bulgur* pilaff was now served with plenty of butter and Ala Temir would eat it with great misgiving. 'This woman is in league with my sons' wives to ruin me,' he would mutter to himself, but there was nothing he could do about it. 'For heaven's sake, Ala Temir,' people would admonish him, 'you're getting old. You've got tons of money, enough to last you a hundred lifetimes and more. Why don't you take it easy? The minute you're dead your sons are going to play ducks and drakes with your fortune.' His tiny eyes narrower than ever he would make no answer, only sighing inwardly. 'Aaah, they don't know, aah, nobody understands other people's problems, aaah...'

But there were certain occasions when Ala Temir would accept without complaint the meat his son had brought into the house. Reverently, their nostrils widening, he and his wife would contemplate the pile of pilaff abundantly topped with meat, as they would their new red boots. Then, closing their eyes, as though performing a sacred rite, they would take their first mouthful, chewing it very slowly with infinite delight, rapt, sitting for hours before this feast, savouring life to the last drop.

One important transformation in Ala Temir was that he now wore a hat, a large-brimmed black felt with a long feather. He would never take it off, not even when he was working in the fields. A spare one, identical with the first, was kept wrapped up in a silk cloth to be worn only when he went to town. He had also had his two front teeth pulled out, though they were perfectly sound, and replaced by gold ones.

Another innovation concerned the money hoarded in the tin cans. Aided by his eldest son they had dug it out of the earth and had travelled all the way to Adana in a hired taxi to place it in a bank. The tin cans were still there, hidden in the closet or buried in the earth, but the big money went into the bank from then on. And whenever Ala Temir visited Adana he would drop in at the bank for a coffee with the manager who would insist on inviting him to lunch at the biggest restaurant in the city. 'Please, Beyefendi,' the manager would fawn, 'please come. Why, if we had just two more clients like you, we'd be the first bank not only in Adana, but in all of Turkey.'

Twice a year, punctiliously, on the same days, Ala Temir would go to see Abdülhalik Effendi who was now a retired pensioner. As in the past he would bring his offerings of butter and honey. 'I've filled in that butter with my own hands,' he would say, sitting upright on the sofa, his two hands as always splayed over his knees. 'The swamp's being dried up, but our butter still smells of narcissus. And the honey from our heather-filled hills . . . Lokman the Physician says . . .' Abdülhalik

Effendi would greet him with warm pleasure and with pride at not having been forgotten, but he would call him Beyefendi now. One thing was not the same. Ala Temir did not prostrate himself before the aged civil servant, he did not kiss his hands and feet. Was it because he was too old for that now? Or had he lost some of his former humility? This was a thing that worried Ala Temir, but he could not explain it.

One day the eldest son bought a Mercedes car without asking his father's permission and kept it hidden from him for a while. But Ala Temir had known all about it from the first, its cost, its make, where the money had come from, everything. He pretended not to know, even ignoring the car when it stopped now and again at the door of their dilapidated house. His son soon realized that his father was just biding his time, so he washed and polished the car till it shone and finally brought it to the front of the house.

'Look what I've bought, father,' he said.

Ala Temir circled the car warily, inspecting its wheels, its steering-wheel, its emblem, its little mirrors. He switched on the motor and saw the green light go on. And the red and the yellow . . . He was like a child. His son watched him anxiously as he got into the front seat.

'Who else has such a car in town?' Ala Temir asked.

'Nobody,' his son answered proudly. 'Well anyway,' he added, 'only Kurtboga has, but not like this one. This is the latest model.'

'So,' Ala Temir commented as he got out of the car, 'you mean there isn't a single car like this in town?'

'No.'

Ala Temir stood staring fixedly into the distance. Then he sighed. 'Call your brothers,' he said. His son was soon back with the three others. Ala Temir took a deep breath, his mouth worked soundlessly. He laughed and clapped his hands, then his face took on a bitter mournful look. 'Your brother,' he said smiling again, but still tearfully, 'tells me nobody's got a car like this one in the whole town.'

'It's true,' the second son said.

'I don't think there are three like it in all of Adana either,' the third son said.

'I don't care about Adana,' Ala Temir said, throwing out his chest.

'Well, not in this town anyway,' the youngest said.

'Then I want you to go to Adana this very day,' Ala Temir said, 'or to Istanbul if necessary, and get yourselves one each, exactly like this one. Your two younger brothers are still at school. They don't need one. You're the ones who're working here. But you must let them ride your cars when they come.'

'Of course we will, father . . .'

Ala Temir's breast was swelling with emotion. His throat tightened. He rushed into the house, hid himself in the closet and wept unrestrainedly. The image of his mother rose before his eyes, of their dire poverty, of his father who had left them to work in the Chukurova and never returned, of his brothers and sisters, always naked and dying of some sickness or other. It was the first time he had wept since leaving his village. He had even forgotten that he could weep . . . After a while his tears dried out and he was filled with joy. He took his town hat from its silk cloth, flicked it once or twice as he had seen it done by the Aghas in the town and clamped it firmly on to his head. Then he went out to his son.

'Drive me into town in your new car,' he ordered. 'To the club.' And opening the door he ensconced himself comfortably in the back seat. For the first time in his life he felt like crossing his legs, but he simply could not manage to keep one fat leg over the other. He thrust his head out of the window. 'What are you all gaping at me for? Why don't you go and get your cars? . . . I see! The money . . . Well, you can give my compliments to the bank manager . . . But no . . . Wait a minute.' He produced his cheque-book. 'Write out the sum,' he told his eldest son. 'For three cars. But exactly like this one. I won't have any other.' The son wrote it out and handed it back. After a whole year of painful efforts, Ala Temir had finally learned how to sign his name, and now, laboriously, the sweat starting on his brow he filled it in at the bottom of the cheque. 'Here you are,' he said triumphantly.

At the club everyone came out to admire his car, the Prosecutor-General, the Kaymakam, the lawyers . . . Jafer Özpolat took his arm. 'Temir,' he said jubilantly, 'I've got good news for you. And I want my reward for it too, you know!'

'Dear Bey, of course, of course!' Ala Temir said, his eyes shining. 'Even without any good news . . . It's for you to command and for me to obey . . .'

Jafer Özpolat was the only Bey in the Chukurova whose tribe had remained intact until recent years. Though his father had died without leaving a penny, the tribe, which had formed twelve villages, always respected him as their Bey and seldom disobeyed him. In one of these villages where the men were especially fierce and devoted to him and made a living mostly out of horse-thieving, the Bey had built himself an imposing mansion, six stories high, which was the subject of songs and ballads in the countryside and which shone brightly with its whitewashed walls and windowpanes among the lowly huts of reeds and rushes all around it. On his father's death Jafer Özpolat was left utterly destitute with his two brothers, both of whom had studied only up to high school. The eldest had drifted from one small bureaucratic post to another and had finally given himself wholly to drink. He had no pretensions whatsoever to be the Bey. The second brother, a daredevil, remained in the village at the head of the horse-thieves and made himself feared by one and all. Jafer Özpolat, a tall well-built dark youth, was the youngest. He loved to wrestle, though that was not considered the thing for sons of Beys, and had even won prizes in contests. He had broad shoulders, a wide forehead and strong chin and walked with a proud, haughty gait, never looking to right or left. He always dressed meticulously with well-pressed trousers, a cravat and bright-coloured kerchiefs in the breast-pocket of his pinstripe suit.

For many years the brothers made a tolerable living from Akchasaz swamp. Most of the village houses in the Chukurova at the time were built of the reeds and rushes and sedge that grew in the swamp. When summer came the brothers would post guards in various parts of the swamp and these would exact money from every villager who wanted to cut anything. Nobody dared ask, now why do we have to pay for this? Those who tried to evade payment were soundly beaten up by the guards, and their cattle and horses butchered. Later, as the swamp began to be drained, the brothers staked a claim on thousands of *dönüms* there and again nobody hazarded to inquire what right they had to this land.

It was during these years that rice cultivation was introduced into the Chukurova by people coming from Marash. Jafer Özpolat had all this land that was wonderfully fertile since it had just been reclaimed from the swamp. He had the population of twelve villages at his beck and call, ready to kill or steal for him, but he lacked the necessary capital for rice-sowing. The paddies were seeded in June and in September they yielded a hundred to one, even a hundred and thirty sometimes. Provided there was no hail or steady rain, the owner would find himself rich overnight, with no ploughing, no harrowing, no trouble at all, just the scattering of the seed over the field and the flooding with the water from the river . . . What matter if whole villages were inundated, infested with mosquitoes, ravaged by malaria? So long as all that money was coming in . . . Jafer Özpolat racked his brains. Where could he get a few hundred thousand liras? It was a friend who gave him the idea. 'Look, Jafer Bey,' he said, 'there's a man in one of your tribe's villages who's simply rolling in money. Why don't you try him?'

'Who's that?' Jafer Bey asked.

'Ala Temir.'

'Ala Temir would die rather than let anyone have a penny of his. He's the greatest miser ever born!' Jafer said despondently.

'Well, there's no harm in trying. How is he with you?'

'Oh, standing at attention, you know, and no end flattered if I deign to greet him . . .'

'Well then! You see what you have to do, don't you?'

'I see . . .'

Jafer Özpolat did not sleep a wink that night. It was the season for rice-sowing and he knew a Marash planter who longed to go into partnership with him . . . Early next day he shaved carefully and anointed himself with perfumed lotions. Then he drew on his riding-breeches and top-boots. He had not worn these in a long time, but today he judged them the very thing to impress Ala Temir. Thrusting a handkerchief into the pocket of his navy blue jacket, he fixed his red necktie with a pearl pin. He picked up his silver-stocked whip and stood twisting his mustache in front of the mirror. His horse was not so good, an ordinary beast pilfered from Urfa. He had just received it. So he borrowed his neighbour's Arab steed and had a silver-nielloed Circassian saddle found to mount it. He cut a really imposing figure when he reined in, an hour later, in Ala Temir's yard in Bajak village.

'Ala Temir! Ala Temir Agha!' he called in a stern haughty voice, very upright on the horse, frowning into the distance.

Ala Temir knew the voice at once. He came rushing out helter-skelter, jerking at his shalvar-trousers. 'Bey, Bey! Welcome! What a surprise! You never honoured us before . . . Wife, wife, look! Look who's come to visit us!' He held the horse. 'Come in, Bey, come in . . .'

Slowly Jafer Özpolat dismounted and stepped into the house. Zöhré had been disposing some cushions on the floor for him. He sank down on them and stretched out his booted legs.

Ala Temir was in a dither. 'Oh dear, oh dear, with the work I have, there isn't any coffee in the house! Or tea . . . Perhaps an *ayran* . . .'

'I want nothing,' Jafer cut him short. 'I've come here just for you, Ala Temir. I've come to my tribe, nothing else. Sit down here beside me.'

Ala Temir complied with alacrity, crouching on the bare floor at his feet.

Jafer Özpolat knew he must press his advantage without wasting time. He signalled for the woman to leave them. 'Now, Temir, listen to me,' he said after she had gone out. 'I've come to you as your Bey, knowing you for our tribe's wealthiest, noblest, most hard-working man. You may have come from the mountains, from the wild forests, yet the whole tribe speaks of you with praise and respect, you who have added to the glory of these villages of ours . . .' For a better effect Jafer began to align bombastic words and phrases in Arabic and Persian whose meaning he only dimly guessed. Ala Temir blinked and nodded attentively, bursting with pride. How beautifully the Bey was speaking, how eloquent he was! Of course no ordinary human being could understand what he was saying . . . 'And for that reason, though you were a newcomer we all accepted you with open arms,' Jafer Özpolat concluded. He fixed his steel-green eyes on Ala Temir who stirred uneasily. Then he pressed his point. 'So now I want you to be my partner. We're going to sow rice. And for this you're to give me . . .'

'But, Bey . . . But . . . But I . . .'

'You're to give me a hundred thousand liras at once,' Jafer pursued relentlessly.

'But, Bey . . . Bey . . .'

'At once . . . I'll give you a promissory note for it. And in the autumn you'll get your money back and your profit too.'

'But, Bey, I haven't got that much!'

'Nonsense, I know you have.'

Still stammering 'Bey, Bey, Bey,' Ala Temir rushed out of the room, flushed crimson, his eyes starting from his head. 'Woman, woman, have you heard? It's money the Bey wants from us. A hundred thousand liras! He wants to be partners with me . . . To sow rice . . .'

'Well?' she said unexpectedly. 'Why don't you give it to him? Think, man, it's our Bey who's come to us, to our very feet! And you stand there hesitating, may you be struck blind! Don't you hear me, man?'

Ala Temir went back. He kneeled at Jafer's feet. 'I can put together twenty-five thousand. Won't that do?'

But Jafer had overheard Zöhré and was now quite sure that he would have his money. 'No,' he said quietly, 'that won't do at all.'

Ala Temir scuttled out again. 'He won't accept twenty-five thousand . . .'

'Well, give him what he wants. Our Bey wouldn't waste your money or not give it back. And even if it was so, he's our Bey, isn't he?'

Once more Ala Temir tried to plead with Jafer Özpolat. But in vain. The Bey simply closed his eyes. 'One hundred thousand is what I need,' he said with finality. 'Not a penny less will I take.'

There was a long silence. 'Bey, Bey,' Ala Temir blurted out at last, 'I want no promissory note from you. Nor any partnership. I'm lending you the money. You'll give it back to me in the autumn, won't you?'

'All right,' Özpolat consented.

313

Ala Temir rose to his feet. 'It's hot in here,' he said. 'If you don't mind, if it's not too much trouble for your honour, we could go out and sit under that mulberry tree . . .'

Jafer Özpolat got the idea. He jumped up at once and walked out, while Zöhré hurried after him to spread some cushions in the shade of the tree. He declined to sit, preferring to pace up and down, tapping his boots with his whip. 'Well, sister?' he said to the woman who was hovering about him. 'And how's life going with you?'

'Thank you, Bey,' she said. 'We're all perfectly all right so long as you're well . . .'

'And the children?'

'They're well too, Bey, may they be your slaves.'

His brow knitted, Jafer fell to pacing the yard again, tapping the whip on his boots.

And inside Ala Temir, having unearthed his tin cans and emptied them over a cloth, was busy counting. On and on he counted, right up to noontime, while Jafer Özpolat kicked his heels outside, his eyes fixed warily on the door, wondering if Temir might not have hoodwinked him and made his escape through the back door. At last he saw him coming out with a bundle clutched tightly in his two hands. Relieved, jubilant, Jafer felt like throwing somersaults on the dung-strewn dust of the yard. Biting his lips to hide his joy, he jumped on to the saddle and took the bundle Ala Temir was holding out to him. 'Many thanks, Temir,' he said as he spurred his horse. 'And to you too, sister . . .' And the horse galloped off out of the village in a cloud of dust.

Jafer Özpolat was now able to enter into partnership with the man from Marash and to sow as much as three thousand *dönüms* of rice-paddies. The rest of the money he obtained by mortgaging a part of his land.

Autumn came and the harvest was brought in. It was a particularly bountiful one and Jafer Özpolat came into such a large amount of money that he had nothing more to fear from now on. In the meantime everyone had got to know that his principal capital had been supplied by Ala Temir. Some were astounded, others disparaging. 'He scrimps on his own food until he's almost starving, the bastard, and has pretensions to making others rich!' Everywhere he went people began to twit Ala Temir. 'So you think you'll see that hundred thousand of yours again, eh? What a simpleton you are, Ala Temir!'

'Hah hah hah! Why, Allah himself couldn't take back the life he gave Jafer Özpolat! And you hope to recover your money!'

'That money you scraped and saved for donkey's years, you poor fool . . .'

'If only, ah if only instead of giving it to that heathen, you'd got yourself some proper clothes, a decent suit . . .'

'That's the way with these Beys, Ala Temir. They don't return what they take, they don't take back what they give . . .'

'You can go home now and take a long draught of cold water to wash it all down.'

'Look, it's ages since the rice was harvested, and sold too. Why hasn't he paid you back yet? Because he's no intention of doing so, that's why!'

'Poor old Ala Temir! Poor old chap . . .'

'It really isn't fair. What a foul trick to play, borrow a man's money, make millions with it, then simply sit on it! At least if he'd given back the half . . .'

'Look, Temir, don't you attempt to go and ask him for your money! These Beys have no scruples about killing people. Not only will you not get the money, but you'll soon be found dead and rotting in some ditch or other.'

'For God's sake, Ala Temir, for God's sake, be careful!'

'They're like wild horses these Beys, you never know which way they're going to kick.'

Ala Temir listened to all this without a word, his tiny yellowish eyes narrowing with worry, his cheeks sunken now, his hands trembling. He would jump out of bed before dawn and rush out to fix his eyes on the road. At sunrise he slipped in, swallowed his soup at one swig and took up his watch again. The Bey would come, of that he was certain. Sooner or later he would bring back the money, but what could be delaying him? . . .

Winter came and the cold weather set in, with the north winds raging over the countryside, and still there was no sign of Jafer Özpolat.

315

'He won't come, Ala Temir. You're just hoping against hope. He won't come.'

'He will, he will.'

The long-legged Chukurova rains had started, steadily untwining from the skies like spools of thread, and still Ala Temir kept up his watch, huddled outside his house, buffeted by wind and hail, soaked by the rains.

One night he decided he must do something. Maybe the Bey had forgotten all about that money. Beys were apt to be absent-minded. He ought to be reminded. So he took up his stick and started off on the road at once. He was wasted to skin and bone now, was Ala Temir. He had hardly eaten or slept in all these days. His knees felt weak and he would stop every now and then to catch his breath. So this is what losing money does to a man, he thought. Worse than death . . . But soon he would be at the Bey's mansion. The Bey would be confounded. I'm sorry, Ala Temir Agha . . . Yes, he'd call him Agha . . . I'm sorry, with all this work I had no time to bring you your money. Here it is, take it . . . Not at all, not at all! I don't really need it. You can give it to me whenever you want. Our soul, our everything is at your service, Bey . . . He'd take the money in the end and stuff it into his shirt, and the Bey would invite him to stay. His wife would spread some wonderful food . . . Roast goose it would be . . . Roasted brown over piles and piles of fat glistening rice-pilaff . . . And *ayran* . . .

Jafer Özpolat spied him coming up the road. His first impulse was to make himself scarce. Then he thought better of it. 'I've got a very important guest coming,' he advised his wife and the servants. 'See that he's given a lavish welcome.' He laughed. 'He's our benefactor, you know . . .'

He greeted Ala Temir in the yard. 'Welcome, welcome, dear Agha!' he cried. 'So you've come at last . . . This house, this high gambrel-roofed mansion has been honoured at last by your bright and precious presence!' Taking his arm he supported Ala Temir, whose legs were weaving under him, up the stairs and made him sit down on a soft sofa covered with a cloth of snow-white soap-scented embroidered batiste. The minute he was seated Ala Temir clamped his legs together, stuck his hands over his knees and sat bolt upright, eyes fixed rigidly in front of him.

'Make yourself comfortable, do, Ala Temir Agha!' Jafer Özpolat urged him. 'This is your house. Do as you would at home.' But the more Jafer exhorted him, the stiffer and tauter he grew.

A buxom green-eyed seventeen-year-old maidservant, her plaited hair swinging over her shoulders, entered the room, a towel over her arm, carrying a basin and ewer. Deftly she untied the straps of Ala Temir's boots and removed one of them. A terrible stench spread through all the house and the girl unwittingly held her nose.

Jafer Özpolat retained his composure. 'Bring me a pair of socks,' he called to another servant. 'One of my new ones.'

And the girl proceeded to wash Ala Temir's calloused feet, rubbing them with plenty of soap, drying them and putting on the socks. She was bathed in sweat.

'Take the Agha's boots down and bring my very newest slippers . . .'

Ala Temir had remained stock-still through it all, his eyes fixed unblinkingly before him. He was proud, flattered, bursting with emotion, but did not show it. Who said this lofty Bey, this proud eagle of a man was going to cheat him out of his money? Of course he wasn't! He was going to give it back of course, but politely, after having treated him to all the hospitality he could muster . . .

A mustached servant appeared in the doorway with a huge butcher's knife in his hand. 'Bey, which sheep am I to kill?'

'Why, the best, the fattest we have, to be sure, for my dear respected guest! This house has never been so honoured before, not even when my noble grandfather entertained Governors and Beys and Vizirs.'

'Please, please,' Ala Temir murmured, overcome with embarrassment. 'Please don't bother . . .' There was a lump in his throat. He wanted to throw himself at Jafer's feet, to beg him to keep the money, to give him all he owned even. Here was a real Bey, hospitable, who knew the worth of a human being, one for whom he could toil a whole lifetime to make him happy.

317

As evening came savoury odours of roast meat began to drift up from the kitchen downstairs and in ones and twos Jafer Bey's villagers entered the room. They greeted Ala Temir with every show of respect, bowing before him, their hands on their breasts, and seated themselves in a row on the sofas. Ala Temir still maintained his stiff position, knees held tight and hands clamped fast over them, but his eyes moved now, dwelling on each newcomer for a while.

The meal was spread on the floor in the old tradition. As the food was brought in, the villagers slipped down from the sofas and squatted all round the long cloth. Ala Temir found himself seated between Jafer Bey and the oldest villager. His heart was dancing with joy. The Bey was giving a feast in his honour, the Bey of twelve villages! At any other time he would have fallen to this luscious fragrant meat with ravenous appetite. But now he was too excited to taste anything at all. It was a good thing that there was no talk during the meal. Villagers always eat in silence.

The conversation began only when they had finished. It ran on various subjects such as cotton and rice prices, politics, foreign and local, bandits, but Ala Temir never proffered a word, only listening avidly, his little eyes flicking from one talker to another.

It was time to go to bed and the villagers took their leave. Ala Temir had never been up so late in his life. The young maid-servant showed him to his room. He had hardly put his head to the pillow when Jafer Bey came in. 'I've come to wish you a good night, my dear illustrious guest . . .'

Ala Temir sprung out of the bed and stood at attention in his underclothes. 'Thank you, thank you, Bey,' he shouted. 'May you live a thousand years.'

Jafer Bey led him back to the bed and tucked the blanket about him. Ala Temir was asleep before he knew it.

The next morning he was up early. Breakfast consisted of butter, cheese and honey and a garlic-scented *tarhana* soup swimming with butter and paprika. Ala Temir forgot every-thing as he gobbled a huge roll of buttered honey, swallowed the milk in the crystal glass and spooned up the soup. His belly felt like a drum. 'May the Lord Halil Ibrahim bless your table,

318

Bey,' he said gratefully, and he took up his position on the sofa again, his hands on his knees. Jafer Özpolat went out into the village and when he returned at noon Ala Temir was there just as he had left him. Lunch was served. Ala Temir ate with the same hearty appetite, then quickly moved back to the sofa.

It was the same that evening, and the next day . . .

On the morning of the third day, Ala Temir fixed his eyes pleadingly on Jafer and never looked away. Jafer was mesmerized by this hunched shrunk figure who seemed to be beseeching with every pore of his body, with the very hairs of his head, and for the life of him could not move either. For how many hours they sat there staring at each other neither of them could tell. Lunch was brought in, which Ala Temir ate without altering his imploring stance. 'Bey,' he blurted out at last when it was over, 'I have to go now . . .'

'But, Agha, of course,' Jafer exclaimed. 'Only you can't go like that! I'll have the carriage harnessed at once.' He rose laughing delightedly. 'You've made me so happy, so happy. You must come again. Would I ever send such a dear treasured guest tramping away on foot? What would people think of me?' On and on he talked while Ala Temir stood swaying, utterly stunned, and when the carriage was announced he held his arm to lead him downstairs. Ala Temir's hand was like ice and his body trembling all over. For the first time Jafer felt a twinge of pity.

A servant was waiting at the foot of the stairs with Ala Temir's boots. He helped him on with them and tied up his laces with practised hands. It took three men to bundle the limp, almost fainting Ala Temir into the carriage. The driver cracked his whip and the horses started up.

Jafer Özpolat was outraged. 'The bastard!' he swore. 'As though he needed the money! Whatever possessed me to borrow from such a snivelling fool? Why, he is almost ready to die! For such a paltry sum! What a skinflint!' Up and down the yard he went until his anger cooled off and he began to laugh as he recalled his victim's mien. His wife, the servants, all those who had seen Ala Temir could talk about nothing else, and the house rang with laughter for days afterwards.

When he came home Ala Temir staggered out of the carriage

like a bag of bones, pale as a sheet and went in to throw himself face down over a pallet.

'What's the matter? What happened?' his wife asked as she knelt anxiously at his side.

'He didn't give me the money . . .'

'Well, it's no use worrying yourself sick over that. He's our Bey, after all. How did he greet you, that's what matters?' She talked and talked, trying to comfort him, and in the end Ala Temir raised his face.

'Zöhré,' he said, 'you should have seen what a welcome I got! The Bey killed a sheep for me. A girl came to wash my feet with scented soap . . . I slept on a high bed with a feather mattress. For three days nothing was good enough for me . . .'

'Well then, what are you fretting about?'

'So, you see, I was ashamed to ask for my money. And he simply forgot, like Beys do, you know. But still . . .'

'He'll give it back,' his wife said. 'And even if he doesn't . . . After the honour he's done you . . .'

'Butter, honey . . .' Ala Temir said. 'And a feast the first evening to which he invited all his villagers! And they all bowed to me with the greatest respect. And you know what the Bey said to them? This house, he said, has seen many great and famous visitors, but none to compare with Ala Temir Agha . . . I simply couldn't ask for the money after that . . .'

'And quite right too,' his wife said. 'You acted like a real man. Now the Bey will know who's who. He'll understand us better.'

'That's true,' Ala Temir said as he rose from the pallet. A whiff of scented soap still clung to him and he breathed it in with intense pleasure.

After this Ala Temir went back to Jafer Özpolat's house every month or so and he received the same enthusiastic welcome. His hands on his knees, he would fix his eyes pleadingly on the Bey who would pretend not to notice. Sometimes Jafer would not be there at all and Ala Temir was not long in realizing that he had made good his escape at his approach. So one day he waylaid Jafer's wife and poured out the whole story. 'Please,' he said, 'tell the Bey I need the money. He's our Bey, he'll understand.'

'All right, Agha, I will,' she said gently. 'It must have slipped his mind . . .'

'I knew it!' Ala Temir rejoiced. 'But if you'll just remind him . . .' Of course the Bey had forgotten, that was all! Now the Lady would tell him and he'd be sure to bring the money home at once.

So once more he fell to waiting and watching the road leading to Jafer Özpolat's village. By now all the villagers were making fun of him. At last, goaded beyond endurance, he appeared again one morning at the mansion. The Bey tried to take his arm, but he shook him away and, marching up the stairs, sat down firmly in his usual place on the sofa. He slapped his hands to his knees and stretched out his neck, fixing his eyes on the Bey like two arrows. 'Why don't you give me back what's mine?' he shouted. 'Haven't you become rich enough with that money I gave you? No one would do what you're doing to me, neither friend nor foe. Give me my money at once! If you don't . . . If you don't . . . I'll . . . I'll . . .'

Recovering from his surprise, Jafer Özpolat sat down too. 'What will you do if I don't?' he asked in a mocking tone.

Ala Temir sprang to his feet waving his hands, his eyes starting from his head and the veins in his neck swollen like rolling-pins. 'I know what I'll do and so do you!' he yelled. His voice was heard all over the village and people began to gather about the house to listen to the quarrel. 'What kind of a Bey are you? What kind of a man? I wouldn't have you for a dog at my door even! You've made yourself with my money and now you're sitting on it. You're nothing but a low-down crooked rascal.'

'You can thank your lucky stars that you're in my house!' Jafer Özpolat retorted, rising and taking a step towards him. 'Otherwise . . .'

Ala Temir suddenly realized he'd gone too far. How could he have insulted the Bey in front of his wife and so that everyone in the neighbourhood could hear? . . . He sat down again, his hands on his knees. 'Bey,' he pleaded humbly, 'give me my money. D'you know how I earned it, with what work of blood and sweat? Eating only *mirmirik* soup and grass, going hungry

321

. . . Saving, saving all the time. Always labouring year in, year out, come wind come weather . . . Even when I was sick I never stopped . . . God forbid that anyone should be like me! For years I saved, laying up five kurush over five, ten over ten . . . How can you have the heart to take this money? And if you do, will God forgive you, d'you think? Isn't there a God above who sees everything?'

'Now that's too much!' Jafer Özpolat exploded. 'Shut up!'

At this, Ala Temir went wild. Cursing like mad, he dashed down the stairs. Out in the yard he stopped and went on howling at the top of his voice, brandishing his fists and hurling insults and imprecations at the Bey. Round and round the yard he pattered saying whatever came to his head, raging, foaming at the mouth. There was no answer, no sound at all from the house.

All day long till evening fell, Ala Temir stood screaming on there, in Jafer Özpolat's yard, cursing all the Beys in the world with bell, book and candle, until his voice turned hoarse and he was hissing like a goose. He felt a deep silence about him and was seized with fright. What had he done? How could he have forgotten himself like this? The Bey would never let this pass unpunished. He might even have him killed . . .

'Bey, Bey, Bey . . .' he croaked. 'I've changed my mind. I give up the money. It's yours. I'm giving it to you. It's yours as your mother's milk.'

This would do the trick, he thought. Now he was saved.

It was midnight by the time he reached home and he was feeling almost joyful.

'Did you get the money?' his wife asked.

Temir smiled. 'The poor man . . . I really felt sorry for him, really quite sorry . . . A Bey, our Bey, so good and kind to me, offering *kurbans** in my honour . . . That he should come to this . . . No, I just couldn't bear it.'

'So you didn't ask for the money?'

'He seemed just like a child about to break into tears . . . I'm not the man to forget favours. So I told him he didn't owe me a penny any more . . . I told him he could come again to me

Kurbans: sacrifices.

322

whenever he needed money. After all he's our Bey, our only Bey. We can't let him go hungry . . .'

Zöhré was bursting with pride. 'That's what one would expect from a man like you,' she cried casting her arms about his neck.

Ala Temir felt that a great load was off his shoulders and for the first time in his life he could not sleep for joy.

And so it happened that Jafer Özpolat came again to borrow money from Ala Temir . . . And Ala Temir gave it to him. Again he waited for months, hoping against hope that the Bey would give it back, visiting his house, sitting in his old place on the sofa, stiffly upright, his hands clamped to his knees . . . He was feasted and his feet were bathed with scented soap. Then one day he would start cursing again and pour insults on the Bey from out in the yard.

For years now it had been like this. Ala Temir would swear and complain, then he would forgive and forget, and Jafer Özpolat whenever hard-pressed for cash would borrow as much as he liked from him.

And in the meantime the two of them were growing richer day by day . . .

'It's now or never, Temir Agha,' Özpolat said. 'Dervish Bey's killed his brother-in-law . . . The villagers are all ready to swear that Kamil just killed himself, but it won't be easy for Dervish to get out of this one. We'll see to that! He'll be needing a lot of money these days. So he'll have to sell some land. You must go to him at once. He'll sell to you. I think he likes you . . .'

'Good!' Ala Temir said, thrusting out his lower lip like an ageing horse. 'It's just what I need. A great deal of land for as little money as possible, and with what I can add from Akchasaz a thousand *dönüms* can become ten thousand.'

'Yes,' Jafer said taking his arm. 'And don't forget my commission!'

'Of course not,' Ala Temir said proudly, leaning on Jafer's shoulder. 'Tomorrow, first thing in the morning I'll be at Dervish's house.'

'First thing in the morning,' Jafer Özpolat said approvingly . . .

38

The dead beetle was still there in the hollow, but lying on its back now with its legs shrivelled up to its belly. There was no sign of the little red ant, and all the ants he had pitted together the day before had separated, except for two tiny ones still struggling with each other at the foot of a slim spurge. The other ants had gone about their business and were dragging grain from the threshing place to their hole.

Suddenly, Mustafa Bey's eyes brightened. Here was the little ant, back again, tackling the beetle once more. 'Bravo!' he cried. 'Brave little ant! It won't accept defeat. It knows it can never move that beetle, yet still it fights on, not to win, only not to be defeated. And as long as it's struggling that means it hasn't lost . . .'

The little ant had seized the beetle with its pincers. Its forelegs were planted firmly to the ground, its hindlegs slipped and scraped obstinately at the earth as it tugged and tugged.

Flitting among the mauve flowers of the agnus castus bush were huge hairy bees, such as he had never seen before, with blue rings and specks. Mestan was lying under the bush propped up on his elbows, his eyes on the road, still cursing away silently at Mustafa Bey.

A clammy heat had set in and the swamp rumbled and boiled with earthshaking booms. There was not a bird in sight, except for a few storks pacing about leisurely on their long springy legs among the large white narcissus and water-lilies on the edge of the swamp. Mustafa Bey, who had lived so many years near this swamp and knew it through and through, had never heard it throbbing so deep and loud, even raising echoes from the Anavarza crags. It gave him a feeling of imminent disaster . . . There was still no sign of Whirlwind Veli, although he had sent Hamdi and three men to look for him in the environs of the Sarioglu mansion. What could have happened to him? At home too, something was wrong. Last night, his mother had looked at him not with her usual compelling killing eyes, but with pity and despair. That hopeless gaze . . . What could be the matter?

Suddenly Mestan gave a shout: 'Here he comes!' Hamdi, Ibrahim Ibo and Mustafa Bey jumped to their feet. A deep rumble from the swamp shattered through the hot air and crashed back from the Anavarza crags.

'Down! Down for heaven's sake! Don't let him see us . . .'

They all crouched behind the agnus castus holding their guns ready as the rider came down the hill, very slowly, clinging to the pommel of his saddle, the reins lying loose over the horse's neck. He was quite near them now. They saw him rise up on the stirrups, searching for something in the reeds. His eyes rested on the bush where they were hiding.

'I'll stake my life it's Dervish Bey's man, looking for us,' Mestan whispered in Mustafa Bey's ear. 'I'll stake my life . . .'

'Be quiet then, or he'll hear us.'

The rider was coming straight at them. He stopped beside the bush and bent down to look. Then he rubbed his eyes, spurred his horse and galloped off in the direction of Hemité Castle.

'He's seen us,' Mestan said. 'I'll swear it's Dervish Bey's man and now they've found our hiding-place, they're going to attack us.'

'I wish they would,' Mustafa Bey said. 'I wish we could simply fight it out, the two of us, like men, face to face, and either one of us die, or still better, both of us . . .'

'But, Bey, what d'you mean?' Hamdi cried. 'Of course you can't do that! We're going to catch him. And then, you know, you'll hold your gun to his eyes and wait like that, one hour, two hours . . . And if he closes his eyes I'll jab him in the shanks with a sacking-needle . . .'

Mustafa Bey sighed dejectedly. 'I'm sick of it all. If it wasn't for that mother of mine, I'd just give up . . .'

'Look, look!' Mestan cried. 'There's another rider!'

This one was coming at a brisk trot, but once again he stopped right in front of them and looked searchingly into the reeds and at the agnus castus bushes before riding on again towards Mount Hemité which floated like a thin wisp of smoke in the heat-haze.

'Something's up,' Mestan said.

'Have we been found out d'you think?'

'Let them find us!' Mustafa Bey said. 'Let Dervish come today, damn him if he doesn't . . . Let's get it over today.'

Towards noon another rider appeared. He was very small on the saddle, like a child. As he approached they heard him calling in a loud clear voice. Mustafa Bey shivered involuntarily and his heart began to beat more quickly. Some calamity was imminent. He had had that foreboding all morning, but what, what could it be?

'Something must have happened to my mother,' he said. 'What if she's dead?'

'Of course she isn't,' Mestan said confidently. 'She'd never die without seeing Dervish Bey's severed head first. Besides this is no one we know. They'd have sent someone from the mansion if it was like that.'

'Mustafa Beeey! Mustaaa . . . Beeey . . .' The voice rang out strong and clear, a voice used to shouting. Mustafa Bey had heard it before somewhere. It sounded like one of those sweet long-drawn-out Chukurova songs. He called to mind the singers and minstrels that he knew. 'Mestan, you go out and see who it is. We'll hide under those willows. Friend or foe, we mustn't reveal our hiding-place.' And he led the way to a green cluster of willows surrounded by a wall-like mass of tall reddish reeds. 'How cool it is here,' he said. 'We were stifling down in that reed-bed.'

'I know this place,' Ibrahim Ibo said. 'There's room enough in that tree for three people to sleep. I hid in it once for a couple of months when the gendarmes were at my heels and they never found me. It's like a paradise in the Chukurova, that tree is, so cool and airy . . .'

'Well, why didn't you say so before,' Mustafa Bey expostulated, 'instead of letting us moulder away in those reeds?'

From way off they heard Mestan calling in his hoarse wheezy voice: 'It's the town-crier! The town-crier's come, the town-crier!'

'The town-crier, Bey!' Ibrahim Ibo cried in astonishment. 'What can be the matter?'

'Something's up,' Mustafa Bey said. 'The town-crier's our

326

friend. He wouldn't leave town like this without important news.'

He came out and stood by a tall mullein studded with bright red flowers and humming with bees. The town-crier dismounted and began bouncing up and down like a ball to relieve the numbness in his legs. Then, running up to Mustafa Bey, he shook his hand like an old friend. His tiny drawn face, the blue shadows under his sunken eyes, his trembling hands, his puckered sullen lips like a child about to cry and the fresh wound on his right temple struck Mustafa Bey at once, but he concealed his anxiety. 'I'm glad to see you,' he said. 'What news?'

'Oh, all's well . . .' But his drooping head belied the words.

'How did you find me here?'

'I went to your house this morning, before dawn. On foot . . . And there they said you were somewhere in Akchasaz, but where they couldn't tell. So I said I'd shout out for you till I found you. The Lady Karakiz gave me this horse. We talked . . .'

'What! She spoke with you?'

'Of course she did . . . She wanted to know why I had come so early, at dawn. Everyone was still asleep, but she was sitting there, perched on a chair, clinging to the balcony post, and her eyes were fixed right in this direction.'

'And what did you tell her?'

'Nothing. Only that the Aghas in the town were going to kill me. And she said, find Mustafa, he won't let them kill you. I guessed you must be here because she never took her eyes off this spot.'

'Wait a minute, brother,' Mustafa Bey said and vanished into the reeds only to appear again a moment later. He grabbed the town-crier's hand. 'Come and look,' he cried as he pulled him into the reed-bed. 'D'you see that little ant here? And look, see how big this beetle is! It's days now that the beetle slipped into this hollow as the little ant was dragging it along, and ever since the little ant's been trying to pull it out, doggedly, tirelessly. And so it will one day, I'm absolutely certain of it.' Then he turned to the town-crier. 'Why do the Aghas want to kill you?'

At last the town-crier could tell his story. He told it all in one breath, not omitting the slightest detail. 'So you see,' he concluded, flushed and sweating, 'they're going to kill me. But I

327

don't care. The ironsmith is my friend, more than a brother to me. He'll look after my children and bring them up and see they don't want anything. That's why I'm not afraid of dying.'

'So we're going to be exiled? When? Does Dervish know?'

'Mahir Kabakchioglu said to me . . . He said, quick, town-crier, if I go the Aghas will be angry with me. You go, first to Mustafa Bey, then to Dervish Bey and warn them of the danger. They're going to exile you to Edirne or Kars, together with all your family and tribe . . . Just to get hold of your lands, you know, and Akchasaz . . .'

'So it's like that, is it?' Mustafa Bey's face was downcast and troubled. But suddenly he burst out laughing. 'I wish I could have seen Kurtboga coming out of that car in all his majesty . . . Hah hah hah!' he guffawed. 'What courage, what a hero! Hah hah hah! And he threatened you with his revolver! And you . . . You . . . What did you say?' He was holding his sides and the tears came to his eyes. The others were soon roaring with laughter too, the town-crier louder than anyone else. 'You defied him . . . Shoot, shoot . . . Hah hah hah! And he stood there frozen, all yellow, while you swore at his wife and mother . . . Hah hah hah . . .' Again and again he made the town-crier repeat his encounter with Kurtboga. 'Oh dear, oh dear, I'm dead with laughing,' he said at last wiping his eyes. 'I haven't laughed so much in all these years. Think of it, that woman-butcher, that money-grubber!'

'But he's going to kill me, Bey. It's not that I'm afraid . . . Not when there's the ironsmith . . .'

Mustafa Bey knew it was useless to offer consolation. The matter had come to such a pass that the Aghas would never rest until they had done away with the town-crier. 'Look, my friend,' he said. 'I've got a suggestion. Why don't you go away? I'll give you some money and . . .'

'Impossible!' the town-crier shouted. 'That I can't do!'

'But wait, brother, listen! Don't get angry . . .'

'You at least, Mustafa Bey, should never suggest such a thing . . .'

'But you're going to die because of us.'

'Yes, I'll die! I'll die but nobody will be able to say I feared for my miserable life and ran away. You at least, Mustafa Bey!

You shouldn't . . .' He stalked off repeating heatedly: 'You . . . You, at least . . .'

'Wait, wait, brother! I'm sorry,' Mustafa Bey said, running after him. 'I didn't mean that. You've got me wrong . . .' The town-crier in his anger seemed larger and taller, even his hump was no longer there.

Just at that moment a rider appeared, galloping hell for leather along the road. As he was passing near them, Mustafa Bey recognized him. 'Why, it's Süleyman Sami!' he said. 'Ibrahim Ibo, you ride after him. He's looking for us too.'

'It's Kabakchioglu who's sent him,' the town-crier remarked.

Ibrahim Ibo was soon back with Süleyman Sami, who jumped from his horse and embraced Mustafa Bey. 'They're plotting to banish you, Bey,' he shouted. 'If not today, then tomorrow . . . Tomorrow, tomorrow! And you unaware of it all . . .' He was tense and on edge. 'Mahir Kabakchioglu sends his regards and says that it all depends now on the Big Judge and he never listens to anyone but Aziz Agha. So Mahir Bey says you must go and see Aziz Agha without fail or, even better, talk to the Big Judge himself.'

They conversed on the events in the town till sundown. Then they all rode back to the mansion where the Lady Karakiz was still waiting on her chair, her hands clasped to the balcony post. As Mustafa Bey slipped in, his head bowed, she muttered something he did not hear.

'What's she saying?' he inquired of his wife who had followed him to his room.

'She's been weeping and lamenting ever since the town-crier came because they're going to banish us . . .'

Suddenly the door crashed open and the Lady Karakiz appeared on the threshold. 'You must be quick, my Mustafa, very quick . . . Before they banish us . . . Retaliation must not wait till Judgment Day. My Murtaza's blood must not be left to lie on the ground, unavenged . . .' She turned away and took up her station on the balcony once more.

After a while they all sat down to dinner. Süleyman Sami was talking all the time. 'They're quite rabid these Aghas,' he said. His eyes rested on the town-crier, very small at his end of the table. 'And now they want to kill this poor little chap!' he cried, pointing a finger at him. 'Kurtboga's armed three huge men just for that! Would a man stoop to lift his hand against him?'

The town-crier glared and muttered something under his breath. The minute dinner was over he jumped up. 'With your permission,' he said. 'I've a long way to go.'

Mustafa Bey knew very well where he was going, but he made no attempt to detain him. He accompanied him to the gate and slipped something into his pocket.

The town-crier took to the road assailed by deep thoughts of death and annihilation, wondering how it would be, how they would kill him, how long he would be agonizing. Sometimes he stopped short in amazement as he recalled his defiance of Kurtboga and the insults he had hurled at him. A chill ran up his spine and his hair stood on end. So Kurtboga had set three armed men to kill him! And he didn't even have a tiny pistol in his pocket . . . A man shouldn't die like this, his hands tied . . . He should kill at least two of those men. Yes, he should. The town-crier was not at all a bad shot.

He reached the Sarioglu mansion before midnight. Hidayet brought the news to the Bey. 'Halil Felek, the hunchback's come,' he said.

Dervish Bey had been apprised of what was going on and he was expecting the town-crier. He greeted him with affection, taking his hand and patting it. 'Bring some food to this humped scamp,' he said laughing. 'Well, man, whatever did you do to that Kurtboga?'

'I've eaten already,' the town-crier said. 'I'm not hungry.'

'I know where you're coming from, you scamp,' Dervish Bey said as he led him into the drawing-room. The colours and designs of the *kilims* that covered the floor were blurred and shadowy in the dim light. And the old walnut chests with their carved and embossed flowers, birds, gazelles, trees, stars and streams were now very dark against the wall and under the windows, their designs flowing into each other. 'Well, you treated that cowardly cuckold just as he deserved . . . They're like women, those people. And so they want to banish us, eh? Let's just see them do it!'

'Mahir Kabakchioglu sent me to tell you that the Aghas are dead serious about it this time. For God's sake, he said, let him

330

go and see the Big Judge, because there's nothing left to do but that . . .'

'Now look here, town-crier, you've got sense and you see everything that's going on. Isn't Mahir himself really at the bottom of it all?'

'Yes,' the town-crier admitted. 'He went to the Prosecutor and planned the whole thing from the beginning.'

'Then why's he trying to warn me now?'

'Because he knows you always get to learn everything in the end and he's dead frightened of you. So he thinks that if he's the first to give you the news . . .'

'The low-down toadying coward!' Dervish Bey muttered, screwing up his face. 'But that Kurtboga's going to have you killed, you know that?'

'I know,' the town-crier said quite calmly. 'He's got three men after me already.'

'Why don't you come and stay here on the farm for a month or two with your family? It'll be a change for them too.'

The town-crier jumped up. 'Bey, anyone could tell me that, but not you! I'd never have expected it of you. It's difficult to accept death, I know. I don't want to, but I can't have it said of me that I ran away from Kurtboga. Not to save my life. Let him kill me . . . The ironsmith . . .'

Dervish Bey rose, took his hand and made him sit again. 'I'm sorry, brother,' he said. 'You're perfectly right. A man can't run away from such a bastard just to save his life, not after having bared his breast to his gun and cursed and sworn at him in front of everyone. Don't be angry. If there's one man in this whole world who can understand this, it's me.'

'I knew it!' the town-crier rejoiced. 'Of course you would.'

'There's still hope in the human race, my friend, that's what you've taught me. So you defied him, eh? You said, shoot, shoot, and if you don't . . . What did he do then?'

'He started trembling all over,' the town-crier replied complacently. 'Quite yellow he was, swaying and looking to right and left as if to say, isn't there anyone to save me . . . And then . . .'

'I know everything. Good for you!' Dervish Bey clapped his hands. 'You treated that bastard just as he deserved. Wait a minute . . .' He left the room and was back in a flash holding a revolver which he handed to the town-crier. Felek rose, put his left hand to his breast and took the revolver from the Bey. He could not believe his eyes. It was an ivory-handled revolver with a longish muzzle and it gleamed and glistened in the faint light. 'This belonged to my brother who was shot,' Dervish Bey said. 'He was a brave, valiant man. And now I'm giving it to my other brave and valiant brother. Take this too.' And he gave him a holster and a red bag full of bullets.

The town-crier sat down again, dazed, running his fingers over the revolver, holding it up to the lamp, beside himself with joy.

'I've heard that you're quite a good shot . . .'

The town-crier looked at him, his eyes shining with gratitude. He was struck dumb, unable to say a word. How could he properly express all that he felt? There was a lump in his throat. 'Never . . . never . . . never . . .' he stammered out at last. 'Bey . . . My Bey . . . Never . . . All my life . . . Just like this one . . .' He gazed in wonder at the revolver. 'I've always wanted one.'

That night he could not sleep a wink. He kept turning the revolver over in his hands, loading and unloading it and whirling the cylinder. Morning found him at the window still in rapt admiration of it. He jumped at the sound of Dervish Bey's voice behind him and quickly thrust the revolver into its holster, a little ashamed at being caught like that. 'Good morning, Bey,' he said, his voice singing with pride. 'I was just waiting for you to rise. I've got to go.'

'But won't you stay for . . .'

'I must go back to town at once,' the town-crier interrupted him. 'At once! Who knows what they may be saying about me even now? Perhaps thinking that . . . I've no time for breakfast. It wouldn't pass through my throat.'

Dervish Bey saw how it was. 'All right then, my friend,' he said. 'I'll tell them to get a horse ready for you. But mind you don't ride it so hard you get a tumble!'

'I won't!' the town-crier said fervently.

'You can take the horse to Ramazan, the refugee. He'll bring it back. He's got to come to the farm today anyway.'

And soon the town-crier was riding out of the yard, whipping up the white horse under him until it flew like the wind, and gazing in ecstasy every now and again at the revolver strapped to his hip. It was still early morning when he entered the town at a gallop, so fast he could not rein in and shot right through the market-place before curbing the snorting foaming horse. He cantered back, very straight on the saddle, his hand on his revolver so that everybody could see it, and stopped before the smithy which stood by itself at one end of the market-place. Quickly he tethered the horse to a bay tree and ran in. The smith was wielding the bellows and the embers glowed and flickered in the forge.

'Look,' the town-crier cried, embracing him joyfully. 'Look!' The smith gave a start of surprise at the sight of the weapon right under his nose, then he laughed. 'It's Dervish Bey who gave it to me, Dervish Bey himself!' the town-crier went on. 'It belonged to his brother who was killed in the feud. And Dervish said to me, he was a brave bold-hearted man and now I'm giving you his revolver, because you've got enemies too now, cruel, treacherous, unscrupulous enemies . . . You'll need it . . .' Suddenly his face fell. 'But what's the use, they're going to kill me anyway . . .'

The smith flared up at this. 'Nobody can kill you, nobody!' he shouted. 'What are we here for then? Just scarecrows in the fields?'

'Don't get angry, brother,' the town-crier said. 'What's the use . . . They're going to kill me.'

The smith's huge hand pulled at the bellows forcefully. 'Hah! So we're just scarecrows, eh?'

People were gathering before the smithy. They had observed the town-crier's lightning course through the market and they felt that something was up. And now they saw the smith rush out in a temper with the town-crier at his heels trying to calm him down. 'Don't be angry, brother,' the town-crier was saying. 'What if they *do* kill me? My children, my wife, I entrust to you. I know you'll take care of them even better than I. With such a friend as you, strong as a mountain, would a man fear death or persecution from those low-down Aghas?'

'There's a bullet for whoever touches a hair of your head!'

the smith roared. 'Or even looks askance at you. What do we have to lose if we die? What are we leaving behind? Only a half-broken anvil and a patched-up bellows, just that! But they? They have wealth and property in abundance that they wouldn't part with easily, and their whorish wives and daughters . . . Just let them touch my brother again and I'll make this world too hot for them. The slimy cowardly bastards! Persecuting poor defenceless people . . .' In his anger he looked taller, his huge hairy hands, large as a man's head, seemed even more formidable. 'Go now, brother,' he said giving the town-crier a gentle push. 'And don't worry. They'll see who they've got to deal with.' He went back to the smithy, seized the bellows and blew them so angrily that the iron was soon red-hot. He placed it on the anvil and began to beat, and at each blow clusters of sparks sputtered up to die out in the air about him.

Outside, the town-crier was still talking to the crowd. 'As if I don't know! Would they ever let me live after this business? Of course not! From now on I'm just a living corpse. But at least I'm ready to meet death with fortitude. And with my revolver on my hip too.' He drew back his jacket to show the ivory handle of the revolver. 'I'll never have the chance to see you like this, all together again. We've had good and bad times together. I've much to thank you for. If I've hurt anybody, even unwittingly, let him forgive me. Because I'm going, brothers. I shall soon be dead. You must relinquish all claims on me.'

'We do, we do,' came the sad murmur from the crowd.

'You wanted me to go away,' the town-crier pursued. 'You collected money for me . . . But if I'd done that, if I'd feared to die, you would all have spoken ill of me. What else could one expect of that little man anyway, you'd have said . . . Now you see me here, waiting for death like a man, as not one of those rich Aghas could do, my honour safe . . . Farewell, farewell . . .'

He walked on, repeating to everyone he met: 'Farewell, brother, you must relinquish all claims on me. These Aghas are going to kill me. Farewell . . .' Then slowly, with great dignity, he took the road that led to the watermills which were situated at the foot of the hills north-east of the town. And soon he could hear the booming sound of water crashing from the turbines to the wheels. He stopped outside one of the mills and watched the white-spumed furious turmoil that surged from the wheels, hurling spray high over the arched troughways. The odour of warm flour filled the air and white particles flew about the rapidly whirling grinding-stones.

The miller was a long man, but bent with age. Only his eyes and teeth gleamed through the layer of flour that covered his whole body. His voice rang out joyously above the deafening roar of the waters and the rumble of the stones. He had not thought to see the town-crier again . . .

'I've come to say good-bye,' the town-crier said. 'You know that I'm marked for death. If not today, then tomorrow . . .'

'I know,' the miller said. 'Why on earth did you get mixed up with those bastards? They'd kill a man just because they don't like the look of him!' Shaking his head sadly, he took the town-crier's arm and led him out to the weeping willows where it was quieter. 'Look, you ought to get away from here for a year or two. I could send you with your family to my village, and when you come back everything will have been forgotten.'

'That's impossible, uncle, quite impossible! I would be branded as a coward for ever if I ran away now. Isn't it better to die with my head held high, like a man?'

The miller made no answer.

'I've come to see you for a last farewell,' the town-crier pursued. 'What can we do, it's fate . . .'

'It's going to rain,' the miller said.

The town-crier looked up at the mountains. 'Yes,' he said. 'And how!'

'Suppose we have something to eat here, the two of us . . .' the miller suggested timidly. How could he tell him, look, you're going to die, let me make for you one last time those really good ash-baked patties that you like so much . . . It had been the town-crier's habit for many long years, when he was in the mood, to drop in at the mill with his *saz*. 'Stop that noise,' he would shout. Then, sitting on the white doorstone, he would huddle over his instrument and play and sing, songs nobody had ever heard before. He had a beautiful voice and in the whole of the Chukurova there was not another who played the *saz* like him. That was how his wife had fallen in love with him. She had heard him singing one day and had not rested until she

335

was married to him. She was reputed to be one of the loveliest women in the town . . . And the miller, each time his friend came, would quickly knead out some dough and make patties filled with onion, pimiento, butter, potatoes, mint leaves and parsley. The town-crier would sit by the hearth, his mouth watering, until the miller carefully raked away the ashes revealing the patties, beautifully browned, delectable. No one could make such delicious patties as this old miller.

'Look,' the miller blurted out. 'I know you like them so much . . . I thought . . . I can make you some ash-baked patties . . .'

'Why, bless you!' the town-crier laughed. 'There's nothing I'd like better than to leave this world with the taste of those patties in my mouth!'

Grey clouds, the colour of ashes, were churning in from over the mountains. A cold wind arose and whipped up the dust of the road. The town-crier shivered. Lightning flashed in the distance, but there was no thunder. Then, suddenly, warm gusts blew in and slow raindrops plopped down, pockmarking the dust. Thunder began to roll through the sky and the rain came down in torrents. The shower lasted forty minutes. When it was over the air was cool and clean, smelling of fresh earth. The town-crier inhaled deeply, his nostrils flaring wide. Mount Düldül was bathed in a pale luminous pink light and circling above it was a wide rainbow, green, mauve, orange, red, reflected faintly over the mountain, orange, mauve, green, pale blue . . . It hovered there well into the evening, shining brightly, emblazoning the clouds and the sky.

As he ate his patty, his eyes closed in enjoyment, the town-crier thought of his wife and children. He would have to explain the whole thing to her so she would understand.

'Look, wife . . . Death is Allah's will. If I die one day, there's the ironsmith. He'll look after the children and see that you do not want. Yes, wife, if I die it'll be to protect my honour. I shall leave behind a glorious name for my children. I shall be a legend on the tongues of men . . . You've heard, wife, what I did to Kurtboga . . . They can't really . . . Don't be afraid. You can trust the ironsmith more than your own brother. My children are his to safeguard . . .'

336

39

'That severed head, those staring eyes . . .'

The origin of the feud was never clear. It might have begun with plunder raids between the two tribes. Or perhaps it was a quarrel over pastures or wintering land. The first incident to be recorded occurred many years after the settlement. Turcomans still talk of that battle and it is the subject of many a song and dirge. The dead were all buried together on a mound in the Chukurova.

It was the time of transhumance. The Sarioglus were descending over Dikenli and Aslantash towards Hemité with the intention of resting awhile at Bozkuyu and then moving on to their customary winter quarters. The Akyollus too had the very same intention.

It must have been in the morning or perhaps at noontime. Who knows . . . The autumn winds had lulled and the heat weighed over the flat plain just as if it was still summer when the two tribes met. Mausers, hunting rifles, pistols, slings, daggers, knives, clubs, everything was good for the fight. Even the women and children joined in. Nobody ever knew who started it. That was not important. The fighting lasted for a whole week, with dogs barking and horses neighing and the cattle bellowing and most of the livestock running wild with terror over the Chukurova plain. No one tried to stop the fray, not even the police force, and least of all the other tribes who were sick of this eternal fighting and fervently prayed they would finish each other off.

The head of the Akyollus at that time was a certain Haji Yakup Bey. And Kerim Bey was the chief of the Sarioglus. He had eight sons of which five were killed in this encounter. Of the three left, one who was still a child went out of his mind. As for Haji Yakup he lost ten of his nineteen sons and three more simply ran away, never to be heard of again.

'Those severed heads, those staring eyes . . .'

The second important encounter took place on the rocky crest of Mount Hemité, near the shrine of Hamit Dedé. The nomads, again returning from the highlands, had come to the shrine to offer sacrifices, with drums and pipes, songs and litanies. Slim graceful Turcoman girls adorned the crags with the red and green, pink and orange and blue of their colourful array. Suddenly, a shot rang out and blood flowed over the mauve rocks. This time the tribes did not enter the fight. The combatants were the sons and grandsons of Kerim Bey and Haji Yakup Bey. They fought on there, around the shrine of the saint for no one knows how long. Three of them threw themselves down a precipice, unable to bear the agony of their wounds. Not a piece of them was ever found again, not even a bone or a bit of clothing. But for three days afterwards the sky over the precipice was thronged with screeching eagles, hawks and other birds of prey. Twenty dead were brought down from the mountain by their people with weeping and keening, while overhead copper-coloured swift-winged eagles whirled incessantly.

For a long time after this there were no more clashes. The Balkan wars and the First World War had intervened. Most of the men who were called up never returned and those who did were either crippled or sick. They were tired of fighting and glad to take up the normal threads of their existence.

But after the War of Independence the clans ran foul of each other again. Hüsam Bey, the grandson of Haji Yakup, was chief of the Akyollus at the time, and Hurshit Bey, grandson of Kerim Bey, that of the Sarioglus. The spark that set off the fire was a quarrel between two shepherds over forage grassland, but that was only a pretext and, though the two shepherds fought till there was not a bone left unbroken in their body, the matter might have stopped there. But Hurshit Bey's son Ali Bey at once laid an ambush in the Narli brake for Hüsam Bey's son Kadir Bey, who had been chosen by the People's Party to serve on the Provincial Council, to the great chagrin of the Sarioglus. They considered themselves better educated than the Akyollus and much more fitted for that position. Moreover Kadir Bey's younger brother, Reshat, was president of the district branch of the party, which meant that the Sarioglus had no backing at all in the Government or the party. This threatened their very existence in the Chukurova. So they caught Kadir Bey and, together with the men that were with him, took him up into the uplands of Mazgach. It was mid-winter. A keen north wind was blowing. They stripped their captives naked and tied them to the trees. Then with sharp razors they proceeded to slash their skin, long narrow slits from top to bottom. The blood had no time to flow. It froze instantly in long red strips . . . Ali Bey and his men never stopped until their squirming victims were nothing but blood-red lacerated rigid blocks. Then they left them there, frozen to the trees, the snow already covering their bodies. But on the way back to the Chukurova Ali Bey was very silent and when they came to the path leading down to Kalé, he suddenly turned to his men and said: 'Wait for me here a little.' He went to a spring that flowed under a pine tree and they saw him perform his ablutions. And afterwards he took off his coat, spread it on the ground and bent down for the *namaz* prayer. When he had finished he leaned against the tree, his eyes closed, and for a long while he did not move.

'Brothers,' he said at last in a dead voice, 'I should never have done such a thing to Kadir Bey. It's unworthy of a human being. And I've dragged you all, too, into this shameful business . . . Even if a man kills himself after this he can never atone. But still the only way out for me is to kill myself.' He drew out his gun. 'After I'm dead,' he told his men who stared at him, frozen to their saddles, 'you're to cut off my head and take it straight to Hüsam Bey. Tell him I send my head to put an end to this cruelty, this savagery. Tell him I said that such abominable baseness is not worthy of a human being . . . And as for you, never be drawn again into these sanguinary feuds and maybe you'll forget this day's foulness . . .' Closing his eyes, he held the gun to his heart and pressed the trigger.

His men did as he had told them. Hüsam Bey was jubilant at the sight of the severed head. 'So this is Ali Bey?' he laughed. 'Good. You bring me the head of a Sarioglu . . .' But when he heard the rest of the story he went mad with rage and started kicking the severed head about. Then he whipped out his gun and shot at the men. One of them dropped dead on the spot, but the others somehow managed to get away.

'His severed head, his staring eyes . . .'

There was a long period of quiet after this, and people had just begun to think that everything had blown over when one day Veli Agha from Anavarza village sent a message to Kadir Bey's brother, Reshat, which set him going at once. He collected his men and they rode off. It was a dark rainy night with the north wind blowing. At midnight they were at Veli Agha's house.

'They're here,' Veli Agha said, 'three of them asleep in that room. I managed to empty their rifles and take all their ammunition too.'

'Good,' Reshat Bey said. 'I'll never forget this mark of friendship, Veli Agha.'

'They didn't realize I recognized them. They just asked to stay like any wayfarers. And then I saw that all three were Sarioglus . . . I've got to inform the Akyollus at once, I said to myself, so I sent my son out to you, riding hard . . . One of them's called Fethi, and the other two Enver and Niyazi. They're the sons of Ali Bey's brother.'

Reshat Bey and his companions burst upon the sleeping men, trussed them up and, after tying them to each other as well, drove them out of Anavarza village towards Chukurköprü.

'If we could only take them up into the mountains, slash them to death with razors just as they did my brother,' Reshat Bey was saying.

'We have no time,' one of the men said. 'The Sarioglus will surely get wind of this soon. We've got to kill them now, to-night.'

The others agreed with him. It would be wiser to finish them off straight away and throw the bodies into the Sumbas Stream.

'Very well,' Reshat Bey assented reluctantly, 'but next time we catch a Sarioglu we've got to slice him to death with a razor.'

'We're on the bridge right now . . .' one of the men said, and before the words were out of his mouth the three captives had flung themselves into the stream.

'My God, they've escaped!'

'Shoot, shoot!'

Fifteen rifles burst out at once, firing into the dark shadows under the bridge. In the village of Chukurköprü everyone was roused. They listened to the sound of shooting that came from the banks of the river and lasted till dawn broke. In the morning the news of the incident spread, including Veli Agha's foul play . . .

The Sumbas Stream flows out towards Anavarza village and the three men were carried on, tied to each other, sinking and floating in the freezing water, until they managed to drag themselves out somewhere above Veli Agha's house. Enver had been shot dead, and Niyazi and Fethi had to haul him up still strapped arm to arm. Veli Agha got the fright of his life when he saw them. 'It's not my fault!' he cried to the villagers who had crowded up to release the brothers. 'Some men attacked my house in the night and took these three away with them.' No one believed him. He was taken straight to the police-station in the town. There he broke down and named as many of the Akyollus he knew who had come to his house that night. 'If you arrest them,' he said, 'they'll name the others . . .' As he was returning from town, he was shot dead at the crossroads of Alikesik. The young peasant who killed him had never had any quarrel with Veli Agha, but in his interrogation he said only: 'What would you have done in my place, officer?' And not a word more could be got out of him.

Eight of the men who had been with Reshat Bey that night were arrested and thrown into prison, but Reshat Bey had thirty-six witnesses to swear that he himself had been in town all the time.

Again, for perhaps the twentieth time, the Beys and Aghas and high officials of Adana, Jeyhan and Kozan tried to mediate between the two tribes, but to no avail. The next year Durmush killed Ibrahim . . . And Ibrahim's brother, Osman, killed Hassan who was over eighty and a distant relative of the Sarioglus. Hassan had seven sons who did not rest until they had wiped out every single male in Osman's family. They even took their heads and stuck them on pikes at the gates to the Akyollu mansion.

'Those severed heads . . . Those staring eyes . . .'

40

The old quarter of the town was quite dilapidated now, the streets muddy, the roofs of the houses caving in and the plaster on the walls cracked and crumbling. Noisy kestrels and wasps nested under the eaves and in the cracks of the high walls of the neglected yards where pomegranate, olive and mulberry trees were beginning to run wild. The olive trees, their dusty leaves tough and velvety, had grown so large that two men could not have joined hands about their trunks, and the pomegranates were all hedged in by their heavy branches, their green leaves smothered in a riot of huge red flowers that dyed the lonely streets a bright red. Bees of all kinds flitted over the flowers. Sometimes they moved in swarms from branch to branch. Sometimes they were quite still under the heavy sun, sluggish, their transparent wings not even quivering, as though forming new combs, as though waiting there for the death, for the slow extinction of these abandoned old trees that drooped forlornly against the crumbling walls.

A rare passer-by, an occasional mangy horse or aged donkey would drift listlessly through the empty streets, pausing in the midst of this ruined desolation to stare vacantly, perhaps yearningly, thinking thoughts no one would ever know.

And yet, in the morning, a little after sunrise, and also in the evening as day was drawing to a close, the solitary streets would come alive with the bees buzzing more loudly and the kestrels darting out of the walls like arrows, spinning crazily in the sky, swooping up and down, tracing long lines over the deep blue and drowning the world with their shrill cries.

Hunting kestrels was a passion with the neighbouring children. They would slip out in the night and scramble up the walls and trees to find the nests and catch these tiny little birds of prey no bigger than a hand, but with beaks as strong as pincers and talons that could tear up anything they closed upon. Many a child met his death in this way, or broke a leg or an arm at the very least. Thus, the two sons of the Chief Justice of the Criminal Court were found dead one morning, splayed over the white cobblestones. Their blood had streamed all over the place. It was dry already and green flies were flashing over it, while yellow ants swarmed over their bloodstained heads. When the Chief Justice arrived he betrayed no emotion. Only his legs trembled a little as he stood over the two little bodies. He laid down his cane and took the hand of his younger son and held it to his heart, then that of his first-born. The Prosecutor and doctors arrived on the scene and he turned away, leaving them to take care of everything. The death of the two children raised a lot of talk in the town. Every single convict sentenced by the Chief Justice was investigated, as were all their relatives. But in the end it was quite clear that the kestrels had been the only cause of their death. For many years the Chief Justice did not go to bed at night. Carrying a ladder he prowled the streets hunting for kestrels in every nook and cranny. In the morning people would wake up and find the streets strewn with dead kestrels, their necks wrung. But hard as he tried, the Chief Justice was never able to wipe them out root and stem, and all his life, on coming home in the evening, he had to listen to their endless squawking, and there were some who swore that even now, at his age, he still took his ladder and went hunting for kestrels in the night.

He never changed his house. He loved that old part of the town, the tumbledown houses, the ancient pomegranates and fig trees and especially the olive trees which he was certain dated back to the time of the Byzantines. And indeed there were mosaics at the foot of these olive trees representing partridges, peacocks, deer, olive branches and human heads. After every long hard rain, when torrents would rumble down the streets carrying away the earth, the Chief Justice would take his cane and walk out into the neglected orchards, looking for mosaics under the olive trees. And whenever he found one he would go wild with joy. He would forget everything and stay there gazing entranced until nightfall. For days afterwards he would take the lawyers and judges and other notables to admire his new find. He knew very well that no one in this town understood anything of the beauty and value of these mosaics, that people only came and admired them to please him and it grieved him not to have one friend at least who could share his joy.

The house was very old, built on two floors with an earth roof that leaked with every rain. In the garden, under the pomegranate, olive, orange and plane trees, mosaics gleamed brightly among the marjoram and the tangle of brambles and wild bushes. On the threshold was a long slabstone dating from the ancient Greeks, blue-veined, carved with roses in bloom and inscribed in a strange script.

It was past midnight and the Chief Justice was still awake when he heard a knock on the door. He raised the wick of the oil-lamp and looked at his watch on the table beside him. It was one o'clock. He got up, unhooked his trousers from the wall and drew them on. The soft knocking on the door was repeated. Without putting on his shirt he took his revolver from under his pillow and went down the creaking stairs.

'Who's that?' His voice was firm and quite incurious, even though in all his twenty-five years as a magistrate no one had ever had the audacity to disturb him in the middle of the night. Nothing that happened to him could surprise him any more.

'Your honour, it's me, Mustafa Akyollu . . . Excuse me for disturbing you at this hour, but I could only come now. Please be so good as to let me in.'

'One minute,' the Chief Justice said. He went up the stairs, took the lamp and returned to open the door. 'Come in.'

'Thank you, your honour.'

There was thunder in the skies and the rain came down in torrents. Mustafa Bey was soaked to the skin. His clothes stuck to his back and his teeth were chattering.

'Where's your horse?' the Chief Justice asked.

'I tied him to an olive tree at the door.'

They went upstairs to a small room with sofas all around its walls and a worm-eaten table right in the middle littered with books. On the floor was a frayed Persian rug. The Chief Justice raised the wick of the lamp a little higher. At that moment the Chief Justice's wife, who was as corpulent as her husband, entered the room. She was dressed up to the nines and had even put make-up on her eyelids and blackened her eyebrows.

'Ooooh!' she cried. 'But you're wet through! Oh dear! What a

344

rain, what a rain!' She held out her hand. 'Welcome to our house. Would you like some coffee?'

'Thank you, Hanum,' the Chief Justice said. 'That is just what we need.'

They sat down facing each other on two wooden chairs.

'What do you say, your honour? You won't sign our death warrant by having us all exiled from here?'

'Would it be so hard for you to leave this town?' the Chief Justice murmured, his lips hardly moving, as though he were putting the question only to himself.

'It would mean death for us,' Mustafa Bey replied just as softly. 'It would finish us for ever. Our enemies know this. They're trying to have us banished only because they want our land and to be able to divide Akchasaz between themselves more easily. That's why I've come at this hour of the night in this dreadful weather. And if I hadn't known you for twenty-five years, if it had been anyone else, I'd never have come, not to save my life.'

'Just so . . .'

'Just so,' Mustafa Bey pursued. 'I've got an old mother with one foot in the grave, but hanging on with her last breath only to see her son's murderer killed . . .'

'Just so . . .'

The coffees were brought in. The Chief Justice held out his cigarette case and producing his lighter he lit first Mustafa Bey's cigarette, then his own. They drank their coffee in silence, their faces vacant as though they had nothing more to say to each other. Then the Chief Justice fixed his eyes searchingly on Mustafa Bey. His face grew longer, his double chin sagged and his eyes widened. He stiffened as though he had just caught sight of some awful thing. His lips opened and closed, his nostrils trembled and he rubbed his temple with his right hand. 'Just so . . .' he muttered.

The sound of rain came louder. They listened to it and heard the muffled call of a bird.

'Just so . . .'

Mustafa Bey could not bring himself to get up and leave, nor could he utter a word of the thoughts that were passing through his mind. His body was paralysed, limp, dissolving . . .

'Just so,' the Chief Justice said again, raising his voice a little.

'It's a senseless business,' Mustafa Bey said at last. 'But what can we do? Everything about mankind is irrational, meaningless. But really everything! Walking, sitting, weeping, laughing, loving, killing, sleeping . . . Ours is just another senseless thing in all this, nothing more, nothing less, just a drop added to the ocean of senselessness of the human kind . . . What difference can it make, your honour?'

'Just so . . .'

'Even being born is meaningless. Everything man does in this world is meaningless . . . And the most meaningless thing about man is his ability to think. It's knowledge makes him irrational.'

The Chief Justice started to his feet as though a pin had just been thrust into the flesh of his large majestic frame. He leaned over and stared into Mustafa Bey's eyes. 'Just so,' he said almost in a shout. Breathing hard, his chest heaving, he walked round the room three times, the shadow of his large paunch covering the whole wall in the orange glow of the oil-lamp. Then he sat down again. 'Just so,' he repeated with finality.

'If man didn't think, he wouldn't feel hatred or the need of revenge. Killing is a conscious act, not instinctive. And to kill consciously is a monstrous thing, a proof of man's senselessness.'

'Just so,' the Chief Justice cried a little angrily. Then he laughed.

'If we're banished what will happen? We'll find each other in the end. My mother will still be waiting, defying death. My mother, your honour, the Lady Karakiz. She . . . She . . . *She* is not irrational! It's her instinct that dominates . . .' He flung his arms out in sudden exhilaration. 'Yes, your honour, she's the only being in the world who's rational. My mother . . . My mother . . .' He hesitated and his eyes gleamed. 'As for us . . . As for us . . .'

'Just so,' the Chief Justice said, smiling broadly.

'Just so . . .'

They fell silent and sat on there, listening to the rain, half awake, half asleep. Day dawned and the Chief Justice's wife came in, bearing a huge tray with breakfast on it. She set the tray on a sofa. 'Help yourselves,' she said. 'It's real Ceylon tea. I got eight packages of it from the smugglers the other day.'

346

She looked at Mustafa Bey. 'Well, your clothes have dried a little. That's a good thing or you'd have caught a cold. I know your lady. She never speaks at all. They say that noble Turcomans never talk, is that so?'

'Well, they do a little,' Mustafa Bey smiled. His white teeth gleamed and his high hooked nose cast a shadow over one side of his face. 'But not always.'

'The tea's piping hot,' she said. 'How good it smells!'

'Yes,' the Chief Justice said. 'Nobody can make breakfast like Nilüfer Hanum. Just so . . .'

'Just so,' Mustafa Bey echoed. He looked admiringly at Nilüfer Hanum, who was highly pleased.

'I've made some honey patties too,' she said.

'Thank you, my dear,' the Chief Justice said, biting into one of the patties, the slim glass of tea steaming in front of him.

There was a knock on the door just as they were rounding off their breakfast with a third glass of tea, and had partaken amply of the honey patties, and also of the toast, Yörük cheese and of the yellow *ayran*-butter with the bubbles still on it.

'I'll go,' Nilüfer Hanum said. The wooden staircase creaked and shook under her heavy step. At the door, holding his horse's reins, was a very tall dark man, slightly stooped, his yellow boots stained by the rain, and water streaming down his back.

'Is the Chief Justice at home?' he asked. His voice was strong and confident. 'My name's Dervish Sarioglu . . .'

'Who?' Nilüfer Hanum asked strangely. 'Who did you say?' She tried to gather her thoughts, to remember. Her eyes rested on the ladder her husband would take out furtively in the night to hunt kestrels, and suddenly it all came back to her. 'Bey, Bey,' she cried hoarsely as she rushed up the stairs. 'Bey . . . He's here . . . At the door . . . He, he . . . He!'

'Who?'

Her hand pointed to Mustafa Bey, then to the door. 'He, he! He, you know! Shall I take him in? What if something should happen? What if . . .'

'Wait, Nilüfer Hanum. What's all this fuss?' the Chief Justice said rising. He laughed. 'Let's go and see who it is that's put you in such a flurry.' He went down the stairs ponderously. 'Oh,

Dervish Bey,' he cried. 'Come in, come in, you're very welcome.'

Dervish Bey had sensed something was wrong. Filled with apprehension he mounted the stairs and the first thing he saw through the open door was Mustafa Akyollu standing in the middle of the room, his hand on the gun at his waist.

'Come in, come in,' the Chief Justice urged him. 'We were just having breakfast.'

With studied unconcern Dervish Bey stepped into the room, brushing Mustafa Bey's shoulder as he went to the sofa.

Recovering from the shock Mustafa Bey turned to the Chief Justice and smiled. 'I must go now, your honour,' he said calmly. 'Thank you. Thank you very much for everything.' He could not keep himself from stealing a glance at Dervish Bey before descending the stairs with great dignity. Suddenly he noticed that his hand was still on his gun. He snatched it away as if it had just touched a live coal. His face red with shame he looked at the Chief Justice to see if he had noticed.

Nothing escaped the Chief Justice's eye. 'Just so,' he said. 'Just so. Force of habit . . .'

41

The oleanders that lined the pebbly little stream had not yet put forth flowers but their red buds were almost ready to burst open. The long blue camel-thistles were in flower and the grass and clover already knee-deep. The large black-eyed narcissus on the edge of Akchasaz swamp and the mountain ash squeezed between the rocks of Alichli valley had blossomed under the spring sun. Clustering blue hyacinths wafted their dizzying fragrance over Mount Hemité and down into the valleys below. The long reeds, the wild rose and blackberry bushes, all of nature was gushing forth in a buoyant efflorescence. The Chukurova earth sang in a riot of colours and scents. Bees, butterflies, birds, insects, well-fed snakes and frogs, all had emerged from their nests and were teeming and coupling under the warm Chukurova sun. The call of francolins sounded faintly from the green cornfields that rippled in the breeze and glistened, forming ever-changing webs of light. Spring torrents swashed down from the valleys. In the trees and bushes and rock cavities birds were busily building new nests or patching up old ones. After the generous winter rains, the rich fecund Chukurova plain was laying open its bounty.

Herds of gazelles roamed freely through the plain. They had come in the middle of February from Syria and the Harran desert and the mountains of Abdülaziz.

From below Dumlu Castle a small herd was pressing east towards the vast reed-bed near Hajilar that extended from Aslanli, Hamam and Chukurköprü right over to Jeyhan River. In the centre of the reed-bed was a stretch of fresh unblemished green and that is where the gazelles were heading. Nowhere else was the grass so soft and juicy. And there they were, still grazing, when a flight of eagles burst out of the Anavarza crags, their long widespread wings flashing like drawn swords, and in an instant they had swooped down over the herd with an ear-rending noise. The gazelles scattered helter-skelter among the reeds and bushes, while the eagles swarmed over whatever prey they had seized, tearing it to pieces on the spot. Those who had caught nothing soared up into the air to pounce down again and again.

One terror-crazed gazelle was tearing along the plain below Deliler village, and chasing it, swift as lightning, was a copper-winged, red-speckled young eagle. The gazelle was young too. Its coat glistened brightly and it streaked like a flame, on and on until it reached the banks of Jeyhan River and stopped among the oleanders. The copper-winged eagle was not long in detecting it. The gazelle would have been lost if not on its guard. The sharp talons of the bird were about to sink into its back when it swerved to the left, too quick for the eye to see. The eagle only just avoided striking the ground and by the time it had picked up speed again the gazelle was way off, fleeting through a meadow of marjoram and nearing Kesikkeli already. It never crossed its mind to hide somewhere, in some hole or thicket. Perhaps hiding did not even exist in its instincts. It trusted only in its long firm slim legs to lead it to salvation and in its ability to bound high into the air, three, five times its own height and shoot onwards . . . And indeed the eagle, though young and strong, could not easily keep up with its speed.

There was a wide expanse of tall bright red poppies about the gazelle now. The bird of prey had been left far behind and the threat of death had receded. But its legs had begun to tremble and its leaps and bounds were shorter. Still it raced on, through the poppies and along green meadows where anemones bloomed, blue, red, yellow, mauve, pink, white, their black eyes, almost human, open in wide amazement in the centre of their large fine five-petalled corollas. The anemones stretched from here, below Endel, right up to the slopes of Mount Hemité like an embroidery over the green, swaying in the gentle breeze. A cloud of blue butterflies rushed past the gazelle, but it never slackened its steady seasoned gait, leaping only at well-appointed intervals, its feet not even crushing the delicate anemones, lightly flowing on like a rippling brook, like a red beam of light over the plain. There was not a bush or thicket in sight, not even a clump of rushes. Its golden coat glistening, the gazelle was still gliding along this flatland when it heard the awesome sound behind it and everything was suddenly changed. The angry young eagle, its copper wings folded back, was diving at lightning speed, the deafening swoosh of its onslaught a harbinger of death. In its flurry the gazelle tripped and fell, and this is what saved it. The bird's talons only grazed its back and passed on. A little blood spurted from the wound, but the gazelle was up and away in the twinkling of an eye, while the eagle, impelled by its own speed, hurtled on, only a little above the anemones, way off to the foot of Mount Hemité. Angrily it soared up once more and from its high stance spotted the bouncing gazelle, a vague zigzagging line in the distance now. It was running for its life in the direction of Bozkuyu, the wound on its back a pricking spur and before its huge sad eyes the flashing copper wings swishing over the anemones, ever larger and more fearsome.

A long line of oxcarts was creaking wearily along the road from the Forsaken Graveyard. The gazelle did not see them, but only heard the grinding of their wooden wheels. It was enough to make it veer back, round Mount Hemité, through Chatal Pass and into the crags. The earth here was red and gritty, but among the red-veined, green-speckled rocks and under the dark-red purplish mastic trees, yellow crocuses grew in clusters, shedding a golden radiance into the blue sky, and beneath the green luxuriant white-flowering myrtle bushes, blue violets wafted their strong perfume over the earth. The gazelle was threading its way through the rocks when it heard the rustling of wings again. It began to skip from rock to rock and this put a tough strain on its slender legs. Its black eyes widened. Like a grieving lament, they were now, filling the whole face.

This time the bird only skimmed over the gazelle, swiftly, at the height of a poplar tree, and rose aloft, poised in the blue, tracing slow wide circles and uttering strident cries like a summons or a warning. Perhaps it was tired too and was resting like that, with its quivering copper wings outspread over the blue.

Suddenly it charged. But the gazelle was ready. It cast itself behind a rock and avoided the swift onslaught. Again the bird only narrowly escaped being nailed to the ground, but three of its feathers broke over the rock.

The gazelle dashed on towards the Adaja crags and there it vanished from sight. High and low the eagle flew, its keen eyes searching in the smallest hollow and under every bush of the narcissus-scented crags. The tenacious bird knew its prey could not be anywhere else and it would not give up the hunt. All night long it circled the moonlit sky, screeching over the jackals, foxes and wild cats that came to drink at the tarns. And as light dawned it caught sight of the gazelle darting in and out of the morning mist along Chatal Pass. Its wings grew tense, its talons and beak crooked sharply and it hurled itself with renewed passion after this prey that had so nearly duped it. But the gazelle had a good start and kept up its lead until it reached a pinkish-mauve expanse of marjoram that grew, man-tall, on the fringe of Akchasaz swamp. There it began to lose speed as its feet slithered and sank into the muddy slippery earth underneath.

When it emerged from the marjoram the noonday heat had descended over the plain. Flies were sticking fast to the wound on its back and the angry bird, its wings whirring furiously, was only ten or fifteen paces behind. It was do or die for both of them now. The gazelle had no chance of escape and the eagle could not fasten its sharp claws into its neck and gouge its eyes out with its beak. For that is the way with these copper-coloured green-eyed birds of prey. First they claw at their victim's back and pierce their eyes, to devour the blind animal afterwards, piecemeal and at leisure. The carcass is then left to the vultures who pick the bones clean, not leaving a trace of blood on them.

The gazelle's leaps were shorter now. Its knees sagged as it touched the ground. The eagle must have sensed this, for it suddenly glided up into the sky and floated there quite calmly, without haste. The gazelle slowed down even more as it encountered a stretch of blackthorns, and at that moment there was a rush of air in its ears and the sound of wings, very close. It redoubled its bounds and skirted the bushes, seeming to have outdistanced its pursuer at last. But the eagle was only gathering force. In an instant, it was on the gazelle's back. With a desperate motion the gazelle shook it off. The bird sprawled away, its wings and talons to one side, its head to the other, only to rise up at once and renew its attack again and again. At the fourth try, its talons were firmly planted in the gazelle's neck and it was ramming its beak from above into its eyes. At each peck, the gazelle gave a long vault and whirled and rushed on madly, struggling to free itself, while the eagle, in a confused flurry of wings, jabbed away without a break, tearing at the eyes bit by bit. Suddenly the gazelle jumped into the air, three times, and fell back. Both its eyes were now two empty holes streaming with blood. And still the eagle kept ramming away, trying to keep its hold on the gazelle as it thrashed about, moaning and spinning on itself ever more quickly.

Everything happened as the sun was setting. The gazelle with a convulsive start threw itself down among the blackthorn bushes. As it fell, one of the bird's open wings was jammed between the gazelle's hard shoulder and the ground. There was a cracking snapping sound and in that instant the talons on the gazelle's back loosened their hold, the heavy weight fell away. The gazelle sprang to its feet and vanished into the night. The eagle remained there, striving in vain to take to the air again. Its copper wing hung motionless, shattered, draggling over the ground.

Day was breaking when Mustafa Bey saw the gazelle. Quickly, he aimed his rifle and was about to press the trigger when he realized there was something strange about this animal. It was spinning like a top and all about its head was a moiling cloud of flies. He lowered the rifle and stood watching.

Round and round the gazelle whirled, its coat dull now, clotted with blood, its slender legs muddy, its head swagging, all sense of balance lost, plunging forwards, swinging to its side, slipping, its legs slithering in all directions, sagging . . . Round and round it went, its slim body writhing in pain, tensing like a bow, rotating on itself until it reached the edge of the miry swamp. For one second its front legs hung in the void, and then it had toppled over.

Mustafa Bey ran up only to see two hind hoofs disappearing among the bubbles and the mire closing over them. For a long time he could not take his eyes off the place where the gazelle had sunk to its death, off this miry swamp that had closed over it like a dark night . . .

42

It was still early morning when the Mercedes drew up before Dervish Bey's mansion house. The black automobile was coated with dust, its colour hardly visible under a thick white layer. First the chauffeur emerged, equally white with dust, and held the door open. Then Ala Temir shot out shaking himself and brushing his shalvar-trousers, his shirt and his hat.

Ibrahim stood watching him with curiosity. He was used to seeing people in all manners of dress, but this balding greying little man with the incredibly enormous hands and feet still surprised him. It was a habit of Ibrahim's, who was bored in the mansion house, to rush out into the yard at every sound of an approaching car or the beat of a horse's hooves. Filled with apprehension, with a foreboding of bad news, of some disaster, he would stand there, tongue-tied, his thin neck stretching out longer and longer towards the newcomer, as though he had never seen a human being before. His eyes would be fixed on the man's right hand, that hand which any minute might shift to the right hip and produce a huge revolver. And if the hand did indeed chance to brush the right hip, Ibrahim would turn and run for his life, crazed with fear, hiding in orchards and tree-hollows, up in the mountains, crouching in bushes, shivering, awake all night long. Sometimes he would find himself high up on a plane tree, clinging to its large trunk, quaking, ears and eyes straining at the darkness. But there were times when nothing seemed to matter any more and, swinging his long legs, he would reach the road, making straight for the Akyollu mansion, enter the yard and stand there watching Memet Ali in his overalls, his hands black with grease, tending his tractors, lost to the world, and he too would forget everything, not even noticing the oncoming dusk, the lengthening shadows. Neither Memet Ali nor anyone else would ask him who he was, what he was doing there, where he had come from. And then, at nightfall, he would turn away, at peace with himself, and slowly as he

354

walked through the darkness the fear would creep back. He would break into a run, and the faster he ran the more terrified he became with the dread certainty of implacable death at his heels.

One night, towards dawn, he was found by the villagers high on the crags of Anavarza, balanced only a foot from the edge of a deep dark precipice, waving his arms, crying for help in the strangling voice of a drowning man. 'They're killing me, killing me! Save me! Help!' he howled, swaying perilously to and fro, his arms flapping desperately, yet unable to drag himself away, as though held there by a spell. The villagers were only just in time to save him from lurching over and being shattered to pieces over the crags.

'If ever Mustafa Bey kills my father,' Ibrahim would say, 'which he will, there's no escaping that, I won't kill Mustafa Bey in return, nor Memet Ali either. I'll make friends with Memet Ali. Our children will never fear death again, never! We've got so much land and Memet Ali needs land, I know, or why would he drive his villagers off his farm? I'll give him the half of our lands, and why shouldn't I? Isn't all this huge Anavarza plain ours?' Then suddenly the fear would grip him again. He would rage at his fear. It would drive him to rush madly through the mansion, foaming at the mouth, his skin and muscles taut, shouting out loud. 'I'll kill them, kill them all! I won't leave a single one of them alive, man or woman! If only our ancestors had thought of it before, if only they'd wiped them out root and branch . . . Then my father wouldn't be . . . No, he wouldn't! And neither would we all be like this, dying of fear every single day of our lives . . . Yes, I'll place a ton of dynamite under their house one night and blow them all up, but all of them. For if just one of them's left, one little girl, she'll grow up and get married and have a son and he'll come and kill us . . . That's why . . . All of them . . . All of them must be killed!' He would stand at his father's door, on tiptoe. 'Father, father, father,' he would say in a low urgent whisper, hardly hearing his own voice himself, 'when will you kill them, when, and save me? Father, they're going to kill me, I know. They're going to kill me . . .'

The talk of banishment had filled him with relief . . . How wonderful! The Akyollus relegated to one end of the country, themselves to another, forbidden to leave, to reach at each other! In a transport of delight, he gave away the nacre-inlaid revolver his father had solemnly presented him with. What would he need it for now? He was saved from being killed, saved to his dying day! Overflowing with joy he went to the town and wandered blissfully through the market, stopping at the smith's, the saddler's, the wheelwright's. He bought two cases of coloured candy and distributed it to the village children. Then, back in the mansion, he heard his father's angry voice. 'Just let them banish me!' he was shouting. 'I'll burn the whole town. I told the Chief Justice I'd wipe it off the map, bring it down in ruins over their heads . . . And my dead body would be found over the ruins afterwards . . .' Night was falling, but Ibrahim turned and fled. On and on he ran, hounded by some beast with bared fangs that wanted to tear him to pieces, up into the Anavarza crags to that same spot on the edge of the precipice, shouting, rocking backwards and forwards over the yawning abyss. The shepherds of Anavarza were used to it by now, on the look-out. They carried him down the crags in a faint. Every time they brought his son back like this Dervish Bey would reward them generously, so they had got into the habit of grazing their goats near Ibrahim's precipice.

'Tell me, my child, is Dervish Bey at home? I've come to see him. Ala Temir is my name . . .'

'He's upstairs,' Ibrahim said, his eyes opening round as saucers. Was this the Ala Temir he'd heard so much about? This outlandish square log of a creature, was he the most industrious, the cleverest, the richest man in the Chukurova, whose only pleasure in life was to pour abuse and curses at the aristocratic Jafer Özpolat for every hundred thousand liras he gave him, who was so miserly that he still subsisted on nothing but *ayran* and dry bread?

Suddenly Ibrahim burst out laughing. He rocked with laughter and Ala Temir's childlike mournful face with its tiny eyes and woebegone drooping lips which always inspired pity in people, turned to anger and changed into something quite different. It became hard and barbed and cutting, yet wavering still between ferocity and innocence, ludicrous in its bewilderment. Angrily, he strode on towards the mansion, just as

356

Hidayet appeared at the door.

'Welcome, welcome, Agha! The Bey's upstairs.' Hidayet was delighted to see Ala Temir. Because his visit could only mean one thing. He wanted to buy land from the Bey. Ala Temir never went anywhere for any other reason. He would pay a good price for the land. And Dervish Bey, who dispensed his money freely when he had it, would give them all a liberal share. Provided, of course, that low-down overseer did not get wind of it. He'd rather they cut his head off, that Zülfikar, than sell an acre off the farm. He'd got Rüstemoglu into such a state after that last deal that the poor man was afraid to set foot on the farm, let alone come to the mansion to buy land again . . .

'Just wait a second here, Agha, and I'll tell the Bey.' He rushed up the stairs two at a time and was back in an instant. 'The Bey's waiting for you. He was at the window and recognized you at once. He's glad you've come, I could see that from his face . . .'

Ala Temir felt better, though still resentful at Ibrahim who was laughing after them in the yard. 'Who's that?' he asked Hidayet. 'That long lad, stretching like a poplar into the sky? And thin as a rake too! Is he mad or what?'

'The one who's laughing, you mean?'

'Yes. He's crazy, isn't he?'

'No,' Hidayet replied apologetically. 'He's the Bey's son, Ibrahim Bey.'

Ala Temir stopped short on the stairs. He'd blundered badly. Imagine calling the Bey's son mad! He looked at Hidayet's face, but was relieved not to find the slightest trace of a frown on it. 'So,' he said, 'that's Ibrahim Bey, is it? The Bey's eldest son? Well, well, God bless him, what a fine lad he's grown into! How could I have dreamt it was he? God keep him, God bless him a thousand times . . .'

Dervish Bey was waiting in the big hall upstairs. Ala Temir rushed up to him, bent in two as though he was going to throw himself at his feet. Dervish Bey raised him quickly and grasped his huge hand. 'Well then, here you are at last, Ala Temir!' he said. 'What's become of you? I thought you'd forgotten us altogether. Why man, your riches seem to have gone to your head!' His voice was condescending, slightly scornful.

'Thank you, Bey, thank you,' Ala Temir replied humbly in trembling tones. 'Thank you . . .'

'Well sit down. How's business?'

Ala Temir complied, straight as a poker, his knees stuck together, his hands clamped tight over them, the fingers wide apart, knobby and wrinkled, with dirty cracked nails.

'Relax, man! Make yourself comfortable . . .'

At this, Ala Temir tensed himself still more and riveted his gaze on the awesome huge-eyed black-mustached portrait on the wall. 'Thank you, Bey,' he said. 'I'm quite comfortable like this.'

Dervish Bey gave up. He knew from long experience that nothing could make Ala Temir unbend from his rigid attitude. 'Eh, man, I hear you're rolling in money now. You've bought a whole fleet of cars, one for each of your sons! Well, God grant you more . . .'

'It's only thanks to you, Bey . . . Under your noble protection . . . We've only done what we could . . . With hard work, with scraping and saving . . .'

'Oh, come off it, Ala Temir! You're as rich as Harun al-Rashid! They say you give Jafer Özpolat one hundred thousand liras every three months just for the pleasure of calling him names, of swearing at a Bey in public. And good for you too . . . Well done, my friend! Go on cursing him up hill and down dale. They deserve it, those bastards.'

Ala Temir smiled deprecatingly, but his voice betrayed his gratification. 'People exaggerate . . . Just because I went a little too far in a moment of irritation . . .'

Dervish Bey roared with laughter. 'Nonsense! I know exactly with what words you swear at Jafer. You mountain folk are the best swearers in the world. Look here, if those people let themselves be called all sorts of names for one hundred thousand liras, and their wives and families as well, they'd be willing to let you go to bed with their women for a hundred and fifty thousand. Think of it, man, for one hundred and fifty thousand you can have Jafer's wife, then his sister, his wife's sister, God knows, all the women in his family! Come on, man, try it! You only live once . . . And if Jafer's women aren't enough, you can always try Mahir Kabakchioglu . . . He'd settle for three

358

thousand apiece, provided no one heard of it . . .'

Ala Temir was squirming. 'Heaven forbid! Heaven forbid!' he cried in great agitation for he knew that Dervish Bey would repeat this conversation to all and sundry. 'Never, Bey, never! How could I . . . Our noble Beys . . . God forbid!'

'Three thousand, Ala Temir! That's all it'll cost you. And you with never another woman but that old frump who's borne thirty children for all I know . . . Think of it, for just three thousand liras . . .'

'God forbid, Bey! God forbid I should bite the hand that feeds me. They're our Beys. Why, our kind aren't fit to lick their boots . . .'

'Three thousand, man, only three thousand! The shroud has no pockets, Ala Temir. You can't take your money with you. Why don't you give yourself a little good time while you're in this world? It's your money, honestly made. And since their god is money, which you have, pay down that three thousand. Their women are beautiful, with silken bodies . . . I should know . . .'

'God forbid, Bey! God forbid!' Ala Temir kept repeating, springing to his feet, sitting down and rising again, never taking his hands from his knees, all bathed in sweat. Dimly he perceived Dervish Bey pacing up and down the hall with his long strides. Through the rush in his ears he heard him shouting: 'Three thousand! Only three thousand! It's your due, the blood and sweat of your toil, the light of your eyes . . .'

After a while Dervish Bey went to the door. 'Hidayet!' he called. 'What are you all about? The richest man in the Chukurova's come to visit me and you haven't even brought him a cup of coffee! A man who can pay one hundred thousand down for a single night with a woman . . .' His voice was fraught with devastating sarcasm. 'Quick, the coffee, Hidayet, and have a sheep killed at once in our guest's honour . . . The most interesting guest in the world . . . Hurry up, you fool!'

Ala Temir felt the storm brewing, about to burst over his head. Desperately, he cast about for a chance to escape, bitterly regretting ever having stepped into this house and silently cursing those who had made him come.

At that moment Zülfikar, the overseer, entered the room. He

was grinding his teeth. Dervish Bey laughed suddenly. 'Well, Zülfikar,' he said, 'what do you want?'

'Only your health, Bey,' the overseer replied, his long creased neck craning goose-like, his green-streaked eyes narrowing. 'I just thought you might be wanting something from me, so I came.'

'Well sit down . . . D'you know this man here?' Dervish Bey said indicating Ala Temir. 'This precious, invaluable man? He's the most worthy guest yet to have crossed the Sarioglu threshold! Yes,' he continued in a subdued voice, 'the Sarioglu House has seen many a worthy guest in its time. Even when we were nomads in the Mesopotamian desert . . . It was the year Sultan Murat* was marching through on his campaign against Baghdad with an army two hundred thousand strong . . . And he heard that a Turcoman tribe was wintering in the desert . . . A tribe as large as any province . . . The Bey's tent, a wonder which had come with them all the way from Khorassan, more beautiful than any palace in all the lands from India to France, of pure turquoise silk, with fourteen vaults supported by tall posts inlaid with pearl, nacre and coral, the floor covered with the most precious rugs and carpets from Khorassan, Bukhara and Persia . . .'

Ala Temir was listening, slack-jawed, entranced, his sweating hands stuck fast to his knees.

'And Sultan Murat cried out: Oh my brave companions, how can we go by without once seeing the Sarioglu tent? Our own forefather, Kayi Bey, was said to have come from Harzem with one just like it. Let us go and live again those glorious days of the tent on this our holy campaign to deliver Baghdad . . . It was already hot in the lowlands and the tribe would soon be moving up into the mountains. The Sultan was sweating and so were the Grand Vizir, the commander of the army, everyone. But lo, when they entered the tent they were refreshed by a cool and pleasant breeze. It was like a paradise. The Sultan was taken around the rooms and was dazzled by the wealth of colour and design that met his eyes. He is said to have particularly

*Sultan Murat: Murat IV of the Ottoman dynasty who conquered Baghdad in the seventeenth century.

admired one room entirely hung with rare skins of elk and fallow deer and red deer . . . They ushered him into the spacious guest-room and spread a gold-threaded tiger-skin for him. And even the all-powerful Sultan was not proof against this. He folded the end of the skin beneath him . . . Ala Temir! D'you know what that means?'

Ala Temir jumped. 'It means, Bey . . . I like this tiger-skin very much . . .' he stammered out quickly.

'Good! That's it. Then the Sultan had some refreshment and was about to leave when my ancestor, Haji Kutulmush stopped him. Sultan, he said, do us the honour of being our guest for the night and your soldiers too . . . The Sultan was astounded. How could the Bey of a nomad tribe accommodate an army of two hundred thousand men? His curiosity got the better of him and he accepted the invitation. And indeed his soldiers were put up and feasted lavishly, and only bird's milk was lacking at their board. So the next morning he summoned Haji Kutulmush and said: Ask anything of me and I will grant it to you. If you wish I can make you the Bey of Beys for the whole of Anatolia. But Haji Kutulmush only kissed the hem of his robe. I wish nothing of you, my Sultan, but your well-being and the expansion of your sway over the earth. Then Sultan Murat took off the ring he was wearing and with his own hand slipped it on Haji Kutulmush's finger. How right you are, he said, not to accept anything from me. Your magnificence is far superior to anything which I, the Sultan of the Ottoman Empire, can ever command . . .'

Suddenly with a sobbing sound Ala Temir covered his face with his hands and burst into tears. Dervish Bey was amazed. 'Now what's the matter? Ala Temir, is anything wrong with you, my friend?'

'No, Bey . . . N . . . n . . . nothing . . . Go on . . . Please, please, go on . . . Those glorious days . . . And now . . . This . . .'

'Yes, Ala Temir. And now this . . .' Dervish rose quickly, depressed by his own story. 'And now this, Zülfikar,' he pursued. 'This Ala Temir, the most valuable guest the Sarioglu House has ever seen, including Sultan Murat . . . Since he can give one hundred thousand liras just for . . .'

Ala Temir's face, as he dried his eyes, wavered between

laughter and tears. He could not make out whether Dervish Bey was serious or just making fun of him. And indeed the Bey's voice varied from sharp pitiless scorn to warm sincere heartiness. On and on he talked while the suspicious overseer wandered in and out of the room, and by midday he had talked himself into a state of good humour again. 'Well now,' he laughed clapping his hand to Ala Temir's back, 'out with it. You don't usually go visiting like this for nothing!'

'May my eyes drop out,' Ala Temir cried, 'for having neglected this house . . . May I be struck blind, Bey . . .'

'Why should you be struck blind? Isn't it a pity for those hazel eyes of yours? Let your enemies be struck blind . . .'

Ala Temir assumed his tearful childlike expression. Was the Bey mocking him again? 'Bey,' he said, his lips thrust out pathetically, 'the Sarioglu House has always showered its blessings far and wide, to all the creatures in the world . . . Though we are mountain folk, the Sarioglu Beys were our Beys too, and when I was a child I would gather thyme for your grandfather, the one who mounted his horse one day and never came back . . . Everyone believes my wife's money was the origin of my fortune, but it was the money your grandfather gave me, may he rest in peace. For every bunch of thyme or wild mint or yellow everlastings that I brought him—he loved those flowers—he would give me a whole fistful of money. There never was another like your grandfather, Bey, so noble, so proud. He was not afraid of death, but he didn't want people to see him once he was dead. That's why he disappeared into the high mountains, never to be seen again. So do the proud old eagles when they feel the end is near . . . Your grandfather revolted against death. He could not reconcile death with human dignity . . .' His eyes filled with tears, his voice broke. 'So I saved the money he gave me, you see . . . If it hadn't been our Bey's money, that blessed money, would God have helped me on? Never, my great Bey, never!' In his excitement Ala Temir's hand slipped from his knees. Quickly he collected himself and sat up, more rigid than ever. 'And now I . . . Your slave who owes everything to this noble House . . . To him who scorned death . . . Who rode out on this noble white steed to meet death on the lofty mountains where the foot of man had never stepped before . . . I, your slave . . . That I should come to this . . . Your blessed hand withheld from me . . . Do I deserve this, Bey? I descend from the Oguz* race too . . .' He rose and sat down, carried away with emotion. 'I too would give my soul, my fortune in the cause of the Nine Oguz . . . That glorious race . . . Your family . . .'

Dervish Bey was observing him closely, not missing a single one of his gestures and expressions. He had never been so fascinated by anyone in all his life.

Now Ala Temir was speaking in a kind of sing-song, as though keening at a wake. 'All the world knows how I've worked, Bey, all my life, never sleeping, never resting, come wind come weather. How I scrimped and saved, eating sour *ayran* and dry bread day in day out, sometimes not even that . . . Yes, my noble excellent Bey . . . And where has it got me? Nowhere. Not if you don't extend your hand to me, Bey. I'm like a little bird that has taken shelter under your wing. Protect me, Bey . . . Like a great Bey should do . . . Do this for me . . .' He gulped and stopped.

'Well, out with it, Ala Temir!' Dervish Bey cried impatiently.

'Bey, what I'm begging from your grace is . . . I want to have that land at Kurtkulak. At any price. You've done it for others, Bey. Do it for me now. Since you're going to sell anyway, why not to me?'

Dervish Bey was on his feet, yelling, even before he had finished. 'Why, you bastard, you wretched fool! How d'you know I'm going to sell Kurtkulak? How d'you know I need money? Carrion-crows, that's what you are, all of you . . . Jafer Özpolat, that low-down dog . . . Haji Kurtboga, that odious murderer, Süleyman . . .' He charged at Ala Temir and dealt him a kick in the shin. 'Get the hell out of here! I've never even thrown a dog out of this house. You'll be the first . . . A dog in human shape . . .' But Ala Temir did not stir. He sat on petrified, his eyes glassy, his hands gripping his knees more tightly. 'Look, just look at this miserable wretch! Get out, I tell you! Get the hell out of here, out of my sight before I . . .' Furiously

*Oguz: name given to the Turkish tribes inhabiting south-western Asia.

363

he strode up and down the room from wall to wall, dealing Ala Temir a fresh kick at every turn. This only made Ala Temir draw himself up straighter, more rigid than ever, his whole flesh so tense that it ached.

'Bey,' he blurted out at last, 'Bey, you can kill me here. Kill me and my blood will still flow towards you . . . But don't drive me away . . .'

Dervish Bey stopped short in front of him. 'Damn you, you dirty skunk!' he howled. 'Allah must have cursed you in your mother's womb . . . Here, take this.' And he spat out into his face.

'Kill me, Bey,' Ala Temir pleaded. 'Do anything to me, but don't let it be said of me that the Bey threw me out of his house. Kill me here, in your high-gabled mansion, and my blood will still flow to you . . .'

Dervish Bey was at a loss. He fell to pacing the room once more. The man simply wouldn't go, whatever he did or said. He couldn't very well draw his gun and shoot . . . He was toying with the idea of having this despicable human caricature dragged down the stairs and thrown out by his men, when he heard Ibrahim's voice. 'Father, father, father,' he was saying, with that note of sadness, of pleading which always had the power to move Dervish Bey. 'Father, dear father, just look at this man! How funny he is, sitting like that. Look, father, look!' And all of a sudden he was laughing away so joyously that Dervish Bey could not help himself. He burst out laughing too. Ala Temir joined them. Even the overseer smiled.

Dervish Bey was calmer now. This Ala Temir, what on earth had possessed him to take him seriously? He was just another of those sick money-grubbers. As mad as all the others, whose only scale of values was to buy at five and sell at ten . . . 'God damn you, Ala Temir!' he exclaimed. 'You were driving me crazy. Thank your lucky stars for Ibrahim, you fool, or I'd have had you thrown out bag and baggage and your bones pounded to pieces.'

Breathing with relief Ala Temir heaved himself up, his hands still on his knees, looking for all the world like a monkey. 'God bless you, Bey, what does it matter . . . And what a fine young man Ibrahim Bey's grown into, may God grant him long life!

I'm sure there isn't another like him in all this land. Ah, the wolf cub's always a wolf and the lake will never run out of water . . .' He sat back, his white teeth gleaming in a happy smile, his mouth watering as he sniffed expectantly at the appetizing odour of roast meat that floated up from below.

'Father! Father . . .'

'Yes, Ibrahim?' Dervish Bey said, embracing him affectionately.

'Father, give Kurtkulak to this funny little man. Look, he's just like a toy tumbler! Rocking all the time . . .'

Dervish Bey laughed out loud. Then his face darkened slowly. 'What a pity . . . What a pity, Ibrahim,' he said bitterly, 'that I have to sell. Every inch of that land is worth the blood of a thousand dogs like him. Or like Rüstemoglu . . .'

'Didn't I tell you you'd regret it, Bey?' the overseer broke in eagerly. 'Selling to the likes of that Rüstemoglu . . .'

Dervish Bey cast him a hard look. Nobody could dare say a word, much less argue with him when he was like that. Zülfikar turned away.

'Father, you needn't sell to Rüstemoglu. Look, this is a good man. Look how he's sitting there, look! Like a wooden puppet . . .'

Hearing this Ala Temir drew himself up still more, closing his fingers in a firm grip over his knees, his neck stretched taut.

'Very well,' Dervish Bey said cheerfully. 'Since you want it.' He walked over to Ala Temir who leapt to his feet and stood at attention. 'Well, Ala Temir, you can thank Ibrahim for Kurtkulak. The land's yours. I suppose you know that it stretches like a dagger right into the heart of Akchasaz, don't you?'

'Thank you, Bey . . .'

'And that when you have this land you can reclaim at least five thousand *dönüms* from the swamp? And that Jafer Özpolat will try coming in for a share?'

'I won't let him, Bey.'

'I know. You wouldn't even let him take a sniff at a handful of that land.'

'Never, Bey!'

'All right, all right. Sit down now.'

Ala Temir slumped to the sofa, his knees folding as though a spring had been drawn beneath him, and Ibrahim started laughing again. This time Ala Temir joined wholeheartedly in the laughter.

Hidayet and a young girl were making preparations for the meal, but Ala Temir had only one thought now, to be back in town a moment sooner so he could tell the whole world of his incredible good fortune. He hardly knew how they sat through the meal, what they ate or talked about. He came to himself in the Mercedes. 'Drive on, drive on quickly,' he urged the chauffeur exultantly. His whole body was tingling with joy from the marrow of his bones to the roots of his hair.

43

There was not the smallest whiff of a breeze in the sultry air. An oppressive heat-haze hung over the plain. The eastern sky turned from purple to mauve, then the mauve slowly paled through lilac to pink. The dawn breeze blew once, cool and pleasant, and subsided, and the heat-haze settled down over the plain again, heavier than before. In a little while the sun would rise, drowning everything in a red-hot blaze. Not a bird, not even a fly would be able to take wing and the bees would remain stuck to their combs. Even now there was no sign of life, not even the croak of a frog or the chirp of a cricket. Only a single water-strider was skimming over the dust-wrinkled chaff-strewn swamp water, travelling at lightning speed from one clump of willows to another.

But above Mount Aladag clouds were piling, darker and darker as they descended over the mountain. In another moment the dawn sky was obscured and the clouds were churning across the plain. There was a distant peal of thunder and a streak of lightning forked out from Aladag to vanish over the Mediterranean. A knifing wind swept in from the north, cold and chilling. Then from all sides warm blasts slapped at the plain whipping up dust and chaff and dried leaves. And the rain began, large slow drops, boring through the soft knee-deep layer of dust right down to the hard earth, so that the road looked like a white sieve. The day turned dark as night and for a while no ray of light filtered through the black curtain of rain. Then slowly the crests of the trees and hills were visible again. The roads and streams lit up and the darkness retreated towards the distant range of mountains. The downpour settled into a thin yellow drizzle, thread-like, barely apparent, but hard as steel. Gusts of wind struck at the yellow steel wires, scattering them here and there in yellow flurries that dyed everything a deep crystal-bright yellow, the trees, the rocks, the hillocks, the streams, the swamp and brakes, the huge wide-open snow-white water-lilies, the Anavarza eagles huddling in the crags, their necks drawn in, the spider-webs, the honey-combs that had dried under the heat of the sun . . .

Mustafa Bey climbed down from his shelter up in the willow tree, lit the samovar and set to wait for the water to boil. Mestan was perched on a hummock on the edge of the reed-bed, his sharp eyes fixed on the road that led to Dervish Bey's farm. Ibrahim Ibo was oiling his gun, while Hamdi sat watching the little ant in the hollow, still obstinately struggling with the dead beetle. 'Bey, Bey!' he shouted every time the little ant succeeded in moving one of the beetle's legs. 'Bey, I swear it's heaving it along at last. This little ant will succeed in the end, it will!'

'It will,' Mustafa Bey said drowsily. 'He will . . .' His head felt heavy as lead. He could not think today, or plan or dream. His brain, his senses, his whole body, even the blood in his veins, were frozen numb. 'It'll make it,' he repeated in a murmur. 'He'll make it . . .' And he himself did not know whether he was thinking of Dervish Bey or the little red ant.

'It'll make it, Bey, it will. I've never come across such a dogged creature.' And even Hamdi was tempted to help it out, to prod the hard glittering dead insect with his finger and push it out of the hollow so the little ant should have an easier task in dragging it off to its hole. But he dared not, lest the Bey should catch him at it and give him hell . . .

The rain let up slightly and Mustafa Bey felt his brain relaxing. Strange thoughts flitted through his mind. The little ant bent on dragging that huge beetle out of the hollow, the bigger ants approaching to sniff at it, then turning away as from a hopeless task, the birds and bees, gazelles and eagles, the fish in the sea, all the creatures of the earth . . . Didn't they all act and feel like human beings? Through the eyes of man every creature in the world, every single thing was human . . .

'He'll come!' Mustafa Bey cried aloud. 'Dervish will come this way in the end . . .' But my mother's weakening, he thought, holding on by the skin of her teeth, yet refusing to die before she sees Dervish dead. Hope and vengeance alone are maintaining her. Once I kill him she'll simply crumble into dust. By killing Dervish I'll be killing my mother too . . . Perhaps this little ant will haul the beetle out of the hollow, but it'll crumble away too, it'll drop dead beside it . . .

Long before the east had begun to pale, Dervish Bey, Hidayet and eight other men, including Zekeriya, had penetrated into the swamp and were creeping soundlessly towards Mustafa Bey's hideout in the reed-bed. Their plan was to surround the reed-bed and, at a sign from Dervish Bey, pounce on the four men and truss them up hand and foot. If anything went wrong they were to shoot and kill the four of them, then cross the frontier into Syria. There, up on Mount Kürtdag, Dervish Bey had friends, relatives of Sultan Agha's, who would die and their whole tribe too, before ever giving him up. But Dervish, un-avowed even to himself, was nursing another, more terrible plan that had matured in his mind during those sweating stifling nights spent in his barricaded room, grappling with the fear of imminent death and chafing with mortification because of it. He would kill these four and, after burying them in the swamp, would attack the Akyollu mansion and exterminate every living thing in it. Then he would do the same with all their relatives in the town and elsewhere. Only afterwards would he retreat, fighting, into Mount Kürtdag.

The yellow rain fell on relentlessly, warm and vaporous, penetrating to the very marrow of their bones, gathering force, a dense yellow torrent, incandescent, limiting their field of vision to less than fifty paces in front of them.

Dervish Bey turned to Hidayet who was crawling along on his right. 'Don't forget,' he whispered. 'You and Zekeriya are to stay with me. You'll suddenly run towards the reed-bed and shout, Mustafa Bey, your mother, your mother . . .'

Hidayet was well prepared. For maybe a month now Dervish Bey had been training him in his room, making him repeat this over and over again . . .

A strong blinding gust of rain lashed out and at that moment the agitated sorrowful voice rang out: 'Mustafa Bey! Your mother, your mother, Mustafa Bey . . .' Mustafa Bey rose in alarm. Too late he saw the three men charging at him and recognized Dervish. He was drawing out his revolver when two hands grasped his wrist from behind. With a swift movement he freed himself, only to stumble and fall right in front of Dervish Bey. He lifted his revolver, but Dervish was already upon him. The revolver exploded three times, then went hurtling through the air. Mustafa Bey tried to rise, but Dervish dragged him down again. They were now locked in a hand to hand fight. Shots rang out in the reed-bed and Mestan was heard shouting.

Suddenly Mustafa Bey was on his feet and running. 'Mestan!' he shouted. 'Turn your gun on me, quick, shoot me, shoot me . . .'

He would be out of the reed-bed in a moment and either Zekeriya or Mestan would shoot him dead. With incredible speed, almost flying, Dervish was at him. They crashed into a pool and the water gushed high above the reeds. Clutching at each other with steely claw-like hands, they thrashed and rolled through the muddy pool.

'Hidayet,' Dervish Bey cried out. 'Hidayet!'

Hidayet rushed up and hurled himself on Mustafa, followed by Zekeriya and four of the others. Mustafa Bey fought like the devil, but in the end he fell back, limp and yellow, sprawled on his back, seemingly lifeless.

'He can't be dead,' Dervish Bey said, panting for breath. 'Undress him quickly. Down to his pants . . . Tie his hands behind his back. His feet too. Quickly! Tear those clothes of his with your daggers . . . And his pants . . . His pants too. I want him stark naked.' And he turned and went out of the reed-bed. 'Mestan!' he shouted. He had spotted Mestan's head showing above a mound and the muzzle of his gun pointed at him. 'Come out of there. I won't touch you. You're a good brave man. There aren't many like you nowadays. I'll never forget that time when you caught me . . . I'll give you more land than Mustafa Bey ever would. Come out!'

'Whirlwind Veli! Whirlwind Veli!' Mestan moaned as he pressed the trigger. But Dervish Bey, prepared for anything, had already thrown himself into a ditch.

Just at that moment Whirlwind Veli emerged from the reed-bed. He was smiling and perfectly calm. 'We've tied him up, Bey,' he said, 'and stripped him, as you said.'

'Whirlwind Veli, Whirlwind Veli! Take this!'

The bullet whizzed by, grazing his ear with a deafening, numbing sound. Whirlwind Veli flinched, but stood his ground. 'Shoot, Mestan, shoot!' he said coolly. 'Shoot, you run-down old dog! What do I care if I live on after this? What do you care? Shoot, man, shoot . . .' Fearlessly he walked up to Mestan and stopped right in front of him. 'Shoot, brother,' he said softly again. 'Why don't you shoot?'

They came eye to eye. Suddenly Mestan stepped out of his cover and took his hand. 'Come, brother,' he said. 'Let's go. God damn these Beys to high heaven. They're no good for us.' And he threw down his gun.

Whirlwind Veli drew the revolver from his hip and cast it down near the gun. 'Come,' he said. 'Let us go, brother.'

And the two old men, without another glance at the reed-bed or at Dervish Bey, walked away hand in hand in the direction of the Anavarza crags.

Dervish Bey climbed out of the ditch and looked after them, shaking his head until they were out of sight. The yellow rain was coming down harder, in eddying gusts, lashing at the plain from all sides with long tight wires of steel, shimmering, crystal-yellow . . .

44

Süleyman Aslansoypenché, Jafer Özpolat, Haji Kurtboga, Ala Temir, Mahir Kabakchioglu, the Schoolmaster, Rüstem Bey, Süleyman Sami and a few others were sitting in the town club. They were silent, in a fever of suspense.

The deep grooved lines of his face stretched taut, Haji Kurtboga was twirling his mustache. Now and again he gave it an angry twitch and his trembling hand went to his paunch and scratched away. His fingers were swollen and pouches had formed under his eyes. But his broad shoulders were as rock-like as ever and he sat up very straight.

Süleyman Aslansoypenché had lifted his feet to a chair in front of him and, his socks off, was assiduously rubbing his toes. Jafer Özpolat had an air of haughty ill-humour as though he was ready to vent his anger on anyone at any moment. This was a way with him at such gatherings, and especially if they were attended by Ala Temir.

The Schoolmaster sat quietly, an absent look on his humble, saintly face, as if unaware of what was going on. But the occasional gleam in his eyes betrayed his impatience.

Ala Temir had stuck his knees together as usual, and clamped his hands over them. His eyes were fixed rigidly on the topmost branch of the mulberry tree outside the window.

Mahir Kabakchioglu was fidgeting nervously, unable to keep still. Every five minutes he rose and crossed the long room to the door, then turned back to sit down again, more restless than ever.

'Can it be true, I wonder?' he said at last, breaking the long silence.

No one answered.

This time he addressed himself directly to Süleyman Aslansoypenché. 'Süleyman Agha, you should know. We've all worked for this, but if Mahmut the Kurd has been caught at last the honour's all yours. No one else could get the better of

372

Dervish but you . . .'

Süleyman Agha only returned an ox-like stare.

'He's been caught for sure,' Süleyman Sami said. 'Once our noble Aslansoypenché has got his clutches into someone, nothing can save him.'

The Schoolmaster smiled his saintly smile. 'It's imperative he should be caught,' he said pinching gently at the crease of his well-pressed trousers. 'Yes, gentlemen, imperative and inevitable. That Kurd and his protector Dervish Bey cannot go on making a fool of a great Government. And a Government that has stood up against the whole world too. It's either them or the Government. Thank heaven for Süleyman Aslansoypenché Agha! If it wasn't for him no one would have found a trace of that Kurdish killer.'

Süleyman Aslansoypenché swelled and leaned back heavily in his chair, that creaked and groaned under his weight. 'Yes,' he said. 'The Schoolmaster's right. Where was the Government when we fought against this country's enemies? By the strength of this fist, by the force of our weapons alone we defeated them . . . Risking our lives, shedding our blood, we won this fatherland, and against what odds! Was it only so that idle Beys should sleep on it? So that we should be forced to kick our heels waiting for the Government to act, to arrest Mahmut and make him talk before they can banish those Beys? And we get a little span of land at last . . . Is that right, gentlemen? Since we're a republic now, since we've sent that Sultan to the devil, isn't that so, my dear Schoolmaster, why can't this Republic which fought against the Great Powers, why can't it round up all these Beys in one night and . . .' He ground his teeth. 'And set up gallows from here to Kayseri to hang them all? Why, why?' Again his teeth grated and his huge hand slapped his knee. 'We'd understand if the Government was reluctant to move against any of its citizens, if they'd told us to take the matter in hand ourselves . . . I alone would have finished them in only one day. One single night for putting them all to the sword, and with God's blessing too . . . Instead we've got to wait here in suspense, wondering whether some piddling Kurd's been caught or not, us, the real patriots of this country. Tell me, do we deserve this? Why don't they simply turn those Beys over to us?' He rose, clenching his fists, the veins in his neck swelling, beads of sweat starting on his flushed brow. 'Why don't they? Why?'

Suddenly, Ala Temir sprang up, shaking his fists like two blocks of wood. 'Why don't they? Why?' he roared. He was trembling with excitement and his eyes were riveted on Jafer Özpolat. 'Why don't they? Why?' he shouted again and the big windows of the room rattled loudly. He sat back and resumed his stiff position, hands on knees, eyes fixed on the mulberry tree.

Mahir Kabakchioglu was quite unmoved by all this talk. 'What I'd like to know,' he said in a subdued voice, 'is whether it's true or not?'

'Who knows?' Haji Kurtboga said. 'You can never tell with Government people.'

But the Schoolmaster was positive. 'This Captain's our man. He wouldn't deceive us. Because he's got his eye on higher things. Mark my words, he'll be a general one day. If he said he'd caught Mahmut, poor Murtaza Bey's cowardly murderer, then he has.'

'I think so too,' Süleyman Sami said. 'I've never seen such a lion of a Captain.'

'We can only wait and see,' Jafer Özpolat said disdainfully. 'Everything will soon be quite clear.'

'Yes, there's nothing for it but to wait,' Mahir Kabakchioglu said.

Only the clatter of the backgammon players filled the large room now. With half-closed eyes they sat on, ruminating, until roused by the clatter of military footsteps on the stairs, accompanied by a jingle of spurs. They all leapt to their feet as the Captain appeared at the door. He was coated with dust. His boots, his clothes, the stars on his epaulets, his cap, even his eyebrows, lashes and mustache were white. He stopped in the middle of the room, smiling, his blue eyes shining with pride, one foot thrust forward, his right hand on his shoulder-belt, his left stuck to his breeches. Then slowly he spoke: 'We've got him,' he said. 'It wasn't easy. It took three days of hard fighting, because we wanted to catch him alive so we could make him talk, but we got him in the end . . .'

Suddenly Kurtboga threw himself at his neck. 'My lion! Bless your lion's balls, my Captain! You're a hero, a saviour of the fatherland! A true son of the Republic . . .' Overflowing with emotion he was squeezing the Captain tighter and tighter until he glimpsed Mahir Kabakchioglu signalling to him behind the Captain's back. He let go at once.

'Please accept our sincere congratulations, Captain,' Mahir Kabakchioglu said. 'If your predecessors had followed up the crimes of these Beys with the same zeal as you we'd long have been rid of them. But nobody before you had a thought for this our last Turkish state . . . Yes, the last to be set up . . .'

Süleyman Aslansoypenché interrupted him. He was eager to drive home to the Captain the glory of his family name. 'Indeed, Captain, those remnants of Ottoman officers who came before you were no better than accomplices of the feudal lords, of those enemies of the fatherland! Why, they never left their table! That Captain Nurettin, for instance, for all his white hair, nothing better than the Beys' ass-licking cur, save your presence . . . And when it came to us, he just ignored us. Nurettin, my lad, I said to him, d'you know who I am? Süleyman Aslansoy-penché's my name! Print that in your memory. I can have you blown to dust from here to Baghdad . . .'

'Stop, Aslansoy, brother,' Haji Kurtboga broke in. 'Stop, so we can go at once to see this Mahmut and question him . . .'

'Aslansoypenché!'

'Aslansoypenché . . .'

'Captain, Captain . . .' Ala Temir was strangling, red in the face. He had rehearsed a beautiful speech, but now he could not remember a word of it. 'My noble lion-hearted Captain . . . Tiger of the mountains . . .' That wasn't it at all. It was on the tip of his tongue . . . But what, what? Suddenly it came back to him and he grabbed the Captain by the arm. The Captain threw him an angry look, and Ala Temir quickly dropped the arm and stood at attention. 'Wait, Captain . . .' he cried. 'You, you . . . You're as high and exalted as our Marshal Fevzi Chakmak . . .' He breathed freely again and smiled proudly. 'Yes, high and exalted, like our own Pasha who killed that heathen . . . As lofty . . .'

375

Schoolmaster Rüstem stepped in. 'Allow me to congratulate you, Captain, from the bottom of my heart. The time has really come to break the power of these feudal lords. And this task falls to the young sons of our country, like you . . .' He slipped his arm through the Captain's and leaned to his ear. 'Has he confessed?'

'No. We haven't interrogated him yet. But we'll make him. At any price . . .'

'We have to,' Mahir Kabakchioglu said, taking the Captain's other arm. 'Let's go to the gendarmerie and start at once.'

'Yes, we've no time to lose,' Kurtboga said.

In all this, Jafer Özpolat never said a word.

They set out, the Captain striding quickly in front, Mahir Kabakchioglu and Kurtboga a step behind him and Süleyman Aslansoypenché trying to get ahead of them. The Schoolmaster came wheezing in the rear, handicapped by his perpetual asthma.

'Have you sent news of your victory to the Kaymakam and the Prosecutor?' Mahir Kabakchioglu asked.

'It's not important, not at all,' the young Captain said modestly. 'For just a mere little fugitive!'

'Not important! Why, Captain, what you've caught today is the powerful feudal system! I shall cable this great achievement of yours to the Minister of the Interior tomorrow, and to the Vali in Adana and the Commander-General of the Gendarmerie in Ankara too, pointing out just how important it is.' He turned to Süleyman Sami. 'Süleyman,' he said, 'go quickly to the Kaymakam and to the Prosecutor and the district doctor. Give them the news and tell them to come at once to the gendarmerie . . .'

The head office of the gendarmerie had been converted from a military ward. There was a long table in the middle covered with green baize and on both sides of it were two rows of wooden chairs, black with grime. The gendarmes on duty saluted them as they trooped in and the warrant officer ran up and halted straight as a bayonet in front of the Captain. 'I've clapped him in chains, Commandant,' he said. 'I didn't take the handcuffs off either. I've put six men on guard and Sergeant

376

Hassan's waiting for your orders, with two men he's trained himself.'

The Captain had had Sergeant Hassan fetched from a mountain post on purpose for this business. He'd been a sergeant for twenty years now and belonged to that class of poor peasants who, on completing their army service, would do anything rather than go back to their village and would stay on to serve as paid sergeants in out-of-the-way gendarme posts. This kind had always proved themselves past masters in flogging and torturing and extorting bribes.

'Tell him to come then,' the Captain ordered, turning to his guests. 'Sit down, sit down please, gentlemen.'

The chairs about the long table creaked as they took their places. Only Ala Temir remained standing at attention, waiting for the Captain to show him to his place. And in that instant he saw himself a boy again, in the field his parents had illicitly sown with tobacco, running into the rocks pursued by a gendarme corporal with a whip in his hand, while the other gendarmes were uprooting the green tobacco plants and hurling them into the stream, his father lying at the foot of a rock, weeping, moaning, steeped in blood, the blood dripping from his long mustache, his mother, her clothes all torn, pleading with the gendarmes who were flogging him . . . He saw himself stumbling and falling over the hard rocks and each time he fell the whip lashed at his back mercilessly. He felt his eyes go black and heard himself screaming: 'Help! Help, they're killing me!' And saw his father leap up at this cry of agony, a figure streaming with blood. 'Stop, Corporal, stop,' he said. 'Don't beat us any more. I've got one cow with a calf. Take them.' And the Corporal leaving off at once, smiling now and saying: 'Well, man, you must have been born under a lucky star, for I tire quickly now. Aaah, I'm getting old, or I'd have had you all lying dead by this time. Aaah, old age . . . Twenty-five years these arms have been beating and flogging and not a minute of weariness have they known till now . . . Is the cow a good one?' And the blood-streaked, still weeping man answering: 'It yields ten litres of milk every morning . . .' 'Good,' the corporal had said. 'Bring it to the station tomorrow. With its calf, mind you.

377

And don't go trying to sow tobacco again.' 'God forbid, Corporal, God forbid! Never again, never . . .'

'Agha, but you're standing!' the Captain exclaimed. 'Here . . .' And he held out a chair for Ala Temir. 'Won't you sit here?'

Ala Temir sat down, drinking in this mark of the Captain's consideration with infinite pride. I must do this Captain a good turn, he thought. Something that'll surprise the whole world . . . He clapped his hands to his knees and drew himself up. 'At your service, my Captain,' he said. But the Captain had already turned away and was seeing to his other guests and giving orders to a gendarme for coffee to be brought in.

Sergeant Hassan appeared and stood planted in a corner of the long room. His military breeches were frayed and patched at the knees, badly crumpled and with the seat sagging like a shalvar's. The jacket was buttoned up all awry so that one end of the collar reached down to his stomach, and his shoulder belt was strapped on in such a way that it was no longer clear whether it was a shoulder or a waist belt. On his feet were a pair of incongruous patent-leather shoes and he wore a silk shirt with the collar carefully drawn out over the jacket. A very thick watch-chain of solid gold dangled out of his breast-pocket right down to his waist. His greying hair was crew-cut with one thick tuft falling over his forehead from under his cap. His bristling mustache was greying too. He had brindled green eyes, hard and vindictive.

It was only while they were drinking coffee that the Captain recalled the Sergeant and saw him standing stiffly in his corner. His eyes went to Ala Temir and he realized with surprise that Sergeant Hassan and Ala Temir were alike as two peas . . .

'Sergeant!'

Sergeant Hassan hurried to the table and stood at attention.

'Well, Sergeant? Will you be able to make that murderer talk?'

'With God's help, my Captain.'

'How long will it take?'

Sergeant Hassan's eyes flicked through the room as though looking for help. They rested on Ala Temir and found something there, something familiar that dispelled the cold atmosphere of the room and emboldened him to speak. 'It's impossible to tell with these people. Sometimes they break down at the first stroke of the stick, sometimes they will die rather than own up . . .'

'Have you really seen people die under the stick then, Sergeant?' Mahir Kabakchioglu asked dubiously.

'Plenty! Why, Bey, I've been a sergeant for twenty years now and what stubborn creatures haven't I come across! You can beat them to pulp, skin them alive and still not get a word out of them. There was one man . . .' The Sergeant was in his element now. 'He'd abducted four girls and tied them to each other and for eight days . . .' He cast down his eyes bashfully. 'He would untie one of them, rape her in full view of the others, tie her up again and pass on to the next . . . Well, I finally got hold of him, but he wouldn't confess. So I gave him the works, and what works, as God's my witness! Then . . .' He did not notice the Captain's eyes and eyebrows motioning him to stop. 'Then I buried him in the earth and pumped air into him. I pumped and pumped . . .'

'Sergeant!' the Captain's stern voice cut him short. 'Go and bring Mahmut here at once.'

Frustrated, the Sergeant touched a trembling hand to his cap and went out.

'It wouldn't matter if he talked in front of us, Captain,' Kurtboga said.

'It's not important, not at all,' the Captain said.

'These people need a stick to their back always,' Süleyman Aslansoypenché declared, 'or the country'll go to the dogs. Thank goodness for Ismet Pasha and all the other Pashas, good patriots every one of them, they've never done anything without the stick. They couldn't!'

'They couldn't,' Kurtboga concurred. 'Try and do without the stick one day, one single minute and see what trouble they'll stir up for you . . .'

Ala Temir forced himself to say something. 'God knows,' he shouted, 'if we stop giving them the stick they'll be sending our heads flying, beginning with the Pashas! Thank God for our gendarmes . . . They break five sticks a day on every peasant's back . . . God preserve us, a peasant who doesn't get the stick is like a poisonous snake. You never know where he's going to bite

379

you. Thank God for our Pashas who've invented the stick. In the name of democracy . . .'

Mahir Kabakchioglu interrupted him just as he was getting in his stride. Ala Temir cast him a black look, but to his great mortification the other simply ignored him. 'Yes, sir, every nation has a distinguishing trait and ours is a long familiarity with the stick. Any other nation would have rebelled for much less, but our people are exceptionally used to the stick. Not only used, but they love it . . . Why, they'd go stark staring mad if we desisted for just one year! Patriotic and gifted administrators of the peace like you, Captain, should always keep this in mind and go on giving them the stick as much as possible, even with no reason at all. That's the only thing they understand. That's what our whole edifice rests upon. That's why the Ottoman administrators have been giving the stick to our people these past seven hundred years. And now with the Republic we've arrived at a scientific understanding of this, and so we've increased the dose ten times, a hundred times more. Otherwise this nation would have been ruined long ago.'

'Allah, Allah!' Kurtboga cried, lifting up his hands in prayer, 'don't ever deprive these people of the stick . . . This nation would go to rack and ruin without the stick.'

'To rack and ruin . . .' Aslansoypenché echoed.

'To rack and ruin!' Ala Temir shouted.

At that moment the Kaymakam entered the room, followed by the Prosecutor and the young district doctor. Everyone rose to greet them, but Ala Temir was still shouting. 'To rack and ruin! They've been beating us for a thousand years. God forbid, if they didn't beat us one day, we'd destroy the whole world. They should kill us, not beat us! Kill us!'

The newcomers stared at him, not knowing what to make of this outburst. Then the Kaymakam turned to the Captain. 'Congratulations,' he said. 'So you've caught the murderer? A great success.'

'Great?' Mahir Kabakchioglu cried. 'Unheard-of, you mean. This is the first time these feudal murderers will be called to account.'

'Mahir Bey's put his finger right on the wound,' the Prosecutor said.

'Congratulations, Captain,' the doctor said. 'I agree entirely.'

'Thank you,' the Captain said. 'And now they're bringing Mahmut here.'

'Here!' Ala Temir cried springing to his feet. 'My God, here, our brave Murtaza Bey's murderer!' His face twitched and his eyes widened with dread. 'Here that bloodthirsty heathen, with his hands steeped in blood . . .' He sat down again, his body tense and rigid as a log, and fixed a glassy stare on the door.

A loud clanking of chains was heard and Mahmut the Kurd entered the room. He was a tall well-built broad-shouldered man with light brown hair, a long curly mustache, slim tapering fingers, jutting cheekbones and full red lips. Two deep furrows ran from his cheeks to the mouth, lending a seasoned expression to his face and there were little wrinkles about his eyes from the sun. On his right temple was the reddish scar of an Aleppo boil. He kept his eyes lowered and nobody could make out their colour. His shalvar-trousers were of brown serge and his jacket of striped black smuggled cloth. A white woollen sash was bound about his waist. He stood before them, very straight, his legs planted wide apart, and a deep silence filled the room. Everybody stared at him, then at each other.

'What a brave handsome lad!' Ala Temir murmured, completely taken aback. 'Who would have thought it?'

The silence would have lasted a long time if Mahir Kabakchioglu had not spoken. 'You murdered Murtaza Bey, didn't you? How could you do such a thing? How could you kill that excellent man? A man who had studied in Istanbul, in Europe . . . Who are you to take such a man's life?'

'How did you have the heart to do it, you Kurdish dog?' Kurtboga thundered. 'To kill that lion? One drop of his blood was worth ten thousand dogs like you. A cultivated man who'd been to Europe and returned, young and eager to serve his country. Not ten thousand, a hundred thousand . . . A million . . .' He rose and strode angrily up to him. Yet deep down he felt unsure of himself. What if Mahmut escaped from here and took to the mountains and came back one day to raid his house? He could not retreat now. His hand shot out, two fingers pointed an inch from Mahmut's face. 'Like this I'll gouge your eyes out. Like this! For killing that brave lion of a man . . .'

Mahmut raised his head. His eyes flashed steel-green, hard and daunting, only for an instant, then he lowered them again, slowly, proudly.

Kurtboga's fingers crumpled and his arm fell back. He swallowed. He could not leave it at that. 'God damn you!' he blurted out, his Adam's apple working up and down. Mahmut's eyes had dealt him a shock. 'Look, you poor misguided man, we know Dervish Bey made you do it. You're not to blame. They'll write out everything on a piece of paper and you'll just sign it. You know how to sign your name, don't you?'

'Mahmut can read and write perfectly,' Sergeant Hassan said. 'He even finished primary school. I know, for I made it my business to find out everything about him while we were hunting for him.'

'Good, good,' Kurtboga said. 'So there you are, Mahmut, my son . . . It's as simple as that. You just say it was Dervish Bey put you up to it and don't worry about the rest.' He leaned over to Mahmut's ear. 'These heathens here will have no mercy. The Captain's quite ruthless. He's had orders from Ankara to make you talk at any price or to kill you. So you listen to me. Save yourself. You're too young to die.'

He said no more and dropped silently back into his chair. However low he had tried to speak, his voice was strong even in a whisper. They all heard him, but chose to pretend they hadn't.

Nobody spoke after Kurtboga. They felt unaccountably subdued, crushed. All eyes were fixed on the prisoner who, for all the chains about his arms and legs, the iron ring at his neck, the handcuffs, stood erect before them, like the statue of pride, handsome, vibrant.

'Like an eagle,' Ala Temir thought. 'A copper-winged eagle . . .'

Mahmut was quite still. Only twice, as he changed his balance, the chains jangled and once as he lifted his manacled hands a little and let them fall again.

Suddenly the Captain came to life. 'Sergeant,' he commanded, 'take this man below. Dervish Bey has already confessed that he made him kill Murtaza Bey. If necessary, you can take Dervish Bey from the next cell and confront them, but

382

treat them both well . . . Just let Mahmut admit Dervish Bey made him do it, and then bring him to me . . . If he won't talk then you know what you're to do. I want you to report to me every two hours . . . We . . .'

'We'll be at my place,' Mahir Kabakchioglu forestalled him. 'I've made preparations and my house is quite near.'

'No, no,' Haji Kurtboga protested. 'I've made preparations too.'

'So have I,' Rüstem Bey said.

'D'you think I haven't?' Süleyman Aslansoypenché bridled.

'Mahir Bey's house is only a step from here,' the Captain cut them short. 'We mustn't go too far. I'm very curious to see if the man'll talk or not.'

'If he confesses, we can arrest Dervish Bey at once,' the Prosecutor said.

'Of course he will!' Aslansoypenché cried heatedly. 'What other choice has he but to confess? With Sergeant Hassan plying him . . .'

They all rose and proceeded to Mahir Kabakchioglu's house where they were greeted by his wife. 'I knew you'd honour us tonight,' she said, 'because I've heard the murderer's been caught. What kind of a man is he? They say he's a monster, but very handsome . . .'

'He's even worse than reported,' Mahir Kabakchioglu said. 'A wild beast . . .'

The sun had set long ago and it was dark by now. A long table had been laid and they sat down at once. *Raki* bottles were opened and the food was carried in, roast chicken, leg of lamb, cucumber salad, white cheese, hot green peppers. Two well-dressed young girls and a youth kept going in and out and bringing more food, water and ice.

'Here's to this **great** success!'

'Here's to!'

'May we see many a happy day like this one!'

Glasses clinked and for a while nothing but the clitter-clatter of knives and forks was to be heard.

'I'll have him paraded up and down the market-place, hand-cuffs and all,' the Prosecutor said. 'He must pay for all those murders he's got at his door, that Dervish Bey.'

'Hurray, bravo!' Kurtboga lifted his glass with enthusiasm. 'It's a great service to the country you'll be doing, Prosecutor. This nation will be so grateful to you. I'll cable Ankara tomorrow and tell them what a Prosecutor we have here, what a lion, what a tiger! To your health! To our great Prosecutor's health! Long life to him!'

'Long life!'

'Good health, good health . . .'

Jafer Özpolat, who had not said a word up to now, was getting drunk. Suddenly, he gave a toast. 'To our health! To everybody's health. Because I know Mahmut the Kurd well and he won't talk. He's a brave loyal man, the best in the world. I've known him since we were children. I would rather have a man like Mahmut than a whole army in full array.'

'Of course he'll talk!' the Captain said. 'I know these paid sergeants. Sergeant Hassan could make the very stones talk.'

'He could make a dead man talk,' Kurtboga emphasized.

'He'll soon be coming, mark my words,' Süleyman Aslansoy-penché said, 'with the news that the Kurd's sung like a nightingale.'

'He's got a hundred tricks up his sleeve, that Sergeant,' Kurtboga pursued. 'He was posted in our village for two years and night and day he would be reading up on new ways of torture and thinking up fresh ones. He was up to date on all the modern American methods and even attended courses in Istanbul and Ankara where they train people for this. Why, he could make a dead man talk, that one, and after working on him for three days he'd even set him on a platform to make a speech! A dead man, I tell you, not just a poor wretch like Mahmut the Kurd!'

Black looks were cast at Jafer Özpolat . . . They had taken great pains, these town Aghas, and spent a lot of money to ensure Mahmut's capture. Dervish Bey's contacts in the mountains were numerous and it had been necessary to bribe them all, one by one, a long and difficult process, and fruitless too, for Mahmut was like mercury, he simply slipped through their fingers. The network of scouts and informers he had built up was stupendous and Dervish Bey kept him well provided with money and ammunition. If it hadn't been for Kurdish

384

Haydar's treachery nobody could ever have captured him alive. In that fatal skirmish Mahmut, suddenly realizing he'd run out of ammunition, had cast himself straight into the range of the gendarmes' fire. But Haydar had grabbed him from behind just in time. 'We'll meet again one day, God willing,' Mahmut had hissed at him through gritted teeth.

'In our epoch,' the Kaymakam declared, 'the man doesn't exist who can hold on to the end without breaking down.'

'It's unthinkable,' the doctor said. 'There's a limit to what the human body can bear.'

But Jafer Özpolat was obdurate. 'No power on earth can draw a word out of Mahmut.'

'Jafer Bey,' the Captain shouted, 'I bet you ten thousand liras that he'll talk, and in less than a couple of hours too. No one can resist Sergeant Hassan longer than that. I'm ready to bet on him.'

'And I on Mahmut,' Jafer Özpolat retorted flippantly.

They all glared as if they wanted to kill him, but someone quickly changed the subject and began to speak about Dervish Bey's sister and her disgraceful reputation, and someone else remarked that there had always been women like that in the Sarioglu family. The doctor explained that this was a kind of disease. Then the conversation turned to the town's mayor, his carousals in the Adana nightclubs, his debauchery, his drinking champagne out of the slippers of nightclub girls. Someone wondered where he got all that money from, but nobody breathed a word of the contraband network he had formed.

The Captain kept looking at his watch. He rose, went to the window, resumed his seat, tossed down a glass of *raki*, looked at his watch worriedly again, then hurried back to the window. At last he summoned the youth who was attending the guests. 'Tell the gendarme on duty outside to go and fetch Sergeant Hassan at once,' he said.

A few minutes later Sergeant Hassan was standing at attention before him. He looked crestfallen and was trembling in all his limbs.

'Well, what's the matter, Sergeant? It's been three hours now!'

'He won't talk,' the Sergeant said. 'I've plucked out every

one of his twenty nails, but he didn't turn a hair. I plugged electric current to his testicles, and still nothing . . .'

'Is that all you did in three hours?'

Sergeant Hassan hung his head. 'There's plenty of time till morning, Captain . . .'

'Well, I'm waiting, Sergeant.'

'He's a tough case, Captain. I've never come across one like him . . .'

'Look, Sergeant,' Süleyman Aslansoypenché cried, leaping to his feet. 'I've laid out a fortune in this business. What if you don't make him talk? You must! There's one thousand liras for you if you do.'

'And a thousand from me too,' Kurtboga said. 'All our future's at stake. Show yourself, my lion.'

'A thousand from me too,' Kabakchioglu said.

All eyes went to Jafer Özpolat. 'He'll never talk,' he said. 'If you can make him, Sergeant, I'm ready to give you five thousand liras.'

'And two thousand from me . . .' Ala Temir said doubtfully. 'If that's the right way . . .'

'He'll talk!' the Sergeant cried, and he hurried off, filled with joy at the prospect of all that money. He'd make Mahmut talk, come what may. He was not at the end of his resources yet . . .

First he tried pleading with him. 'Look, brother,' he said, 'if you confess, I'll be promoted. They'll give me a lot of money, more than I've ever seen in all my twenty-five years at this job. I've got a family too . . . It's their daily bread you'll be playing with if you don't. What's Dervish Bey to you? But I . . . I'll never forget it if you help me now. I'll arrange for you to escape from prison. I'll snatch you from the gallows even. Just say it was Dervish Bey made you kill Murtaza Bey. Don't deny me this and mess up my whole life . . .' On and on he went, but there was no response whatsoever from the blood-stained man before him. It was too much for the Sergeant. 'Well then,' he roared, 'on your own head be it!'

'He'll talk,' the Captain asserted angrily.

'The Turkish Republic . . .' the Kaymakam began.

'Long live the Republic,' Ala Temir broke in. He was not drinking, and sitting like that stiffly with his hands on his knees all this time had tired him out.

'Well,' Jafer Özpolat said. 'I'm ready to bet.'

Suddenly the doctor exploded. 'But this is shameful, infamous! To stand up for a murderer! What does it mean?'

'Are you talking to me, doctor?' Jafer Özpolat inquired with deadly calm.

'Of course not!' the others cried quickly. After that the doctor and Jafer Özpolat kept their peace.

Haji Kurtboga looked at his watch. 'It's four o'clock,' he cried. 'It'll be light soon and still no news from Sergeant Hassan . . .'

'It won't be long now,' the Captain said. 'Don't worry.'

'Look, Captain, allow me to go to him. I'll have him talking in less than no time.'

'Certainly,' the Captain said. 'Whether it's you or Sergeant Hassan . . .'

Kurtboga left the room, lurching heavily as he went. He knew the place where Mahmut was being tortured and knocked on the door. Sergeant Hassan opened at once. There were six gendarmes inside and Mahmut was lying on the slimy floor, still as a corpse. An oil-lamp on the wall shed a tremulous light over the cell, striking up fugitive gleams from his chains.

'Get out, all of you,' Kurtboga ordered. 'I'm going to talk to him with kindness . . .' As soon as the door had closed behind them, he went up to Mahmut and took his hand. It was wet with blood and warm. 'You remember Osman? He died right here, where you're lying now. They emptied out all the blood in his veins . . . At Saricham, and this too you know very well, they shot dead Haji Veli and his gang, thirty-three people in all, on the pretext that they had tried to escape. Were there any questions? They cut off Resul's head and sent it to his mother, as an example to the whole village. No questions asked . . . In Tanishli village the gendarmes flogged eight people to death in full view of everyone, and what happened? Nothing . . . Haven't you heard about these things? Don't you know how it is? And now, you too will be dead in a few hours. The doctor's even drawn up the medical certificate . . . Isn't it a pity for you? Why should you die? Let Dervish die. I'll save you. I'll give you land from Akchasaz and help you to farm it. I'll settle a salary on you for life . . . Come, Mahmut, say it . . . Speak! Just say it was Dervish made you kill Murtaza Bey. Come, brother . . .' On and on he talked in warm deep-felt tones, like a father, a brother, a sympathetic friend, but there was not the slightest sound from Mahmut.

In the end he could contain himself no longer. 'Are you dead, man? Damn you, damn you!' Furious, he fell to kicking the silent Mahmut. 'Take this, you pig-headed Kurd! And this . . . And this . . . Sergeant!' he howled. 'I give up. You can kill the bastard if you like.'

When he entered Mahir Kabakchioglu's house again he was trembling with frustration. 'He won't talk,' he groaned, snatching up his glass of *raki*.

'Let me try too,' Jafer Özpolat suggested. 'We used to be friends when we were young. Perhaps he won't deny me . . .'

'Yes, yes, go!' they all urged him. 'He wouldn't deny his childhood friend . . .'

Jafer Özpolat rose. He tipped his glass and drained it to the last drop.

The east was slowly lighting up and a few tardy cocks were still crowing as he came to the door of Mahmut's cell. He heard a noise inside as of something breaking and his heart twitched. Sergeant Hassan opened the door. 'He hasn't said a word, Jafer Bey,' he said despondently. 'He won't talk. Ah, I won't be able to make him . . .'

'Get out, all of you,' Jafer Özpolat said. 'Let me have a word with him.'

Mahmut was twisted up on the wet cement floor, seemingly dead. His blood had gathered into little pools in the cracks of the cement. A noisome stench filled the whole cell and Jafer Özpolat held his nose. 'Brother,' he said, 'what have they done to you, those heathens! You must speak, Mahmut. They'll never let you out of here alive if you don't. Think! If they sentence Dervish, it'll be for eighteen years. And the same for you. And then there'll be an amnesty, as there always is, and you'll both

388

be free. Don't let yourself be killed for Dervish, in vain . . .' He could not go on. The putrid odour of the cell was piercing his lungs. He threw himself out and ran back to Mahir Kabak-chioglu's house. 'He's in no state to talk any more,' he said, tossing down a full glass of *raki*. 'He's dying . . .'

Mahir Kabakchioglu rose. 'Let me see if I can't do something,' he said, but when he entered the cell his knees felt weak. 'Mahmut, Mahmut!' he cried. 'If you just pronounce Dervish Bey's name, I'll make you the owner of two thousand *dönüms*, a huge farm. If you don't it'll be all over with you . . .'

After him, Süleyman Aslansoypenché decided to try his luck. He drew the inert blood-stained body of Mahmut on to his lap and began to entreat him. 'You'll die. Die! Isn't it a pity for a brave handsome man like you? A thousand dogs like Dervish aren't worth one nail of yours . . .' In the end, he too turned away. 'A pity,' he sighed.

'It's no use,' he told the others. 'He'll die without breathing a word.'

'He'll talk,' the Captain said. 'The Turkish Republic has the power to make even the dead talk.'

Jafer Özpolat jumped up and shouted: 'Turk, be proud, be diligent, be confident . . .'*

'Bravo!' they all applauded.

Ala Temir rose, dragging his numb hands wearily from his knees. 'Let me have a go at that Kurd too,' he said.

It was nearly day outside, but his eyes blinked as they peered through the dimness of the cell and rested on Mahmut. 'Alas,' he exclaimed, 'they've killed you . . .' He crouched down beside him and leaned to his ear. 'Hold on, brother,' he whispered. 'It's nearly morning. Don't inform against Dervish Bey, because whether you do or not, they'll still kill you. The doctor's standing by to inject poison into you . . . We've given him a ton of money for that. You're dying. Don't let Dervish be killed too. Forgive me, my lion, my brave lad . . .' His breast heaving with sobs he turned away. He could not stop his tears and had to wait at the door of Mahir Bey's house until they had dried.

*A much-used slogan during the first years of the Republic.

'There's no pity, no mercy, no humanity left in these Aghas and Government people,' he was thinking. 'They kill thousands of poor folks like this year after year. They kill and kill and kill . . .'

'Well you did take your time!' they greeted him when he went in. 'What happened?'

'He'll talk,' Ala Temir said. 'He has to . . .'

The doctor was tired and sleepy, and besides, the sick must be crowding at his door by now. It was five years since he'd been posted to this town. He came of a poor Erzurum family and had studied medicine in Istanbul, living from hand to mouth and sleeping in Moslem hospices, and this had generated in him a bitter rancour against all mankind. He was the only doctor in the district and every day he would administer quinine shots to hundreds of malaria-ridden patients. Town gossips would have it that most of the time he simply injected water, in order to cut down on his quinine expenses. At any rate one thing was evident. In these five years the doctor had grown rich. He now owned two large houses, a seventy-five-*dönüm* orange grove, and a farm on the Anavarza plain that covered six thousand *dönüms*.

He yawned, his mouth gaping wide, and stretched himself. 'Well, I must be going,' he said. 'That stubborn Kurd won't be talking so soon. I'll just write out the certificate . . .' He produced a sheet of paper and a pen from his pocket and proceeded to write. When he had finished he read it over several times, then nodded. 'Here you are,' he said, handing the paper to the Prosecutor. 'It says he died of heart failure as he was being brought to the gendarmerie. On horseback . . . That's the medical certificate if he dies. If he doesn't, just tear it up.'

Haji Kurtboga started up. 'Wait, doctor! I've just had an idea . . .'

'What is it?' the doctor asked curiously.

'All these Aghas here will agree with me . . . Our good teacher, Rüstem would say . . .'

'What? What did I say?' Rüstem Bey mumbled, startled out of sleep.

'The only thing to do is to draw up a deposition just as if Mahmut had confessed, and sign his name to it.'

'That's good!' Aslansoypenché said.

'By God!' Jafer Özpolat cried. 'Why on earth didn't we think of that before instead of worrying ourselves sick all night long!'

'Oh dear, oh dear,' Ala Temir murmured. 'Then it's all for nothing they killed him, that brave valiant Kurd . . .'

Kabakchioglu was silent.

'No!' the Captain thundered. 'A man who defies us . . . He'll talk yet.'

'We can't allow anyone to defy the State,' the Kaymakam asserted. 'And to forge a document would be to admit to weakness. The State cannot commit frauds.'

The Captain shot up like a drawn bow. 'The integrity of our country . . .' The whole place rattled loudly. 'The well-being and happiness of the Turkish nation are at stake. Never, never will we suffer defiance of this, the last Turkish State! Never, not even from a dead man! We cannot allow the tiniest fly to encroach on the sacred interests of this country. Forgery!' He sat down breathing hard, his lips trembling with rage. 'D'you know what that means, gentlemen? Forgery!'

The Prosecutor rose, trying to imitate the Captain and to work himself into a passion. 'Even if it's a fly that defies us, an insect, an ant, we will summon all our forces to crush it. What kind of talk is that? Forgery!' He flung his arms out wide as though he wanted to fly and began to swing backwards and forwards. 'What kind of talk! Forging documents for a mere Kurd! Of course our Government has the power to make him talk.'

'Yes, yes,' Kurtboga said hastily. 'What kind of . . . Yes, the power . . .'

'All the power in the world,' Özpolat said.

'Yes, all the power . . .' Aslansoypenché echoed.

'To commit forgery!' Mahir Kabakchioglu spoke out in shocked accents. 'And thus disgrace the authority of the State! Who could ever suggest such a thing?'

'Who indeed?' they all chorused.

'Kurdish Mahmut will end up by confessing,' the Captain declared with authority.

'Well, if he doesn't and if he dies,' the doctor said, 'you've got my certificate.'

The sun was quarter-high when Sergeant Hassan appeared at

the door, all spattered with blood and mud. His face was drawn and yellow. It had taken on a rusty hue. His eyes had sunk into their sockets, his skin hung about him, sack-like. There was nothing in common between this weary mortified man and the Sergeant Hassan of the evening before. He came forward with dragging steps and stopped in the middle of the room.

'What happened? He talked at last, is that so?' The Captain was almost dancing with impatience around him.

'I buried him in the ground up to his neck,' the Sergeant blurted out, so low they could hardly hear him. 'And then . . .' He stammered. 'And then I pumped him up . . . American style . . .'

'And then? Then?'

'He's very stubborn . . .'

'All right, he's stubborn. We know that. What happened then? Did you get it out of him?'

'I . . . I . . . I've never seen such a stubborn man . . .'

'What happened, you fool?' the Captain shouted, giving the Sergeant's arm a wrenching shake. 'The result?'

'He's so stubborn . . . He . . . He . . . On purpose . . .'

The Captain dealt him a sharp kick in the knee. 'Are you going to speak, man?'

'He died,' the Sergeant said tearfully. 'Just to spite us . . . As we were pumping air into him . . . We'd hardly begun yet . . .'

The Captain went mad. 'You . . . You . . . And I'm going to kill *you*!' he yelled as he went at the Sergeant with fist and boot. The Sergeant, who was dead tired anyway, fell to the ground. Foaming at the mouth, the Captain began to stamp all over his prostrate body in a kind of frenzied dance. It seemed as though he would never stop.

At last, the Prosecutor could stand it no longer. 'You're wearing yourself out, Captain,' he said, 'for these scum . . .' He took him by the arm and made him sit down. The Captain was bathed in sweat and panting like a bellows. 'So,' he muttered, 'the might of a great Turkish Republic was not enough. He got the better of us by dying . . .' He was on the point of letting fly again, but kept a hold on himself. 'Get up, Sergeant,' he said dully. 'Go and get that dead dog's carcass and carry it out into the market-place. Since everyone will know how he died, let's make an example of him at least . . .'

And so, for two and a half days, Mahmut's bloody corpse, mangled beyond recognition, was exposed in the town square, laid out on the lid of an ancient Greek marble sarcophagus. And all about him steel-green flies kept flashing, up and down, up and down . . .

45

The Anavarza crags were already steaming hot, impregnated with the odour of parched yellowing thyme. Bees with glittering steel-green bodies and lucent blue wings flitted about the asphodels. Rumbling sounds arose from the depths of the purple white-flecked rocks on which a flower, carved by some ancient Greek, bloomed mauvely here and there. The old castle wall with its large slabstones, thick and solid, defying the passage of centuries, rose among the tangled wilderness of blackberry bushes, dwarf oaks and prickly pears, and the ground was strewn with broken pieces of pottery, brown with stripes of blue and black and white. A blunt-headed spotted snake was slithering slowly through the broken pottery. It vanished into the crack of a rock. Swift-footed lizards, their red tongues sticking out, scurried to and fro as though making off with a stolen flame. At the foot of a long, red-veined rock a covey of partridges, with their lustrous blue breasts, their reddish beaks and legs, their white-streaked black wings and plump greenish bodies, were scraping at the sandy earth and sending it flying over their backs.

And still it grew hotter. The rocks were like iron in a furnace now, impossible to touch, and even the faint breeze that had been blowing a little while ago laden with the scent of thyme dropped away.

They took the three naked men from the horses and cast them down over the rocks just as they were, hands and feet firmly bound. Not a sound came out of them as they hit the burning rocks, not a movement to betray any pain.

Pacing up and down in his accordion boots Dervish Bey was watching Mustafa Bey from the corner of his eye. Hidayet had trussed his legs up to the knees and tied his hands behind his back, and he lay there as if impaled to the searing rock surface. Involuntarily, Dervish Bey's eyes went to his genitals. The penis was crumpled up and very small, contracting and darken-

394

ing even as he looked, as though it would disappear between the legs any minute. So it is with men and horses of noble stock, Dervish Bey thought. Their penis puckers up in sleep and when they awake it grows larger and larger. In ancient times a man's nobility must surely have been measured by his penis. Any other part of the human body by which blue blood is rated, the nose or lips, the chin, long limbs, delicate wrists, all these may change, but not a man's penis. For the ancient Greeks and Romans the criterion of nobility was that the second toe of a man's foot should be longer than the others. They knew nothing of the penis, these degenerate Greeks and Romans, whereas the Sumerians, the Urartus, the Hittites were certainly aware of its significance. His own penis was just like Mustafa Bey's and so it must have been with their fathers and ancestors. He bent down beside Mustafa Bey's tense twitching body and examined his feet. Damn it all! The second toes were longer than the others . . . Quickly he retreated behind the wall, out of sight, and pulling off his right boot observed with amazement that with him too the second toe was longer. It filled him with pride. Yes, he thought, there is such a thing as nobility, but it must be measured both by the penis and the second toe. If a man satisfies only one condition then he is only half noble . . . And there is courage and valiance too. The noble man does not fear death. He will never forfeit his honour for a few days' lease on life.

'Now we'll try our noble brother Mustafa,' he muttered as he quickly drew on his boot. 'What kind of nobility is his, of the toe, or the penis, or what . . . We'll soon see.' He went back to the flat stretch of rock on which the three naked men were lying.

'Hidayet!'

'Yes, Bey?'

'I'm going to kill these three one after the other, beginning with Mustafa Bey. They were planning to torture me for days on end before killing me. Well, I'm going to kill them right away.'

Ibrahim Ibo who had been weeping silently all this time, fell to pleading. 'Don't kill me, Bey! What have I done? It's only because I told Whirlwind Veli where we were that you caught us. You'd never have found us otherwise. Is this my reward?

395

Bey, have pity on me. I've got a wife and family . . . Please, Bey, let me kiss the soles of your feet . . .'

Hamdi began to beg for mercy too. It was unbearable. Dervish Bey's men, lined up at the foot of the castle wall, were watching in silence.

'Take these two somewhere I won't have to listen to their whining. And as soon as you hear me shoot, bring them along. I'm going to kill them with my own hand, these heathens who've been killing me with a thousand tortures every day . . .'

The two naked men were borne away through the rock-hewn portal of the castle wall.

'Hidayet, Zekeriya, lift Mustafa Bey up. Don't hurt him, mind you. Just stand him up against that wall and go.'

They propped Mustafa Bey up against the high rampart of Anavarza Castle. From there the plain below seemed very distant, the cars and carts, horses and people on the roads small as birds, squirming at the bottom of the heat-haze that hung over everything. Then they went away and all was still. Only a faint rumbling drifted in from afar, but Dervish Bey did not hear it.

Mustafa Bey's face and body were waxen, his eyes closed, the lines on his face deepening and lengthening. He might have been a corpse tied there to the wall, but for the uncontrollable tremors that shook him.

Dervish stood six paces away, his legs planted wide apart on the rugged rock surface veined with blue like a spider's web. He drew his revolver from his waist, emptied the cylinder into his hand, rattled the bullets loudly and loaded them again. Mustafa Bey's eyes remained closed. Dervish Bey waited patiently in perfect silence for him to open them.

The sun rose to quarter-high. Mustafa Bey's shadow was stuck to the wall. Dervish Bey's shadow stretched to Mustafa's feet and fell over his body. Suddenly, Dervish Bey rejoiced. His enemy's chest was heaving more and more rapidly. His face sweated and went cold, flushed and paled, the lips became blue and moved, the nose quivered like a bee's wings and under the closed eyelids the eyeballs rolled and rolled like a blind man's. Dervish aimed the muzzle of his revolver straight at his forehead and held it there. His hand did not tremble or shift an inch. He

396

waited. The revolver gleamed and glistened under the smiting sun, its sheeny steel flashing in a thousand sparks. The face and body of the naked man tautened and jerked convulsively. This was what Dervish Bey wanted. If it went rigid, if it was quite still there would be nothing left to do but to empty the revolver into it and leave. The knees too were sagging. He's capitulating, Dervish exulted. But just as he was thinking this Mustafa Bey's trembling stopped and the rolling of his eyes too. His face became stern, knife-like, and his body hard as a rock. So! Dervish Bey thought, he's resisting . . . Let's see how long he'll bear up, how strong is the human body, the power of the will . . . I won't shoot until he opens his eyes. I'll wait here like this, the revolver pointed right at the centre of his forehead. He must have seen it from under his eyelids. He's heard me unload and load it again. He must feel the muzzle on his forehead, its impress deeper and deeper, gouging a hole in it from this distance even. No, I'll make him cry mercy, yes, mercy, before I kill him. I'll make him open those eyes of his. If he holds out for ten days and ten nights, I'll hold out too . . .

The noonday heat was upon them now. Hot whiffs of wind blew in, wave after wave, like scorching flames. The scent of thyme clung heavily to the ground and only the odour of burnt earth and rock filled the air. Dervish Bey's throat was dry with thirst.

'Hidayet!' he shouted. 'Water.'

Hidayet rushed up with a flask.

'This side. To my left.' He held out his left hand and drank with loud gurgling gulps, never taking his eyes off Mustafa Bey's face. As he returned the flask to Hidayet he had the satisfaction of seeing his enemy licking his lips furtively while a violent spasm shook his body and his skin darkened and shivered. Gradually, imperceptibly he began to sweat. It started at the roots of the hairy down on his shoulders, then broke out in beads on the deepening furrows of his brow and spread to all his body, streaking down ever more quickly to form a wet circle at his feet. Then the sweat dried, the skin shrivelled and sagged, contracting as though enveloped in a cold mist. The eyeballs kept spinning under the closed lids, in perpetual motion.

Dervish Bey knew that Mustafa Bey wanted nothing more than

397

to hear some sound, some movement from him, so he kept quite still. He was sweating also, profusely. His clothes were wringing wet, the insides of his boots quite soaked and the sweat dripped steadily from the hand that held the revolver to dissolve in vapour even before hitting the torrid rock surface.

There was a sudden flurry of yellow rain. It came and passed, and the red-veined purple rocks, the black parched earth, the incandescent ashen sky, the Jeyhan River that flowed below like molten tin, were all dyed a deep yellow. A fresh gust of rain passed over them and then the rain settled into a steady drizzle, crystal-yellow.

Mustafa Bey's body was all yellow too, but Dervish Bey saw with amazement that it was slowly tightening into a kind of rigid resistance. Easy, he thought, yes, very easy to die like this with your eyes closed! No pain, no agony, just one single bullet and it's all over. Anyone could do it! No, no, my lion! I'll wait here with this revolver in my hand till you open your eyes. Only then will I shoot, with you looking me in the eye like a man. I must see fear and prayer flickering in those eyes of yours, my noble enemy . . .

At last Mustafa Bey began to give again. The sweat broke out over his brow and temples and flowed down his shoulders and arms. The eyeballs under the blank closed lids were spinning ever more quickly. Dervish Bey had the impression that he half-opened his eyes for a fraction of a second. His lips were blue and his mustache drooped in a triangle about his gaping mouth.

With incredible noise and speed a fat black bee swooped down and buzzed three times about Mustafa Bey's head, then zoomed up, zigzagging over the rampart to vanish into the crags. It brought Mustafa Bey to himself, but only for a second. After it had gone he sank back into the emptiness of death, alone, abandoned, and felt again the muzzle boring into his brow, now searing hot, now cold as ice. His heart was bursting in an agony of waiting for the bullet that did not come. His head whirled, his knees trembled and beneath him the earth shook and slipped and flowed past, oily, polished. He held his breath. Shoot, shoot . . . What are you waiting for? Dog, dog!

he kept repeating to himself. He had to look, he had to, once more . . .

The first thing he saw was a tall cardoon growing out of the rock with six round blue thistles glistening in the sun. The blue globes glowed and whirled under his eyelids, their blue deepening and gathering the sun's light in rings about it, a thorny round mass surrounded by a rainbow sheen, and over it the shimmering revolver, its dark muzzle yawning like a deep well, all that brilliance, the thistly blue brightness, and that pitch-dark mouth . . . The mad longing to cast himself into it . . . Rigid, panting . . . A lancinating pain stabbing at his heart . . . Cursing his own helplessness, in a fury of self-pity . . . Waiting . . . Waiting breathlessly, madly for death to come . . . Casting about desperately for a way to hasten it . . . In vain. His muscles straining, numb and cold now, the deafening beat of his heart abruptly arrested . . . Falling, falling into a razor-edged void, shattered into a thousand agonizing pieces . . . And the swift acceptance of surrender, resigned, sweating, almost smiling, burning to open his eyes again, to cast another glance.

He waited. Behind his eyelids the burning glare of the sun grew stronger, an intense orange glow. And as the glow increased there was a rushing in his ears, a sound like laughter or sobbing, the flap of a bird's wings, the shuffling of many feet, ever louder, like a gathering storm.

Dervish Bey realized Mustafa Bey was weakening, slowly losing every vestige of resistance. Now he would open his eyes. What would those eyes say in the face of the coming bullet? He looked at the penis. It was shrivelled black, sunk into the flesh under the belly, almost invisible.

The sun was at its noon height, boring into Dervish Bey's brain and he was beginning to be tired. How much longer could he hold on like this, with the revolver aimed, ready to shoot, in the midst of these red-hot crags? The sweat ran down his body like a river. His clothes were wringing wet one moment, then dry stiff the next and filmed over with a thin white powdery layer.

A flock of birds passed overhead with loud screeching cries. Mustafa Bey staggered and his body was racked with violent spasms. His heart throbbed, pounding at his chest as though it would leap out. The shrill hiss of a snake sounded from the crags. And suddenly his green eyes flashed open, all the strength he could muster gathered in two steely pinpoints in the pupils. Dervish Bey was astounded, his initial triumph shattered. But Mustafa Bey had caught that fleeting look of triumph above the dark muzzle ready to spew out death. He relaxed a little, and seeing this Dervish Bey decided to finish him. Now's the moment, he thought. Press the trigger . . . Right at his forehead . . .

But what was this? Mustafa Bey's eyes were widening in a pallid glassy stare. His face darkened, then paled. The nostrils fluttered, the mouth tautened in stark expectation of inevitable death and that convulsive trembling seized him again.

Dervish Bey hesitated. Wearily the hand that held the revolver sank to his side and in that instant Mustafa Bey's face changed once more. It was suffused with relief, with a mad joy at just one moment's lease on life. His trembling stopped. Swiftly Dervish Bey levelled the revolver, and again that pallor of dread, those glassy frozen eyes . . .

Dervish Bey was suddenly sickened by it all. He felt a wave of nausea come over him. And the same nausea hit Mustafa Bey. A slimy greyish liquid issued from his mouth and trickled down his chest.

Some time passed and it seemed to Dervish Bey that Mustafa was laughing. His lips were drawn in what looked like a smile, his eyes fixed somewhere on Dervish's body, a button perhaps . . . Or was it the tiepin? Dervish looked down and saw a very small ladybird on the left lapel of his jacket. Gritting his teeth he gripped the revolver so tightly that it hurt and pointed the muzzle straight at Mustafa's heart. His eyes met Mustafa's and they were pleading, pleading desperately . . . Dervish Bey's stare must have betrayed his amazement, because Mustafa flushed with shame and quickly lowered his eyes. He looked up again and saw the triumphant face, the lowered arm. Dervish was savouring his victory, the infinite satisfaction of having brought his enemy to his knees at last.

Sickened, utterly disgusted, Mustafa stiffened with loathing. His eyes flashed greenly and the steely pinpoints settled in his pupils again. He drew himself up and braced himself to wait for death without a sign of fear.

Quickly, Dervish Bey levelled the revolver. But what was this? He could not believe his eyes. Mustafa Bey had not faltered. His face remained hard, unyielding, his eyes narrow, defiant. This was not the same man who only a minute ago had been imploring with his eyes, his drooping mustache, his crumpled penis, with every pore of his body.

An eagle swished down over them. A group of huge rock lizards with slit backs, their red tongues sticking out, scuttled up the rampart and scaled it. A large bee, its squat body ringed with bright yellow, whizzed round Mustafa Bey's head with a deafening noise. He did not move. His eyes glinted in fierce defiance of fear or death, of the heat and the bullet that was going to blast him any moment now.

It's because he's convinced I won't kill him, Dervish Bey thought. The low-down cur, the coward! Quivering with fury, he took a firm aim and closed his eyes. But he could not help himself. He had to look before pressing the trigger . . . He opened his eyes and stared in wonder. Mustafa Bey's head had dropped to his chest. His face was piteous, stricken beyond recognition. Dervish Bey's arm fell and in a rush of joyous relief Mustafa Bey smiled. He smiled with his eyes and white teeth, his hair, feet, hands, his whole body. Against his will Dervish found himself sharing this joy, the relief of being able to breathe a little while longer. But only for a moment, and the next he was raging at himself, at his inexplicable hesitations. Mustafa Bey felt the change and knew that all was lost. He reeled as though struck by lightning and closed his eyes. Dervish Bey had closed his eyes too. They opened them in the same instant. A white luminous cloud was drifting overhead, shedding its shadow over the rocks. Mustafa Bey followed it with his eyes and Dervish Bey automatically did the same. Slowly the cloud floated past. Its shadow skimmed over the plain, the streams and mounds, the swamp and the dusty roads and fell over the Taurus range. Tiny green-bellied bees flitted up and down among the sun-dried thyme, humming noisily, and lizards came to rest on the rock at Mustafa Bey's feet, with small flies on their tongues, too lazy even to swallow. A white-striped black spider with very long legs was lying in wait for its prey, motionless in a web that hung between three rocks and a dwarf oak. It had the proud stance of an old-world Sultan, confident that the web it had spun could withstand the boisterous winds of the Anavarza crags. Through his narrowed eyes Mustafa Bey saw it all, but distorted, blurred as in a dream.

Dervish Bey too seemed to be in the throes of some strange dream, unable to move, his eyes going from the spider to the glowing blue globes of the cardoon and then to Mustafa Bey's penis, his sweating body, his harrowed eyes. Suddenly he began to walk. Up and down he went with hard angry strides between the rock and the rampart, and Mustafa's eyes followed him as though tied fast to his body, as though anxious to fix his image indelibly in his mind. Dervish Bey's legs as he walked seemed to be independent of the body, disjoined. Fitfully, the hand that held the revolver waved in the air as though it had touched some filth and could not get rid of it. He quickened his pace, almost running now. Mustafa Bey's head whirled, his knees began to tremble, and when Dervish pulled up abruptly his eyes were arrested too, fixed in a wide glassy stare on Dervish Bey's legs. They were trembling as much as his . . .

The yellow rain gathered force and swashed down over them, razor-like.

Was Dervish smiling? Mustafa Bey smiled too, a fawning smile and Dervish gripped his revolver so tightly that the blood froze in his palm. The yellow rain turned as blue as the cardoons, a glowing spiked blue downpour, and cataracted down the age-old ramparts and over the white, red and green-veined rocks. The whole world was bathed in a blue light. But from over Mount Aladag a churning black pile of clouds was advancing, shattered by long rumblings and rent by bright sharp flashes of lightning. A night-darkness spread over Anavarza plain and the blue rain was lashed this way and that by the mad force of the storm.

The blood settled in the palm of his hand and Dervish Bey swayed like a drunken man. Slowly, as in a dream, he lowered the revolver that had been pointed at Mustafa's brow and started pacing up and down again, hurriedly, his head bent, deep in thought. And Mustafa's eyes followed him, up and down, up down, until suddenly he retched. With a tremendous effort he held back the vomit that rose to his throat. Dervish Bey stopped short and looked at him with contempt, but his own breast was heaving as heavily as Mustafa's and his heart beating just as fast.

And the rain turned yellow again, falling with a steady swishing noise.

Mustafa Bey's eyes narrowed. His face hardened. He drew himself up, his body taut, his legs, arms, private parts, even the hairs of his body and head stiff and rigid. Filled with infinite loathing he looked straight at Dervish Bey, all the accumulated hate of his race blazing in his eyes, a fearless, implacable, murderous look, more telling than any word or movement or action of the terrible anger, the boundless rancour and unforgiving vengefulness that was in him.

Dervish Bey was thunderstruck, frozen to the marrow. He tried to laugh. He sent out peal after peal of laughter, but he could not dispel the weight of that freezing anger, the crushing hate he read in his enemy's eyes. I must kill him now, he thought, at once . . . Turning his back on Mustafa Bey, he slumped down on a rock, panting as if he had only just rushed up the crags. Kill him, kill him . . . But how to do it now, when he was facing him fearlessly with all the force of hate and revenge, defying death . . . Would he not remain like this for all eternity, the image of valiance and fortitude? A man's last attitude as he dies is surely what he will forever be . . . When he could have killed him a little while ago, grovelling, pleading, limp with fear . . . Those venomous, unflinching eyes were boring into his back now, angry, oppressive, and Dervish shrank from turning around to look again . . .

A burst of yellow rain swept through the crags bending the round blue radiance of the cardoons to the ground and redressing them again, whipping them this way and that. Yellow torrents rumbled down the rocks into the plain.

How long he remained there, sitting on the rock, tense under the searing weight of those eyes in his back, he did not know. The first thing he felt was the numbness of the hand that held the revolver. Then a lightening, the lifting of a weight. He looked behind him. Mustafa Bey's body was slumped against the wall, in a moribund attitude. His eyes were glazed, sunk in a maze of wrinkles, the black irises filmed with grey, utterly lifeless.

Slowly Dervish Bey turned around, still sitting, the sharp rock piercing into his flesh. He could not detect the slightest tremor in that frozen gaze, that sagging body. Could it be that he was dead? But then he would have dropped to the ground. Asleep perhaps? He's dead, Dervish decided. No use wasting a bullet on him. The only thing to do is unbind him and leave him there. The coward, the dirty low-down craven . . . Dying even before I could shoot . . . And even if he isn't dead, how can one kill such a cowering wretch? Killing must have its rules too, even if it is only a bird, an ant . . . The plucking of a flower . . . One cannot touch a flower in the bud, a woman with child. Nor can one shoot a man already half dead . . . What would Mustafa have done in my place? The answer came to him at once as he recalled the deadly hatred he had seen in those eyes only a while ago. Mustafa would have killed him a thousand times . . . Yet after all his defiance he had broken down at last . . .

Dervish Bey was on the point of calling to Hidayet to come and untie him when, lifting his head, he was astounded to see Mustafa alive again, his face drowned with relief. Swiftly he levelled the revolver and in that very instant all the blood drained from Mustafa's face. It paled and shrivelled, and Dervish Bey was so startled he could not press the trigger. Damn him, he thought in disgust. God damn such a creature. I mustn't look at him, that's all. He turned away and began pacing up and down, quickly, ever more quickly. And now Mustafa Bey realized that all was lost. His lips moved soundlessly in a last prayer and the quicker Dervish went the more rapid was the patter of his lips. Suddenly they froze. Dervish Bey had swerved and was bearing down on him in a fury of determined loathing. The hot burning oily iron of the revolver struck his brow and his head was dashed against the wall, three times. It was do or die now for Dervish Bey. He stepped back, exultant, resolute. They came eye to eye. His finger moved on the trigger . . .

'Enough, enough, enough!' Mustafa Bey cried in a moan. 'Kill me, kill me . . .' And he crumpled down over the hard rock surface, his eyes closed, his face devastated, greying . . 'Kill me, kill me,' he repeated faintly, his lips hardly moving. 'Enough! Kill me, Dervish, kill me . . .'

But Dervish Bey was no longer listening. Lost in a transport of ecstasy and pride, he thrust his revolver back to his waist and turned away without a further look at his prostrate enemy.

There was another cloudburst and the yellow rain lashed out again. The crags, the ramparts, the castle towers, the ruined church, the great entrance portals, the wide amphitheatre with its granite seats still intact, the roads and streams and greening swamp below were drowned in the surging rush of yellow torrents that streamed down the gullies. A dark yellow shroud spread over the mountains and over the boundless expanse of the ancient Chukurova earth.

They reached the Akyollu mansion at daybreak. The Lady Karakiz was on the balcony beside the marigolds and sweet basil, clinging to the post. All night long she had sat there, her heart burning with anxiety, waiting for her son who had disappeared two days ago without leaving a trace.

Mustafa Bey, Hamdi and Ibrahim Ibo had been thrown face down over the horses just as they were, stark naked, hands and feet bound, and their heads hung limply.

The Lady Karakiz seemed to recognize her son, but she would not believe her eyes.

Zekeriya threw open the gate and Dervish Bey rode into the courtyard, very erect on his horse, with Hidayet following. They stopped by a blue tractor and kept a wary watch while Zekeriya led in the three horses and tied them to the door of the mansion. He stole a glance at the Lady Karakiz and his heart twitched. Dervish Bey saw her eyes as she rose with her bent back and leaned over to look at the three naked men on the barebacked horses. He turned his horse's head and slowly rode out of the yard. It was only when they were well away from the mansion that they spurred on to a gallop.

The yellow rain was still pouring down, hard as cords.

46

His hump stuck out higher than ever and his head was sunk so low between the broad shoulders that it seemed pasted to his chest. His huge eyes shone with a melancholy lustre, like those of a noble horse, in the smooth, almost transparent pallor of his long sad face. But the lips were fresh and full, and the teeth white as a child's, and when the town-crier laughed he changed into an entirely different person, even the hump no longer there, wiped out altogether. He was like an oversized long-suffering child who has always been buffeted and ill-treated.

'Where are you off to at this time of the evening, with darkness coming on?'

'To the agnus castus brake.'

'You look very worried . . .'

'Does it show?' the town-crier said, taken aback.

'Show? That face of yours is a mirror to your thoughts!'

'I must kill him,' the town-crier said. 'I must, and in broad daylight too, in the market-place under the big plane tree . . .' As he performs his ablutions . . . Three bullets aimed at the same spot, the very centre of his brow . . . Flat on his back he'll fall, stretched mouth up in the dirt and dust . . . And green flies whizzing madly over him, in and out of his nose . . . Haji Kurtboga killed! And who killed him, who? That tiny little man! The falcon, too, is small, but will never let go its prey . . . His fame would spread all over the Chukurova and into the Binboga Mountains . . .

'But why did he kill him? Why? Why?'

'Why did you kill him, you wretch, that lion of a man? He was worth a thousand of you.'

'Why don't you speak, dog?'

'I'll make you speak if I have to pluck out every tooth in your mouth, if I have to tear out that serpent tongue of yours.'

'It's Mustafa Bey and Dervish Bey who put you up to it, isn't that so? Confess, you hunchbacked dog!'

Kurtboga's forgotten all about it. Why should a powerful Agha trouble to kill you? He's got plenty of other business to attend to, I can assure you. It was just a passing fit of anger. You're making too much of this, brother. Forget it. And don't go about any longer with that revolver stuck to your waist. It's downright provoking the man, what you're doing. You're not a warrior, are you? And what's the use of raising a hue and cry every goddam day and telling whoever you come across that he's going to kill you? If he kills you, then that's that. Let him kill you. A man should hold his head high and not be so afraid to die. Shame on you, town-crier. Death is there anyway. It'll come sooner or later. The children? They've got a good mother, the best in the world. And what about the ironsmith? Isn't he more to you than a brother? Won't he look after them better than you would yourself? And he makes a good living too. He could provide for ten more children like yours. The ironsmith . . . His broad shoulders . . . His powerful biceps, his huge calloused hands . . . Such beautiful hands he has, the smith!

The early morning light had already crept into the solitary market-place and the shadows of the great plane trees were dappling the white cobblestones. Long, slim, bright-blue damsel-flies skimmed swiftly over the stones, pausing here and there as though suddenly nailed to the ground, their pellucid wings quivering. The town-crier stood here, all alone, looking at the distant peak of Mount Düldül. It seemed closer in this early light. Its pale pink flanks were slowly turning to lilac.

'I must kill him.'

'Who'll look after the children?'

'You, wife, you. I have to kill him. Or he'll kill me . . .'

'Now you're raving again. Why should he kill you? And if you go to prison, how can I support both you and the children?'

'What about the smith, then? My friend . . .'

His unsmiling face . . . Never so much as a joke with him. A faithful friend, but . . .

'He's human too. Who knows how he'll act once you're gone . . .'

'Hush, don't talk like that, wife. He's my own true friend, the staunchest man that ever lived . . .'

The agnus castus brake was strewn with pebbles scattered

407

among the thick-growing blue marjoram by the little brook flowing through it. The fragrant scent of marjoram and agnus castus pervaded the whole brake that gleamed mauvely under the radiant Chukurova sun and hummed with the noise of many bees and insects. White butterflies fluttered here and there in dazzling clusters. His face glazed, his eyes glittering, the town-crier paused near a tussock of large-flowered, heady-scented marjoram. Hundreds of butterflies fluttered up in a bright orange whirl, bathing the town-crier in an orange glow one instant, then lifting into the sky the next. Another group of butterflies, lilac-coloured, swirled up to him and for a while he was plunged in a lilac flurry, a moist lilac vortex that made him shiver. He threw out his arms in bewilderment.

'Of course I can depend on him! My friend Mustafa, my brother the smith . . . I can serve a fifteen-year sentence without worrying my head about a thing. Isn't that so, Mustafa, brother? You wouldn't forget me there in prison, like a stone at the bottom of a well, would you? . . . Why, you low-down hunchback, that's just what one would expect of you! And that's why God made you a hunchback too! To show the whole world the dirty abjectness of your mind. Who knows what pains he took, poor God, to fashion such a revealing hump . . . Stop, stop! You're right, Mustafa brother, of course I can rely on you . . . I'll kill him then, that villain, that murderer of women. But what if he . . .'

Swords slashing at his hump, slicing it up . . . An agonizing pain . . . His eyes gouged out, hanging by a thread, swimming in blood . . .

The pure filtered ultramarine sky was studded with stars, large and small. In the east Mount Düldül's flint-like pink mass seemed nearer, glimmering and glinting with the reflected light of the stars that teemed about its peak. To the left the dawn-star whirled in a coruscating brilliance. Suddenly a light burst forth like the flash of a hundred thunderbolts, illuminating the whole brake, the pebbles at the bottom of the stream, green, yellow, mauve, the fish with their spangly scales, the flowers of the agnus castus and marjoram with their dark black eyes. Struck with fear the town-crier raised his head. A star, perhaps the largest there was, was cleaving through the sky. Nearer and nearer to the town-crier it streamed and shattered into dazzling shivers only a little way above him. For a long time his eyes were blinded. Again and again he rubbed them until at last they returned to normal again.

'I must kill him. I must, wife, I must!'

'Don't, Halil, don't do it! Please, Halil, think of your children . . .'

And your wife so beautiful too, Halil . . .

But if I don't, *he* will kill me.

Kurtboga's ox-like eyes . . . It must be in the market-place so everyone should see . . . Riding at a gallop . . . In his hand the shining revolver, Dervish Bey's present . . .

'Stop, dog! Stop just where you are. Open your mouth . . .' And bang bang bang!

'What, what, what did Halil say? The town-crier . . .'

'He said open your mouth, you dog of an Agha . . .'

'Say your last prayer . . .'

'You're good only for killing your poor wives . . .'

'What did you do with so many of them? Where did you bury them?'

'He said, who d'you think I am? Just a hunchback? Halil, the town-crier, they call me! Take this and this and this . . .'

Kurtboga bellowing like an ox . . . Streaming with blood . . . Hurling himself at the town-crier . . .

'Here, take this, and this, and this . . .'

Right in the middle of his forehead . . .

'Who killed him, who?'

'Halil! Halil, the town-crier!'

'Like a rotten tree he toppled over . . .'

In the early dawn a crowd is streaming, surging into the empty market-place . . . The white cobblestones are chequered with the dark heavy shadows of each separate leaf. And here, at the foot of this tree, a few feet away from the fountain, is where the smiths have always disposed of the ashes from their furnaces, a wide space enclosed like a fold with prickly pears on all sides. Green moss gushes forth in places from the heap of ashes, fresher, more vernal, greener than any other, and the yellow, mauve, pink and red flowers of the cactus bloom brightly all round. It was Osman who first caught sight of the reddish gleam in the green moss among the ashes. He called to Murat, the street-sweeper. It was a very small trickle of blood. How had Osman detected it? It was Osman's habit to collect the half-burnt coals from the ashes every day before sunrise.

The crowd came streaming in, thronging ever more thickly under the big plane tree in the ironsmiths market, men, women, children, old and young, and stood about with stricken horrified faces. The peak of Mount Düldül reddened and glowed and over it the sun came to sit like a drop of blood.

'The ironsmith! They've killed the ironsmith . . .'

His left hand was clasped tightly to the anvil. His right, still gripping the hammer, dangled under the bellows. His head drooped to the ground. On his right flank the blood had congealed in a large patch. The huge hand that held the hammer was also bloodstained, and so were the cracked soles of his bare calloused feet.

'The ironsmith! They've killed the ironsmith . . .'

The town-crier whirled. Round and round he went like a dervish. 'The ironsmith! The ironsmith!' His eyes widening, his long triangular face glazing . . . 'They've killed the ironsmith!' Trembling as in the throes of death . . .

The smithy hummed like a bee-hive. People crowded in and went out again, weeping, their faces drawn in pity and horror.

'They shot him in the back. In the back!'

'The bullet pierced his back and came out in front, shattering his lungs . . .'

The town-crier could not bring himself to go in. He stood one moment at the door and saw the large bloodstained hand grasping the hammer, the massive feet, bare and dirty, then turned away and went to sit on the granite stone under the prickly pears.

'I killed him, I!' he cried. 'They didn't kill me, those vicious Aghas. I wasn't good enough for them. Haji Kurtboga wouldn't deign to kill me. So he killed him instead . . . I killed him, I . . .'

'Everyone knows who killed him, Halil. Don't you go . . .'

'I killed him, I! Whatever anyone says, I did it, I . . .'

'You?'

'Yes, Ali, I . . . Three shots . . . In the back . . . Three dum-dum bullets . . . Ali, will you do something for me?'

410

'Whatever you wish . . .'

'I'll never forget it if you do. If I'm still alive, that is . . .'

'What is it?'

'His feet were bare, Ali, and dirty. He was a bachelor. He had no one . . . Take this money, Ali. Go, buy a pair of socks and slip them on to his feet. And a set of underclothes . . . So the doctor should find him clean when he undresses him. He was a bachelor, my brother Mustafa, the ironsmith . . .'

Green flies had made their way into the smith and were whizzing round and round the dead man. The sunlight hit the hand that held the hammer. It fell also over the town-crier where he sat hunched on the stone, frozen numb.

Haji Kurtboga made his appearance. He held a long cigarette between his fingers. Its smoke floated in the early morning light, pale blue. All eyes were turned on him as he walked, his body canted backwards, his head held high, slightly smiling. Bending a little he entered the smithy. After a while he emerged again puffing complacently at his cigarette.

Five armed gendarmes with the Sergeant at their head were standing at attention under the plane tree. Kurtboga strode up to the town-crier and stopped before him. 'You killed him, you, hunchback! *You* killed the ironsmith. Don't give me that stupid stare! You know you killed him. Sergeant, arrest this man! Handcuff him at once, this murderer, still at large when he's killed that mountain of a man, the ironsmith . . .'

The gendarmes closed on the town-crier, lifted him up, more dead than alive, passed the handcuffs over his wrists and dragged him away. The crowd looked after them, dully, uncomprehendingly.

'He's killed the ironsmith!'

'His closest friend!'

'But why?'

'There's a woman in this!'

'He was always haunting the town-crier's house.'

'They were such close friends . . .'

'But it wasn't for that wretched hunchback's black eyes he went there!'

'How mad the hunchback must have been! Three dumdum bullets! Mustafa's whole body was smashed to smithereens . . .'

411

'Good for the town-crier! This is a question of honour. It isn't because he's a hunchback that he's not a man, and a brave one at that! Hasn't God made them all, the blind and the lame and the hunchbacked?'

'She's a real beauty, the hunchback's wife . . .'

'As God's my witness, if I'd been in his place it's thirty-three bullets I'd have rammed into him, not just three!'

'I heard him with my own ears. He kept repeating, I killed him, I killed Mustafa . . .'

'No, he never tried to hide it. Everyone heard him . . .'

'He was seen rushing all over the town last night crying, I killed him, I killed my brother Mustafa . . .'

'But it's impossible. His wife's an honest woman . . .'

'What! With that misshapen crooked creature?'

'What on earth did she ever see in him?'

'She never loved him one bit . . . And this is the result.'

'Well, he cleared his name, the town-crier . . .'

'As a real man should do.'

The Captain walked into the market-place and went straight to the smithy. As he came out again, his face impassive, Kurtboga waylaid him and took his arm. Together they proceeded to the gendarmerie. Sergeant Hassan was waiting at the door, a wily look on his face, like a wolf making ready to pounce on its prey. 'I've clapped him in chains and put an iron collar round his neck too,' he said. 'And set a whole squad of armed men to guard the monster.'

'Come in, Haji Agha.'

'After you, my Captain . . .'

'You first,' the Captain barked out as though giving a military order. 'You're my guest.' He held the door open for Kurtboga. 'And you're older too . . .'

Haji Kurtboga smiled modestly and stepped in, his body canting back still more.

'Yes . . .' The Captain's face was stern and tense. 'This time, Sergeant, I want a confession. I want you to make that town-crier confess he murdered the ironsmith. What's his name, anyway?'

'Halil Felek, my Commandant.'

'Now listen. You've got a month to make this Halil Felek

412

speak. I mean without killing him . . . If he doesn't, well then, the rest is up to you, Sergeant.'

'Very well, Commandant.'

'You can start right away. And report to me in a little while. Let's see how long he'll resist, this hunchback. These cripples can be very difficult sometimes . . .'

'I don't know about hunchbacks, but the deaf! My God! And I had a one-armed fellow once, and did he make me sweat! But let's tackle this hunchback now.'

'Good luck.'

Sergeant Hassan left the room.

'Coffee?'

'With pleasure, Captain.'

A few minutes later a white-aproned gendarme brought in the coffee.

'Will he talk?'

'This hunchback's worse than Mahmut. He'll die rather!'

The Captain scowled. At such moments his eyes had a tendency to squint and his speech betrayed the origin of a Balkan immigrant. 'I'll make this one talk, Haji Kurtboga,' he vowed. 'If Sergeant Hassan can't do it, I'll step in. We've got very perfected instruments of torture now, and for that we must be grateful to the Americans. Such means and methods they've taught us that we can make the very stones and trees and earth talk. Mankind can never forget the service that America has rendered to humanity.'

'Never,' Haji Kurtboga agreed.

'If our great friend, America, hadn't invented these methods and instruments of torture, if they hadn't let us have them too, think how many crimes would have remained unsolved!'

'Exactly!' Haji Kurtboga said proudly. 'America is our wise, resourceful, clever friend. Such a friend that . . .'

'Without America,' the Captain interrupted him, 'we'd all have died of hunger . . . Without America . . . The airplanes, the ships . . . Who do we owe these roads to? And the Injirlik airport? That's something! What planes they have there! That can reach to the moon even . . .'

'America's our very soul.'

They were still expatiating on America when Sergeant Hassan

413

returned, red in the face, cowed, almost in tears, like a child whose toy has been taken away from him.

The Captain leapt up. 'What's happened? What's the matter?' he shouted, his eyes squinting. 'Is he dead?'

'No,' Sergeant Hassan said dully. 'He's not dead, but . . .'

'Well, what? Has he escaped?'

'He's confessed,' the Sergeant said despondently. 'He said he killed the ironsmith . . .'

There was a dead silence. The Captain's eyes squinted more than ever.

'The reason?' he asked at last. 'Didn't you ask him why he killed him?'

'I did, but he wouldn't say.'

'Listen now. Go back to him and make him sign his confession.'

'I've done that already, my Commandant.' And Sergeant Hassan handed over the sheet of paper he was holding.

The Captain took it and read it through. He looked up. 'Well now! What d'you say to this, Kurtboga?'

'What d'you expect of that wretched hunchback? Those who employed him to kill the smith should have known what kind of a coward he was. But they don't know, those low-down feudal lords . . . They even make presents of revolvers to such sneaking weaklings. And keepsake revolvers too . . . Well, let them see their hunchback now, their brave trigger-man, how he sings like a nightingale before the gendarmes . . .'

'Have you found the revolver?'

'I asked him, Captain. He says he hasn't got a revolver and that nobody ever gave him one.'

'All right. Now go back to him, Sergeant. I want that revolver and also the reason why he committed this crime.'

Haji Kurtboga leaned back and burst out laughing. He held his sides and hooted with laughter. The Captain broke into laughter too.

A little after midday, Sergeant Hassan appeared again. His face was yellow and he looked utterly worn out.

'Well, Sergeant?'

'He won't talk, Captain . . .'

'What did you do?'

'The American method . . .'

'And what happened?'

'He just fainted away, Captain. He won't say why he killed the ironsmith, nor where he's hidden the revolver. He's a hard nut.'

The Captain stood up. 'Don't stop,' he said firmly. 'Carry on, Sergeant. Tonight, I'll start working on him with the newest American methods. We'll see who's a hard nut! Go down again. He's come to by now. Keep at it all the time.'

'All right, Captain . . .'

47

Soaring high above the flattened range of hills that stretched like flimsy pale blue gauze to the east, Mount Düldül stood out as though etched on copper, clouds swirling about its snow-capped peak, the dark copper-purple shadows of its valleys and the flinty copper-green of its crags now sharply clear-cut, seemingly only a stone's throw away, now fading into a vague gently swaying mass.

Ala Temir and Memet Ali were descending the Anavarza crags through the withered thyme and mint and asphodels. The plain was already greening, with fresh swards of grass everywhere and the flowers ready to burst forth. An undefinable scent wafted on the soft breeze. Bursting with exuberant verdure, Akchasaz swamp rumbled deeply in the distance, laden with a wealth of birds and insects and odours. But its shrinking process was visible from day to day, as more and more dry soil appeared on its borders, new land pregnant with riches, spreading its fecund bounty generously under the sun at last after these many shivering burning years of sterile passive waiting, ready now to receive a thousand and one seeds and colours and scents, offering itself with moist open lips, eager to make the very stones take root and sprout.

'Oh my, oh my, oh my!' Ala Temir kept repeating as his red boots sank into the soft earth. 'What a soil, my God, what a soil! Don't stop too long, Memet Ali, or you'll take root. Yes, you will, son! Your feet will take root and your head will sprout leaves. Oh my, oh my, what a soil, what a soil . . .'

He was full to the brim with ineffable joy, walking on air, not knowing what to do in his excitement. Memet Ali was astounded. Here was a new Ala Temir, neither cringing, nor standing at attention, but laughing, relaxed, in his element, his yellowish eyes a clear green now, his white teeth gleaming, his face bright with happiness, clapping his hands like a child at the sight of a rare flower or some large bright-coloured butterfly, ready for all his advanced age and short breath to break into a run and follow its flitting course . . .

'Oh my, oh my, oh my!'

'Look, Uncle Temir Bey, we must buy up as much land around Akchasaz as we can. That was a master-stroke of yours to obtain that Kurtkulak field from Dervish Bey. It's no use paying a lot of money for acres and acres. Just the parts along the border, and then as the swamp dries up . . . Do you know, Uncle Temir Bey, there's a hundred thousand *dönüms* of land in this swamp, maybe a hundred and fifty. Think, just think . . . Fresh new soil . . . It'll yield a hundred to one . . . It'll be ours, ours! Think, Uncle Temir Bey, think . . .'

Ala Temir stopped short, lifting up his flushed sweating face and thick calloused hands. 'I *have* thought,' he shouted. 'Oh my, oh my, oh my . . .' He fell to his knees and fixed his eyes unblinkingly on the sun. His lips moved in a prayer and he stretched his arms out wide as though to embrace the whole sky.

Memet Ali stood by at a complete loss. Ala Temir's face was bathed in ecstasy, quite clear of wrinkles now. His hands moved to his face and he blew into them superstitiously, muttering prayers all the time. He did this several times. Then he bent down, his forehead touching the earth and remained like that for a long time.

The sun had already risen to a bird's flight when he slowly raised himself again.

'Uncle Temir Bey . . .'

Ala Temir looked at him, love and affection shining in his eyes. This was the first time anyone had shown any sincere respect for him. Respect was not the word. This young man simply idolized him. He could not do enough to mark his esteem. He talked to him as though he was a great man, calling him Bey too . . . Here was a real human being, not in the least like those arrogant, conceited Beys, fatuous nonentities every one of them . . . Your Uncle Temir will do anything for you, anything . . . He'll teach you what it means to work on this soil, under this beautiful sun. He'll show you that only work counts in this world and that all the rest is hollow and false. Work, and also the soil, this young fresh earth opening before us like the dappled dawn . . . Those people think that all there is to life is eating and drinking and performing that other business . . . Your Uncle Temir will show you the real things, Memet Ali . . .

'Look, Uncle Temir Bey, both Dervish Bey and my father are mad. And that Kurdish Ali Bey, you know, who's so old and whom everybody says is so wise, well, he's stark staring mad. All those old Beys have taken leave of their senses. As for my grandmother, my father's mother, she's just ripe for the asylum. Everybody's crazy in our house, Uncle Temir Bey, but really, really crazy . . .'

Ala Temir's eyes opened like saucers. 'Really?' he cried, grasping Memet Ali's arm. 'Is it true what you're telling me?'

'Unfortunately,' Memet Ali replied bitterly.

Ala Temir hesitated. He wanted to say something, but could only look dumbly with questioning eyes at Memet Ali.

'Tell me,' he blurted out shyly in the end, 'what d'you think of me, my Memet Ali?'

Memet Ali smiled at him affectionately. 'Uncle Temir Bey . . .' He had sensed that Ala Temir was excessively gratified by this appellation and he used it as often as he could. 'Uncle Temir Bey, may I ask you a question?'

'Of course, of course,' Ala Temir cried with enthusiasm. 'Ask me anything you like . . .'

'They say that you give Jafer Bey money every year, huge sums, a hundred thousand liras, two hundred, three hundred thousand . . .'

Ala Temir's face was suddenly drained of all blood. His lips turned blue and he lowered his eyes. Memet Ali regretted instantly having ever broached the subject, but it was too late now. 'Every year . . .' he stammered. 'And that he . . . That he never repays his debt . . . And that you go to his house and curse and swear at him in front of his wife and children and villagers, and after having called him by all the names in the world for a whole day long you then make him a gift of that money. People say that for days afterwards you are wild with happiness, that you offer sacrifices of sheep and distribute the meat to the villagers . . . That's what I've heard . . .'

Ala Temir lifted his head and fixed a dull gaze on Memet Ali.

418

The colour was slowly returning to his face. 'It's true,' he said at last soberly. 'But that's a different matter . . .' He stopped, embarrassed.

'How different?'

'He . . . He's our Bey . . .'

'But he's not mad, that one,' Memet Ali said triumphantly. 'He's going to buy up the whole of the Chukurova . . . He'll be very rich one day. Don't you see, Uncle Temir Bey, how he's already got the title-deeds to a whole chunk of land on the fringe of Akchasaz?'

'That's true,' Ala Temir hesitated, then smiled ingratiatingly. 'And what about me, then? . . .'

'You're very clever, uncle. You've achieved everything with your brain, with hard work and parsimony. You've made yourself.'

Ala Temir was delighted. He began to repeat, made yourself, made yourself . . . Yourself, yourself . . .

'If it wasn't for that business with Jafer Bey . . .'

'That's different,' Ala Temir said quickly.

'You know best, Uncle Temir Bey,' Memet Ali said humbly. 'You're so clever. You know what you're doing. I see.' He decided never to refer to this matter again.

They walked up to the edge of the swamp. Here the water was clear and they could see right down to the black muddy bottom. Ala Temir pointed to a group of elm trees to the east. 'Should I buy up to there, Memet Ali?'

'Of course, Uncle Temir Bey. Dervish Bey's finished. He'll have to sell all his land within three to five years. It's because he won't use modern cultivation methods and still employs share-croppers, when one tractor could do the work of a thousand men. Yes, Dervish Bey's at his last gasp. You keep going at him. He must like you because he turned Rüstemoglu away and sold to you instead. And he'll go on selling. He has no choice. This is the end for Dervish Bey . . .'

'The end!' Ala Temir repeated sadly, his face twisting with pity. 'The end . . .'

'As for me, uncle, I plan to buy three combines . . .'

They sat down, each on a tussock of reeds. Memet Ali was

looking admiringly at Ala Temir. He had been looking at him like that ever since he had met him. But he was thinking too. They were both thinking. Now and again they turned their heads to the east where Mount Düldül, swathed in a grey heat-haze, its pink washed out now, seemed to have receded far into the distance.

'You know, Uncle Temir Bey, I love tractors and combines and cars ... So what do I do to buy them? I sell some of our land to the villagers, especially to the Kurds. They've got tons of money. It's a mystery how they ever made that much.' He paused and looked reflectively at Ala Temir. He tried to speak, opened his mouth, then closed it again, swallowing.

'What is it, my Memet Ali? Say it. I'm your very own uncle, closer to you than your father even. You can confide in me freely. Tell me everything that's on your mind.'

Memet Ali looked at him doubtfully, then suddenly took courage. 'Uncle Temir Bey,' he said breathlessly, his face flushed with excitement, 'I'm going to propose something to you ... Those fields I was telling you about that the villagers are buying up ... I'm selling them anyway because I need the money for farm machinery. Why don't you buy them instead? It's very good land ...'

Ala Temir jumped up, then sat down again. He laid his hand on Memet Ali's shoulder. 'But of course, Memet Ali, my boy, of course. Whatever you want from me, I'll do it.'

Memet Ali was jubilant. Ala Temir would give him a good price for the land, he knew it, and this would enable him to modernize his farm in a very short time. He began to walk up and down, talking very quickly, disconnectedly, almost raving in his joy.

'Poplars, Uncle Temir Bey,' he was saying ... 'A forest of poplars ... For the timber. And eucalyptus ... Eucalyptus trees grow to full size in only ten years ... And a factory. I must have a factory. Many factories, operating day and night ... I'll do it all, I must, Uncle Temir Bey. Land is only the foundation stone ... Then the factories ... And a bank! Without your own bank you can do nothing. Money produces money, you know that better than anyone, Uncle Temir Bey ...'

'So it does.'

'Money that's left to lie unused is bound to die. Money must procreate, more and more, every day . . . Money . . . Money's like the earth, like men, like all living creatures. They must procreate or die . . . The Irrigation Department now . . . I know the chief engineer there, a modern-minded man. He told me we could open a canal from Akchasaz so that all the water would be drained into the Jeyhan River in just one year. And if we deflected the course of the Savrun River as well, then the swamp would be quite dry in no time . . . But I said to him, no no, not now, for God's sake. Of course I didn't tell him that with my Uncle Temir Bey we have to secure the land around the swamp first! The rest is easy . . . I only told him about you. I know him, he said. A self-made man. I wish there were more like him in the Chukurova . . . As for Dervish Bey . . . Letting all that land he owns run to seed . . . We must take it away from him. If it wasn't for that overseer of his, that obstinate Circassian, he'd have sold it all already. Perhaps we can bribe him . . . And then, one must get to know the world of commerce . . .'

Ala Temir was watching him with fond eyes. If only God had given me such a son, he thought. I'd have sacrificed all my fortune, all my other sons for him. What marvels could be wrought with a business partner of this kind!

Memet Ali was tired and bathed in sweat by now. He sank down beside the silent, pensive Ala Temir and began to scratch at the earth with a twig. And so they sat, thinking their separate thoughts, till they were roused by the beat of hooves. It was getting on to noon. They looked up and saw three horsemen riding straight at them.

Ala Temir's eyes widened with fear. 'It's Dervish Bey, Dervish Bey!' he said faintly. 'He's coming this way. He must be in one of his tempers. Quick, let's hide in the swamp.'

In the twinkling of an eye Memet Ali had vanished into the trees. Ala Temir was still lumbering after him, heaving his fat stubby legs with difficulty, when the horsemen drew up about two hundred yards away and lifting their rifles emptied them in his direction. Then, with shouts of laughter that rang out against the Anavarza crags, they swung around and galloped off towards Jeyhan River.

At the first crack of bullets Ala Temir had hurled himself into a ditch. There he lay, bellowing without a break, trembling like a leaf, his hands casting feverishly about his body for the wound that must be there, the blood, something. And trembling even more, crazed with fear at finding nothing . . .

48

Uso, I said, rise, Uso. Rise and go . . .

There, in front of the tent was a greyhound with a curly auburn coat, long firm legs and a body arched like a bow. Its large eyes were black-rimmed and it had a slender neck and flagged ears. Its shadow fell over the desert sand and stretched into the distance.

The desert was hot. A yellow flower had bloomed, very large. Its petals and leaves were opening and spreading still more as the heat increased, its glowing brightness deepening.

And Uso could not tear himself away. Round and round the tents he prowled as though tied to the greyhound by a fast rope. The Arab women were singing in a shrill monotone as wide-ranging and unending as the desert itself.

Uso, Uso! Rise, rise up and go . . . It's only a greyhound after all. But the greyhound's auburn coat glistened irresistibly as it stood there beside the black long-legged Arab horse in front of the black goathair tents. Black tents left over from olden times, from the age when the tent was first invented . . . Black-browed, black-eyed, long-legged Arab women . . . And tall, dark, hollow-cheeked, long-faced, flame-eyed men, walking with long swinging strides, their robes swirling about them, daggers stuck to their waists.

Uso came from the high mountains up north. It was all like a dream to him. He loved the desert, but he was mortally afraid of it too.

Uso, Uso, rise, rise up and go . . . He ran. Round and round the tents, his sharp eyes glued to the greyhound, seeing the glistening coat change from auburn to tawny yellow, gleaming in the fading mist-swathed greening blue of the desert. Round and round and round, tied to the greyhound, whirling on its axis . . .

'Give me this greyhound, my Agha. Give it me and may I be

your slave till I die. Emir of Emirs, give it me. I've lost my heart to it . . .'

The Emir was silent, swathed in his white silk *kaffiyeh*, with his stern coal-black eyes, his hawked nose, his curly beard.

'Give me the greyhound, Emir of Emirs. I'll do anything for you, anything . . .'

All day long, till sunset Uso kneeled before him. But the Arab never spoke a word. Impassive, he stared into the distance. A large-winged bird was wheeling above the tents. He followed it with his eyes.

Uso, Uso, rise! Rise up and go . . .

'Take my horse, Emir of Emirs, and give me the greyhound. He's a handsome noble steed. His pedigree goes back to more than three hundred years . . .'

The Arab's face remained frozen, as though he never heard him. And Uso was filled with anger. In the dead of night, under the huge sparkling stars of the desert sky he untied the greyhound from the stake, lifted it on to his horse and rode away. In that instant the night was rent with screams, and as the dawn shed its first reddish glimmer over the sky and undulating sands, the streaking horses of the Arabs caught up with him. Sharp-pointed daggers flashed in the dawn light. The sands had a red glint. And the greyhound was wrenched out of Uso's arms. He was thrown to the ground, motionless. His noble horse stood at his side, its eyes wide and mournful. Suddenly, fastening its teeth on Uso's clothes, it raised him up, threw him over its back and galloped like the wind in pursuit of those who had taken the greyhound away. Uso awoke on his horse's back. Once more, in the night, he held the greyhound in his arms. The yellow flower bloomed more strongly, its scent wafted, wave after wave, through the desert air, and they overtook him again . . .

Rise, Uso! Rise up and go . . . Three days and three nights Uso keened for the greyhound, and left him to the desert. And came to lofty distant Mount Süphan where it soared into the azure sky and floated in the blue of Lake Van . . . And there, beneath the tall poplars, on flower-laden Patnos plain, was a girl, her hair braided into many long plaits, her eyes huge and sad as a gazelle's, her neck slender and graceful as a swan's . . .

He saw her standing in the swiftly changing colours of the lake, pale blue, grass-green, streaked with lightning flashes of red, glowing in an orange light, blurred in a milky whiteness, swaying in a flimsy evaporating silvery drift into the blue. He saw her there at the foot of Mount Süphan. He saw the fresh child-like face, the white teeth, the pouting lips, the luminous oval eyes crinkled at the corners in a smile that carried all the sadness in the world, and her beauty trickled into his heart, warm and tender. He shouted out loud to the mountains, the flowing streams and flying cranes, and when the new day dawned, the sky was a thousand times more blue. Lake Van, Mount Süphan's pale heights, the green expanse of Patnos, Erjish and Muradiye plains turned a bright blue too. All the world was blue, the light, the clouds, the sun, even red Mount Esrük with its trees and birds, its teeming people emerging into the sun from their underground dwellings . . . From the red crags and earth of Sor valley red-legged partridges started up and they, too, were blue. Blue cranes streamed through the sky in long luminous formations, crying their age-old soulful song. And in the middle of all this blue was a huge eye, jet-black, radiant.

Swinging lightly on his long legs, his curly beard waving, his hollow cheeks dimpling, his red lips parted in a smile of joy, Uso walked up to the tall poplars which seemed to turn blue as he approached them, while in the distance Mount Süphan was a flash of blue. He knelt down and spoke.

Tell me your name, Uso said. But the girl was silent. Your name, your name? He asked the earth, the trees, the clouds, the herds of gazelles sprinting by, the wild horses, the streams, the wedge-like trains of cranes winging above. A light rain fell, deep blue. Uso laid his head against the age-old rain. Her name, her name? Gazelé, the rain whispered. Gazelé, sang the clouds, the flowers, the cranes, the spiring crags and red earth of Sor valley, the whole billowing blue world. Gazelé, Gazelé, the gazelles chorused. And Uso called her Gazelé. Gazelé, too, he named the greyhound he had left behind in the desert. All that was dear to him he called by the name of Gazelé now. And he sang out his love, forty days and forty nights, kneeling before her on the immemorial earth of love, with beautiful words that broke from his heart to spread over the world.

Uso, Uso arise! Uso you must go . . . His heart was on fire. Gazelé coursed in his veins. She was whatever he touched, wherever he looked, and he saw it with his own eyes how she turned and vanished forever together with the herd of gazelles.

And Uso never forgot. Never, never, never!

And one day, in the market-place of a little town, as he stood near the blacksmith's shop with his greyhound beside him, Uso saw the Captain with three gendarmes at his heels. His boots were polished so bright you could mirror yourself in them. Like a premonition of evil he appeared to Uso and he quickly drew back behind the tree. But the Captain had already seen the greyhound.

'You there! Stop! Where did you find that greyhound?'

'I brought it over from the desert, Bey, from Arabia. I wanted one so much, but they would not give it me. At last they let me have one of the puppies . . .'

'Good, very good. Give it to the gendarmes, they'll take it to my house. Good, good, very good.' His right leg thrown forward . . . Like a blond wolf . . . Erect, looking at Uso as he would at an ant, a tree, the earth, or nothing at all, as though he was not there, as though Uso was only some strange pitiful object.

Uso had caught the greyhound by its collar. The gendarme tried to kick him away. The other two gendarmes rushed up and began to kick him too.

'Why, you mean wretch, so you'd grudge a paltry greyhound to a Captain of the Republic!' The Captain was livid. 'Throw him down!'

The three gendarmes pinioned Uso flat to the ground.

All the market had thronged up to the blacksmith's shop under the tree. A murmur went through the crowd as the Captain jumped upon Uso and began to stamp on him, pounding him flat.

'A paltry greyhound . . . To a Captain . . . A Captain of the Republic! And you a savage, hardly able to speak properly . . .' Like a blond wolf he was, the Captain, trampling his prey before swallowing it. He grabbed the greyhound's collar and stepped down at last, smiling proudly at the people around, his

blue eyes flashing. But the crowd was silent, like a blank wall
. . . 'Wretches!' he roared. 'You too? You'd grudge a little
greyhound to a Captain? Dogs, all of you . . . Quick now,
disperse!'

The crowd broke up in silence.

Uso, get up. Rise Uso and go . . .

Uso was frantic. The greyhound haunted his thoughts night
and day. He had named it Gazelé . . .

A year later at the peep of spring, in the market-place of this
little southern port, the Captain stopped dead, his right booted
leg fixed firmly in front of him, and swung around to face the
man who had been trailing him like a shadow for the past three
days. He was frightened, but the man was smiling at him and
his face was familiar. The Captain's fears were dispelled.
'Hello,' he said. 'What d'you want?'

'I'm Uso . . . From Lake Van . . . The greyhound . . . My
greyhound, Gazelé . . .'

The Captain stiffened. His face went dark and the blood
rushed to his head. 'Why, it's you then, you dog! So you've
been following me, have you, all the way from Van . . .' His
curiosity got the better of him. 'But how did you come here?
How did you know I'd been posted here?'

His eyes lighting up with hope, Uso eagerly explained to the
Captain all the trouble he had gone to in order to find him, how
he had walked all the way from Van to here, Iskenderun, this
port on the Mediterranean, how it had taken him a whole
month and a half to do so . . . 'You see, my Captain, that
greyhound is dearer to me than my two eyes . . . Give it me,
Captain.'

'Why, the rascal! For a greyhound . . . To me, a Captain . . .
Gendarmes!'

Four gendarmes rushed up and hurled Uso to the ground . . .
And the Captain bounced up and down over him in a mad rage,
and Uso's blood-stained face was reflected on his shining boots
. . . And the gathering crowd watched on in silence. At last the
Captain cast a triumphant smile about him. He met only frozen
sullen faces and his anger knew no bounds. A shiver ran down
his spine and he trembled as he saw the hatred in those many
eyes.

'He grudges a wretched greyhound to me, a Captain! That ignorant savage has been after me a whole year, following me everywhere I go, under the pretext of getting back a greyhound . . . If I don't teach him a lesson now, God only knows what he's capable of doing later on in life. A man who walks all the way from Mount Süphan for a greyhound! Given the chance wouldn't he assault the very existence of the State, our last Turkish State? The last, the last . . .' He was foaming at the mouth, shouting, but there was not the slightest sound from the grim silent wall of people around them. Sparks flew from the Captain's venomous green eyes. 'Get away from here, all of you,' he thundered, waving his arms over the crowd. 'Quick now, clear out!'

Slowly the crowd flowed out of the market-place and Uso was left lying alone on the concrete pavement, the sour smell of his blood spreading into the warm evening air.

Uso, rise, Uso! Rise up and go . . .

How beautiful, how slender the greyhound! How its body arched like a bow over the long slim legs . . . That long golden muzzle, the huge lovely eyes . . . Always and always it was there in his mind's eye, streaking like a flame from the Arabian desert to Patnos plain and Lake Van.

He could not sleep, he could not breathe. He came back to Iskenderun once again. But the Captain was gone. He's been posted somewhere else, they told him. And Uso set out in search of the Captain, convinced that he would get his greyhound back in the end. I'll explain to him. He'll understand. He's human too. What's the greyhound to him? Only a dog . . . But to me it's something else. It is the wide Arabian desert. It is Gazelé, and Lake Van and Patnos plain, my whole lifeblood.

Seeking and questioning he found the Captain at last, here, in this little town on the foothills of the lofty Taurus Mountains. He looked upon Mount Düldül, all etched out in copper, with its snow-capped peak, and likened it to his own Mount Süphan. He found the Captain's house and stood in the shadow of the trellised vine at the garden gate. Two days he stood there, and the Captain went in and out without seeing him. On the morning of the third day, the Captain awoke to the sound of singing, a man's voice, mellow, vibrant, crying out in a bitter pealing lament . . . He looked out of the window and saw the singer squatting in front of the gate, his hand held to his ear, swaying endlessly to the rhythm of his song, a gaunt dried-up figure wasted to the bone, his neck thin and scraggy, stretching out still thinner as he sang. Something rang in his memory. He dressed and went out to the crouching man, and suddenly it all came back to him. He burst out laughing. He held his sides and laughed himself red in the face.

'So it's you again? You've come after that greyhound, eh? The golden greyhound? Well, it's dead,' he shouted. 'I killed it with one bullet . . .'

Uso shot up like a steel spring and clamped his hands about the Captain's neck. They rolled to the ground. The Captain's eyes bulged, his lips went blue. Uso squeezed and squeezed until the eyes were almost out of their sockets and the Captain sagged limply under his clasp. Then suddenly seized with fright, he fled, leaving him lying there only half alive.

He fled into the mountains. Seven years he roamed there, and saw the great caravan routes, the lofty Taurus heights, the Mediterranean Sea . . . He saw machine-guns and bombs and rifles, and many gendarmes and soldiers. His band of outlaws was a large one, but down in the plain the captains and soldiers were more numerous. People died and were butchered in clash after clash. Houses were burnt, hearths destroyed. And one day, in a mountain pass among sharp flint-like white rocks he fell down over the dead bodies of his comrades at the foot of his machine-gun, his shoulder shattered by a bullet. And there the gendarmes captured him.

And Uso saw the Big Judge. And he said not a word, struck dumb, more terrified by that frozen lethargic rock-like being before him than he had been of the Captain, the gendarmes, the blood and the bullets. All through the trial, the Big Judge dropped off at leisure. He even had dreams. Uso's heart fluttered like a bird's whenever he dared to steal a glance at that nodding bald pate. In his dreams the Big Judge saw swirling flames and hundreds of kestrels burning in them . . . All night long he had toted his ladder from wall to wall, throwing burning brands into the nests, watching with gloating pleasure the shrieking birds being consumed by the flames. Only towards dawn had he returned to his house to sip his coffee before the rising sun, at peace with himself, and to relive it all again in blissful dreams during the proceedings . . .

'Uso, son of Hassan, found guilty . . . Sentenced to death . . .' Roused from his doze, wrinkling up his face as though he had swallowed some bitter potion, quickly signing the paper before him, then reluctantly snapping the pen in two . . .

And Uso saw the prison. His wounds healed and, though he looked death in the face, he laughed. And he heard a song. It floated in from very far, from the heart . . .

To the ramparts of Diyarbekir city I came and knelt over its ancient stones. Three times I called out to beyond the ramparts and three times I brought them down. Three times I razed Diyarbekir prison to the ground. And three times I saw Uso and held his hand and kissed him and stroked his wounds . . . And I went before the Big Judge. I am Gazelé, I said, the gazelle of the desert. My father's stables are full of noble Arab steeds. Take them, they are yours. My brow, my breast, my arms are laden with gold. Take them, they are yours. But spare Uso's life. I am Gazelé with the golden hair. I will cut off my golden hair. Take it. I am Gazelé, the gazelle-eyed, take my eyes, they are yours. Only spare Uso's life.

Wild figs grew at the foot of the parapets, and pomegranates and blue roses were in bloom. Forever after, a song shall tremble there under the blue-flowering rose bushes . . . Diyarbekir city is laden with the smell of roses and violets and tyranny. Violets and roses are sold in its streets. Blue and pink and many-petalled . . . Only a hundred paras the bunch, only a hundred paras . . . I will sell violets in the market of old Diyarbekir. I will gather all the violets of the fields. I will save Uso. I will save his life . . .

In the early dawn light Gazelé is there as though chained to the prison gate . . . I am Gazelé, the gazelle of the plains and the desert. Selling violets to the judges, the captains . . . The flowers of love have blossomed in my heart, in my earth and ramparts. I have planted them in the stone walls of Diyarbekir prison and even there they have bloomed . . .

And Uso saw Alijik too in the prison. Alijik had set fire to his own house. To other houses, to the mansion, to the whole

Anavarza plain . . . In a fit of mad frenzy he set fire to whatever he came across, and to himself in the end. He was brought into the prison unconscious, a charred mass of flesh.

Uso, rise, Uso! Rise and tend to Alijik with the salves and balms your mother and grandmother taught you to make . . . And Alijik's burns healed.

And Uso saw the town-crier when they threw him into the prison yard, a mangled bloody heap, hardly breathing, his face long and wizened, all bone. Then he opened his eyes three times, huge tender mournful eyes that filled his whole face. Grotesque were the heavy chains that hung about him . . . As though they had been shackled to the hands and feet of a little child . . . Too large that iron collar for the frail neck that seemed about to snap . . .

Uso, Uso, arise . . . The town-crier began to moan. Uso took his hand and held it to his heart. 'Brother,' he said, 'brother, don't! You'll get well, you'll see. You will, you will . . .'

And then the town-crier spoke, not a sound, only a breath. 'I killed him. I killed the ironsmith. Never will I tell why. Never, not to anyone . . . Kill me, kill me, kill me, but I'll never tell.'

All these things Uso saw. The Captain, the greyhound, Gazelé, Alijik, the town-crier, the mountains, the flying cranes, blood and flames, the Big Judge, chains and prison and tyranny . . . He saw tyranny, Uso. He saw the long golden hair of his dear love, of Gazelé whose eyes were like those of a gazelle . . .

431

49

'He will die, Mistik will die . . .'

The Lady Karakiz was the daughter of a Turcoman Bey of ancient stock from the region of Kozan, a captivating beauty, with slanting oval eyes, high cheekbones, a pointed chin, a long slender neck, dimpled cheeks and a complexion like a clear limpid pool. But it was the sunny smiling quality about her that always bewitched people. The only girl among six brothers, she would ride, hunt, wield a gun and play the *jereed* games as well as any man.

One day as the east was only just lighting up, as the yellow spikes of wheat swayed gently in the dawn breeze, as the camel-thistles shed their mauve over the dawn, as Mount Düldül's snow-capped peak drowned in a copper glow seemed only a stone's throw away, the Lady Karakiz rode out into the plain. And saw Mistik for the first time. He was swinging his sickle in a wheat field. Mistik was a gentle dark youth with timid eyes that shone with a strange fervour in his dreamy face. The Lady Karakiz reined in. Her eyes were on him as though held there by a spell. He lowered his head in embarrassment and still she did not move. They remained motionless, bathed in the early morning light, until the sun rose up to meet her gaze. Suddenly she turned her horse's head towards the mountains and galloped away.

But she came again the next day, and the next. Each day at the first peep of dawn she was there. And one day, when Mistik had finished reaping and was threshing the wheat, as the sun blazed down and the pungent odour of cut straw filled the air, he saw her jump from the horse and run to the wheat-rick. He felt a warmth gushing from his heart, enveloping his whole body. They came together in a melting ecstasy. She was like a raging fire, the Lady Karakiz, that seared through his flesh. She left him lying there, half in a faint on the heaped wheat.

She never came again. And soon after she was betrothed to

Mustafa Bey's father. Night after night Mistik wandered about the mansion. She saw him from her window, standing under the plane tree and turning away with the first light of day. It pleased her, this constancy of his, but she never once went out to him. And so Mistik pined away day by day. The light went out of his large dark eyes and his curly black beard was dull and lacklustre now.

The wedding festivities for the Lady Karakiz lasted seven days and seven nights. Mistik fled into the Anavarza crags and remained there all the while, perched on the rocks with eagles flapping all about him. When at last he came down, he went straight to the Akyollu farm. She saw him standing in the yard, pale and wan, and her heart went out to him.

'This young man is from our village,' she told her husband. 'I want him to stay on the farm.'

So Mistik was given some work. Every day the Lady Karakiz would go out to the balcony and stand in that same place where the sweet basil and marigolds grew now and he would be there, his eyes fixed on her adoringly, unable to tear himself away. She would come and go, ride out over the plain, visit the town, and Mistik would still be waiting there by the wall when she returned. It seemed as though he had never moved.

'Ah, he will die! Mistik will die . . .'

Months passed and Mistik was now wasted to skin and bone. And one night the Lady Karakiz rose from her husband's side. A mist had fallen over the warm autumn night. It was pitch dark. She groped her way along the wall, found Mistik and clasped him to her in a transport of passion. In an instant she had stripped him naked and undressed herself too. They lay down over the bed of marigolds and sweet basil, lost in an all-consuming flame. In the end Mistik sank back with a desperate moan. Slowly, kissing him again and again, she dressed him and went away as day was about to dawn.

'Mistik will die . . .'

It grew light and still Mistik did not move from where she had left him, a small huddled shadowy heap at the foot of the wall.

'Mistik is dead . . .'

Forever afterwards the Lady Karakiz mourned in her heart

433

for him. Her first son she named Mistik which is short for Mustafa.

And here he was now, her Mustafa, her first-born, lying naked, face down across the back of his horse. She fell away from the balcony post, half in a faint, thinking he was dead. When she learnt that he was alive, but unconscious, she prayed to God that he should die after suffering the ignominy of being stripped naked by an enemy who had not even deigned to kill him. She shut herself up in her room, refusing to see anyone, asking nothing, motionless on her bed, a waxen agonizing shrunken figure.

Mustafa's body was black and blue all over, as if it had been pounded in a mortar. They carried him to his bed and the Kurdish Physician was sent for. He came at once. Huge copper cauldrons were set over fires under the wide-spreading plane trees in the Akyollu yard, beside Memet Ali's bright-coloured tractors. For days, all kinds of herbs, flowers, oils and liquids were boiled to make poultices and salves, and strange odours, bitter, pungent and sweet pervaded the mansion, the trees, even the people. Every day, two or three times, the Kurdish Physician rubbed these ointments into Mustafa's body, making sure that every pore was impregnated with them. 'One must not lose faith in Allah,' he kept saying dejectedly. 'This man's in a bad way, but with Allah's mercy . . .'

Every other day the Kurdish Physician would visit the Lady Karakiz. He would take her cold limp hands in his and hold them for a long time, his eyes fixed on her spent ravaged face. He had known the Lady since her youth and it grieved him to see her come to such an end. 'Everyone dies only once, but the Lady Karakiz has died a thousand times. Would that she would die now and be at peace . . . Death is the only good thing left for her. Oh Allah, take her life . . . Take the life of the beautiful Lady Karakiz . . .' And he would kneel by her side and pray in his native Kurdish tongue.

One morning, how many days later nobody knew, the Lady Karakiz opened wide her sunken lifeless eyes and looked unseeingly about her. The sun was dawning over the mountains beyond and Mistik was there in a heap at the foot of the wall. His large black eyes were bright and brimful with love and he

434

was smiling. And the Lady Karakiz was fluttering over him with shrill, bird-like cries. Unto my dying day, my love, unto my dying day . . . Mistik standing amidst the sun-drenched yellow wheat, chasing her and she chasing him . . .

'Physician!' she cried. 'I have no need for potions and salves. 'Bring me food. Quickly . . .'

His hands trembling, the Kurdish Physician staggered out. A miracle . . . 'Quick, food for the Lady! *Tarhana* soup first, then chicken broth with the white meat. And honey . . . Honey . . . Quick! She's going to live!'

In a couple of days she was out of bed and walking about the mansion. She went to her son's room and kissed him as she had never done since he was a child. A long-forgotten embrace . . . Mustafa Bey felt it. His heart lifted with gladness and he came to. The Kurdish Physician's ointments had healed the bruises on his body, but he was too weak to think, to wonder why his mother had kissed him like this, in a transport of delight, why, after all their misfortunes, she was so suddenly overflowing with love.

The Lady Karakiz summoned her daughter-in-law. 'Have them heat up the big bath,' she said. 'I want to wash myself. And prepare some henna for my hair and hands.'

All day long she roamed about the house peering into every nook and cranny like a cat prowling through a new place, lingering over the old oakwood chests, purple-veined, embossed with large roses, the oak tables and chairs, slim-legged, brought over from Marash, the Turcoman *kilims* and hangings that adorned the walls from ceiling to floor, the delicately embroidered saddlebags, sacks and black goathair mats, the hunting-cloths for snaring partridges and francolins, the carved wooden guns with nacre-inlaid stocks, the ancient Turcoman gilt swords, engraved with verses from the Koran . . . And she would take out of their chests the many remnants of her bridal trousseau, cherished over the years like a sacred trust, and contemplate each one of them with a glad smile on her face.

Mustafa Bey was quite restored now. But he did not get out of bed. He was content just to feel alive again and to see his mother her old self. He lay there smiling, and the Kurdish Physician sat by his side talking to him, retelling marvellous tales about the old Chukurova Beys and the hawk-like Beys of the east. It was as though he had no recollection of all that had befallen him. Dervish Bey was consigned to oblivion.

As the days passed the Lady Karakiz seemed reborn, a different person altogether. The web of wrinkles was wiped from her face. Her back was straighter, her eyes shone brightly and even her gait had recovered some of the buoyancy of youth. Every morning she would lock herself up in her room, and taking from a chest the revolver which had been her husband's she would oil it carefully, load it and aim at the birds on the plane tree outside the window. Then, at the last moment, she would refrain from shooting and lay it back in the chest.

'Bring out a horse for me,' she ordered one morning.

A bay steed, the best of the thoroughbreds in the stable, was saddled for her. Leading it to the mounting-block, she mounted it without asking for help and rode away. On the road she drew the revolver from her waist and fired three shots at a small branch of a mulberry tree. The branch broke off and fell. The years had not blunted the Lady Karakiz's skill at shooting. She rode on proudly, overflowing with joy, and it was only when her horse stopped of itself in the yard of the Sarioglu mansion that she realized what she was doing. A strange thrill ran through her body, but she felt perfectly cool all the same. A young man had materialized before her.

'Is this the famed Sarioglu mansion?' she asked him in a clear voice. 'Is Dervish Bey at home? I'm an old friend of his father's and I've come a long way to see him.'

The young man greeted her with pleasure. 'Welcome, venerable lady,' he said, holding the horse. 'My father just left for a ride. He'll be back by noon. Come in and rest a little until he comes.'

The Lady Karakiz went pale. Her hands shook and a nervous twitch passed over her face. 'And who are you?' she asked softly, her voice strangling. 'What's your name? You look to be a goodly lad . . .'

'I'm Dervish Bey's son, Ibrahim. Won't you come in now, venerable . . .'

Swift as lightning the Lady Karakiz had drawn the revolver and discharged all the bullets, shot after shot, into Ibrahim's body. Only one long scream, and he had crumpled to the ground in a heap on the grass, quite still, as though asleep.

The horse had reared in a panic at the first shot, but the Lady Karakiz managed to curb it until the last bullet was fired. Then it bolted. It flew like the wind along the Anavarza plain, its belly grazing the ground. The Lady Karakiz let go of the reins and clung to its mane, flat over its back, trying to hold on against the lashing wind raised by the horse's speed. Round and round the plain it raced, on towards Tozlu, shying away from a bramble bush, hurtling back towards Kesikkeli, on towards Yalnizdut, down Jiyjik valley, until at last it found its way to the Akyollu mansion and came to a stop in the yard, all lathered in sweat, panting like a bellows. The Lady Karakiz was still lying flat on its back. Then slowly she slipped down the saddle . and fell at the horse's feet.

People came rushing out of the house. The Kurdish Physician was the first to reach her. He took her hand in his.

'It's all over,' he said. 'She's cold already.'

She lay there turned on her right side, as though asleep, almost smiling.

'Mistik will die. Mistik will die, Lady, oh he will die . . .'

50

Something is moving under the turbid surface of the stream. His wide-open frozen eyes are floating, now elongated and oval, now contracted and round, and the shadow of his head trembles at the bottom, over the pebbles. Water fills his boots and blood . . . Blood too, frothing . . . And there is the dog's shadow also, falling over the greenish moss-grown pebbly bed, folding and unfolding, large as a water-buffalo, its eyeballs rolling with the flowing water. The dog is licking its chops, its eyes are fixed on those frozen, glittering drowned eyes. A fish shoots up and flashes away, cleaving the swirling water to hide in some nook on the bank. Only a moment, and it is out once more, darting swiftly at the head, pecking at it again and again. Blood is trickling out of those boots. From the nose too, staining the water, forming two long rivulets that flow down and away under the bridge. One of the rivulets passes just below his right ear. But just below . . .

The bullets spilled out of the revolver in front of him, pat pat pat, with dull little thuds. One two three . . . Seven. Seven drops of light dancing before his eyes . . .

But see him rise from the water and stagger away on the dry pebbles, skidding, slipping . . . Blood squirting out of his boots, squelch, squelch, blood dripping from his nose, suspended in long red filaments . . .

Three times he stumbled among the crags at the foot of the hill near the reed-bed bordering the swamp, and lay there sprawling.

'Up you get, dog!'

He rose at once, as though wound up.

'Walk before me!' And he scrambled up into the crags. 'Straighter! Straighter! Hold yourself up. Don't stop!'

His two hands stuck to his sides, rigid, advancing with groping steps . . . A yellow haze lay over the swamp, and behind the haze the sun was only a vague wavering shape, the trees,

438

bushes, reeds, dust-devils swayed dimly, the cars and trucks moved in a dull flicker, all their headlights on, with far-off muffled sounds. Large water-lilies, white and yellow, undulated over the gently wimpling water.

The shiny bullets flowed back into the cylinder of the glistening revolver, his fingers hardly touching them, those swift deft fingers . . . And out again once more, spilling, tap tap tap, over the quilt, sinking into its softness . . .

'Stop!'

The sweat gushes from his shoulder-blades. The crags are crackling in the torrid heat. They are like live embers to the touch.

'Look down that precipice . . .'

Dark and deep as a well . . . The trees below, the swamp, the villages are tiny objects that could fit into the palm of a hand, the streams thin strips . . . All melting in the light . . .

'Don't move! Mestan, strap these sticks of dynamite to his legs. Whirlwind Veli, don't be so afraid! Take the fuses and fasten them to him.'

Mestan works fast, but Whirlwind Veli is all yellow with fear. He knows, better than anyone, that he will meet his doom too in a little while. After the Fiend . . . But suppose he casts himself into the precipice before . . .

'Whirlwind Veli, lash him to that tree, as tightly as you can.'

The tree is an old mastic, growing out of a cleft in the rocks on the very edge of the precipice.

'Quick, Mestan.'

'It's done, Bey. He's all plastered with dynamite, his legs, his body . . . Give me that Veli. There!'

Two fuses, one to each leg . . .

'Ready now? As soon as I shoot you'll fire the fuses. No, no . . . I'll do it.'

The fuses are long. Draw them as far from the tree as you wish. We must ignite them from a great distance. The flame must creep on slowly, very slowly. He must see death coming, inch by inch, inexorably . . .

He bent down, struck a match, was holding it to the fuse when he straightened up again. There was plenty of time. Calmly he walked up to the tree and sat down a few feet away.

439

The Fiend's eyes were closed. The rope was coiled fast about his body. Blood trickled from his nose in thin red threads that grazed the lips. Blood frothed from the leg of his boots, forming a pool on the ground. Green flies flashed all about him in hundreds. He burst out laughing. Mestan laughed too, very loud, a speaking cursing laugh . . . Whirlwind Veli laughed, a sobbing laugh, for he knew what was coming to him. But the Fiend's eyes remained closed.

His hands trembled. The seven bullets suddenly flowed back into the cylinder . . .

Three times he fired into the tree above the Fiend's head. Sparrows pattered to the ground. And still the Fiend never opened his eyes.

They hewed into the rock, a large crevice. It took a long time. Till noon . . . And filled it with dynamite . . . Green flies were flashing over the frothing blood, whizzing like bullets through the air. The dynamite was ready now. It would explode any moment.

'I must be near him. I must see his eyes. His open eyes . . .'

He stopped three yards in front of him. Round and round and round went the revolver's cylinder. The bullets clattered into his hand and, like so many drops of water at his fingertips, flowed back into the cylinder . . . The eyeballs under the blank lids were spinning now, the skin over the high cheekbones twitched. The Fiend's lips were dry and cracked. His tongue flicked out, very red, to lick his mouth and mustache. He is trembling too, yes, trembling from head to foot . . . And the tree trembles with him. Its leaves and branches are all a-quiver, fluttering ever more strongly, jerking convulsively.

The dynamite exploded. An earth-shaking blast, followed by long deafening echoes from crag to crag. And still those closed eyes, clamped tight, crinkled at the corners. There were more bursts, very near, as more and more sticks of dynamite were fired. Chips flew from the rocks and the echoes boomed through the skies like thunder. Under those closed eyelids even the eyeballs were still now, sunk into their sockets, leaving two deep hollows in place of the eyes. The tree shook more than ever. It pitched and plunged as though hit by a storm. Its leaves rustled and broke and flew.

'Whirlwind Veli! This time I'm going to fire the last fuse . . .'

The bullets poured out of the revolver, then once again, slowly, easily, they flowed back into the cylinder, as of themselves . . .

He ran to the fuse behind a rock. Now he would fire it and everything would be over in a minute, the head, the limbs, the body shattered through the air in a thousand pieces, falling in flabby calcinated scraps over the rocks.

But first . . . His boots crashing over the sharp-edged rocks, he ran back with dagger drawn. 'Here,' he cried, gritting his teeth, 'take this. And this . . .' The dagger sank deep into the flesh of his thigh, three times, three thin slits from which blood oozed out and trickled down the leg. A noisome smell hit his nostrils, but from where he could not tell.

'Fire the fuse!' he shouted. 'Quick, Mestan, quick, Whirlwind Veli, fire the fuse and blow this Fiend to pieces . . .'

But Whirlwind Veli was far below, at the bottom of the precipice, running as fast as he could, his long arms and legs wheeling like a windmill.

'Whirlwind Veli! Stop!'

Snatching up his rifle he crouched down. The sharp needle-like rock bruised his knee. Five times he aimed, right in front of Whirlwind Veli. A long scream echoed from rock to rock, and Whirlwind Veli tossed through the air three times to fall back at last, quite still, sprawled mouth up, on the ground.

My God, he had forgotten all about the Fiend, strapped there to the tree! He turned and saw that he had opened his eyes and was looking at him with a contemptuous sneer.

'Mestan, Mestan, quick, fire the fuse.' No answer from Mestan . . . 'So you've run away too, Mestan!'

He looked down to where Whirlwind Veli was lying. There was no one there! But way off, a tiny figure was sprinting at top speed along the stream. He aimed his rifle again and took five shots at him. Whirlwind Veli fell and rose once more . . .

And back to the tree . . . Was he smiling, the Fiend? His eyes were blurred by the rippling stream, frozen again, widening, now round, now stretched into a thin line. He ran to the fuse and ignited it. The flame travelled along the rope, nearer and nearer to the Fiend.

441

'Open your eyes! Open them! Look, it's coming, the fuse is burning . . .' Shouting, running around him desperately . . . But the eyes clamp down more closely. They vanish into the sockets . . . And the flame is creeping up, up . . . On a sudden impulse he pulled at the fuse, tore it off and hurled it away. It fell at the foot of a rock and burnt itself out there. A flimsy wisp of silvery grey smoke hung for a while over the rock.

'Smiling again, eh? Well, I'll show you this time. You'll see how I'll blow you to smithers . . .'

He took another coil of fuse, fixed it to the dynamite strapped to the Fiend's body and uncoiled it until he was back behind the rock. Without losing a minute he lighted it and ran back, only to stop short in amazement. The Fiend's eyes were wide open, glazed, fixed on the burning fuse. His neck was straining, thinner and thinner. It could not be! Could a neck reach out that far? And the eyes! Bulging, jumping out of their sockets. Even the lashes are stretching out, spiky, far apart . . . Only fifteen metres left. The Fiend's face is purple, beaded with sweat. Five paces now. But what's that? The face has gone yellow, the eyes are closed . . . He jumped at the fuse and tore it away. His throat was dry, his hands trembling.

Sparrows were twittering in the tree just before his window. Slowly the bullets slipped from his trembling fingers and lay there over the soft cotton quilt.

After a while he attached the fuses again to the sticks of dynamite on the Fiend's body and waited while the burning fuses drew nearer and nearer, watching his bulging eyes, his drawn sweating purpling face, seeing him go pale, close his eyes and slouch forward, resigned to oncoming death. And at the very last moment, he snatched them away.

All through the day, till evening, this game went on and the dynamite on the Fiend's body did not explode. His nose stopped bleeding. His boots, too, were no longer overflowing with blood and the green flies had disappeared into the dusk. The night began to frazzle away. Coral-eyed snakes slithered ponderously over the rocks. The rattling of a rattlesnake came from down below. He untied the Fiend from the tree, trussed him up again, but taking away the sticks of dynamite first. Then he dragged the limp spent body to prop it up against a rock. This time he fastened the dynamite to the mastic tree before running back to his shelter.

'Look,' he said. 'Look how I'm going to blow it up. Look at that tree, how there won't be a particle left of it afterwards.'

The smoke travelled along the fuse and reached the trunk. There was a thunderous blast. The rocks pitched against each other and the Fiend was hurled into the air to fall back again a few yards away with an agonized scream. There was not a trace of the tree now. Even the rock it had grown out of had been blown off.

'See? That's what I'm going to do to you. Whether you open your eyes or not . . .'

Was he smiling?

A murky sun rose behind the yellow mist, flashing only for a moment, then settling over the mountain which trembled behind the curtain of mist, gleaming with a pale mauve and copper glow.

'You think I'll take pity on you, eh? Just because I let you sleep all night through . . .'

Dew had fallen. He felt as if all his blood had frozen in his veins . . .

He chose another tree on the edge of the precipice, with a thicker, rougher trunk and dragged the Fiend up to it. His body was worse than dead, flabby, boneless, slipping through his hands. He lifted it up against the tree, but it plopped down again. Again and again he fell, the Fiend. This time he passed a rope under his armpits and hung him up to a bough. His feet only grazed the ground, his head drooped to his chest.

'Soon soon, my fine fellow . . . Right away, don't you worry . . .' As he strapped the sticks of dynamite all about him . . . 'You'll be rid of me in a minute, and I of you . . . That's enough. I've given you as good and more than you gave me. We're quits now.'

He fastened the fuse. This time he retreated very far. It must take a long long time. Half an hour . . .

He was tired. He took a cigarette from his case and lit it. A large dark mauve butterfly flecked with orange and black alighted on the long mullein flower in front of him. The flower swayed. And more and more butterflies fluttered up. The

443

mullein turned from yellow to purple.

And the bullets came and went, came and went from his hand into the cylinder that whirled and clicked in a perpetual monotone . . .

His face stretched and contracted as though immersed in a stream, the eyes closing and opening, two huge rolling eyeballs with glittering whites, a frozen glitter under the swirling water. A fish flitted up, took a peck at the eye and darted away, only to return in an instant. Then there were more fish hanging in a swarm about the opening and closing frozen eyes. The swarm of fish moved with the rippling stream, dashed away, then slowly, timorously, clustered up again, their dark green shadows dancing on the bright moss-grown pebbles, shattering with the gentle waves, then still again, smooth. Only for a moment . . .

51

'They have mounted those beautiful horses, all the good people . . .'

A misty yellow rain was falling, very thin and straight, like steel wires uncoiled from the depths of the skies, taut-drawn, brightening in places, flashing briefly in the distance. Like a curtain, the rain, and the trees indistinct shapes behind it, the reeds shedding their spikelets, and thousands of tiny blue birds hurtling this way and that, spilling through the air . . .

Then the rain thickened and poured down like viscous mud, hard, stifling. A copper-winged eagle floated very low in the sky, its wide wings outspread, motionless, glittering wetly.

Ibrahim's dead body lay stretched on the sticky mud of the yard. His eyes were open, large and glassy, frozen in stark staring fear. Fear is stamped on that face forever, under the yellow rain, fear on those arms and legs and that ever-lengthening emaciated body. His blood oozes into the sticky earth, fresh, mouldering already . . . The rain washes clean the trickle of blood from his mouth. White-flowering myrtle branches spread their odour everywhere, but mingled with the rusty yellow smell of rain and rotting bark. Ibrahim, who loved to watch the tinsmiths working . . . Always that look of fear on his face . . . But sometimes joy and gladness too . . . His body stretched out there, smelling of gunpowder . . .

And the keening began. Meyro's voice, in a long, unending, unbroken lament, reaching out to beyond the mountains and echoing back in a scream . . . Meyro, who had stood numb and still before her husband's mangled body, her lips pursed tight, her face twitching only a little . . . While Mahmut's relatives howled out their wild foreign laments, never-ending . . . And now at last Meyro, in a long screaming agonizing lament . . . That will never stop . . .

Dervish Bey's hands are clasped over his breast, defeated, pitiful . . . He sways silently, yellow behind the sheet of yellow

445

rain . . . Nailed there, right below the motionless copper-winged eagle . . . Never taking his eyes off the dead body of his son.

Blood drips from the boots and the stirrups, denting deep into the dust of the earth . . . 'Sultan Agha, Sultan Agha!' Slowly he sank to the feet of his horse and lay there in the rain, over the dead leaves that covered the yard, knee-deep. The crack of rifle shots burst out behind the wall of the yard. There was a sound of approaching hoofbeats. Three men entered the room. They did not sit down, they did not speak, they only stood there with bent heads and clasped hands.

'Bey,' they said at last, 'give us Sultan Agha. It's true he has claimed sanctuary under your high-gabled mansion and you will not want to surrender him to us. But you must, Bey . . .'

Again they left, vanishing into the darkness of the night. Sleep is death . . . In their sleep they came upon them, unawares. All night long daggers struck through the mansion, at babies in their cradles, at children and women and men, old and young . . . No one was spared. And when morning dawned the mansion was steeped in blood from top to bottom.

'This is Sultan Agha, Bey. This is what he does to people. And still you refuse to surrender him. But we will take him from you at any cost. All of Harran plain will flow to this place to get him. We must have him, we must! Give him to us . . . If only for the sake of your dear one who lies dead there in your yard . . . For his dear memory . . .' Dark flickering shadows in the night, mournful, their hands locked over their breasts, speaking in a silent monotone, their lips hardly moving, their teeth clamped tight . . .

And more and more they came, on horseback, in carriages, trucks, tractors, and surrounded the mansion, waiting for the night. And the night descended from the mountains. A long whirling, glistening dust-devil stopped at the gate in the dark of the night.

'Sultan Agha! Sultan Agha . . .'

Sultan Agha was burning with fever, delirious, straining out to some unseen being. His dark curling lashes were wet with sweat. His face was growing yellow.

Meyro's keening screams rang out, coming from very far, from the very confines of the night . . . And Mahmut's mangled body trembled in a strange paleness, spilling over the sticky earth in shreds of bloody flesh. While overhead, more and more coppery eagles gathered, motionless, as though nailed to the sky, their huge wings outspread, screeching . . .

Dervish Bey was numb, in a dream-like state, emptied of all thought, sinking ever deeper into a void, into the nothingness of after-death. He mounted his horse. And in the stirrups he saw the feet of the Lady Karakiz, her head grazing the ground beneath the horse's galloping hooves, bloody, spattering blood over the stones and hollows, the bushes and thistles and flowers . . .

On the edge of Anavarza swamp a small diaphanous dust-devil hovered on the bank of Jeyhan River, gently swirling, fading away. A gazelle, all skin and bone, floundered in and out of the beds of narcissus. And in the grey dawn Dervish Bey galloped madly around the mansion. Round and round he hurtled, shouting out loud, screaming, what, to whom, firing at windows frenziedly.

In the middle of the yard she lies, the Lady Karakiz, one foot in the stirrup, her head sunk into the dust, her eyes closed, not a wrinkle now on her smooth calm face . . . And the town-crier too, he sees, behind some salty watery screen, a tiny ball with his hump, his drawn skintight face . . . Only his eyes are widening, larger and larger all the time.

The screaming and the keening . . . And Memet Ali is gone. Gone, leaving his tractors, his machines, his land on Akchasaz. Gone without a word, where, nobody knows.

And always that thin yellow rain falling in long taut-drawn compact steel wires over the gluey earth in the all-pervading odour of myrtles.

Dervish Bey's dark shadow falls over the earth under the blazing heat. Alone in the middle of the plain, sitting on his sweat-lathered horse . . . Before him rises the Akyollu mansion, etched out in the sweltering sky. And in the fields all around he sees the labourers, ant-like, slow-moving in the yellow heat, distant. And distant too Mount Düldül's coppery mass, swathed in smoke, glittering like smelting copper.

And they came again and stood at the gate.

'Sultan Agha! Sultan Agha . . .'

447

'Wait! I'm coming,' Sultan Agha is crying out. 'Wait, you wretches. I am one and you are a thousand, but still I'll come out to you.' His ebony beard, his flaming coal-black eyes . . . He rises, but only to fall back again . . .

The old man's white beard was dirty, unkempt. There he sat, leaning against the sunny wall of a tumbledown inn . . . His eyes were closed . . .

Dervish Bey rode up to the mansion and began to gallop madly round and round and round, firing again and again at the windows. There was no response from the mansion, no sign that any living creature was there any longer.

The old man opened his eyes. He opened his eyes as the gathering south wind swept up the dust-devils and sent them swirling over the roads, as the shadows of the swelling snow-white sail-clouds raced through the plain. And still Dervish Bey galloped in a frenzied whirl, the void inside him growing deeper and deeper . . . Like the nothingness of after-death . . .

'They have mounted those beautiful horses, all the good people, and ridden away.'